Mary Shelley's Fictions

Mary Shelley's Fictions
From *Frankenstein* to *Falkner*

Edited by

Michael Eberle-Sinatra
The Northrop Frye Centre
Victoria University

with an Introduction by

Nora Crook
Anglia Polytechnic University
Cambridge

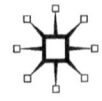

Selection and editorial matter © Michael Eberle-Sinatra 2000
Introduction © Nora Cook 2000
Text © the various contributors 2000, with the exception of Fiona
Stafford's essay © Edinburgh UP and the Editors of *Romanticism* 1997, and
Daniel E. White's and Lidia Garbin's essays © the Editor of *Romanticism on
the Net* 1997
Softcover reprint of the hardcover 1st edition 2000 978-0-333-77106-8

All rights reserved. No reproduction, copy or transmission of
this publication may be made without written permission.

No paragraph of this publication may be reproduced, copied or
transmitted save with written permission or in accordance with
the provisions of the Copyright, Designs and Patents Act 1988,
or under the terms of any licence permitting limited copying
issued by the Copyright Licensing Agency, 90 Tottenham Court
Road, London W1T 4LP.

Any person who does any unauthorised act in relation to this
publication may be liable to criminal prosecution and civil
claims for damages.

The authors have asserted their rights to be identified
as the authors of this work in accordance with the
Copyright, Designs and Patents Act 1988.

Published by
PALGRAVE MACMILLAN
Houndmills, Basingstoke, Hampshire RG21 6XS and
175 Fifth Avenue, New York, N. Y. 10010
Companies and representatives throughout the world

PALGRAVE MACMILLAN is the global academic imprint of the Palgrave
Macmillan division of St. Martin's Press, LLC and of Palgrave Macmillan Ltd.
Macmillan® is a registered trademark in the United States, United Kingdom
and other countries. Palgrave is a registered trademark in the European
Union and other countries.

ISBN 978-1-349-65499-4

This book is printed on paper suitable for recycling and
made from fully managed and sustained forest sources.

A catalogue record for this book is available from the British Library.

Library of Congress Catalog Card Number: 00–033266

To my mother

Contents

Editor's Preface and Acknowledgements	ix
Abbreviations and Sigla	xii
Notes on the Contributors	xv
Introduction by Nora Crook	xix

Part I The Craft of Writing

1 In Defence of the 1831 *Frankenstein*   3
   Nora Crook

2 The Ends of the Fragment, the Problem of the Preface:
   Proliferation and Finality in *The Last Man*   22
   Sophie Thomas

3 Mary Shelley and Edward Bulwer: *Lodore* as Hybrid Fiction   39
   Richard Cronin

Part II Gender

4 'Don't Say "I Love You"': Agency, Gender and
   Romanticism in Mary Shelley's *Matilda*   57
   Anne-Lise François and Daniel Mozes

5 Mary Shelley's *Valperga*: Italy and the Revision of
   Romantic Aesthetics   75
   Daniel E. White

6 Gender, Authorship and Male Domination: Mary Shelley's
   Limited Freedom in *Frankenstein* and *The Last Man*   95
   Michael Eberle-Sinatra

7 'The Truth in Masquerade': Cross-dressing and Disguise
   in Mary Shelley's Short Stories   109
   A. A. Markley

Part III The Contemporary Scene

8   'Little England': Anxieties of Space in Mary Shelley's
    The Last Man 129
    Julia M. Wright

9   Mary Shelley and Walter Scott: *The Fortunes of Perkin
    Warbeck* and the Historical Novel 150
    Lidia Garbin

10 Mary Shelley and the Lake Poets: Negation and
    Transcendence in *Lodore* 164
    David Vallins

11 *Lodore*: a Tale of the Present Time? 181
    Fiona Stafford

Part IV The Parental Legacy

12 The Corpse in the Corpus: *Frankenstein*, Rewriting
    Wollstonecraft and the Abject 197
    Marie Mulvey-Roberts

13 Rehabilitating the Family in Mary Shelley's *Falkner* 211
    Julia Saunders

14 Public and Private Fidelity: Mary Shelley's 'Life of William
    Godwin' and *Falkner* 224
    Graham Allen

Index 243

Editor's Preface and Acknowledgements

The idea for this volume originates in my attending a number of British and North American conferences devoted to Mary Shelley during the bicentenary anniversary of her birth. I was very much impressed by the quality and diversity of new work done on Shelley by both established and emerging scholars from Canada, England, Ireland, Scotland and the United States of America. I decided to put together a volume of essays that would reflect the vitality and richness of current Shelleyan criticism.

The sub-title, 'From *Frankenstein* to *Falkner*', could have lent itself to a purely chronological arrangement, and indeed it is literally true that the first essay is on *Frankenstein* and the last on *Falkner*. While this would have been one way of attempting to unite the Other Shelley to her *Frankenstein*ian Self, and thus to reassemble a single Being, this collection has eschewed simple linearity and adopted another method: that of grouping contributions thematically into four main sections. Within each section essays primarily on the 'early' Shelley (from *Frankenstein* to *The Last Man*) are juxtaposed to those primarily on 'later' Shelley (*Perkin Warbeck* to *Falkner*). The sections are not intended to be watertight. Each hooks on to the other; there are several currents running across all boundaries. Several of the essays might, with equal appropriateness, have been assigned to sections other than the ones in which they are to be found.

Most of these essays are based on papers (since extensively rewritten), which were first offered at these following national and international conferences in Britain, Canada and the USA: 'Beyond *Frankenstein*' (University of Bristol, England, 22 February 1997), convenor Timothy Webb; 'Mary Wollstonecraft Shelley in Her Times' (Keats–Shelley Association of America, in conjunction with the University Center and Graduate School of the City University of New York, 21–24 May 1997), convenors Betty T. Bennett and Stuart Curran; the Fifth British Association of Romantic Studies (BARS) Conference, 'Romantic Generations' (University of Leeds, 24–27 July 1997), convenors Vivien Jones and John Whale; 'Mary Shelley: Parents, Peers, Progeny' (Anglia Polytechnic University and the Open

University, Cambridge, 12–14 September 1997), convenors Nora Crook and Marilyn Brooks; North American Society for Studies in Romanticism (NASSR) Conference, 'Romanticism and Its Others' (McMaster University, Hamilton, Ontario, 21–24 October, 1997), convenor David Clarke; and MLA 1997 (Toronto, 27–30 December 1997).

Earlier versions of Lidia Garbin's and Daniel E. White's contributions appeared in *Romanticism On the Net*, 6 (May 1997), since when they have been substantially revised. Fiona Stafford's essay was published in *Romanticism*, 3.2 (1997) and is here reprinted, with a few changes, by kind permission of the editors and Edinburgh University Press.

Many persons have assisted me, directly and indirectly, with this volume. First among these I must mention Jonathan Wordsworth, who gave me some extra time on a different project in order that I might accommodate this one. Without his friendship, patience, and mentorship, this book would not have seen the light. Charles E. Robinson generously gave invaluable scholarly advice in the middle of an exceptionally busy schedule. I would also like to thank Betty T. Bennett, William D. Brewer, David Chandler, Pamela Clemit, Syndy M. Conger, Stuart Curran, Marilyn Gaull, Nicholas Halmi, Chris Koenig-Woodyard, Lucy Newlyn, Michael O'Neill, Joel Pace, Seamus Perry, Matthew Scott, Nicola Trott, Timothy Webb, Astrid Wind, and Duncan Wu. It has been a real pleasure to work with Charmian Hearne, my editor at Macmillan, whose support throughout I have greatly appreciated. Thanks are also due to Eleanor Birne, Ann Marangos and everyone at Macmillan who has helped with production. I would also like to thank all the contributors, for the cameraderie, good humour and professionalism that have made this project such a gratifying experience.

Special thanks are due to Nora Crook for her acceptance of my invitation to write the introduction. But her contribution to this volume goes beyond what goes under her name, beyond scholarly inspiration and valuable suggestions; it extends to her taking on the role of temporary editor when my other commitments threatened to stall the project at an advanced stage. She has left the impress of her expertise throughout. On my own behalf, and on behalf of the other contributors, I wish to express my deep gratitude for all the work she has put into this volume.

Last, but not least, I would like to acknowledge the constant support, encouragement, and patience of my wife Wendy. For a comparatist, she has probably heard more about Mary Shelley over the last three years than she may have wished. For her endless patience, and for much more, I am endlessly grateful.

MICHAEL EBERLE-SINATRA
The Northrop Frye Centre
Victoria University
Toronto

Abbreviations and Sigla

Quotations from Mary Shelley's novels and pagination are taken from *MWS Pickering* (see below). Volume and chapter numbers of the *first* editions are, where appropriate, given in square brackets after the primary reference in order to facilitate the location of quotations in a range of editions other than *MWS Pickering*. Following what appear to have been Shelley's final intentions, the spelling 'Matilda' is used for the title of the novella. 'Mathilda', however, is used for the character, following the spelling in Shelley's fair-copy manuscript.

Bennett, *Evidence*	Betty T. Bennett, 'The Political Philosophy of Mary Shelley's Historical Novels: *Valperga* and *Perkin Warbeck*', in *The Evidence of the Imagination: Studies of Interactions between Life and Art in English Romantic Literature*, eds Donald H. Reiman, Michael C. Jaye and Betty T. Bennett (New York: New York University Press, 1978), pp. 354–71.
F	Mary Shelley, *Frankenstein, or the Modern Prometheus*, ed. Nora Crook, vol. 1 of *MWS Pickering*. [1818 edition, with collations]
FN	——, *Falkner, a Novel*, ed. Pamela Clemit, vol. 7 of *MWS Pickering*.
Frankenstein Notebooks	*The Frankenstein Notebooks: a Facsimile Edition of Mary Shelley's Manuscript Novel, 1816–17 (with alterations in the hand of Percy Bysshe Shelley) as it survives in draft and fair copy deposited by Lord Abinger in the Bodleian Library, Oxford (Dep. c. 477/1 and Dep. c. 534/1–2)*, transcribed and ed. Charles E. Robinson, 2 vols (New York and London: Garland Publishing, 1996).
L	Mary Shelley, *Lodore*, ed. Fiona Stafford, vol. 6 of *MWS Pickering*.
LM	——, *The Last Man*, ed. Jane Blumberg with Nora Crook, vol. 4 of *MWS Pickering*.
M	——, *Matilda, Dramas, Reviews & Essays,*

	Prefaces & Notes, ed. Pamela Clemit, vol. 2 of *MWS Pickering*.
Mellor	Anne K. Mellor, *Mary Shelley: Her Life, Her Fiction, Her Monsters* (New York and London: Routledge, 1988).
MWSJ	*The Journals of Mary Shelley, 1814–1844*, eds Paula R. Feldman and Diana Scott-Kilvert, 2 vols (Oxford: OUP 1987) [corr. and repub. as one vol. with same pagination (Baltimore and London: Johns Hopkins University Press, 1995)].
MWSL	*The Letters of Mary Wollstonecraft Shelley*, ed. Betty T. Bennett, 3 vols (Baltimore and London: Johns Hopkins University Press, 1980–88).
MWS Pickering	*The Novels and Selected Works of Mary Shelley*, General Editor Nora Crook, with Pamela Clemit, introd. Betty T. Bennett, 8 vols (London: William Pickering, 1996).
MWST	Mary Shelley, *Collected Tales and Stories*, ed. Charles E. Robinson (Baltimore and London: Johns Hopkins University Press, 1976; corr. pbk edn, 1990).
Other MS	*The Other Mary Shelley: Beyond Frankenstein*, eds Audrey A. Fisch, Anne K. Mellor and Esther H. Schor (New York and Oxford: Oxford University Press, 1993).
PBSL	*The Letters of Percy Bysshe Shelley*, ed. Frederick L. Jones, 2 vols (Oxford: Clarendon Press, 1964).
PW	Mary Shelley, *The Fortunes of Perkin Warbeck, a Romance*, ed. Doucet Devin Fischer, vol. 5 of *MWS Pickering*.
Sunstein	Emily W. Sunstein, *Mary Shelley: Romance and Reality* (Boston: Little, Brown, 1989; corr. pbk edn, Baltimore and London: Johns Hopkins University Press, 1991).
TW	Mary Shelley, *Travel Writing*, containing *History of a Six Weeks' Tour* and *Rambles in Germany and Italy*, ed. Jeanne Moskal, vol. 8 of *MWS Pickering*.

V ——, *Valperga: or, The Life and Adventures of Castruccio, Prince of Lucca*, ed. Nora Crook, vol. 3 of *MWS Pickering*.
< > Encloses deletion in MS.
˄ ˄ Encloses insertions in MS.

Notes on the Contributors

Graham Allen is a college lecturer in the Department of English, University College, Cork. He is the author of *Harold Bloom: a Poetics of Conflict*, and has published various articles and chapters in the fields of Romantic studies and literary theory.

Richard Cronin teaches at the University of Glasgow. His latest book, *The Politics of Romantic Poetry: In Search of the Pure Commonwealth*, was published in 1999.

Nora Crook, Reader in English at Anglia Polytechnic University, Cambridge, is the General Editor of *The Novels and Selected Works of Mary Shelley* (1996) and *Mary Shelley: Literary Lives and Other Writings* (forthcoming 2002). She recently joined Donald H. Reiman and Neil Fraistat as a member of the team currently editing *Complete Poems of Percy Bysshe Shelley* for Johns Hopkins.

Michael Eberle-Sinatra is an Associate of the Northrop Frye Centre, Victoria University. He is the founding editor of *Romanticism On the Net*, and a former junior fellow of St Catherine's College, Oxford. He is the General Editor, with Robert Morrison, of *The Selected Writings of Leigh Hunt* (forthcoming). He has published articles on the Shelleys, Leigh Hunt, the French Romantics and science fiction. He has recently completed a book-length study of Leigh Hunt and is currently working on a project on French and British Romantic writers.

Anne-Lise François is an assistant professor in the English and Comparative Literature Departments at UC Berkeley. She is currently completing a book on passive agency and the ethics of reserve entitled *Open Secrets: the Literature of Uncounted Experience*.

Lidia Garbin has recently completed her doctoral dissertation on the interrelations between the works of Walter Scott and Shakespeare at the University of Liverpool. She has given papers and published on Scott and his influence on his contemporaries (Mary Shelley, Byron, Manzoni) and successors (Hardy and Forster).

A. A. Markley is Assistant Professor of English at Penn State University, Delaware County. His research interests include William Godwin's novels and Mary Shelley's fiction, particularly her short stories. He has published essays on the poetry of Alfred, Lord Tennyson, has co-edited, with Gary Handwerk, editions of Godwin's novels *Caleb Williams* and *Fleetwood*, and is a volume editor of *Mary Shelley: Literary Lives and Other Writings*.

Daniel Mozes graduated from Columbia University and the Graduate Center of the City University of New York. He has taught for six years in the City University, and is an Adjunct Assistant Professor at Lehman College of CUNY. Dr Mozes is writing a memoir of teaching at CUNY.

Marie Mulvey-Roberts is a Senior Lecturer in English at the University of the West of England, Bristol. The author of *Gothic Immortals*, she has edited *The Handbook to Gothic Literature* and a special issue on Mary Shelley for *Women's Writing*, which she co-edits.

Julia Saunders graduated from Girton College, Cambridge in 1990. She joined the British Diplomatic Service and spent five years working in London and Warsaw, Poland. Returning to academic life in 1995, she is now studying for her doctorate at Wolfson College, Oxford.

Fiona Stafford, Tutor in English at Somerville College, Oxford, is the author of *The Last of the Race: the Growth of a Myth from Milton to Darwin* (1994) and the editor of the Pickering *Lodore* (1996). She has research specialisms in eighteenth- and early nineteenth-century Scottish literature and publications in these areas.

Sophie Thomas is Lecturer in English at the University of Sussex. The essay included here is part of a forthcoming book on the fragment, tentatively entitled *Undoing Romanticism: Coleridge and the Ends of the Fragment*.

David Vallins studied at Cambridge, Sussex and Oxford Universities, and is currently Research Fellow in English at the University of Hong Kong. His book *Coleridge and the Psychology of Romanticism* was published in 1999, and his articles have appeared in *JHI*, *ELH*, *Modern Philology* and *Prose Studies*.

Daniel E. White is Visiting Assistant Professor of English at the University of Puget Sound, where he teaches eighteenth-century and Romantic literature and culture. He has published essays on the early Romanticism of Thomas Gray, Charlotte Smith and Anna Barbauld. He is writing a book about religious Dissent, politics, and literary communities during the late eighteenth century.

Julia M. Wright is Assistant Professor of English at the University of Waterloo. She specializes in British and Irish literature of the Romantic period, and has published on that subject in a number of journals and collections. She co-edited (with Tilottama Rajan) *Romanticism, History and the Possibilities of Genre*, and is currently editing Sydney Owenson's *The Missionary*.

Introduction

The year 1997, the double bicentenary of Mary Shelley's birth and Mary Wollstonecraft's death, proved that Shelley had in some sense 'arrived'. Special exhibitions were held at the National Portrait Gallery, London, the New York Public Library and the Horsham Museum in Sussex. An ugly British postage stamp depicting Frankenstein's monster was issued, Shelley's mythological dramas were premiered (in Cambridge and Bologna) and plays about her were written and performed. *Pour comble de merveille*, a lost children's story, *Maurice*, was found. In national and international conferences entirely or partly devoted to one or both Marys – in Bristol, New York, Leeds, Calgary, Cambridge, Bologna and Parma, Toronto – this elusive writer was celebrated, analysed, explicated, contextualized, theorized – a situation unthinkable twenty-five years ago.

If we look at the landmark collections of essays on Shelley over this period in order to map the growth of her canonicity, we find three distinct phases. The first may be called 'Author of *Frankenstein*' phase. This built up during the 1970s, when *Frankenstein* rose in eminence as a studied feminist, Gothic and science-fiction text, and was consolidated by Levine and Knoepflmacher's *The Endurance of Frankenstein* (1979). For the public at large and for most university students this phase has, of course, never passed away; Shelley remains the originating cause of a series of *Frankenstein* films and author of the most widely studied novel in the universities of the USA – and that is that.

In academia, however, the very success of the canonization of *Frankenstein* itself provoked what I call the 'Not *Frankenstein*' or 'Other Mary Shelley' phase, after the title of the landmark collection of 1992. Pointing out the irony that Shelley was now in danger of being 'obscured even by her own renown'[1] the editors, Fisch, Mellor and

Schor, offered their book as a corrective. As Levine and Knoepflmacher had drawn on work of the 1970s, so this collection drew on that of the 1980s – an explosion of Mary Shelley scholarship: monumental editions of Shelley's *Letters* (*MWSL*, 1980–88), Shelley's *Journals* (*MWSJ*, 1987), biographies by Spark and Sunstein[2] and influential critical overviews such as Poovey's *The Proper Lady and the Woman Writer* (1984) and Mellor's *Mary Shelley: Her Life, Her Fictions, Her Monsters* (1988). *The Other Mary Shelley* was followed up by *Iconoclastic Departures: Mary Shelley after Frankenstein* (1997),[3] which focused on challenging/modifying the view that Shelley was a defeated radical, crippled by gentility, the society of Dead (male) Poets, and her own idealization of the bourgeois family. However, the 'Other Mary Shelley', despite being a necessary and valuable historical response, produces its own form of distortion.

Complicating the 'Other Mary Shelley' phase has been the virtually simultaneous emergence of a 'Early Mary Shelley'. The increased availability of the novella *Matilda* (written 1819, first published 1959), of her apocalyptic *The Last Man* (1826), and (more recently) of her feminist historical novel *Valperga* (1823) has promoted recognition of Shelley as a three-book – maybe four-book – author,[4] while her novels of the 1830s – *Perkin Warbeck* (1830) and her two 'domestic' novels, *Lodore* (1835) and *Falkner* (1837) – remain in comparative obscurity. This phenomenon is, nevertheless, symptomatic of a readiness for progress beyond a simple *Frankenstein*/Not *Frankenstein* binary opposition and towards a synthesis, where her oeuvre might be restored to its wholeness. Such a progress has been advanced by Betty T. Bennett and Charles E. Robinson's anthology, *The Mary Shelley Reader* (1990) and by the first collected edition of all her novels (1996). The surprising number of 1997 conference papers on *Lodore* and *Falkner*, especially on *Lodore*, was another portent. We are now in a phase of transition towards – let us say – 'The Inclusive Mary Shelley'. This collection is, I believe, partly its product, and, I hope, partly its producer.

'From *Frankenstein* to *Falkner*', Betty T. Bennett has written, 'Mary Shelley's novels dwell on questions of power, responsibility and love.'[5] Here is common ground, but once we step beyond it we find debate and controversy – indeed, we do so even as we probe the terms. What, for instance, *was* Shelley's attitude towards power? What is the relationship in her work between 'love' and 'self-sacrifice'? Michael Eberle-Sinatra takes no sides; he has, of course, his own views and leanings, but with his editor's hat on he does not set out to be a 'judge of controversies';[6] his approach to selection is that of the broad church, of an opening-up of a space where views may clash, coalesce or co-exist. Upon examining the four parts into which these essays have been arranged, we find that each raises a controversial key issue or issues. We observe markedly differing assumptions and alignments among the contributors. Yet it would be an exaggeration to say that contrariety and debate are defining features of this collection. Some of the essays seem almost intentionally to form a complementary pair – those of Cronin and Stafford, or Thomas and Wright, for instance.

Part I, 'The Craft of Writing', engages with the question of how far it is appropriate to regard Shelley's prose as *writerly*, as produced by a self-conscious artist, as distinct from its being a vehicle for large concepts and ruling themes, obsessively pursued – consciously or unconsciously, as may be. While none of these essays tackles the question head-on, each does so implicitly. My own contribution assumes that the dichotomy between writing-as-craft and writing-as-vehicle here posited is a false one. Scrutinizing Shelley as a self-reviser, it argues that her often minute alterations for the 1831 *Frankenstein* simultaneously offer aesthetic satisfaction and concentre, not weaken, the energy of the 1818 text. Approaching Shelley as an experimental writer and using a formalist methodology, Sophie Thomas illuminates a rich subject: the temporal ruptures and displacements in *The Last Man*. She presents the text as a fragment, but not as the typical 'Romantic fragment'. The novel has been rendered unfinishable by the very nature of the relationship of the author's introduction to the rest of the text; it is 'a compelling meditation on the ends of writing' which may be read 'as a reflection on the infinality of writing itself'. Richard Cronin's essay is that rarity, an analysis of the actual characteristics of Shelley's style, a technique which has scarcely advanced since Jean de Palacio's pioneering 1969 study[7] and which is almost never applied to her later prose. He pinpoints what he calls the hybrid sentence, at once sentimental and 'styptic', as a prominent and significant feature of *Lodore*. His terms (one hopes they will catch on) help both to define new developments in the 1830s novel and to identify Shelley as one of the avant-garde of that decade.

'*Gender*', the title of Part II, on the other hand, is for many critics the issue which is *par excellence* associated with Shelley. Is she a victim of patriarchy? Does her work constitute a critique of Romantic male egotism – indeed of Romanticism itself? Or did her 'critique' work from within an alternative tradition of female Romanticism? Did she espouse an ideal of androgyny, and if so, was this empowering or enfeebling?

A notable feature of this section is the extent to which contributors continue to react to Anne Mellor; the agenda she set a dozen years ago is still sparking. Assenting to Mellor's view that *Matilda* is Shelley's most radical critique of her commitment to the bourgeois family, Anne-Lise François and Daniel Mozes nevertheless question any uncomplicated view of the heroine's victim status. This can be squared with the arguments advanced recently by critics such as Charlene Bunnell and Charles E. Robinson,[8] but François and Mozes come from a different direction. Drawing on the work of feminist moral philosophers such as Baier and Butler, they examine the concept of agency, and the manner in which gender interacts with emotional/philosophical problems of the self. Daniel E. White, discussing Shelley's most overtly feminist novel, begins with a contextualization of *Valperga* in post-Napoleonic Italy. White elaborates both Bennett's thesis that Shelley proposes an alternative politics based on love and the Poovey/Mellor thesis that Shelley's work subverts Romantic Prometheanism; nevertheless, he articulates a complementary truth and reclaims transcendence, divine music and the thirst for immortality – the supposed prerogatives of the male poet – for a feminist aesthetic. Michael Eberle-Sinatra, resisting *revanchisme*, restates the thesis that Shelley was indeed threatened, as an author, by male dominance. Drawing on Genette's narratology, he, like Thomas, but for entirely different purposes, analyses the paratext of *The Last Man*. Taking on board the question of Shelley's literary androgyny, he concludes that it was a strategy to transcend her exclusion; similarly, he interprets the conspicuous absence of a surviving female in her novel as a device to lay bare gender inequalities. A. A. Markley, spanning the period 1819–37, continues with a theme related to literary androgyny, that of cross-dressing, which, he points out, is often associated in Shelley with pilgrimage. Exploring whether Shelley reaffirms contemporary gender constructions while seeming to unsettle them, he concentrates on her *Keepsake* tales, in which cross-dressing and disguise are remarkably prevalent. His essay prompts the revaluation of an area of her work which has been frequently ring-fenced in anthologies of supernatural tales, or, where taken seriously, discussed primarily as the product of 1830s literary consumerism.

Part III, 'The Contemporary Scene', dwells on Shelley's responsiveness to developments in the public sphere and her alignments in the literary world. Here what is chiefly at issue is whether she increasingly moved towards conservatism during the 1820s and 1830s.

Julia M. Wright places Shelley within the big picture of cultural history. England's emergent sense of itself as an imperial power on which 'the sun never sets' (a 'singular fact', noted by Shelley's ill-fated friend, Edward Williams, in 1821),[9] is the starting point for her examination of spatial anxieties in *The Last Man*. Fear of the inadequacy of 'Little England' to manage or even imaginatively to grasp the immensity of the globe, constitutes, she establishes, as potent a source of menace in *The Last Man* as 'the infectious East or the dangerous Other'. The next two contributors, Lidia Garbin and David Vallins, bravely take on a somewhat thorny subject, Shelley's relationship to older male canonical Romantics in the 1830s. That 'The Author of Waverley' was a writer whom 'The Author of *Frankenstein*' greatly admired is well known, but has not been followed up very often. Garbin documents the influence of Scott's *Ivanhoe* upon the seldom-discussed *Perkin Warbeck*. She presents Shelley as having learned from Scott his technique of using historical romance as displacement narrative and sees embedded in *Perkin Warbeck* a call for a revival of true chivalric virtues. As Vallins maintains, taking *Lodore* as his example, very little has been said about the important presences of Wordsworth and Coleridge in Shelley's texts. Accepting that Shelley's work critiques 'Romanticism', he argues that her targets are primarily the Romantic individuation of P. B. Shelley and Byron, whereas Wordsworth and Coleridge are more sympathetically regarded. In them, as her work moves towards pessimism, Shelley finds the consolations of philosophy and the recuperation of the lost. Like White, Vallins defines a space in Shelley for the celebration of Romantic transcendence. Fiona Stafford, offering a more politicized Shelley, relates her, like Cronin, to the young literary lion, Bulwer, rather than to her elders. Locating *Lodore* in the turbulent state of Britain during the run-up to the 1832 Reform Bill and the virtual collapse of the book-trade, she depicts a Shelley responsive, indeed, to the demands of the market-place, but using the silver-fork novel as a mask whereby to engage in contemporary analysis of aristocratic degeneration.

With Part IV, 'The Parental Legacy', one confronts biographism – the assumption of 'a transparent relationship between text and life' and vice versa.[10] Few writers have been more subject to having their work interpreted as disguised biography than Shelley, and this has provoked, in turn, an extensive literature of protest against such reductionism. I sense, however, that the high tide of this controversy has ebbed, leaving militant anti-biographists less embattled and old-style biographists ... hidden in the woodwork. Moreover, the emergence of lifewriting studies has done much to dissolve the old distinctions between 'reality' and 'art', making possible new negotiations and nuancing of an old problem.

Marie Mulvey-Roberts grasps the nettle. Much has been written on the subject of the dead mother in *Frankenstein*, yet Mulvey-Roberts, uniting psychobiography with research in the archives of the Royal Humane Society, and the Kristevan theory of the abject with the peculiar practices of reviving the drowned in the 1790s, infuses this subject with new life. Appropriately, her essay moves literally from *Frankenstein* to *Falkner*. Shelley's remarkable last novel dominates this section, and the contributions enable us to understand the author's high hopes that it would prove 'my best ... I believe'.[11] Julia Saunders proposes a Shelley who is not the familiar self-accommodator to Early Victorianism but an isolated figure still fighting the battles of the 1790s and winning small victories. The Shelley of *Falkner*, she argues, so far from idealizing the bourgeois family, points to its limitations from the standpoint of a latter-day heir of Godwin and Wollstonecraft. Graham Allen considers the problematics of Shelley's parental legacy. Juxtaposing *Falkner* with Shelley's unfinished 'Life of William Godwin', he argues, through an analysis of the novel's plotting, that Shelley found a fictive solution to a problem which she was unable to solve through lifewriting. Many explanations have been offered as to why Shelley did not finish this 'Life'. Allen's is surely among the most convincing.

Allen's essay dissolves the frame of 'From *Frankenstein* to *Falkner*', reminding us of the inadequacies of all frames and of what has had to be left out of this collection. Every anthology leaves ungathered flowers in the meadow. Absent from this one are, for example, pieces on her reviewing, her beautifully crafted and melodious lyrics, her final book, *Rambles*, and, still unrepublished, her literary biographies. But these are instanced only to suggest the possibilities for an as-yet-unrealized but not unimagined 'Plural Mary Shelley'.

Let us, finally, take a quick glimpse at this 'Unrepublished Shelley'. At the beginning of her 'Vittoria Colonna', one of the brief lives of celebrated Italians which she wrote for Dr Dionysius Lardner's *Cabinet Cyclopaedia* in 1835,[12] she evokes fleetingly a shadowy but intriguing historical figure: the daughter of a fourteenth-century professor who herself lectured in the University of Bologna, albeit behind a veil. Shelley finds much to salute in this circumstance: the relative openness of medieval Italy to female learning, the modesty of the 'young girl' and, finally, her willingness to 'impart her knowledge to the studious'.

This 'young girl' is *there* in the text as a harbinger and type of Shelley herself, daughter of a celebrated philosopher, who shrank from the public gaze yet who could not refrain from imparting – veiled behind anonymous publication, behind the sobriquet 'The Author of *Frankenstein*', behind her own protestations ('I cannot teach – I can only paint')[13] and behind the pleasing mask of fiction itself – what she thought and knew: of history, of the secret springs of action, of good and evil, of her forebodings and hopes for her generation and the next 'new-sprung race', of vindication of the traduced. If in the last quarter of a century Shelley has come to resemble the Bolognese professor's daughter even more closely than she did in her own lifetime, when academia, as such, paid her scant respect and attention, we, her readers, have come to resemble the Trecentisti 'studious'. Today, her constituency is increasingly those, who, like the writers and readers of this volume, pay close attention to what she has to impart to us from behind her many veils.

NORA CROOK
The English Department
Anglia Polytechnic University
Cambridge

Notes

1. *Other MS*, p. 3.
2. Muriel Spark, *Mary Shelley* (Constable, 1987; rev. edn of *Child of Light*, 1951); Emily W. Sunstein, *Mary Shelley: Romance and Reality* (Little, Brown, 1989).
3. Syndy M. Conger, Frederick S. Frank and Gregory O'Dea, eds (Fairleigh Dickinson University Press, 1997).
4. Key texts here are Jane Blumberg, *Mary Shelley's Early Novels* (Macmillan, 1992 and University of Iowa Press, 1993), paperback editions of *The Last Man* (Morton D. Paley, ed., Oxford World's Classics, 1994; Anne McWhir, ed., Broadview, 1996) and of *Valperga* (Stuart Curran, ed., Oxford, 1997; Tilottama Rajan, ed., Broadview 1998). I am not talking here about editors' or critics' intentions but, in Godwinian phrase, the *tendency* of these works.
5. Betty T. Bennett, Introduction, *MWS Pickering*, 1, p. lxviii.
6. See Mary Shelley's 'Note on *Queen Mab*' (*M* 261).

7. Jean de Palacio, *Mary Shelley dans son œuvre* (Paris, 1969) pp. 572–92.
8. Charlene Bunnell, '*Mathilda*: Mary Shelley's Romantic Tragedy', *Keats–Shelley Journal*, XLVI (1997) 75–96; Robinson's paper, given at the New York Bicentennial Conference 'Mary Wollstonecraft Shelley in Her Times', May 1997, is included in the volume of the conference procedings (Johns Hopkins University Press, 2000). Both treat *Matilda* as dramatic monologue rather than as self-expression.
9. *Maria Gisborne & Edward E. Williams, Shelley's Friends: their Journals and their Letters*, ed. F. L. Jones (Oklahoma, 1951), p. 109.
10. Graham Allen 'Beyond Biographism: Mary Shelley's *Matilda*, Intertextuality and the Wandering Subject', *Romanticism*, 3.2 (1997) 170.
11. *MWSJ* II, p. 548.
12. *Lives of the most Eminent Literary and Scientific Men of Italy, Spain and Portugal*, 2 vols (London, 1835) I, p. 75). A four-volume edition under my general editorship of Shelley's *Cabinet Cyclopædia* biographies and other uncollected works, including the 'Life of Godwin' is contracted for by William Pickering for publication in 2002; volume editors are Tilar Mazzeo, Lisa Vargo, Clarissa Campbell Orr and A. A. Markley.
13. Letter to Trelawny of 26 January, 1837 (*MWSL* II, p. 281); in context, this comes over as conscious irony at Trelawny's expense.

Part I
The Craft of Writing

1
In Defence of the 1831 *Frankenstein*
Nora Crook

> You must certainly have lost that simplicity that was once your characteristic charm.
>
> (Letter IV, *Frankenstein*, 1818)

Did Mary Shelley, in revising *Frankenstein* in 1831 for Colburn and Bentley's Standard Novels, tame her 1818 text and stifle its characteristic charm with superfluous elaboration? Did she transfer sympathy from the oppressed Creature to the oppressing Victor and thus confuse her original conception? Certainly, that the 1831 *Frankenstein* is both less ideologically clear *and* 'a smoother, more sociably presentable work' – more sexually proper, politically quietist and religiously orthodox – is at present the dominant view.[1]

It is with some diffidence that I dissent, especially since, as General Editor of the recent *Novels and Selected Works of Mary Shelley*, I have helped to promote the 1818 *Frankenstein* as normative by choosing it as base text. Editorial consistency was a crucial determinant, but, conveniently, this coincided with current critical preference. Upon publication, the monstrous shadow of the 1831 *Frankenstein* rose up, as it were, to accuse the editor of injustice and neglect. However, in this act of quasi-reparation, I am arguing – I wish to stress – not for a reversal of a consensus but for parity of esteem between the two texts. They differ, I believe, less than has been contended, and very little as regards ideology. Major revisions tend to be directed towards making the action more plausible and the two main protagonists more 'interesting' (i.e. psychologically complex); there is a greater concern with exploring 'the mysteries of our nature'. More regard is paid to the principle of 'keeping' – foregrounding the principal characters while leaving secondary ones relatively undeveloped.[2] Politics, with the possible exception of the omission of some of Elizabeth's social criticism, have not been made blander, but they have been partially updated.[3] Irony is thickened: an addition or verbal change is often proleptic, intended to ring its bell only many chapters later. These features may imply a slightly more sophisticated envisaged readership, but do not, I consider, introduce confusion. Rather, the 'confusion' was present from the start and is crucial to the work.

There is no extrinsic evidence, only supposition, that Shelley altered *Frankenstein*, voluntarily or under pressure, in order to accommodate it to Tory and 'popular' interpretations. The nearest approach to such evidence that I have found – an 1834 advertisement that the Standard Novels list included only novels 'written in accordance with morality and decorum', involving not 'the slightest danger of contaminating the minds of their readers'[4] – implies that the titles had met the publishers' purity standards at the selection stage, i.e. before revision. The sparse information available concerning Shelley's intentions provides a very different motive. She had once planned, probably as early as December 1818, to rewrite the first two chapters in order to make them less 'tame' and more artistically satisfying.[5] Her introduction to *1831* states that her alterations were 'principally those of style'. Her further protestation that she had 'changed no portion of the story, nor introduced any new ideas or circumstances' has been deemed specious, but, true or not, the disclaimer seems addressed to a readership which wants and expects, not a smoother, mellower *Frankenstein*, but assurance that it is getting the original brew.[6]

Turning, then, to the intrinsic evidence of *1831*, we find a text that is wide open to interpretation. Changes which might give against the view of a more conformist Shelley often go unnoticed, while those that might support it are summoned to bear a heavy burden of proof – sometimes too heavy. The accumulation of small examples can often build up into a weighty argument. However, it is also liable to produce a 'halo effect' in which neutral or ambivalent material is marshalled in support of the initial proposition. That *1831* is a 'tamed text' is a proposition which, in my view, has benefited from such an enhancement. An example is the omission of the dedication to Godwin and the epigraph from Milton. While these alterations do ratchet down the provocation of *Frankenstein* by a notch, they were not initiated by a prudent Shelley in 1831, but by Godwin in 1823.[7] Obviously she did not feel so strongly as to make a positive decision to re-instate them (which she would have had do, as *1823* was her copytext), but we cannot know whether she had actively wanted them to go; their absence in *1831* casts little light on her general revising strategy.

Another example concerns the near-universal acceptance of the proposition that in *1831* Elizabeth was turned from a first cousin into an orphan so that an incest theme might be erased. This is a case of conjecture hardening into fact without supporting evidence. No reviewer had even hinted at finding incest in *Frankenstein*. First cousins married each other in early nineteenth-century novels without shocking the public, as in *Mansfield Park*. Had reviewers sniffed out incest, a cosmetic change to 'orphan' in *1831* (Victor and Elizabeth continue to address each other as 'cousin') was not likely to have appeased them, any more than they had been appeased when P.B. Shelley altered 'sister' to 'orphan' in his own *Laon and Cythna* (1817). Certainly, Shelley disliked 'coarseness' in contemporary writing. But with non-contemporaries – as with the *Cenci* family story – or where sexual content was inexplicit, she could be surprisingly robust. At one point, *1831* is actually less 'decent', more like Sterne, than *1818* – the scene in the barn where the Creature inserts the mother's portrait into what he awkwardly describes as 'the folds of [Justine's] dress', i.e. her pocket.[8] In *1818* the Creature implausibly slips in the portrait unperceived as Justine is walking along; *1831* improves on this manoeuvre, and heightens the reader's sense of the Creature's thwarted sexual desire – one can infer that he has touched the thigh of the sleeping girl through the fabric. That the Shelley who made this discreet but indelicate change should half-heartedly attempt to expunge overtones of incest that no one, apparently, had accused her of introducing, seems unlikely. Indeed, it would be possible to argue that she was sailing closer and more confidently into the wind in *1831*.

More plausibly, it was Shelley's wish to introduce the theme of Italian liberation, one of the great causes of her life, that prompted the change to 'orphan'. For Elizabeth's father (in *1831* a martyr for Italian freedom) to have voluntarily given away his own daughter would have been to raise doubts concerning the value of his patriotism. The change aligns Elizabeth more firmly with Victor's mother as it is Caroline who determines to adopt her. It also reiterates the motif of seeking the illusory or unattainable earthly paradise – here, the villa Lavenza in the warm South, which the owner–bride who should have been its presiding genius never sees.

The perception of Shelley as increasingly politically conservative during the 1830s is at odds with her known sympathies in 1830–31

6   *The Craft of Writing*

with radicals such as Frances Wright and Robert Dale Owen, her hopes for the Reform Bill and her growing support for the Italian Risorgimento.⁹ This last surfaces in *1831* with the quotation '*schiavi ognor frementi*' – 'perpetually restless slaves', the tribe to which Elizabeth's father, the energetic Italian patriot, belongs. Shelley was fond of this tag, which she may first have encountered in 1815, when she read Germaine de Staël's *Corinne* (*MWSJ* II, p. 678). It appears in her 1826 'The English in Italy' and in an 1830 letter to Frances Wright (*MWSL* II, p. 124). In *Corinne*, the heroine spiritedly defends Italians against the charge of supineness:

> Other peoples ... have less of the imagination which can create visions of another destiny:
> *Servi siam, sì, ma servi ognor frementi*
> We are slaves, but perpetually restless slaves *says Alfieri*, the proudest of our modern writers.¹⁰

The mention of Elizabeth's father, 'lingering in the dungeons of Austria', is brief, but it had particular topical resonance for 1831 readers. The years 1830–31 saw violent Carbonari uprisings in Northern Italy and the release of Silvio Pellico, the Milan-based dissident and dramatist, after eight years in the most notorious of Austrian prisons, the Spielberg.¹¹ The incuriosity of Victor about the fate of Elizabeth's father (dead? languishing in a Spielberg?) is, in this context, remarkable. One wonders, and, I think, we are intended to wonder, how Frankenstein *père* came to have so much credit with the Austrian authorities as to get back the Villa Lavenza for Elizabeth.

The culpable political unawareness of Victor is made clearer in *1831*. In a highly significant revision to the first chapter, he praises his parents for allowing him to choose his own educational pathway and confesses that 'neither the structure of languages, nor the code of governments, nor the politics of various states, possessed attractions for me' (*1831*, ch. ii). Ignorance of what one might consider an essential part of civic education is treated by him as an uncorrupted youthful preference which it would have been tyranny to interfere with. Significantly, political quietism is presented as a Swiss national characteristic in 'History of a Six Weeks' Tour', Shelley's contribution to the co-authored *History of a Six Weeks' Tour* (1817), a curtain-raiser for *Frankenstein*. Shelley finds 'no glimpse' of the spirit of William Tell' among the modern Swiss, who appear 'a people slow of comprehension and of action'. However, they are not altogether sunk, for 'they would, I have little doubt, make a brave defence against any invader of their freedom' (*TW* 31).[12]

This passage interestingly illuminates Shelley's decision to change Ernest Frankenstein from a sickly boy whom Elizabeth destines to be a farmer in *1818* to a healthy would-be soldier in *1831*. Marilyn Butler has suggested that this, advantageously for the family's reputation, helps remove a suggestion of degeneracy.[13] However, the change is actually *more* damning. Elizabeth, in an *1831* addition to her first letter to Victor, fears lest he should have to attend him only 'some mercenary old nurse' (ch. vi) – which is exactly what later happens to Victor as he awaits trial.[14] In the next paragraph she remarks that Ernest 'is desirous to be a true Swiss and enter into foreign service'.[15] The juxtaposition throws a most ironic light, lost on Elizabeth, upon Ernest's ambition. Ernest is himself proposing to become a mercenary. The Swiss in the late eighteenth century were frequently labelled military prostitutes, ready to sell their services to anyone. What foreign service will Ernest see? Protecting some Bourbon? We take our leave of Ernest with Switzerland on the threshold of the Napoleonic invasion of 1797; let us hope that the need to defend his country will relight the spirit of Tell dormant within him.

More crucial to *1831*'s 'taming' than propriety or politics, however, is the issue of whether critics and stage-adaptors of the 1820s obliged Shelley to impose on the revised book an orthodox moral – an awful warning against blasphemous 'presumption'. That *1831* adds another instance of the word 'presumption' to the three already present is often adduced to show the direct influence of Richard Brinsley Peake's depoliticized stage play *Presumption or the Fate of Frankenstein* (1823), which Shelley herself attended.[16] Religious orthodoxy is also descried in Shelley's recollection in her Introduction to *1831* of the originating 'waking dream' at the Villa Diodati: the sensations of the 'pale student of unhallowed arts' were 'supremely frightful' as 'would be the effect of any human endeavour to mock the stupendous mechanism of the Creator of the world'. Including the above, *1831* adds three instances of 'unhallowed' to the already existing two.[17]

However, the religious frame of reference that this language evokes is not necessarily an orthodox one; the terms are compatible with heterodoxies such as pantheism, Spinozism, Shaftesburyan scepticism, Romantic Deism[18] or even Godwinism, which on occasion assumes a religious register. While contemporary Christian readers might well have supposed Mrs Shelley to be affirming that it is wicked to 'mock' God Almighty, the sentence curiously fails to satisfy the criteria of strict orthodoxy. The word she actually uses instead of 'blasphemous' or 'impious' is the Gothic 'frightful'. Warnings against 'presumption' are not the prerogative of Christian humility or of political reaction; indeed, one often finds in Deist *philosophes* (Volney, for instance, one of the educative influences on the Creature) animadversions against anthropocentric and, specifically, *Christian* presumption. The title 'Presumption' may well have been suggested to Peake by instances in *1818*, and by Victor's warning:

> Learn from me, if not by my precepts, at least by my example, how dangerous is the acquirement of knowledge, and how much happier that man is who believes his native town to be the world, than he who aspires to become greater than his nature will allow.
> (F 36 [I. iii])

That is to say, 'Beware of presumption.' A conventional 1831 Shelley might have been expected to excise Victor's very last words ('I have myself been blasted in these hopes, yet another may succeed'), which undercut this edifying admonition. But no, the *1831* Victor is still allowed his presumptuous exit. Rather than adding pietistic gracenotes, the new instance of 'presumption' in *1831* heightens the 'interestingness' of Victor and allows Shelley to display her mature powers of psychological analysis. It is worth a closer scrutiny.

On the morning of Justine's trial, Victor reflects that the circumstantial evidence is insufficient for a conviction. In *1818* he then calms himself – she will be acquitted (F 57 [I. vi]). In *1831* the belief in the insufficiency of circumstantial evidence remains, but not Victor's calmness. Instead, he frantically rehearses excuses for concealing his story – listeners will think he is mad, no one, except 'I, the creator' will believe in 'the living monument of presumption and rash ignorance which I had let loose upon the world' (*1831*, ch. vii). In *1818*, Victor is simply complacent. In *1831* he is less simple and less innocent. Incompatibilities – cold calculation and blind panic, self-exoneration and self-blame – compete in his bosom. The self-abaser is simultaneously the self-aggrandizer ('I, the creator'). Despite his protestation, he evidently *does* foresee that the evidence might somehow go against Justine and works out *in advance* that if it does he will remain silent. In short, what we have here is not Shelley's confusion but her dramatization of Victor's self-division.

Another *1831* addition, often interpreted as evidencing Shelley's bowing to convention, is placed after the Irish trial. Victor (not his father, as in *1818*) insists on returning immediately to Geneva. Duty, he tells Walton, had triumphed over his 'selfish despair'. He will protect his family, carrying weapons so that, if he meets the Creature, he 'might, with unfailing aim, put an end to the existence of the monstrous Image which I had endued with the mockery of a soul still more monstrous' (*1831*, ch. xxi). 'Mockery of a soul' would seem to have been inserted solely to reassure censorious readers that Victor is not to be supposed to have created a *real* soul, capable of knowing God.

However, this complex and cleverly written insertion points in quite another direction, that of proleptic irony. That '*might* put an end' enfeebles the force of 'unfailing aim' and foreshadows Victor's wedding night, when his aim will indeed fail. Another effect is to develop the theme of Victor's increasing self-mirroring of his adversary. The phrase '*mockery* of a soul' anticipates the '*scoffing* devil' that he will later call the Creature. Unwittingly he represents himself as a diminished type of his parody-Adam. The insertion continues; immediately after the sentence quoted above, Victor calls himself 'the shadow of a human being. My strength was gone. I was a mere skeleton; and fever night and day preyed upon my wasted frame'. *He* is becoming what he declares the Creature to be, an abhorrent 'Image' of a man ('a shadow of a human being', 'a skeleton') inhabited by a 'mockery of a soul' ('fever'). His disease, caricaturing the animating principle, propels him towards his revenge and death, burning the brighter as it frets his body to decay.

'Soul', a word of unstable meaning in the early nineteenth century, could mean 'self', 'principle of life', 'seat of the emotions' as well as 'immortal spirit'. It serves Victor's purposes very well at this point to suggest to Walton (rather than to Shelley's worried readers) that the Creature does not have a soul that can survive its body; how, otherwise, could he reassure himself with the thought that shooting the Creature would end its 'existence'? But of course Victor shifts between rationality and irrationality throughout the book; introducing the idea of the 'soul' here shows him in the act of making such a shift and betrays his suppressed fear that, despite his bravado, the Creature might after all continue to have some kind of metaphysical existence after its physical death. There is a passage, present in both *1818* and *1831*, in which slippage between the various possible senses of 'soul' again occurs, this time in a context where Victor envisages his own continuing existence as a vengeful spirit. In the final words of his narrative, he makes his climactic appeal to Walton:

> His soul is as hellish as his form, full of treachery and fiend-like malice. Hear him not; call on the manes of William, Justine, Clerval, Elizabeth, my father, and of the wretched Victor, and thrust your sword into his heart. I will hover near, and direct the steel aright.
>
> (III. 159 [III. vii]; *1831*, ch. xxiv)

Indeed, when the two passages are collated, it looks as though Shelley made the *1831* insertion in order to adumbrate the above, in a manner similar to the 'mercenary nurse' passage. Common elements are the Creature's 'soul' and the intention to kill its mortal form with a single, penetrating blow. And the *1831* addition, if anything, underscores rather than softens one subversive implication of *1818* (never spelled out, merely insinuated to those with ears to hear and blood to curdle at it): if Victor even half-believes that he has given the Creature an immortal soul, then he is ready to send that soul to perdition.[19] He is fast perfecting his imitation of a retributive creator-God who ensouls beings and then places them in circumstances where they will heap crimes on their heads until they deserve eternal punishment.

But the chief point at issue is whether Victor has free will (and thus responsibility) in *1818* but not in *1831*. In Anne Mellor's words, in *1831*, 'Mary Shelley now presents Victor Frankenstein more as a victim of circumstances than as the active author of evil' (Mellor, p. 174). His diminished responsibility is accompanied by greater remorse and regard for his parents. Anyone so filial, so guilt-ridden, and so excusable is surely to be pitied rather than censured. Mellor links this kinder view of Victor – a good man condemned by Destiny to do bad things – to what she perceives as a increasingly pessimistic determinism in Shelley's mental outlook.

Undoubtedly Shelley was tempted strongly at times to reify 'destiny' or 'fate' as an actual power, debilitating and overpowering her.[20] Mellor tellingly quotes from a letter of 1827:

> The power of Destiny I feel every day pressing more & more on me, & I yield myself a slave to it ...
>
> (*MWSL* I, p. 572)

However, Shelley also constantly asserts her creed that, while action and disposition are subject to unalterable circumstances, the will and the imagination are still able to envisage other possibilities, and that it is ones duty to exert these faculties. The same sentence, also quoted by Mellor, continues with a Corinne-like affirmation. Shelley may be a slave, but she is one of the *ognor frementi*:

> ... a slave to it, in all except my moods of mind, which I endeavour to make independent of her, & thus to wreathe a chaplet, where all is not cypress, in spite of the Eumenides.
> (*MWSL* I, p. 572)[21]

Mellor considers, but rejects, the possibility that the foregrounding of Victor's submission to Destiny might be 'introduced to emphasize Victor Frankenstein's capacity for self-deception, rationalization, and self-serving attempts to win his audience's sympathy' (Mellor, p. 172), on the grounds that in *1831* the sympathetic female characters – Elizabeth and Justine – express the same deterministic sentiments, apparently voicing Shelley's own views. But their supine submissiveness to Destiny may indicate, rather, the tendency of a Frankensteinian upbringing to encourage female family and household members to be amiably slavish.[22]

Is it, in any case, true that the *1818* Victor is represented as possessing free will while the *1831* Victor is not? The *1818* Victor on several occasions presents himself as a pawn of destiny and circumstance. He tells Walton that 'nothing can alter my destiny: listen to my history, and you will perceive how irrevocably it is determined'. After the execution of Justine, Victor visits the Alps. He reflects disconsolately:

> Alas why does man boast of sensibilities superior to those apparent in the brute; it only renders them more necessary beings [i.e. beings more subject to Necessity]. If our impulses were confined to hunger, thirst and desire, we might be nearly free; but now we are moved by every wind that blows and a chance word or scene that that word may convey to us.
> (*F* 72–3 [II. ii]; *1831*, ch. x)

So already in *1818* we find Victor expressing Necessitarian views, impressed as he is by the workings of nature's laws – the irresistible power of the avalanche which has destroyed pine trees and the 'tremendous and ever-moving glacier'. His mind then moves to the fluctuating laws of Chance, which imperceptibly interweave the light but binding threads of circumstances.

Working against this Necessitarian thrust is another which asserts the freedom of the will. The reader is at every turn allowed to glimpse paths which might have been taken, alternative choices open to the protagonists. Victor did not have to *make* the Creature, nor devote his life to pursuing him. He deliberates whether to make a spouse for the Creature; no reader of *Frankenstein* but wonders what would have happened if he had refused. Murderous thoughts may have inevitably arisen in the Creature's brain, but was he obliged to commit murderous acts?[23]

Tellingly, Walton's second letter, almost at the very beginning, recounts a paradigmatic story which warns the reader that 'Destiny' is a name given to the predicted or the intended, and has no real existence. Walton extols the 'heroically generous' ship's master who has bestowed his unwilling bride upon her true-love against strong paternal opposition just before the 'destined ceremony'. No one had anticipated the moving effect of the bride's tears – an example of what may be done when the wills of a man and a woman combine to thwart a father's will. This Scipio of continence then sacrifices his chances of domestic felicity by endowing his rival with his entire prize-money. Now his mind revolves around 'the rope and the shroud',[24] but his new 'destiny' (a death-or-glory mission) is one which he has chosen. This is only the first of many incidents in which 'the destined' proves to be what does *not* happen.

When we turn to *1831*, we find the same split. What *1831* does is to accentuate it, sometimes obviously, sometimes more subtly. The number of times that Victor refers to 'Destiny' is very obviously increased, and the concept is reified by him. 'Destiny ... and her immutable laws', Victor states in a new addition, 'had decreed my utter and terrible destruction' (*1831*, ch. ii.). These 'immutable laws' are later explicitly linked to those governing matter. *1831* expands his Alpine musings (quoted above) with a passage describing the 'cracking ... of the accumulated ice', rent and torn at the behest of 'silent working of immutable laws' (*1831*, ch. x).

Again we see Shelley in *1831* writing in a new passage which is to have its repercussions many pages ahead. This example has a dynamic effect on an episode carried over from *1818* virtually unchanged, in which Victor, near death, vehemently attempts to motivate the crew (who wish to return home) to continue north. Victor asserts that they could push on with their mission if they really wanted to: 'This ice is not made of such stuff as your hearts might be; it is mutable, cannot withstand you, if you say that it shall not.'[25] The new addition of *1831* ('cracking ... of the accumulated ice') now pointedly anticipates this passage, and thus shows more clearly than *1818* had done what lies behind Victor's plea. He is attempting to persuade the sailors that their wills work exactly like those laws of nature which he has previously observed at work in the Alps; as accumulated ice inevitably cracks in obedience to these laws, so the Polar ice will inevitably crack in obedience to the will of the sailors' concerted hearts.[26]

However, that Victor is here attempting to act as a Prime Mover (and the *1831* addition helps to make this clearer), provokes the suspicion that his brand of determinism is self-serving sophistry or a delusion. Moreover, *1831* retains all the incidents which had called into question the irresistible power of Destiny in *1818* and introduces some new ones. One such is the introduction of Elizabeth's energetic father, the restless slave. Another is Justine's deposition. In *1831* the 'Guilty' verdict is actually less 'inevitable' than in *1818*, even though everyone, including Justine, is more resigned to it. In *1831*, Justine does not pass a completely sleepless night but, she testifies, dozes off in a barn for a few minutes; an opportunity has been created, not present in *1818*, for someone to have planted the picture on her unawares. A Justine with her wits about her, a Victor less preoccupied with self-exoneration, a judge more concerned with saving an innocent life than securing a conviction – all could have put the case for reasonable doubt, and, given the Geneva magistrates' preference for not convicting on circumstantial evidence alone, might well have secured an acquittal.

This double trajectory – one which hastens readers to the conclusion that events in the story are inevitable, the other which counterfactually beguiles them with might-have-beens – constitutes an important source of *Frankenstein*'s enduring readability and probably that of all major nineteenth-century novels. In *Frankenstein* this dual motion has a correspondence in the protagonists' extremes of self-exoneration and self-excoriation. Victor and his Creature in *1818* both present themselves as subject to irresistible obligations; their persuasiveness is enhanced by the pace of the narrative, the interest of which, as P.B. Shelley's review puts it, 'gradually accumulates, and advances towards its conclusion with the accelerated rapidity of a rock rolled down a mountain'.[27] Both try to disclaim responsibility for their actions – the Creature, even at the end, cannot say 'I killed Elizabeth', but exclaims 'Yet when she died!' as if her death had been a terrible surprise.[28] Yet both execrate themselves without measure as if they were at fault. They do the same in *1831*, and, if anything, more extremely. What is one to make of this?

We find a polarization between the consciousness of necessity and belief in free will starkly expressed in Godwin's novel *Mandeville* (1817), written at the same time as *Frankenstein*.[29] The heroine, Henrietta, Mandeville's sister and mouthpiece for what P.B. Shelley called 'the genuine doctrine of *Political Justice* presented in one perspicuous and impressive view',[30] attempts to arouse her brother from his depression with a medicinal dose of Necessitarianism. Consider, she tells him:

> that man is but a machine! He is just what his nature and his circumstances have made him; he obeys the necessities which he cannot resist.
>
> (*Mandeville* II, p. 143)

Nevertheless, Henrietta continues, the human will resists the consequences of this doctrine:

> It is the prerogative of man, to look on outward circumstances with scorn ... we have the source of our satisfaction or unhappiness within us, and are the masters of our own fortune. ... He that is truly worthy of the powers with which nature has endowed us, is of no thin and airy substance to be turned by every wind that blows.
>
> (*Mandeville* II, p. 145)

Godwin was to dilate further upon the position outlined in *Mandeville* in *Thoughts on Man* (1831). There he drew a sharp distinction between theory and practice. 'In the sobriety of the closet, we inevitably assent to [necessitarian] conclusions.' Reason produces the 'unreserved conviction, that man is a machine, that he is governed by external impulses'. Mind, like matter, is subject to immutable laws: 'the decisions of our will are always in obedience to the impulse of the strongest motive'. It is on this assumption that one person attempts to overpersuade another.[31]

But in 'the society of our fellow-creatures' we are guided by our sentiments and behave as though possessed of free will. We cannot escape from the 'delusive sense of liberty',[32] and it would be 'pernicious' if we did. From it springs 'what we call conscience in man, and a sense of praise or blame due to ourselves and others'. Love, hatred, duty (very importantly), 'debt, bond, right, claim, sin, crime, guilt, merit and desert' all derive from it. It energizes, whereas the doctrine of Necessity instils inertia. The delusion 'turns a man into what we conceive of a God ... inspires him with a resolution and perseverance that nothing can subdue'. It forms 'the genuine basis of self-reverence, and the conceptions of true nobility and greatness, *and the reverse of these attributes*. The doctrine of necessity 'can never form the rule of our intercourse with others'. What, then, is its utility? Godwin's reply is that it moderates our excesses of judgement. Under its influence 'We shall make of our fellow-men neither idols to worship, nor *demons to be regarded with horror and execration* ... most of all, we shall view with pity, even with sympathy, the men whose frailties we behold, or by whom crimes are perpetrated', satisfied that, like ourselves, they are 'driven forward by impulses over which they have no real control'.[33]

As an account of an intellectual impasse, this is surely a classic.[34] What Godwin does not do in *Thoughts on Man* is to pursue the question: suppose the criminal is oneself? Will not necessitarianism require self-compassion? And will not the 'delusory sense of liberty' lead to self-blame? What then?

Shelley's protagonists, Victor and his Creature, are in this situation. Both describe themselves in terms of being 'driven forward by impulses over which they have no control' *and* apply to themselves terms that derive from an assumption of the 'delusion of liberty': debt, bond, right, claim, sin, crime, guilt, merit and desert. On a high mountain hut, a ship's cabin and other variants of the philosopher's closet, they reflect on cause and effect and express necessitarian views. Acting in the world, they behave as though they have free will and are responsible for their deeds. When they recount their histories, the two doctrines collide. Detached assessments of self and of fellow-humans rapidly collapse into idolizing and demonizing. These self-contradictions are not due to Shelley's confusion but arise from her initial assignment to her protagonists of equal adherence to conflicting positions, neither of which can be dispelled or subordinated. Her changes to *1831* point up more sharply the philosophical dilemma at the core of *Frankenstein*, but not so as to reduce the novel to a *thèse*, which it never is. We do not find, as we do in *Mandeville*, passages of didactic exposition in which 'issues' are laid bare. The increased emphasis also raises to a higher pitch the tension between sympathy and judgement with respect to the two protagonists. All versions of *Frankenstein*, including Shelley's draft, reveal a concern to intensify these tensions. Both Victor and the Creature in *1831* are made more deviously manipulative *and* more emotionally engaging.

An example illustrating the minute care that Shelley could take in this respect concerns the promise exacted from the Creature in return

16 *The Craft of Writing*

for a mate. In all versions, the Creature makes an initial offer. Victor then reasons with the Creature, who reiterates the offer, but on increasingly worse terms. The underlying, triadically structured type-story of such bargaining is the Roman legend of the Sibyl who offers King Tarquin 12 books at a high price.[35] Tarquin refuses, hoping to beat her down; the Sibyl burns three books, and repeats her offer twice, burning a batch of three each time. At length Tarquin is forced to buy the last three unburnt books for the same price as the original 12.

From draft stage right through to *1831*, duplicity, menace, and self-justification, are written, along with pathos, into the conception of the Creature, and these qualities are matched against Victor's own self-justifications and agonizing. The Creature, unlike the Sybil, uses ambiguous words which obfuscate the fact that he has withdrawn certain items from the offer. At first, he volunteers to go to South America for good; the second time, he does not specify that he will leave Europe but offers merely to dwell 'in the most savage of places'. When Victor puts up his third objection to the Creature's plea, the *1818* Creature retorts:

> How is this? I thought I had moved your compassion, and yet you still refuse to bestow upon me the only benefit that can soften my heart and render me harmless.
>
> (*F* 110 [II. ix])[36]

Victor, after reflection, agrees, provided that the Creature reaffirms his promise to quit Europe for ever and 'every other place in the neighbourhood'. The Creature, however, makes no such reaffirmation. Instead, in *1818* (and *1823*) he says

> I swear ... by the sun, and by the blue sky of heaven, that if you grant my prayer, while they exist you shall never behold me again.
>
> (ibid.)

No mention now of leaving Europe or even the habitations of men! The letter of the vow could be fulfilled if the Creature were to blind Victor or to visit him on a pitch-dark night. Significantly, 'Saying this, he suddenly quitted me, fearful, perhaps, of any change in my sentiments.' *Perhaps*. The alert reader can see that the Creature could be making a quick get-away before Victor realizes that his creation has promised, like one of Waldman's 'modern masters', very little, while he himself is committed to performing a great deal.

The ambiguousness of the Creature's words is more obvious in the draft, where Shelley at first made him swear 'by the sun and by the clouds that while they exist you shall never behold me'. To swear by the *clouds* was perhaps to tip too broad a wink to the reader that the Creature's vows were mutable. But perhaps the disingenuousness is a shade too occluded in *1818*. In *1831*, however, Shelley finds a precisely intermediate degree of suggestiveness. The Creature swears by the sun and by the blue sky but also by 'the fire of love that burns my heart'.[37] Could there be a more sincere and exalted vow? But whereas the sun and the blue sky exist somewhere even when unseen, no mortal can promise to burn with love forever; indeed, the prime reason for manufacturing the hideous lady is to end the torture of the Creature's burning desire. Once the fire is extinguished, the pledge becomes worthless.

Yet critics who see Shelley as presenting a seductively 'nicer' Victor in *1831* may have a point, although not for the reason usually advanced. Both Shelleys seem to have anticipated that making the Creature sympathetic would be the really difficult challenge. P.B. Shelley's review is largely an apologia for him. But sympathy-for-the-monster has a long history, antedating Boris Karloff by well over a century; an early reviewer pronounced 'his natural tendency to kind feelings' as among *Frankenstein*'s 'very interesting and beautiful' features; another stated roundly: '*my* interest in the book is entirely on the side of the monster'.[38] No reviewer declared for Victor, whose image worsened over the following decade. A dramatic version of 1823/26 added seduction and abandonment to the tally of his crimes,[39] while the Creature became a pantomime Beast in need of a woman's gentle influence. Shelley may have found that, unexpectedly, a genuine dilemma had been all too easily resolved and sentimentalized, and took corrective action. Logic – the law of Necessity, if valid, applies to both the Creator and the Creature – and intensity of interest demanded that both protagonists be allowed to compete for readers' sympathy on a more nearly equal basis; if the Creature was ultimately to win, there should at least be a contest.[40]

Be that as it may, the most important determinant of the changes made for *1831* is the dynamic of the *1818* text itself. The *1818 Frankenstein* has a stark, pristine, 'expressionist' texture which one sometimes misses in *1831*. But in dismissing as a white lie or wishful thinking Shelley's claim that her revised version did not make any major change to her original novel, might we not be behaving like Dr Johnson's 'poring man' who, on discovering a mere five apples and

18 *The Craft of Writing*

pears in an orchard, triumphantly declares that they are wrong who say that the orchard has no apples and pears? Could we not, applying Johnsonian criteria, take her seriously?

Notes

Quotations and references, unless otherwise stated, are taken from the 1818 *Frankenstein*. I am grateful to Pamela Clemit and Maurice Hindle for reading this essay during the evolutionary process. An earlier version was presented at 'Mary Wollstonecraft Shelley in Her Times' (New York, May 1997).

1. 'A Note on the Text' in *The Annotated Frankenstein*, ed. Leonard Wolf (New York: Clarkson N. Potter, Inc., 1977); revised as *The Essential Frankenstein* (New York: Penguin Books USA, 1993), n. pag. Godwin made over 120 small changes for the rare 1823 edition; Shelley kept almost all in 1831. For a collation of all three editions (hereafter *1818*, *1823* and *1831*) and the hand-corrected so-called 'Thomas' copy, see *MWS Pickering*, vol. 1. Among critics, Butler, Palacio, Rieger, Poovey, Mellor, Macdonald and Scherf agree broadly that Shelley weakened the *1831* text. A dissenting voice is Elizabeth A. Bohls, *Women Travel Writers and the Language of Aesthetics, 1716–1818* (Cambridge: Cambridge University Press, 1995) p. 288n. The pro-*1818* shift is mirrored in publishers' lists. While cheap, plain editions usually have an *1831* text, *1818* now dominates annotated editions.
2. See 'keeping' in *F*, Letter II (all edns) explained in Walter Scott's review of *Childe Harold*, Canto III (*Quarterly Review*, XVI [October 1816] 181–3). 'Interesting' is taken from Ludwig Tieck's essay on *Hamlet*; see *The Romantics on Shakespeare*, ed. Jonathan Bate (Harmondsworth: Penguin, 1992) p. 335.
3. While the *1818* Elizabeth's indignation in Justine's cell is forceful, it abruptly collapses, almost ridiculously, into world-despisal (*F* 62–3 [I. vii]). Shelley may have justifiably felt in *1831* that it would be giving mixed messages to the readership for tyrant-hatred to be thus compromised.
4. Endmatter to Theodore Hook, *Maxwell*, Standard Novels XXXV (London: Colburn and Bentley, 1834).
5. *Thomas* copy; see *F* 34n.
6. Colburn and Bentley normally required living authors to make revisions for their Standard Novels, the chief motive being, apparently, to establish a new copyright (information from William St Clair). However, there were exceptions. Revisions to the Standard Novels *Caleb Williams* (1831) are very minor.
7. The epigraph might have been omitted to accommodate 'by/Mary Wollstonecraft Shelley' without crowding the title page; notably, too, the title-page epigraph from the third (1797) and subsequent editions of *Caleb Williams* was dropped for no obvious reason. In 1823 Godwin might have felt that to publish the dedication, when the author was widely known to

be his daughter, looked like vanity or that it took away from her own remarkable talent.
8. *F* 107 (II. viii; *1831*, ch. xiv). The portrait was found in Justine's 'pocket' (*F* 56–7 [I. vi; *1831*, ch. vii]), a word the Creature uses when recounting the discovery of his 'parentage' in Victor's laboratory dress (*F* 97 [II. vii; *1831*, ch. xv]). The two pockets are evidently intended to be compared. The episode recalls parodically Sterne's 'The fille-de-chambre, Paris' in *A Sentimental Journey*, when the narrator slips a volume of an erotic novel into a young woman's pocket.
9. See *MWSL* II, pp. 3–5, 16–17, 122–5 for supportive letters to Wright and Owen. In 1839 Shelley was bracketed by Crabb Robinson among the 'ultra-Liberals' patronized by Mary Gaskell; see *MWSJ* II, p. 608.
10. *Corinne*, bk. IV, 'Rome', ch. iii (my translation). The phrase (adapted by both De Staël and Shelley) derives ultimately from Victor Alfieri's *Misogallo* (1799).
11. Shelley's *Rambles in Germany and Italy* (1844) scornfully contested revisionist attempts to belittle Pellico's sufferings; see *TW* 275 (*Rambles* II, pp. 87–8).
12. Also found in *History of A Six Weeks' Tour* [etc.] (1817); facsimile rpt. introd. Jonathan Wordsworth (Oxford: Woodstock Books, 1989) p. 50.
13. *Frankenstein* (1818), ed. Marilyn Butler (Oxford: Oxford University Press, 1994), Appendix B, p. 200.
14. *F* 137 (III. iv; *1831*, ch. xxi).
15. Cf. *F* 45 (I.v) and *1831*, ch. vi. For a genuine 'true Swiss', see Godwin's Ruffigny, a reverse Ernest: 'Like a true Swiss of the earlier times, I have returned home, and bidden adieu, without a sigh, to the refinements and ostentation of other climates' (Godwin, *Fleetwood* [1805] 1832 Standard Novels edn, p. 71).
16. See, for instance, Chris Baldick, *In Frankenstein's Shadow: Myth, Monstrosity, and Nineteenth-Century Writing* (Oxford: Clarendon Press, 1987) p. 61.
17. 'Unhallowed' occurs thus in *1818*: 'the unhallowed damps of the grave' (*F* 37 [I. iii]); 'any curious and unhallowed wretch' (*F* 169–70 [III, Walton, 12 Sept.]). The other two *1831* additions are: 'my unhallowed arts' (*1831*, ch. viii, last sentence); 'my unhallowed acts' (*1831*, ch. xxii, para. 1). St Leon calls his alchemical lore 'unhallowed pursuits' (Godwin, *St Leon* [1799] 1831 Standard Novels edn, p. 290).
18. See Maurice Hindle, *Frankenstein*, Penguin Critical Studies (Harmondsworth: Penguin Books, 1994) p. 173.
19. Shelley herself never writes anything in endorsement of the retributive doctrine of eternal punishment.
20. Apparent also in her letters of 30 December 1830 and 26 January 1837 ('fate has been my enemy throughout'); in both she struggles towards some kind of affirmation, dreaming of a better destiny in a warmer clime or disowning her 'low spirits' (see *MWSL* II, pp. 124, 281).
21. Mellor, p. 170. That *Corinne* is in Shelley's mind is suggested by the references to 'slave' and 'chaplet'. In *Corinne*'s most celebrated passage, the inspired poet–heroine is crowned with laurel and myrtle in the Capitol.
22. Bohls (see n.1 above) considers that *1831*'s blue-eyed victim more tellingly indicts the Frankensteins than does the semi-bold *1818* Elizabeth. She is

also more in keeping with plot demands (Why does the 'stronger' Elizabeth not become Victor's confidante and comrade?) A previous name ('Myrtella') in the *Frankenstein* draft indicates that from an early stage she was conceptualized as a sweet domestic plant; see *Frankenstein Notebooks* I, p. lviii.
23. Shelley is sporadically drawn to counterfactual history, as, for instance, in her pondering the alternative fate of Europe had Wallenstein not become a Catholic (*TW* 232 [*Rambles* II, pp. 8–9]), or the following: 'Had [Louvet's measures] been followed up on the instant, France had been spared the reign of terror' ('Madame Roland' in *Lives of the Most Eminent Literary and Scientific Men of France*, 2 vols [London, 1838–39] II, p. 284 [*Lardner's Cabinet Cyclopædia*, 133 vols]).
24. *F* 14 (Letter ii); a black and brilliant pun – a regrettable loss in *1831*. Shelley's heightening of the master's savage torpor – 'silent as a Turk' – is inadequate recompense.
25. *F* 163–4 (III, Walton, 5 September).
26. The result leaves the question unresolved. The sailors hold firm to their resolution to go south, back home to loved ones, and overpersuade Walton. Victor's assertion that the men's resolution can literally crack ice is fallacious, yet after the crew wins the ice *does* crack. The necessitarian might take this as proof that necessity governs both mind and matter. Believers in freedom of the will can also claim a triumph. So can those who believe that Love is the law which necessarily rules the universe; for a similarly unresolved discussion of the issues of freewill and necessity, see *LM* 55 (I. iv[a]).
27. P. B. Shelley, *The Prose Works of Percy Bysshe Shelley*, ed. E. B. Murray, 1 vol. to date (Oxford: Clarendon Press, 1993– ; hereafter PBS *Prose*) I, p. 28.
28. *F* 168 (III, Walton: 12 Sept.).
29. *Mandeville: A Tale of the Seventeenth Century in England*, 3 vols (1817); ed. Pamela Clemit, vol. 6 of *Collected Novels and Memoirs of William Godwin*, 8 vols (London: William Pickering, 1992), hereafter, Godwin, *Novels*. Mandeville, like Victor, is a self-justifying, self-condemning protagonist. J. G. Lockhart praised Godwin's skill in inducing readers to 'sympathize in the emotions without being deceived by the speciousness of his hero' ('Review of *Mandeville*', *Blackwood's Edinburgh Magazine*, II [December 1817] 273).
30. PBS *Prose* I, p. 278. The similarity of 'turned by every wind that blows' in the ensuing *Mandeville* passage and 'moved by every wind that blows' in Victor's Alpine reverie, cited above, suggests mutual influence.
31. William Godwin, 'Of the Liberty of Human Actions', *Thoughts on Man* (1831); ed. Mark Philp, in vol. 6 of *Political and Philosophical Writings of William Godwin*, 7 vols (London: William Pickering, 1993) p. 166. If the will is free, Godwin wrote, repeating his argument in *Political Justice*, choices could be made without motives; persuasion would be an irrelevant activity.
32. Godwin took this phrase from Lord Kames's *Essay on the Principles of Morality* [etc.] (1751).
33. Godwin, 'Of the Liberty of Human Actions', pp. 165–71 (my emphases). Godwin's inclusion of 'sin' may explain why the Creature's final speech in

1831 refers to his 'sins', the sole instance in the *Frankenstein* texts. Locke points out that Godwin's modification of his necessitarianism had began as early as 1800 (Don Locke, *A Fantasy of Reason: the Life and Thought of William Godwin* [London: Routledge and Kegan Paul, 1980]) p. 326.

34. The philosophical jury is still out on the question of free will vs determinism. For a recent survey of the state of play, see Galen Strawson, 'Luck Swallows Everything', *TLS*, 26 June 1998. He concludes that 'the debate is likely to continue for as long as human beings can think, as the ... argument that we can't possibly have free will keeps bumping into the fact that we can't help believing that we do'.
35. See *FN* 75 (I.xii) and *PBSL* II, p. 400 for the Shelleys' allusions to this legend.
36. Godwin in *1823* heightened the Creature's exasperation at this critical point of the interchange: 'How is this? I must not be trifled with; and I demand an answer.'
37. *Frankenstein Notebooks* II, pp. 411, 415–17; *1831*, ch. xvii.
38. *Scots Magazine and Edinburgh Literary Miscellany*, n.s. II (March 1818) 249–53; *Knight's Quarterly Magazine*, III (August 1824) 195–9; both partly rptd in *Frankenstein. The 1818 Text: Contexts, Nineteenth-Century Responses, Modern Criticism*, ed. J. Paul Hunter (New York: W. W. Norton, 1996) pp. 191–200.
39. *Frankenstein, Or, the Man and the Monster*, described on the title page as 'partly based on *Le Magicien et le Monstre*, by H. M. Milner' (London: J. Duncombe, n.d.), facsimile rpt in *The Hour of One*, ed. Stephen Wischhusen (London: Gordon Fraser, 1975), n. pag.
40. Shelley elsewhere treats the polarization of readers' reactions as a merit. In her unfinished 'Life of William Godwin' (c.1839) she praises *Caleb Williams* for this effect: 'those in the lower classes saw their cause espoused and their oppressors forcibly and eloquently delineated – while those of higher rank acknowledged and felt the nobleness, sensibility and errors of Falkland with deepest sympathy' (Abinger MSS c. 606/1–5, quoted in introd. to *Caleb Williams*, ed. Pamela Clemit, vol. 3 of Godwin, *Novels*, p. viii).

I am grateful to Charles E. Robinson for making me aware of James O'Rourke's 'The 1831 Introduction and Revisions to *Frankenstein*: Mary Shelley Dictates Her Legacy' (*Studies in Romanticism* 38 [autumn 1999] 365–85), which unfortunately appeared too late for me to engage with it. While we use very different examples and arguments, I salute Dr O'Rourke as a fellow-vindicator.

2
The Ends of the Fragment, the Problem of the Preface: Proliferation and Finality in *The Last Man*

Sophie Thomas

For many of its contemporary readers, Mary Shelley's 1826 novel *The Last Man* came too late: it treated a theme whose imaginative power had all but vanished in a brief storm of popularity. Its apocalyptic possibilities had, it seemed, by virtue of their over-representation in a proliferation of 'Last Man' narratives, become slightly ridiculous.[1] This turning of the tide, however, was largely a response to the fundamental unrepresentability of the theme of lastness: that such an idea could not only be represented but received – by a reader, for instance – would contradict, logically speaking, any claim to lastness. Indeed, the very idea, in spite of its inherent attractiveness, quickly became the object of scorn. As the writer of an essay in *The Monthly Magazine* pointed out, not only is the word '"last" ... insufficiently final', but last things in general are 'the last things in the world that are last'.[2] And yet, the incommensurability of lastness and finality, the problematic relation of 'the last' to 'the end', far from providing grounds for dismissing Shelley's efforts, helps us to come to terms with the most problematic – and arguably the most central – aspects of her novel: first, the relationship of the prefatory fiction, with its discovery of the Sibyl's prophetic fragments, to the tale of the extinction of humanity narrated in the future by Lionel Verney; secondly, the resulting temporal ambiguities; and finally, the relation of both of these to the impossibility of ending, the difficulty of concluding, which, under the pressure of its subject matter, profoundly affects the novel.

The Last Man is afflicted, however, by a greater problem than the unrepresentability of lastness, its insufficiently *final* quality, for at work in the novel is the paradoxical dynamic of an endgame in which narrative finality, the reduction – in this case, of the human race – to an implicit nothingness, involves a peculiar *plenitude*. Reduction is, paradoxically, accomplished through multiplication, insofar as there is a potentially infinite reproduction of the very condition that ostensibly ushers in closure. The plague, for example, brings on the destruction of man, his (shall we say) progressive diminishment, at the same time as it is a figure for the forces of proliferation. It manages this through its uncontainability, through its capacity to reproduce its destructive effects. This uncontainability is, on the one hand, prefigured by the scattered Sibylline leaves of the preface – while the narrative situation, on the other, is propelled by the overwhelming *presence* of an end that is by definition absent. This suspension of the end, and of ends, is precisely what constitutes a fragment, but it is also a compelling meditation on the ends of writing: the last man – both the novel and the situation of its hero in his function as writer – may be read, particularly when viewed through the proliferating fragments of the Sibyl's cave, as a reflection on the infinality of writing itself.

Since fragmentation is central, as I will argue, to the novel's concerns, it is worth sketching out now the general implications of such a claim. It is an obvious generalization to observe that forms and figures of fragmentation proliferate in Romanticism. Proliferation is perhaps in the very nature of fragmentation: that is, the phenomenon of the uncontainable is itself uncontainable, in the manner of the plague in *The Last Man*. At issue in the novel, however, is not the boundless aspiration of the poetic imagination – the obvious province and provenance of the Romantic fragment – but boundlessness *as such*. Perhaps the most striking difference between the Romantic fragment and Shelley's treatment of fragmentation in *Frankenstein* and *The Last Man* is that with Shelley, fragmentation no longer has to do with the integrity of the poetic persona and its coherent production, but rather with human community. In the shadow of the plague that reduces human civilization to its last man, the central epistemological problem that the poetic fragment represents is re-inscribed on the body (and the body politic), so that the organicist postulate becomes not what makes the work of art whole, but what makes a person (and, by extension, a collective of persons) 'whole'.

In *Frankenstein*, the creature *is* a body of fragments, an assemblage of dead body parts that apes a monstrous whole; it embodies life at the margins of life: a life to be lived only in and through death. Death also looms larger than life in *The Last Man* and explicit questions are raised there about the relative completion and incompletion of being. Starvation and disease of the body are set against models of plenitude:

fullness of the mind, for example, is to be gained through the completing capacities of thought and of love. Working against this ideal at the very moment of its articulation, however, is the reduction of human civilization to a fragment, a mere leaf, of Sibylline prophecy. The dispersal of life itself raises a rather different problem for the fragment than did the dispersal of poetic vision: the problem of finality itself. The resulting generation of fragmentation makes reduction to the one, the *none*, infinitely problematic. Wholeness is no longer to be achieved constructively, but is arrived at through a process of reduction. The essence of one-ness, so to speak, is a product of diminishment – a process contrary to that of Frankenstein's creature – so that the problem is no longer of the unfinished, but rather of *finishing*.

I

Metaphors of fragmentation (and of parts, wholes, ruins, and so forth) occur with remarkable frequency in *The Last Man*. Shelley exploits the considerable power of the opposition between parts and wholes to figure forth the ideal interconnectedness of things, as well as to describe their disintegration. Early in the novel, the particular (Shelleyan) ideal that the character of Adrian is to embody is described in precisely these terms: 'Adrian felt that he made a part of a great whole'; he feels his life 'mingle with the universe of existence' (*LM* 38 [i. iii]). This harmonious negotiation of all the world's parts is an apt reflection of the inherently related nature of *all* things. 'We go on,' Adrian argues, 'each thought linked to the one which was its parent, each act to a previous act. No joy or sorrow dies barren of progeny, which for ever generated and generating, weaves the chain that make[3] our life.' This totalizing enchainment has, however, a darker side, as lines Adrian cites from Calderón suggest: 'A day calls to another,/And in that way is linked/Grief to grief and sorrow to sorrow' (*LM* 39 [I. iii]).[4] These lines offer, it seems, an analogy for the actual spread of the plague in the fictional world of *The Last Man*, as well as for the accompanying narrative enchainment, both generated and generating, that propels the story forward through ruin toward terminus. The lines emphasize, moreover, the relationship of minor events to a situational whole in which they proliferate infinitely, since they are inextricable from, among other things, the progress of time. With just one example, then, we have moved from a specific instance of the part/whole metaphor to a dynamic impelling the 'whole' novel. That is, the question of 'connectedness' in Adrian's view of things may be linked to the question of narrative structure, and particularly, narrative *completion*.

Metaphors involving fragmentation are frequently deployed with regard to both personal and political relations. The breakdown of a relationship, for example, is described as 'the disunion of an whole which may not have parts' (*LM* 111 [I. ix]). The political state is characterized in terms of dismemberment and restoration. When Raymond argues for a return to a monarchical state, he speaks of England's 'broken sceptre', which Adrian's father 'yielded up', and affirms that he will 'join its dismembered frame' (*LM* 47 [I. iv]). Some of the most pointed uses of fragment metaphors, however, are with respect to individual decline and, in extreme cases, death. Early in the novel, Raymond describes Adrian, who has been falsely declared 'mad' by certain interested family members and friends, as a human ruin, whom he wishes to see 'restored to himself' (ibid.). In a later conversation with Lionel Verney on the same subject, Raymond's metaphors apparently proliferate. He refers to Adrian as 'that melancholy ruin, which stands in mental desolation, more irreparable than a fragment of a carved column in a weed-grown field' (*LM* 57 [I. iv(a)]). Raymond's own dramatic death in the burning Constantinople is perhaps all too fitting when (in what is perhaps my favourite example) he was 'thrown from his horse by some falling ruin, which had crushed his head, and defaced his whole person' (*LM* 163 [II. iii]). Clearly there is some infectiousness at play on the level of metaphor, as characters are ruined by ruins, defaced, so to speak, by the already defaced. Perhaps Shelley is merely expressing her familiarity with the aesthetic discourses of her time, but the language of fragmentation, dismemberment, ruin, and restoration, is working overtime in a novel charting the decline of civilization.

This decline, marked as it is by a paradoxically proliferating force, is accompanied by equally marked chronological ambiguities. In spite of the apparent predictability of the enchainment model of (narrative) time just mentioned – the progress of time that, generated, generates its effects – there is nevertheless a great deal of indefinition surrounding what we usually think of in fairly certain terms as 'before' and 'after'. There is the obvious interest aroused by setting a first-person account of past events in the distant future of the twenty-first century, while prefacing that account with another first-person narrative, that of the author's discovery in 1818 of the text that will follow – long before the events that are prophesied as having taken place possibly *could* have. The preface, we recall, tells the story of the author's visits to the Sibyl's cave, where she and her companion find verses inscribed on leaves and fragments of bark, out of which they assemble the ensuing work. The problem of chronology intersects with the peculiar status of the preface in general, and I will return to it later. But right from the first pages of the novel, we perceive that the characters are already the inhabitants of an afterworld. The status of the principal players as variously orphaned, disinherited, or otherwise estranged – 'Lord Raymond was the sole remnant of a noble but impoverished family' (*LM* 34 [I. iii]) – makes the world of the novel something of a 'post' world: post-family as well as post-monarchy. This provides the characters, of course, with the necessary isolation to live out their domestic utopia in Windsor, but it presents them as quite detached, for a time at least, from encroaching socio-political realities so that they may be seen to constitute a fragment whose very fulfilment is predicated upon detachment – a detachment that is not unrelated to a pervasive, if illusory, sense of temporal immunity.

Some of the novel's chronological ambiguities involve that ultimate end, death itself. Several of the main characters have a 'near death' experience, in which they seem to die, but then live on for a time in an ambiguous afterlife, before finally dying (again). Raymond is reported (falsely, as it turns out) to have died in the Greek wars; Lionel and Perdita discover him still alive, but just, and although he recovers to a degree, he is never fully 'restored'. Both Adrian and Lionel virtually die during serious illnesses. Lionel, having apparently contracted the plague, is for several hours declared clinically dead: 'On the third night animation was suspended; to the eye and touch of all I was dead.' Miraculously, however, he returns to life, and furthermore, returns with increased strength and vitality (*LM* 268–9 [III. iii]). Immune, so it seems, from the plague, and the only one to have survived it, we feel him to be immortal. Lionel's resurrection, however, marks another stage in the disintegration of his wife Idris, who collapses in horror at his unlikely recovery. She, we recall, was thrown onto the path of progressive decline by the serious illness of their eldest son, Alfred, and although he too recovered and lived on for a time, her security and peace were allegedly shattered beyond repair.

In another pattern of female response, Raymond's death is the direct cause of his wife Perdita's. Between the time of his death and her own, she declares herself to be living a living death, living in 'another world' from the one she inhabited previously. 'Look on me as dead', she says, as she argues her desire to live out her life in close proximity to Raymond's grave, 'and truly if death be a mere change of state, I am dead' (*LM* 166 [II. iii]). In that place of living death, she claims she may 'hold communion only with the has been, and to come'. She may, then, sustain an extratemporal, a prophetic perhaps, relationship to her past life. She feels compelled to this; it is not, she says, a matter of choice: 'I can live here only. I am a part of this scene; each and all its properties are a part of me' (*LM* 167 [II. iii]). Made to de-part from that place of death, drugged by Lionel (in yet another counterfeit death) and taken on board a ship bound for England, Perdita's suicide by drowning is, so to speak, a foregone conclusion. There is another moment much later in the novel when the interchangeability of death and life is reflected upon. The dwindling band of survivors contemplate the inevitability of the death that awaits them, and wonder if it is not rather to be sought eagerly than procrastinated. 'Death is a vast portal,' comments the narrator, 'an high road to life: let us hasten to pass; let us exist no more in this living death, but die that we may live' (*LM* 320 [III. vii]).

The finality of death, then, and the certainty with which it establishes a before and an after, a beginning and an end, becomes increasingly ambiguous. This ambiguity is felt through a number of contradictions that plague, shall we say, the progress of the novel. One of these is the way in which death, the progressive destruction through diminishment of the human race, does its work amid relative plenitude. Several times in the novel the discrepancy between event and situation is remarked upon. Seasons come and go, the natural world flourishes, while the human world is depopulated. Riding for the last time through the streets of London, Lionel remarks: 'everything was desert; but nothing was in ruin' (*LM* 260 [III. ii]). The passage cited above, in which Lionel reflects on life in and through death, is preceded by reflections in the form of a series of questions, for which there can be no final answer, about the possibility of the world continuing unperturbed by the disappearance of man:

> But the game is up! We must all die; nor leave survivor nor heir to the wide inheritance of earth. ... Will the earth still keep her place among the planets; will she still journey with unmarked regularity round the sun; will the seasons change, the trees adorn themselves with leaves, and flowers shed their fragrance, in solitude? Will the mountains remain unmoved, and streams still keep a downward course toward the vast abyss; will the tides rise and fall, and the

winds fan universal nature; ... when man, the lord, possessor, perceiver, and recorder of all these things has passed away, as though he had never been?

(*LM* 320 [III. vii])

The end of humanity, then, will take place incompletely, or at least in a partial context in which nature and the animal kingdom apparently continue to thrive. Fulfilled nature, it is speculated, will remain indifferent to the disappearance of man, yet it is inconceivable that the loss of such a part will not obliterate the whole that it possesses, perceives, records. Finality is neither, then, a totalizing nor an absolute concept, and the last line of the passage just cited evokes a temporal ambiguity, making what has passed away ('as though [it] had never been') indistinguishable from what is not yet come.

Interestingly, though, 'harmony of event and situation' are achieved when the plague (rather inexplicably) dies out. It is buried with its last victim in a cave of ice beneath the ever-moving glaciers of Chamounix, a 'fitting costume' for what Lionel refers to as their 'last act'. The sublime grandeur of the scene, which accords so well with their sense of desolation – their existence at a limit, at the very limits of life – is highly appropriate since the experience of the sublime is itself located at the threshold of the sensible. The passage through the Alps of what is now the very last remnant of the race of man functions, Lionel claims, as a boundary between their former and future states (*LM* 331–2 [III. viii]). This passage marks, however, an end before the end, or perhaps an interim ending, as it is here (there) that the drama is said, by its participants, to have been closed: 'Majestic gloom and tragic pomp attended', notes Lionel, 'the decease of wretched humanity' (*LM* 329 [III. viii]). If this 'last' death is ambiguously designated as the end of man, what, then, comes after? Is the final ending merely deferred, or are Adrian, Lionel, Clara and Evelyn released into an afterlife from which the plague has miraculously disappeared? What is certain is that release from the threat of the plague brings with it, ironically, a heightened sense of the end, as each of the four look round themselves and wonder which of them is fated to be the *very* last man. The game, then, far from being up, has changed course.

The END, though difficult to approach, much less arrive at, shadows the novel from early on, indeed from its preface. The end *is* the future, and the two terms are perhaps interchangeable in a novel where the future is first and foremost that which will usher in the end. But just as the future is, by definition, always before us and never where we are now, perhaps the end, in theory, will never come. Such reflections, however, are no consolation to Shelley's characters, who spend a great deal of time thinking about the end. As the plague spreads, Lionel expresses his natural desire to stave off futurity (this is recorded, of course, after the futurity he has in mind has already come): 'futurity, like a dark image in a phantasmagoria, came nearer and more near, till it clasped the whole earth in its shadow' (*LM* 201 [II. vii]). It is the *shadow* of the thing, rather than the thing itself, that 'clasps' the 'whole earth', so we are still at some remove from futurity as such. The end of time has become visible to the characters, but only in the form of a yawning gulf – a nothingness – before them. Formerly, they had measured out their lives in years along the road of life, through a 'lengthened period of progression and decay', while the road's terminus in the Valley of the Shadow of Death had been hidden 'by intervening objects'. Now, however, the hours propel them towards the chasm, the 'deep and precipitous' gulf, that has opened at their feet (*LM* 214 [II. viii]). This revelation is, significantly, a revelation of nothingness, since what is no longer hidden is nothing. Such a curious state of affairs accords, moreover, with Adrian's arguments for leaving England as the plague enters its final stages. The end of time, he felt, was come: 'he knew that one by one we should dwindle into nothingness' and it was 'not adviseable to wait this sad consummation in [their] native country' when travelling, on the other hand, would distract their thoughts 'from the swift-approaching end of things' (*LM* 256 [III. ii]).[5] In what sense, though, can this approaching end be viewed as a 'consummation': what kind of consummation is a reduction to nothingness? Here too, we find the idea of the end expressed through the paradox of fulfilment achieved by emptying out, or voiding.[6] The lines ascribed to Cleveland that Shelley cites a few pages earlier (after an extended farewell to England and everything it represents) are indeed apt: 'Farewell, sad Isle, farewell, thy fatal glory/Is summed, cast up, and cancelled in this story' (*LM* 254 [III. ii]).

At a crucial juncture in the novel, it is suggested to the narrator (by an internal voice, clear and articulate, which suddenly seems to speak) that the victory of the plague over mankind was inevitable:

> Thus from eternity, it was decreed: the steeds that bear Time onwards had this hour and this fulfilment enchained to them, since the void brought forth its burthen. Would you read backwards the unchangeable laws of Necessity?
>
> (*LM* 310 [III. vi])

Like a text, like *this* text, Shelley's novel, which cannot be read backwards, the chariot of Time and all that is chained to it, runs on in one direction – though its provenance is eternity, and its destination is the consequence decreed of nothingness. It is significant that this motion and its meaning are expressed in textual terms. At times, the characters seem literally to inhabit a text, a (prophetic?) text in which 'horror and despair' are 'written in glaring characters' on the faces of all (*LM* 311 [III. vi]). Frequent metaphors involving writing and reading ground us in the narrative situation by reflecting, often explicitly, on Lionel Verney's undertaking, and on its putative ends. They remind us, too, of our position as readers of Shelley's text, and of the position of the implied author as decipherer of the fragments out of which the text is constructed.

The narrator, for example, occasionally refers to events as though he is *reading* them. He describes the events in Greece as an 'animated volume' that he peruses attentively, reading his tale on 'the new-turned page' (*LM* 139 [II. i]). He writes of 'the pages of the earth's history' – writes of Raymond, alluding to Shelley's *The Mask of Anarchy*, as the '"hero of unwritten story"' (*LM* 154,159 [II. ii]).[7] But the more telling examples are those that refer the moment of writing to the problem of time, as they bring into sharper focus the problem of narrative conclusion in a text that must defer its end. Now, if we accept Peter Brooks's reading of Freud's *Beyond the Pleasure Principle*, the circuitous search for the right end is as much a feature of narrative plots as it is of our lives, and in Shelley's novel, of course, we have a conflation of the two.[8] But by the same token, deferral, in the case of *The Last Man*, is made doubly necessary by the novel's content, as well as by its chosen mode of presentation. Verney comments at one point that elapsed time, and the corresponding distance and disjunction between what was and what is, are precisely what enable him to 'comprehend the past as a whole'. Initially, he writes his journal of death as an opiate, a process that soothes with its 'melancholy pleasure', at least while it describes his friends in their prime. As his narration progresses, however, its 'long drawn and tortuous path' leads to an 'ocean of countless tears' and he reflects on the task that falls to him of picking through the ruins of his history, selecting 'leading incidents, and disposing light and shade so as to form a picture in whose very darkness there will be harmony' (*LM* 208–9 [II. viii]). This is an extraordinarily painful process, one which the endpoint of the narrative – the final ruin of mankind that leaves him in his solitary 'present' – threatens continually to subvert: 'Oh my pen! haste thou to write what was, before the thought of what is, arrests the hand that guides thee' (*LM* 66 [I. v]).

For the narrator is indeed in a precarious position, and one that foregrounds his vexed relationship to time. He has experienced, effectively, a *second* resurrection, having only just survived the shipwreck that took the lives of his last two companions (although their deaths are a matter of inference; their bodies are not found washed up on the shore). He has woken up alone, for the first time, in a dead world (*LM* 346 [III. ix]) – with time, so to speak, on his hands (this is, of course, what it is to be a writer). For him, the future will be a perpetual burden: he begins by marking time with notches on a peeled willow-wand, then leaves off in despair, realizing that 'the unveiled course of [his] lone futurity' was far more obscure than death (*LM* 354 [III. x]). For a time, Lionel replaces futurity with antiquity in Rome, a city of which every part is 'replete with the relics of ancient times' (*LM* 357 [III. x]). The choice of Rome is significant for several reasons, one of which is that it evokes Lionel's early (pseudo-pastoral) life as a shepherd, 'as uncouth a savage, as the wolf-bred founder of old Rome' (*LM* 360 [III. x]). Now, at the 'end' of his life, he rambles in 'undiminished grandeur'; he seeks oblivion amid the fragments of an ancient culture, fragments which, however empty and ruined, are nevertheless full of significance as the signs of cultural continuance. This is only, however, a brief if enchanting episode, a waking dream, from which he falls into 'the abyss of the present', into 'self-knowledge' (*LM* 359 [III. x]). For a time, he occupies himself by reading volumes contained in the libraries of Rome. Then, upon the chance discovery the necessary materials in an author's study, he sets about writing, so that he may 'leave in this most ancient city, this '"world's sole monument," a record ... a monument of the existence of Verney, the Last Man' (*LM* 362 [III. x]). Interestingly, the author whose study he enters had written a treatise on the Italian language, with an 'unfinished dedication to posterity' (ibid.). This almost comical detail both asserts and questions the supposition that language will endure. Undeterred by the fact that his text will in all likelihood suffer the same lack of readership as the learned disquisition (Lionel, however, dedicates *his* to the 'illustrious dead'), he embarks upon his task. Having read what he has written, we reach the moment at which he begins to write: 'I will write' (ibid.), he asserts (so very near the end), in an attempt to keep alive what has been lost.

This is not, however, his first attempt to seek consolation (and construct a future) through writing. In every empty town he passed through on his road leading to Rome, he wrote in some conspicuous place, in white paint and in three languages (recalling the multilingual, fragmentary inscriptions of the Sibyl's cave), 'that "Verney, the last of the race of Englishman, had taken up his abode in Rome."' In Verney's account, then (in which he quotes himself at the – obviously earlier – moment of this undertaking), he describes his future movements in the past tense and the third person. To this message of a future past, directed toward a future present, he adds the adjuration: '"Friend, come! I wait for thee"' (*LM* 353 [III. x]). This, too, recalls the situation described in the preface, in which the implied author, part way through the task of translating and ordering the fragments gathered from repeated visits to the Sibyl's cave, loses her companion, and must, like Lionel, complete the task alone.[9]

It is the presence, then, of a threatening but unknowable futurity that propels the narrative at its later stages. We must keep in mind the difference between the time of writing and the time of the story: as the two begin to meet, as Lionel searches for 'words capacious of the grand conclusion', he doubts his capacity to accomplish what he has undertaken. He invites 'black Melancholy' to accompany, in an apocalyptic consummation of his narrative, both the writing and the reading of these (his) pages, bringing with it murky fogs from hell that will extinguish light, and 'blight and pestiferous exhalations' that will fill every crevice and cavern of earth with corruption, while the 'everlasting mountains' will be decomposed, and while the 'genial atmosphere which clips the globe, [will] lose all powers of generation and sustenance' (*LM* 338 [III. ix]). This vision of the end, provoked by arrival at the end of narrative, is one of both filling up and decomposing, of a poisonous plenitude that strips nature of its capacity to generate life, and by extension withdraws the power of the narrator to compose his story. This passage is clearly the expostulation of a moment, a scenario driven by despair, but it is fed by a very real threat that is also a desire for the oblivion that the end will bring. The ends of narrative composition, are, however, a reading, and the possibility of a reader mitigates the end of the end. Several questions are raised by Verney: not only who will read his lines, but what context is fit for their transmission? His suggestion?

> Seek some cave, deep embowered in earth's dark entrails, where no light will penetrate, save that which struggles, red and flickering, through a single fissure, staining thy page with grimmest livery of death.
>
> (*LM* 339 [III. ix])

With this remark, I would like to return to the beginning, to the preface that these lines revisit in a more desperate mode, for the work of Lionel Verney, unlike that of the author, *is* work without hope. The cavern Verney evokes is an imaginary place, the product of his dark fancy, but we, as readers, have passed through its more literal manifestation. And yet, the framing narrative of the author's journey to the Sibyl's cave remains open-ended: the *novel* does not return to it, but opts, understandably, for a more suggestive ending, in which the narrator sets sail for unspecifiable destinations (although among them are 'the libraries of the world'), and toward an unknowable future that lies beyond the confines of the narrative. This is precisely how, or rather why, the novel degenerates into the structure of a fragment, as the end of the fragment is always, of course, outside and beyond itself. With all the world now before us, though, it is easy to overlook, or even forget, the confined passages through which we entered the novel. And yet it could be argued that the preface itself is one of the novel's principal destinations.

II

While some readers have viewed the author's introduction, or preface, as a convenient, if extravagant, fiction that can be quickly forgotten once it has done its work of facilitating the reader's entry into Lionel Verney's world, closer examination reveals how tightly interwoven it is with the material of the novel, and particularly how bound up it is with the main issues isolated here: the relation between fragmentation, conclusion, and the temporal dynamics of the novel. Leaving aside for a moment the merits of introducing a work of futuristic fiction with a frame that declares it an ancient prophetic text, let us look quickly at some of the preface's claims. It begins factually enough: the author and her companion, on 8 December 1818, visit Naples in order to view 'various ruined temples, baths, and classic spots', some of which are the 'fragments of old Roman villas', now submerged in the translucent and shining waters of the sea – hardly an insignificant detail, given the importance of the sea at the end of the novel. At length, the travellers enter 'the gloomy cavern of the Cumæan Sibyl'. The actual Cave of the Sibyl is apparently inaccessible; however, they abandon both their guides and, eventually, their torches, to force their way, through a series of steep ascents and narrow passages, through darkness toward an increasing, but dim light, to that unvisited and unvisitable place: a wide cavern with a dome-like roof, and a veiled aperture permitting the light of heaven, as it were, to enter. And what do they find? Sibylline leaves: literal fragments (such as 'leaves, bark, and other substances') that are 'traced with written characters'. Some fascinating details are related at this point. First, these writings, to the astonishment of the travellers, are in several languages: some old ('ancient Chaldee, and Egyptian hieroglyphics') and, stranger still, some modern (English and Italian). Here begins a remarkable proliferation of contradictions: the writings are said to contain prophecies, but these prophecies are 'detailed relations of events but lately passed'. They involve well-known names, but of modern date. The author asserts that this is indeed the Sibyl's cave, though not, admittedly, as Virgil describes it, and accounts for their curious discovery as the result of convulsions of the earth (such as earthquakes and volcanoes), 'though the traces of ruin were effaced by time' (*LM* 7 [Introd.]).

The curiously modern 'English dress of the Latin poet', at which the author wonders, is clearly a thin disguise for the author's identification with the Sibyl, but it also identifies the fragments with the work of translation, adaptation, and ordering that must be carried out – that is, it blurs the line between the ancient fragments and their modern recuperation. 'Sometimes I have thought,' remarks the author, 'that, obscure and chaotic as they are, they owe their present form to me, their decipherer.' An implicit debate ensues over the value of the author's completing efforts *vis-à-vis* the disordered state of the original fragments. In their pure, 'pristine', condition, the fragments were apparently 'unintelligible', and thus invited, demanded perhaps, the transformation they have undergone. Having raised, then, the question of what follows as a consciously manipulated and constructed text, the author leaves the reader to judge whether his/her time has been well spent in 'giving form and substance to the frail and attenuated Leaves of the Sibyl' (*LM* 8–9 [Introd.]).

There is a wealth of associations and meanings attaching to the choice of a cave, and the invocation of the myth of the Sibyl (though relatively unexplored by critics) is itself rich with possibilities.[10] Here, however, I would like to draw attention to the importance of the preface as an exemplary location for launching, or instigating, the central dynamics of the novel, particularly as they relate to the problematic status of time. The Sibyl's fragments are said to be fragments of prophecy, and there appears to be an interesting relationship at work here between prophecy and fragmentation. Both a prophetic text, and a fragmentary text, are documents of *what is not*: the fragment is a document of what was, the prophecy a document of what will be (although this temporal orientation could be reversed); and here, where fragments of prophecy are discovered before the time of the prophecy's putative fulfilment, we have a document of what *will have been*. Is there an essential relation between the temporal category of prophecy, as a statement of the non-existent, and its representation by the fragment?

The gesture of the preface, the work of prefacing in general, is caught up in the same temporal ambiguity of both fragment and prophecy. The intention of a preface is normally to represent in some form what is to come, to say something of what will, logically speaking – and paradoxically – already have been written, since in the course of writing, it is the preface that is the last thing. As Derrida remarks in *Outwork* [*Hors livre*], his own essay on prefaces collected in *Dissemination*, the preface is to 'announce in the future tense ('this is what you are going to read') the conceptual content or significance ... of what will *already* have been *written*'.[11] The preface thus makes present *and* absent what is to follow. Having anticipated everything, Derrida points out, it cancels the need for the main text. The difficult status of the preface, then, is both temporal and conceptual, and its *difficulty* is in no small part related to its status as a fragment in relation to the work it introduces.

The general problems of prefacing are not only illustrative of the peculiarities that mark Shelley's preface, with its explicit relation to fragmentation and prophecy but also helpful when we consider the temporal structure of the novel. Written in the peculiarly negative moment of the future anterior, *The Last Man* ends only because it exists (or runs, perhaps) out of time. The essential conditions of its fragmentary structure make it impossible for the preface to be an adequate container for the novel (and vice versa), particularly since the problematic status of lastness infects and undermines both. The mutual unworking that the preface and its text perform upon each other is only emphasized, then, by the temporal incommensurability of preface and novel. This unworking is present from the very *outset*, preceding even the preface, in the epigraph from *Paradise Lost* with which the novel opens:

>Let no man seek
>Henceforth to be foretold what shall befall
>Him or his Children.
>
>(*Paradise Lost*, XI. 770–2)

In the passage's context in Milton, Michael has shown Adam a vision of the future of human history, a future filled with horrors that he will be unable to prevent. While history has, in this prophetic vision, become a function of the future, the novel's first word has the ring of a *final* pronouncement – a definitive assertion, the last word on the subject. Indeed the temporal doubleness of Milton's passage could not be bettered, as it effectively urges man, hereafter, not to seek to know before.

The ambivalence of Shelley's own view of the future is perhaps apposite here (for as she once remarked, 'if I am to be the judge of the future by the past and the present, I shall have small delight in looking forward'). Indeed her use of the future anterior tense is especially haunting in light of its obvious biographical resonance: it is difficult *not* to suspect displaced autobiography in a novel in which the implied author revisits the past in order to rewrite the future. But there is more than the personal at stake if, as critics often suggest, she reveals herself in *The Last Man* to be the 'unwilling prophetess' of a tragic human destiny.[12] While it may be, as Giovanna Franci suggests, the futuristic nature of her novel that calls for the conventional verb tenses of science fiction – the use of the past to describe events of the future – one feels that there is nevertheless more involved than either 'prophetic intonation' or the need to keep both memory and regret at bay. This *something more*, the very thing the novel demands, is clearly related to the fragments of the preface and the gaps they engender – openings that the 'subsequent' narrative cannot foreclose upon.

There are, then, a trio of factors (fragment, prophecy, preface) that are working together in Shelley's *The Last Man*. To the extent that the novel may be read as the playing out of the temporal ambiguity, even the impossibility, of the prophetic fragment, it presents a world that can, perhaps, only be expressed as a broken textual record. This is precisely what makes finality so problematic: the novel functions in a world where the end has, necessarily, always already taken place, while having been (always already) subverted by the proliferating effects of ruin. Rather than regarding the relationship of preface to novel as an ideal one in which the whole of the novel is expressed in the parts or fragments of the preface (a conventional Romantic prescription),[13] instead of the harmonious dialectical movement between the two this model implies, I suggest that the novel is in fact driven by, or generated from, the dynamic established by its relation to the preface, while remaining unable either to fulfil or complete it, or even in a sense to arrive at it. Narrative fulfilment, at the end of *The*

Last Man, is the result of an emptying out that is itself a function of its implicit excess, so that as we bid *adieu* to our hero, scattered now across the pages of the world, it is the incompleting effects not only of writing, but of ending, that are felt to be everlasting.

Notes

A previous version of this essay was presented as a paper at 'Romantic Generations' (University of Leeds, July 1997).

1. Morton D. Paley, whose observations I am adapting here to my own 'ends', remarks that Shelley's novel appeared at the wrong time, and briefly examines the earlier works on the subject that soured the reception of her work; see '*The Last Man*: Apocalypse Without Millennium', *Other MS*, pp. 107–10.
2. 'The Last Book: with a Dissertation on Last Things in General', *The Monthly Magazine*, n.s. II (1826) 137–43; cited by Morton Paley (*Other MS*, p. 108). Of course 'lastness' is a theme with a certain currency now, as we approach the millennium – and so, in an era of AIDS, is the plague. See Audrey Fisch, 'Plaguing Politics: AIDS, Deconstruction, and *The Last Man*', *Other MS*, pp. 267–86. Also in the same volume is Barbara Johnson's remarkable essay, 'The Last Man', in which she takes up the problem of the 'ends' of man (Derrida) through questions of reading and writing.
3. Thus in all editions. There is a strong case for emending to 'makes' as the first edition contains a number of typographical errors; there is, however, a possibility that Shelley may have intended the subjunctive.
4. *El príncipe constante*, II. iv [1129–31].
5. Travelling, however, is not merely undertaken for its own sake, but rather for the sake of a particular, and highly significant, destination: 'sacred and eternal Rome'.
6. This paradox would only be confirmed by a possible pun here on 'consumation' and 'consummation', since the plague is clearly the ultimate consumer.
7. *The Mask of Anarchy* was also in 1826 an unpublished poem, and remained unpublished until 1832. Verney quotes from a work that 1826 readers of *The Last Man* will not have seen, but which, it is anticipated (prophesied?), will have become a citable text by the 21st century.
8. Peter Brooks, *Reading for the Plot: Design and Intention in Narrative* (New York: A. A. Knopf, 1984).
9. The biographical significance of this situation is self-evident, and expressed in the often-cited journal entry for 14 May 1824:

> The last man! Yes I may well describe that solitary being's feelings, feeling myself as the last relic of a beloved race, my companions, extinct before me –
>
> (*MWSJ* II, pp. 476–7)

'Relic' has the appropriate double resonance of something at once anachronistic as well as fragmentary – a temporal remnant.
10. Anne McWhir's unpublished PhD dissertation, 'Portals of Expression: An Approach to Shelley's Caves and Their Romantic Context' (University of Toronto, 1976) is particularly useful on the question of caves. For example, in the underworld, the classic cave of prophecy is the place where past and future meet, where timelessness and the experience of chronological time can be brought together. On the importance of the Sibyl, see Steven Goldsmith's excellent treatment of the subject in *Unbuilding Jerusalem: Apocalypse and Romantic Representation* (Ithaca and London: Cornell University Press, 1993).
11. Jacques Derrida, *Dissemination*, trans. Barbara Johnson (Chicago: The University of Chicago Press, 1981) p. 7.
12. See, for example, Giovanna Franci, 'A Mirror of the Future: Vision and Apocalypse in Mary Shelley's *The Last Man*', in Harold Bloom, ed., *Mary Shelley* (New York: Chelsea House, 1985) p. 183. Franci uses Shelley's remark about judging the future as the epigraph for her article.
13. See, for example, Friedrich Schlegel's remark: 'A good preface must be at once the square root and the square of its book', Critical Fragment 8 in *Philosophical Fragments*, trans. P. Firchow, foreword by Rodolphe Gasché (Minneapolis and Oxford: University of Minnesota Press, 1991).

3
Mary Shelley and Edward Bulwer: *Lodore* as Hybrid Fiction
Richard Cronin

Lodore, as Mary Shelley recognized, represented a new departure for her as a novelist. Her reputation was as a writer of 'wild fictions',[1] but *Lodore* was to be both a thoroughly contemporary novel, 'a tale of the present time' as she described it in her preferred subtitle, and a novel that embraced all the 'dingy-visaged, dirty-handed, realities' (*L* 200 [II. xvii]) that had been excluded from her earlier fiction. Foremost among these dingy realities is the reality of hard cash, the fact that even those staying in cheap suburban inns must go hungry if they do not have the wherewithal to pay for their dinner. *Lodore* is the only novel by Shelley that fully recognizes that the study of human personality is inseparable from an understanding of economics. *Lodore*, like her earlier novels, finds room for the 'tortures of passion', but in *Lodore* Shelley is prepared to allow that such tortures are rarely felt by those 'whose situation in life obliges them to earn their daily bread', and are indulged in chiefly by the 'rich and great' who find in such suffering convenient 'resources against *ennui* and satiety' (*L* 58 [I. xi]).

In *Lodore*, the 'cash nexus' is the crucial point at which the material and the spiritual coincide, but there are others. For example, as one would expect of the author of *Frankenstein*, Shelley is attentive to the pressure of the physical body on the inner world of the emotions, but whereas the myth of the monster offers an analysis of that relationship, in *Lodore* it is rendered more feelingly, located in experienced or remembered moments of poignant physical contact, as when the new intensity with which Lady Lodore feels her estrangement from her daughter (she has just learned that her daughter is to be married) takes the form of an intimate physical memory: 'she felt the downy cheek of her babe close to her's, and its little fingers press her bosom' (*L* 146 [II. vii]). Best of all, there is the moment (*L* 179 [II. xii]) when Lady

Lodore, in an intimidatingly formal, public setting – the Visitors' Gallery of the House of Lords – fastens her daughter's ear-ring, and, for the first time since her infancy, Ethel feels her mother's hand on her face.

Shelley is interested in almost all her fiction in the point of contact between inner feeling and material fact, and between the workings of the spirit and the workings of society, but in *Lodore* that interest is expressed differently, and I want to suggest that this difference can be best explained by pointing to the influence of a novelist seven years her junior, Edward Bulwer. By 1831, when Shelley began work on *Lodore*, 'the accomplished author of Paul Clifford' (*L* 149 [II. viii]) was only 28, but he was already the most popular novelist in England, and startlingly fertile – five novels published by 1831, eight by the time that *Lodore* finally appeared, not to mention volumes of verse, plays, and a non-fictional report on the state of the nation, *England and the English*.

The letters of these years reveal clearly enough that Shelley's life was heavily punctuated by humiliations. There are the letters to William Whitton, Sir Timothy's man of business, in which she is often reduced to cringing displays of civility in her efforts to secure a competence for herself and her son, and there are the letters to the publishers and the editors of the great periodicals in which, when her own proposals are refused or ignored, she is reduced to offering to undertake almost any literary commission, and even then usually without success. When John Murray refused *Perkin Warbeck*, she offered him a life of Madame de Staël (*MWSL* II, p. 89), and the following year gave him a choice of a life of Mahomet, a history of the conquests of Grenada and Peru, a history of eighteenth-century literature, or a collection of lives of the philosophers, though 'this would hardly be so amusing' (*MWSL* II, pp. 113–14). A month later she was suggesting a book on the earth's prehistory, or the lives of famous women, or a history of chivalry, and even offering to write for the *Quarterly*, persuading herself that this was not just a 'clever and distinguished' periodical, but had also become acceptably 'liberal' (*MWSL* II, p. 115). She can only have felt a painful contrast between her own status in the world of letters and Bulwer's, whose novels had made him in just a few years a very rich young man.

But it was not just Bulwer's commercial success that Shelley admired, it was the novels themselves. The evidence is clear that there was no novelist whose work she read more avidly and looked forward to more eagerly. She asked Ollier to send her a copy of Bulwer's fourth novel, *Devereux* (1829), adding, 'I want it very much' (*MWSL* II, p. 80). She was even more emphatic in asking for his sixth, 'Do not forget Eugene Aram – every day *earlier* that I get it will be a debt of gratitude to you' (*MWSL* II, p. 151). But it was the fifth novel that prompted her most emphatic tribute, in the journal entry for 11 January 1831:

> I have been reading with much encreased admiration Paul Clifford – It is a wonderful, a sublime book – What will Bulwer become? the first Author of the age? I do not doubt it – He is a magnificent writer.
>
> (*MWSJ* II, p. 517)[2]

It is not very surprising, then, that Bulwer's influence is so evident both on *Lodore* and on Shelley's final novel, *Falkner*. But it is influence of a complex kind, because Bulwer, as his poems reveal, was an admirer of Byron and of Shelley's husband. As editor of the *New Monthly Magazine* he sought information from Mary on her husband's life and work. His own early works often contain admiring references to the poet. In chapter 57 of *Pelham* (1828) Vincent leads a discussion of Percy Shelley's *Posthumous Poems*, in which, for all the faults of the poems, Vincent finds that 'the master-hand is evident upon them'.[3] In chapter 14 of *The Disowned* Percy Shelley is paired with Wordsworth as the leading poet of the age, 'a great but visionary mind' whose work contains rare 'treasures' for all its irregularity,[4] and in the survey of literature included in *England and the English* Percy Shelley is again singled out for praise.[5] Shelley must at once have recognized the importance of finding a champion of her husband's work in the most successful novelist of the time.

Bulwer was also one of the last in that long procession of young men who over the years came to sit at the knee of her father to receive the benefit of his advice. He was drawn to her father, it seems, not so much by his philosophy, for Bulwer was at this time a convinced Benthamite, but by his novels, and most of all by *Caleb Williams*, which is the most important single model for most of Bulwer's early fiction, as it was, of course, for Shelley's. Bulwer's first novel pays transparent homage to *Caleb Williams* in the very name of the character who gives the novel its name, *Falkland*, and, like Godwin's Falkland, Bulwer's is an honourable man who is guilty of an action for which he can make no reparation. He persuades a married woman to elope with him, and, when her husband discovers the affair, she suffers a haemorrhage and dies. The plot of *Pelham* hinges on the murder of a brutish squire, and the suspicion that falls on Pelham's admired friend, Glanville. In another act of homage the squire is named Tyrrell. In *Paul Clifford* (1830) the attack on a judicial system that punishes youthful misdemeanours by sending the culprit 'to a place where, let him be ever so innocent at present, he was certain to come out as much inclined to be guilty as his friends could desire', and of which 'the especial beauty' is its aptness 'to make no finedrawn and nonsensical shades of difference between vice and misfortune' (I. vii),[6] develops one of the major themes of *Caleb Williams*, and Clifford himself, a man of energy and talent who finds that the only profession available to him in which he can express these virtues is that of the highwayman, is a character who owes much to Godwin's Captain Raymond. To use Pamela Clemit's term, both Shelley and Bulwer were exponents of 'the Godwinian novel'.[7]

In the relationship between Shelley and Bulwer, then, influence eddies, it flows both ways. It seems likely, for example, that Shelley's final novel, *Falkner*, is modelled in part on Bulwer's first. Both Falkner and Falkland try to persuade married women to elope with them. Both attempts result in the woman's death. Both men are stricken with remorse, and both respond by engaging in a foreign war of independence, Falkner adopting the cause of Greek nationalism, and Falkland fighting with the Spanish liberal insurgents. Falkland finds the heroic death he seeks, and Falkner recovers from wounds that had seemed fatal. But the lineage is complicated by the fact that both characters are indebted to the study of grief and remorse that Godwin had offered in the character of his own Falkland, and becomes more complex still if we allow that Bulwer probably knew Shelley's earlier novels. In *The Last Man* it is Raymond who seeks to atone for a sexual transgression, betraying his wife in an affair with Evadne, by engaging in the Greek War of Independence. There is no absolute proof that Bulwer read Shelley's novels, but, given that he knew her and so admired her father and husband, it seems extremely likely, and there is a piece of internal evidence that strongly supports this conjecture. In chapter 4 of *The Disowned*, the exultation of Bulwer's hero, disowned by his family but feeling the whole world open before him, prompts an unexpected comparison:

> he felt, like Castruccio Castrucani, that he could stretch his hands to the east and to the west, and exclaim, 'Oh, that my power kept pace with my spirit, then should it grasp the corners of the earth.'

'Lodore' as Hybrid Fiction 43

No such anecdote occurs in the only life of Castruccio that had contemporary currency (that of Machiavelli). Indeed, outside his native Lucca, Castruccio Castracani in the nineteenth century was, as now, a fairly remote figure. However, for a brief interval during the 1820s, he became slightly better known to the British reading public, and this higher profile would seem to have been an effect of Shelley's *Valperga*.[8] Moreover, there is a passage in *Valperga* – the point where the ambition of the exiled 17-year old Castruccio emerges for the first time – that Bulwer seems to echo:

> Thus, in solitude, while no censuring eye would check the exuberant vanity, he would throw his arms to the north, the south, the east, and the west, crying, – 'There – there – there, and there, shall my fame reach!'
>
> (*V* 23 [I. ii])[9]

The extraordinary popularity of Bulwer's early novels was, as it is in most cases of brilliant and immediate success, produced by a simple but striking originality, and it was this, too, in addition to the personal animosity that Bulwer seemed so successfully to provoke, that caused the novels to be so violently abused, most notoriously in *Fraser's Magazine,* in which the editor, Maginn, and his group of extraordinarily talented associates who included Carlyle and Thackeray sustained a campaign against Bulwer unexampled for its length and its ferocity. Put briefly, Bulwer combined two apparently antithetical kinds of fiction. One was the sentimental novel, the dominant form of English fiction from the mid-eighteenth century either in its naturalistic mode or in its Gothic inflection, and the other was a kind of novel for which I have no simple description, since the preferred contemporary terms, 'silver-fork fiction' or 'fashionable novels', seem unhelpful and misleading. The prototype of this kind of novel is Disraeli's *Vivian Grey* and the novel by Bulwer that most completely conforms to the pattern is *Pelham* (1828), though even this, Bulwer's second novel and the first that he gave his name to, is already a hybrid, including as it does a sentimental sub-plot centred on Pelham's schoolfriend, Reginald Glanville. The hero of these novels is a young man intent on using his dazzling social skills to advance himself in the world. But his appetite for society is already when the novel opens, or quickly becomes, prematurely jaded. His most characteristic mood is *ennui*, and in this mood he views the society around him from a stance of cynical, amused detachment. Lord Lodore, at that time of his life when he returns to England from Europe and his European mistress, is clearly a version of this character. He suffers, Shelley tells us, from a 'palled appetite'; his is a 'satiated soul' (*L* 37 [I. vii]). The fact that Disraeli and Bulwer both grew up as ardent Byronists suggests the origin of this kind of fiction, but the influence, I think, is less the Byron of *Childe Harold* than the Byron of the country house cantos of *Don Juan*.[10] It is through the clash within his novels between this kind of fiction, social and satirical, and sentimental fiction that Bulwer produces the effects that secured his success and provided the fuel for hostile critics such as those at *Fraser's*.

The objection is most amusingly formulated by Thackeray in his spoof of *Eugene Aram*, in which he identifies Bulwer as 'the father of a new "*lusus naturae* school"' of novelists.[11] Thackeray, posing as Bulwer's grateful disciple, has been taught by *Eugene Aram* how 'to mix vice and virtue up together in such an inextricable confusion as to render it impossible that any preference should be given to either, or that the one, indeed, should be at all distinguishable from the other'. In particular, he has learned from Bulwer a novel technique of characterization that requires, if an adulterer is wanted, to look for him in 'the class of country curates', and 'being in search of a tender-hearted, generous, sentimental, high-minded hero of romance' to find him 'in the lists of men who have cut throats for money'. The position is more temperately stated in the *Edinburgh* in its 1832 composite review of Bulwer's first five novels,[12] but it is recognizably the same. The technique produces characters which seem to the reviewer to result in a 'moral anomaly', most strikingly evident in the protagonist of Bulwer's fifth novel, *Eugene Aram*, in which a notorious eighteenth-century murderer is represented 'in the romantic garb of a refined lover, of an enthusiastic scholar, living quite as much in the ideal as the actual world'. The novel asks us to believe that 'this romantic enthusiast is, after all, a murderer, and *for money!*'. Compare that with the response to *Lodore* of a particularly interested reader, Claire Clairmont:

> Good God to think a person of your genius, whose moral tact ought to be proportionately exalted, should think it a task befitting its powers to gild and embellish and pass off as beautiful what was the merest compound of Vanity, folly, and every miserable weakness ...[13]

Claire Clairmont was, of course, an interested witness in both senses – she believed, surely mistakenly, that the plot of *Lodore*, in which an infant daughter is removed from the mother by the father, alluded to her own and Allegra's treatment at the hands of Byron,[14] but her personal interest does not blunt her critical perception. For her, Shelley's Lord Lodore represented exactly the kind of moral anomaly that the *Edinburgh* found so distinctive of Bulwer's fiction, and she is surely right. *Lodore* is Shelley's experiment in the kind of hybrid fiction that Bulwer had invented, and that was to prove one of the decisive influences on the development of the Victorian novel.

But again caution is needed, because both Thackeray and the *Edinburgh* reviewer are conscious that the construction of characters who embody moral anomalies is a characteristic of Bulwer's fiction that reveals its indebtedness to the Godwinian novel. '*Eugene Aram*', Thackeray recognizes, 'has certainly many qualities in common with the Anglo-German style of Mr. Godwin's followers.' The *Edinburgh* insists on a distinction between Aram who murders for money, and a 'Falkland, goaded into assassination by a brutal and irreparable outrage to his honour, yet retaining his native chivalry of soul, his lofty demeanour and tenderness of heart'. But even this admits the kinship, and it is not clear how Falkland's chivalry can remain unbesmirched by his willingness to allow the Hawkinses, both father and son, to be executed for the crime that he had committed. In Falkland, in Victor Frankenstein and in Beatrice Cenci, Mr Godwin and his followers had shown their interest in producing characters designed to induce in their readers a 'restless and anatomizing casuistry'.[15] Bulwer's originality lies less in the nature of his characters than in that of the prose through which they are represented, and it is in its prose that *Lodore* most clearly reveals Bulwer's influence.

The prose of *Lodore* is very often marked by a pointed, unillusioned wit quite unlike anything to be found in the earlier novels. For example, on the death of his father Lodore returns to England and is prevailed upon by his devoted sister, Elizabeth, to stay on for a few weeks after the funeral before going back to his Continental mistress. As a consequence:

> Elizabeth had the happiness of seeing the top of his head as he leant over the desk in his library, from a little hillock in the garden, which she sought for the purpose of beholding that blessed vision.
> (*L* 34 [I. vi])

46 *The Craft of Writing*

Or there is Lodore justifying to himself his decision to remove his daughter from her mother. He begins by reviewing 'impartially' the failings of his wife and mother-in-law, the mother-in-law's 'worldliness', the wife's 'frivolity and unfeeling nature', until 'almost against his will, his own many excellencies rose before him; – his lofty aspirations, his self-sacrifice for the good of others, the affectionateness of his disposition', etc. (*L* 62 [I. xi]). Just occasionally this prose manner is lent by the narrator to one of her characters, as for instance when Lord Lodore is trying to explain to his wife that he must flee the country immediately or be obliged to fight a duel against his own natural son. Lodore makes his confession, but couched in a declamatory sentimental rhetoric that effectively obscures all significant facts, and properly merits Lady Lodore's response, 'This sounds very like a German tragedy, being at once disagreeable and inexplicable' (*L* 56 [I. x]). But it would be hard to claim that Shelley writes this kind of prose as well as either Disraeli or Bulwer.

More interesting are those passages in which two styles, the sentimental, and what I shall call, for want of a better term, the styptic, are brought together, to produce a prose that tends both towards the antithetical and the oxymoronic. A simple example is the sentence that records Lady Lodore's response to the news that her daughter has joined her husband in his confinement in a debtors' prison: 'She was grieved for her daughter, but she was exceedingly vexed for herself' (*L* 247 [III. ix]). The first clause sentimentally allows Lady Lodore to respond sympathetically, and the second looks askance at her egotism, but the sentence remains a true hybrid: that is, the styptic coexists with the sentimental, it does not expose it as a sham. Ethel's willingness to marry Edward despite his lack of money is recorded in a very similar sentence:

> Love in a cottage is the dream of many a high-born girl, who is not allowed to dance with a younger brother at Almack's; but a secluded, an obscure, an almost cottage life, was all that Ethel had ever known.
>
> (*L* 152–3 [II. viii])

Ethel's idealism is first mocked, and then tenderly acknowledged. It is a prose that lends itself to antithetical characterization, as, for example, in the contrasting responses to Lodore's death of his daughter and his sister. Ethel is racked by her grief, whereas Mrs Elizabeth flourishes in mourning:

Though sincere in her regret for his death, habit had turned lamentation into a healthy nutriment, so that she throve upon the tears she shed, and grew fat and cheerful upon her sighs.

(*L* 98 [I. xvi][16])

This may remind us of Jane Austen's Mrs Musgrove, but it is the difference that is significant: the comfortable plumpness of Mrs Elizabeth's grief is not at all an indication of its insincerity, but just another instance of 'the strange riddle we human beings present, and how contradictions accord in our singular machinery' (ibid.), and it is those contradictions that this kind of prose is peculiarly adapted to explore.

But this kind of hybridity does not just mark Shelley's prose: it gives her a principle of characterization. It allows Lady Lodore's act of renunciation, when she resigns almost her entire fortune to her daughter, and retreats into a life of obscure poverty to be at once an exercise of heroic greatness of soul, and an act taken in obedience 'not to a high moral power, but to the pride of her soul' (*L* 272 [III. xiii]). Lady Lodore is constructed as a person who, almost until the final page of the novel, can support equally well violently contradictory judgements of her character; from Mrs Elizabeth's certainty that she is irredeemably wicked, to Ethel's husband's judgement that she is 'a worshipper of the world, a frivolous, unfeeling woman' (*L* 255 [III. xi]), to the response of Horatio Saville, who is Edward's cousin and best friend, and is inspired by Lady Lodore to a lifelong devotion. Lodore's unhappy marriage is paralleled in the novel by the marriage of his old schoolfriend, Derham, and the characterization of Derham's wife, though much slighter than Lady Lodore's, is produced by the same principle. Lodore first hears of her in America, just before his death, when he learns from an Englishwoman that Derham has been rejected by his family because of a 'més-alliance': he had married an 'unequal partner'. 'She was illiterate and vulgar – coarse-minded, though good-natured' (*L* 78 [I. xiv]). The thought that his old friend is bound to such a woman fills Lodore with a tender sadness. It is not until much later in the novel that we meet Mrs Derham, when Ethel takes lodgings with her in London, and she emerges as a kind, motherly woman with much practical good sense, 'a little, plump, well-preserved woman of fifty-four or five' (*L* 195 [II. xv][17]), and a woman of whom her daughter Fanny can say, 'My mother ... is the kindest-hearted woman in the world' (*L* 212 [III. i]).

The most complete characterization of this kind is, as one would expect, that of the man who gives his name to the novel, Lord Lodore. Lodore's courtship of Cornelia, and the history of their married life together is narrated in a style in which the styptic predominates. He returns to England at the age of 32 suffering from a 'palled appetite'. Having tired of his mistress and apparently uninterested in his son by her, he becomes convinced that all is 'vanity' (*L* 37 [I. vii]), and, feeling haughtily misanthropic, he retires to Wales. There he first meets Cornelia. She is just 15, and he sees her as 'a vision of white muslin' (*L* 39 [I.vii]). Her extreme youth and the material of her frock prove a potent combination for Lodore, whose favourite metaphor for his 'ideal of a wife' is 'white paper to be written on at will' (*L* 41 [I. vii]). Lodore's relationships with women have hitherto been complicated by the fact that he nurtured a high 'ideal of what he thought a woman ought to be', without much liking women: 'he had no high opinion of woman as he had usually found her' (*L* 45 [I. viii]). This proves no barrier to his courtship of Cornelia, because he takes the precaution of not speaking to her much – they 'conversed little' (*L* 41 [I. vii]) – before he proposes. On his marriage he transports his wife and her mother to London, and introduces them to his own fashionable circles, only to find that his wife develops an irritating liking for evening parties, and that he cordially detests his mother-in-law. Cornelia, just turned 17, gives birth to a daughter, and Lodore is outraged by her failure to display proper maternal feelings. He introduces her to his ex-mistress, and is rendered insanely jealous by the friendship that develops between his wife and his natural son, who is entirely ignorant that Lodore is his father. He insults the young man, strikes him, and is forced to flee abroad to escape the charge of cowardice that would be brought against him if he refused to offer satisfaction to a man he had insulted. He offers his wife the chance to join him in his exile, stipulating only that she must sever all relationship with her own mother, and, when she refuses, spirits her infant daughter from their house and emigrates with her to America, convinced in his own mind that he is motivated solely by a tender concern for the welfare of his child.

And yet, framing this acerbic novella, is the account of the years that father and daughter spent in the wilds of Illinois, an almost wholly sentimental narrative in which Lodore finds fulfilment in tenderly nurturing his child and comes to embody for Ethel an ideal of manhood that can only be supplemented, not effaced, by the man she eventually marries. There is no attempt to articulate a relationship between the two narratives, by, for example, representing the years in

America as assisting Lodore in a passage towards self-knowledge. To the very last he remains as convinced that he has been ill-treated by his wife, as is Cornelia that she has been cruelly used by him. Nor is he morally transformed. He dies in a duel which he had himself provoked, the desire to recover his reputation as a man of honour more precious to him than his responsibility to a 15-year-old daughter separated by 2,000 miles from her kindred. Lodore remains to the end a man who properly merits Saville's revulsion at 'the inexcusable cruelty of his conduct' (*L* 120 [II. iii]), and yet he is also and equally the refined and tender father who merits his daughter's exalted and idealizing love.

In Lodore Shelley produces her most extreme version of the kind of character that Bulwer invented, the character that embodies the *Edinburgh* reviewer's 'moral anomaly', and in doing so she escaped, like Bulwer, from one of the more inhibiting conventional constraints of the novel, its placing of its characters within a single hierarchy of moral judgement. We are not asked to choose whether Lodore is a cruel or a loving man, high-minded or self-deceived, but to accept that he is all these things, and that it is in the acceptance of such anomalies that we are brought into a proper confrontation with the 'singular machinery' of human nature in which 'contradictions' may 'accord' (*L* 98 [I. xvi]).

I have already suggested that Bulwer's hybrid fiction marks a significant point in the development of the Victorian novel, but in one respect Shelley is the more prescient of the two. She recognizes that the new technique opens a new subject matter for the novel: it allows the novel of courtship, in the 1830s still the commonest of all kinds of novel, to develop into the kind of novel practised by the great Victorians, the novel of marriage, and more particularly, of unhappy marriage. *Lodore* is importantly a marriage novel, a novel which places at its centre not political, but 'domestic revolutions' (*L* 119 [II. iii]). The courtship of Ethel and Villiers is only a necessary prelude to the account of their married life together, and the history of their relationship, though central, functions only to bind together the more vivid accounts of other marriages, of the Derhams, of Saville and Clorinda, and most importantly of Lord and Lady Lodore. The hybrid style lends itself to the marriage novel in part because marriage is itself a hybrid, both a sentimental state, and an institution that is embedded in social and economic practices. Ethel and Edward are all in all to each other, finding each the only happiness in the other's arms, so much so that when they set up house in London, 'they were always satisfied with one or two parties in the evening. Nay, once or twice in the week they usually remained at home' (L 176 [II. xii]). It is a style, then, that can accommodate marriage in both its aspects. But, much more importantly, it is a style that can accommodate contradictory perspectives, and hence can admit the truth that only happy marriages admit stable description, for the reality of a marriage is only constituted by the manner in which the marriage is experienced by the two people joined in it, and in an unhappy marriage the experience of the two people will be, of necessity, inconsistent and incommensurate. The Lodores' marriage is not either a relationship in which the man suffers his conjunction with an unfeeling, worldly woman, or a relationship in which a woman suffers the tyrannical abuse of her husband, but both of these, for every unhappy marriage is, as Shelley would say, a 'strange riddle' in which 'contradictions accord'.

Finally, Shelley found in Bulwer's kind of novel the possibility of a new authorial stance, a manner of surveying people and their doings sharply different from anything to be found in her mother's work, or her father's, or her husband's. Take, for example, the elaborate comparison between Ethel's and Fanny Derham's upbringing (L 217–19 [III. ii]). Both have been educated exclusively by their fathers. Lodore offers Ethel very much the kind of education that Rousseau gave to Sophie. Hers is, we are told, 'a sexual education': her father moulds her into conformity with 'his ideal of what a woman ought to be', that is, 'yielding', devoted to her male protector, and obedient. Fanny, on the other hand, is educated to be 'complete in herself', 'independent and self-sufficing'. There is very little doubt as to which educational system Shelley prefers – she remains her mother's daughter – but she restrains herself from pressing her preference. We are allowed to smile at Ethel's inability to understand money, and her utter reliance on first her father, and then her husband, but we smile, too, at the 'platonic notions of the supremacy of mind' (L 284 [III. xv]) that Fanny has imbibed from her father. Shelley is content to admire both women, despite the difference of their education, and despite the very different personalities that their education has produced, with a kind of smiling equanimity.

In *Lodore* Shelley develops a narrative manner that is always alert to difference, always sharp in its discriminations, but reluctant to pass final judgement. Her development of the hybrid novel issues in the end in a large and calm tolerance, which is the more persuasive because it is arrived at not by ignoring but by examining the human capacity for self-deception, for inconsistency, and most of all by recognizing that irremediable egotism that for all of us makes 'the ideas of our own minds ... more forcibly present, than any notions we can form of the feelings of others' (*L* 129 [II. v]). This is not much like Mary Wollstonecraft, or Godwin, or Percy Shelley, but it does prefigure the work of another writer. In *Lodore* Shelley can sound oddly like George Eliot. Both writers interrogate the metaphor by which a just perception of the real is compared to a mirror's faithful reflection, George Eliot by offering in chapter 27 of *Middlemarch* the 'parable' in which the random scratches in a mirror are arranged by a lighted candle into 'the flattering illusion of a concentric arrangement', and Shelley by pointing out that no mirror is true, that no two mirrors are alike, and that all mirrors, like prisms, refract the light that they reflect:

> Our several minds, in reflecting to our judgements the occurrences of life, are like mirrors of various shapes and hues, so that we none of us perceive passing objects with exactly similar optics.
>
> (*L* 62 [I. xi])

In Chapter 5 of *Amos Barton* George Eliot turns to confront the reader who finds her central character 'palpably and unmistakably commonplace', and Shelley anticipates her by rebuking those who would rather 'embark on the wild ocean of romance' than suffer the novelist 'to describe scenes of common-place and debasing interest' (*L* 201–2 [II. xvii]), but the commitment of both novelists to 'dingy-visaged, dirty-handed realities' is moderated by a lingering attachment to the ideal. Shelley trusts to the 'youth and feminine tenderness' of her heroine, Ethel, to irradiate the coarse realties of her poverty by shedding 'light and holiness around her', and Amos's wife, Milly, performs an exactly similar function in *Amos Barton*. It is the compromise that George Eliot announces in her review of Goethe's *Wilhelm Meister*, in which she insists that the right of the novelist to treat 'every aspect of human life' has its 'legitimate limits', and that only those truths are fit to be represented that are redeemed by the presence of 'some twist of love, or endurance, or helplessness to call forth our best sympathies'.[18] These resemblances are not accidental, nor simply the result of a shared interest of the kind that might prompt one to compare the final paragraphs of *Valperga*[19] and *Middlemarch*, which both end with an elegy for a heroic woman whose name has escaped public notice. The narrative stance that aspires to a wise, restrained disinterestedness, the willingness to recognize that such disinterestedness is difficult of attainment, and that most of us see the world refracted through the prism of our own egotism, and a commitment to realism that is always tempered by a sentimental attachment to the ideal are all of them distinguishing characteristics of a distinctive kind of novel. They remind us that George Eliot writes a more developed version of the same kind of novel as *Lodore*, the novel that Bulwer seems to have been the first English novelist to write, and that, because it is produced by a prose style that swings between the sentimental and the styptic, I have termed the hybrid novel.

Notes

Earlier versions of this essay were presented as conference papers at 'Mary Shelley, Parents, Peers, Progeny' (APU and OU, Cambridge, September 1997) and at 'Mary vs. Mary' (U. of Bologna, November 1997).

1. From the notice of the novel in the *Courier*, no. 13635 (16 April 1835).
2. The only books that inspired her with a similar enthusiasm in this period were Washington Irving's *The Conquest of Grenada* (1829) and Thomas Moore's *Letters and Journals of Lord Byron* (1830). She was closely involved with Moore's book, having provided him with information, and for Irving she had a *tendresse*. Her admiration for Bulwer is the more remarkable because she firmly categorized him as 'my acquaintance but not my friend' (*MWSL* II, p. 261). She found him inordinately vain, had met his wife, Rosina, and was at least partly aware of Bulwer's mistreatment of her (*MWSL* II, p. 202). Rosina, the unusual name of Bulwer's wife, is also the title character of her short story 'The Invisible Girl', first published in *The Keepsake for 1833*, though it may be that the title of the plate for which the story was written determined the name. It is even possible that Shelley drew on her knowledge of Bulwer's miserable marriage for her representation of Lodore's. It may be, however, that she had initially found Bulwer more attractive than she subsequently judged him to be. In May, 1831, she wrote to Ollier asking him to send her the current copy of the *New Monthly* 'containing Mr. Bulwer's portrait' (*MWSL* II, p. 135).
3. Edward Bulwer, *Pelham*, 3 vols (London: Henry Colburn, 1828), III, p. 62. Bulwer revised his early novels, but the chapter numbers given in the text here and subsequently will allow the passages to be located in later editions of the novels.
4. Edward Bulwer, *The Disowned*, 3 vols (London: Henry Colburn, 1828) is also remarkable for including what is surely the first fictional representation of Keats, in the person of the artist, Warner, a consumptive young man fired with a dangerously intense ambition to win immortal fame, which crumples when he overhears Joshua Reynolds' coolly dismissing the painting on which he has pinned his hopes. The reference to Keats is fixed

by the quotation from *Endymion* which serves as the epigraph to chapter xxiv (I, p. 284).
5. Edward Bulwer, *England and the English* (Paris: Baudry's European Library, 1834) pp. 249–50. Wordsworth and Percy Shelley are identified as the joint 'founders of a more profound and high-wrought dynasty of opinion' than that founded by the more popular poets, Byron and Scott. Feldman and Scott-Kilvert believe that Shelley was alienated from Bulwer by the comments on Percy Shelley's poems included in his 'Life of Schiller', but there the attack on the 'effeminate barbarism' and 'gaudy verbiage' of modern poetic diction is directed at the poet's imitators rather than the poet himself. The accusation that Percy Shelley produces 'glittering and fantastic lines' which 'only distract the reader from the comprehension of the general idea' is entirely consistent with all the earlier references to his poetry. See *The Poems and Ballads of Schiller*, trans. Edward Bulwer Lytton (Edinburgh and London: William Blackwood and Sons, 1844) p. cxlvii, and *MWSJ* II, p. 605.
6. Edward Bulwer, *Paul Clifford*, 3 vols (London: Colburn and Bentley) I, p. 147.
7. Pamela Clemit, *The Godwinian Novel: The Rational Fictions of Godwin, Brockden Brown, Mary Shelley* (Oxford: Clarendon Press, 1993).
8. Thomas Jefferson Hogg, in 'Journal of a Traveller on the Continent: VII', *London Magazine*, VI (September–December, 1826) 23–4, wrote of Lucca as famous for Castruccio 'who is known to many, because his life was descibed by Machiavelli, and to all as the hero of Valperga' (quoted in *V* xv). That 'all', however, must be interpreted as a generous exaggeration, understandable in a friend of the late Percy Shelley and lover of Shelley's friend Jane Williams.
9. My initial inference that Bulwer had read *Valperga* has been strengthened by further information supplied to me in a private conversation by Nora Crook, to whom I am grateful.
10. Bulwer took his Byronism to the unusual lengths of engaging in an affair with Lady Caroline Lamb. See Michael Sadleir, *Bulwer: A Panorama* (London: Constable, 1931) pp. 55–62.
11. 'Elizabeth Brownrigge: a Tale', *Fraser's Magazine*, VI, 21 (August 1832) 67–88. My quotations are drawn from the dedication 'To the Author of "Eugene Aram"'.
12. 'Mr. Bulwer's Novels – Eugene Aram', *Edinburgh Review*, LV, 109 (April 1832) 208–19.
13. Letter of 15 March 1836, *The Clairmont Correspondence*, ed. Marion Kingston Stocking, 2 vols (Baltimore and London: Johns Hopkins University Press, 1995) II, p. 341; also quoted in Robert Gittings and Jo Manton, *Claire Clairmont and the Shelleys* (Oxford and New York: Oxford University Press, 1992) p. 131.
14. See Jane Dunn, *Moon in Eclipse: A Life of Mary Shelley* (London: Weidenfeld and Nicolson, 1978) pp. 306–7.
15. P. B. Shelley's preface to *The Cenci*. This point was well made by Pamela Clemit when I offered a version of this paper at the conference 'Mary Shelley: Parents, Peers, Progeny'.
16. Actually chapter xvii, but misnumbered.

54 *The Craft of Writing*

17. Actually chapter xvi, but misnumbered.
18. George Eliot, 'The Morality of *Wilhelm Meister*', *Leader* (21 July 1855) 703, rpt. in George Eliot, *Selected Essays, Poems and Other Writings*, eds A. S. Byatt and N. Warren (London: Penguin, 1990) pp. 307–10.
19. That is, the final paragraphs of the last numbered chapter of *Valperga*, before the Conclusion.

Part II
Gender

4
'Don't Say "I Love You"': Agency, Gender and Romanticism in Mary Shelley's *Matilda*

Anne-Lise François and Daniel Mozes

> On this earth, out of which nature has made man's first paradise, dread exercising the tempter's function in wanting to give innocence the knowledge of good and evil.
>
> (Rousseau, *Emile, or On Education*)[1]

> Undoubtedly no person can be truly dishonoured by the act of another; and the fit return to make to the most enormous injuries is kindness and forbearance, and a resolution to convert the injurer from his dark passions by peace and love.
>
> (P.B. Shelley, Preface to *The Cenci*)[2]

> I believed myself to be polluted by the unnatural love I had inspired, and that I was a creature cursed and set apart by nature. I thought that like another Cain, I had a mark set on my forehead to shew mankind that there was a barrier between me and they.... [I] should have fancied myself a living pestilence: so horrible to my own solitary thoughts did this form, this voice, and all this wretched self appear; for had it not been the source of guilt that wants a name?
>
> (*M* 60–1 [ch. xi])

One of the most notable characteristics of Mary Shelley's *Matilda* is that the protagonist becomes a self without performing a definite action. Within that violent novel, the locus of violence is shifted away from physical acts of injury. Instead, Shelley focuses upon a violence in communication that may intrude upon or even determine a listener's feminized subjecthood.

In so doing, Shelley's narrative challenges Enlightenment optimisms about reason's power to save humankind. For in its short span, *Matilda* manages to present a broad response to such Enlightenment projects as Rousseau's call to educate the whole man in *Emile*, while also re-writing one of the centrally defining tropes of Romanticism – the exile. It accomplishes this by defining responsibility for the feminine ethical subject not in terms of her own acts and volitions, but in terms of her responses to the thoughts, desires and words she elicits from others. In the process, the novel asks us to reconsider what makes a victim, and looks forward to some of our recent struggles to redefine Romanticism's genders.

Three main critical perspectives set the stakes for this reading of *Matilda*: first, the attention paid over the last 15 years to the trope of feminine passivity in Romanticism,[3] especially where this pertains to Romantic disenchantment both with Enlightenment claims for self-definition through action and with the high valuation of the transcendent self (as in Wordsworthian egotism); secondly, dissatisfaction with the contractualist bent of much liberal philosophy as set out recently in the work of the feminist moral philosopher Annette Baier; thirdly, the increased interest within critical studies of Romanticism and gender to the agency of the *object* of romantic love. Julie Ellison, for example, in her book on Romantic hermeneutics, has carefully examined the relevance for a feminist politics of an 'ethics of understanding' that pays attention to how the confessional Romantic self informs and interferes with the listener's own desires and claims to power).[4]

A maxim in Rousseau's *Emile* voices one of the background assumptions against which Shelley sets *Matilda*: 'To live is not to breathe. It is to act; it is to make use of our organs, our senses, our faculties, of all the parts of ourselves which give us the sentiments of existence.'[5] Though standing in equivocal relation to Rousseau's thought (he was, after all, the master of reverie), this passage expresses a familiar prejudice which excludes passive bodily states from the moral life and grants moral value exclusively to what a person does or makes of his faculties. Among Romantics of the period following the French Revolution (when people had killed and had been killed in the name of the Rights of Man and freedom of choice) the moral value of action-in-the-world becomes problematic. Even domestic action, as in *The Cenci*, *Matilda*, and elsewhere, becomes the occasion for exploring ambivalent attitudes to action in general.

As Annette Baier has argued, the desire to base ethics on the intentional *acts* of allegedly free and equal individuals has led modern liberal ethics, especially as defined by Kant, to ignore the experience of a significantly large proportion of individuals – namely those not in a position to claim control over the use of their faculties nor expected to act in their own name – women, dependants and slaves. Baier writes:

> [E]quality of power and interdependency, between two persons or groups, is rare and hard to recognize when it does occur. ... the moral tradition which developed the concept of rights, autonomy, and justice is the same tradition that provided 'justifications' of the oppression of those whom the primary rights-holders depended on to do the work they did not wish to do themselves.[6]

Liberalism, thinking only of the already empowered male subject, pretends that everyone has choices; Shelley presents the experiences of a feminized object of another's desires in the tragically unfinished process of becoming a liberal subject.

Baier's criticism of Kantian intentionalism applies to *Matilda*'s radical re-invention of the Romantic exile (of which Coleridge's Ancient Mariner may stand as an exemplar, a point to which we shall return) who suffers remorse for actions he does commit. Though Shelley's novel is by no means a levelling antidote to Romantic performances of individuation, *Matilda* gives these male exiles a twist: in the intensity and melodrama of *Matilda*'s language, the shock of hearing Mathilda's self-recrimination doubles when one realizes that unlike these men she has perpetrated no crimes.[7]

Or has she? *Matilda* is told in retrospect by the dying titular character to Woodville, a grieving Shelley-like poet who would be her lover, but with whom she cannot bring herself to speak her history. She only writes her autobiography after she knows that before anyone can read it and respond, she will be dead. She tells how her aristocratic father married Diana, the daughter of a gentleman of 'small fortune.' Diana's death in childbirth sends Mathilda's father into an unbearable grief. He exiles himself from England, leaving Mathilda to be raised by his sister in Scotland. There Mathilda remains innocent, friends only with the landscape and books, thinking of running away to find the absent father whom she idealizes. Finally her father returns when she is 16, takes her to London where she enjoys a brief period of filial bliss and where she begins to be courted by other men. The father, then discovering his own incestuous love for Mathilda, becomes overwrought but in shame refuses admit his desire. Mathilda goads him into telling her his secret. The father flees her, asking for forgiveness in a letter. She overcomes her initial loathing of him to pursue him to the sea, but he reaches it before she can prevent his suicide. Mathilda then wanders, mentally blasted and full of remorse, unable to live with others. She stages a fake death in order to retire to the country alone where she dies in a Clarissa-like semi-suicide by withering away.

But *Matilda* breaks from *Clarissa*'s separation between actor and acted upon. While in Samuel Richardson's novel, the ultimate conduct book, Clarissa allows herself to die because of an act done to her body while she was unconscious, Shelley's heroine insists on the immateriality of the action – a speech act – which produces her own death. As she says, 'I disobeyed no command, I ate no apple, and yet I was ruthlessly driven from [paradise]. Alas! my companion did, and I was precipitated in his fall' (*M* 17 [ch. iii]). Re-interpreting and reversing a misogynist tradition of Eve as the precipitator of the fall, Shelley writes a story in which the characters lack agency and consummate no passions – for her father's illicit passions never become sexually overt. But Mathilda's disclaimer aside, the parallel between her fall and Eve's remains: both grasp at forbidden knowledge. However, as our third epigraph makes explicit, Mathilda figures herself after the male exile Cain: she knows that if her father's speech was an act, then so was her own speech, and if his desire alone constituted disobedience, then she too disobeyed, as she seems to imply at her narrative's end:

> In truth I am in love with death; no maiden ever took more pleasure in the contemplation of her bridal attire than I in fancying my limbs already enwrapt in their shroud: is it not my marriage dress? Alone it will unite me to my father when in an eternal mental union we shall never part.
>
> (*M* 65 [ch. xii])

In her desire for an absolutely internalized social ritual – marriage to her father – and more generally in her mental life, Mathilda is far more active than she admits, even as she announces her withdrawal from the world. And if she is mentally active, consciously or not, the novel suggests that she is still guilty, dramatizing the way in which merely forming and possessing subjectivity requires acts of perpetrating egotism, even if only in self-defence and in retreat.

Indeed, Mathilda does blame herself for involuntary criminal action in eliciting her father's secret of sexual love from him. As she says, 'I alone was the cause of his defeat and justly did I pay the fearful penalty' (*M* 24 [ch. iv]). Being her father's sole child, Mathilda alone could have inspired incestuous sexual love, but that identity involves no volition on her part. Yet even in eliciting his secret, a much more active state than merely *being* his daughter, she intends, not the harm she causes, but a sympathetic hearing, a 'talking cure'. *Matilda* challenges our Freudian optimism that to talk is to begin to enact a cure, to get everything out in the open, and it does so armed with the scepticism that so much feminism has adopted against the male psychoanalyst who pries information from the female 'hysteric' or, in other words, the melodramatic subject. Sometimes revelation leads to personal catastrophe by materializing rather than exorcising the gap between self and other.[8]

The climax of the novel, in which Mathilda elicits her father's secret, exemplifies Shelley's designed confusion about who is the actor, who the victim. Mathilda's father, knowing what Mathilda asks, since it is *his* secret, must also hear the ironies we hear in her accusations. He may be considered villainous for giving into her importunities to speak and in his apparent requirement of her to behave like the very pattern of the obedient daughter that Mary Wollstonecraft attacked in the *Vindication*. He calls her 'presumptuous' and bids her 'wait in submissive patience the event of what is passing around you'. Her response is a bitter refusal to sit tight and pretty: 'Oh yes!' I passionately replied, 'I will be very patient; I will not be rash or presumptuous: I will see the agonies, and tears, and despair of my father, my only friend, my hope, my shelter, I will see it all with folded arms and downcast eyes' (*M* 26 [ch. v]). Her sarcasm parodies her society's picture of feminine passivity. But her father has a legitimate reason for withholding his secret. As he says, 'Yes, you are the sole, the agonizing cause of all I suffer, of all I must suffer until I die. ... One word I might speak and then you would be implicated in my destruction' (*M* 27 [ch. v]). Her father is not just asking her to play the feminine role or to beat her down into submission. Since she is the object of his secret, his attempt to bar her from it may be his one attempt, however feeble, to continue to address her as a subject, to preserve her autonomy from his intruding desires.

Mathilda refuses to acknowledge her father's superior position here, saying:

> Speak that word; it will bring peace, not death. If there is a chasm our mutual love will give us wings to pass it, and we shall find

> flowers, and verdure, and delight on the other side. ... Yes, speak, and we shall be happy; there will no longer be doubt, no dreadful uncertainty; trust me, my affection will soothe your sorrow; speak that word and all danger will be past, and we shall love each other as before, and for ever.
>
> (*M* 27 [ch. v])

Mathilda speaks as if they both had 'doubt', which is true, but not in the way that she thinks. Ironically she is not in a position to be 'trusted' and the father cannot help but 'doubt' whether she has the strength, born of experience, to forgive his taboo desire. In figuring herself as the bearer of wisdom she claims a position for which she is not qualified. Here Shelley may be ironizing what is naive about Wollstonecraft's condemnation of feminine pliancy. Though Mathilda is not submissive according to society's oppressive dictates, her active role fails to deliver Wollstonecraft's promised agency in the world. When her ignorance is lifted, she is momentarily empowered to forgive her father, or not, but the self-confrontation that his revelation has forced upon her leaves her too stunned to employ this power. The novel, then, bleakly avoids assigning usable social power, whether to achieve benevolent or selfish ends, to any subject in any state of ignorance, knowledge, desire, or loathing.

Perhaps the central irony of the climactic scene of importunity consists of the way in which Mathilda seeks to wrest her own identity – to become a subject – from her father even while she remains ignorant of the foundations of her identity in her father's secret. In her heroine's idealistic search for confirmation of her selfhood in another, Shelley dramatizes the way in which over-confidence in the self, and the transcendent powers of love, sympathy, and language to communicate selfhood, can lead to crushing disaster. Mathilda, before her fall, is not yet aware of the necessity of certain kinds of ignorance; as she says, 'the agony of my doubt hurries me on, and you must reply' (*M* 27 [ch. v]). She emphasizes not what she can do to alleviate her father's suffering, but what he should do, as her father, to shore up her identity and alleviate her doubt concerning her value in his eyes:

> Alas! Alas! What am I become? But a few months have elapsed since I believed I was all the world to you; and there was no happiness or grief for you on earth unshared by your Mathilda – your child.... In the despair of my heart I see what you cannot conceal: you no longer love me. I adjure you, my father, has not an unnatural

passion seized upon your heart? Am I not the most miserable worm that crawls?

(*M* 28 [ch. v])

In figuring herself as the 'miserable worm', Mathilda puts herself in the place of the vile creature that she had assumed he had fallen in love with. She had previously supposed that the most probable explanation for her father's behaviour 'was that during his residence in London he had fallen in love with some unworthy person' (*M* 24 [ch. iv]). She thinks her father's secret is an inability to acknowledge an unseemly passion for a stranger – a demirep, perhaps – who has alienated his affections, while his secret in fact is a transgression of the domestic boundaries which make the patriarchal family possible. As Anne Mellor has written, '*Matilda* constitutes Mary Shelley's most radical critique of her ideological commitment to the bourgeois family' (Mellor, p. 191).[9] Part of Mathilda's impulse, then, to force her father's speech, is her fear of becoming an abandoned child once more. When she asks, 'What am I become?' like Frankenstein's monster, Mathilda already sees herself in the light of her father's repulsion and recalls the monster's hysteria upon not finding himself within a structure like that which he sees in the De Lacey family. But since Mathilda's impulse to demand that her father speak to her is her downfall, the novel suggests that her desire to solidify her filial identity by insisting on the father's overt love is a shortcoming, not a natural necessity.

Like the monster in *Frankenstein*, Mathilda, the offspring, is treated by the way she looks, as object, not equal subject. Like Victor, too, her father has a myopic streak born of class privilege which prevents him from fully understanding her position:

> I do not say that if his own desires had been put in competition with those of others that he would have displayed undue selfishness, but this trial was never made. He was nurtured in prosperity.... By a strange narrowness of ideas he viewed the world in connexion only, as it was or was not related to his little society. He considered queer and out of fashion all opinions that were exploded by his circle of intimates, and he became at the same time dogmatic and yet fearful of not coinciding with the only sentiments he could consider orthodox.
>
> (*M* 7 [ch. i])

Combined with the father's semi-incestuous past (he is the only son of a doting mother), this 'narrowness' is an unselfconscious egotism which sets the stage for his sexual love of Mathilda. The father seems an exemplar of the universalizing complacency we see in both Enlightenment claims for reason and the solipsism upon which Romanticism meditates. Later, when he does admit his love for her, he tells her that it is because she reminds him of her mother, Diana, a woman he considered ideal partly because 'he felt as if by his union with her he had received a new and better soul'. Mathilda's father, then, loves women whom he can imagine as utterly devoted to the improvement of his mental and spiritual state, and Mathilda's words indicate her readiness to fill this role. His desire disgusts Mathilda once she becomes aware of it, yet she overcomes her impulse to shun her father partly because she sees that he is not as self-reliant as his philosophy would have him be; he is still a 'victim' of the grief caused by Diana's death.

The text offers further complications in reading the father as *the* villain, for all his solipsistic, insensitive bungling. Throughout her life Mathilda vainly yearned for her absent father, but now he pines for her knowing that he cannot have her in the way he possessed her mother. The difference between their unfulfilled desires emphasizes the fallen nature of knowledge and ironizes agency itself. Knowledge of his own desires, far from lending him any more agency, leads to his fall and removes his choices. As the man, he had been able to come and go as his passions dictated, but now he is trapped by that very freedom to determine where both he and Mathilda will go, since he cannot resist keeping her with him. As a female and a child Mathilda never had this power, for she could not summon the will or resources to run away in hopes of finding her father. In her ignorance she does not have true power – either to cure or to reject him – analogous to the power he threw away when he abandoned her, and yet Mathilda, as object, wields power, and this is what compromises her. In unconsciously trading power plays with her father, she unwillingly and unknowingly comes to exemplify Judith Butler's recent observation:

> As a form of power, subjection is paradoxical. To be dominated by a power external to oneself is a familiar and agonizing form power takes. To find, however, that what 'one' is, one's very formation as a subject, is in some sense dependent upon that very power is quite another ... [P]ower is not simply what we oppose but also, in a

Agency, Gender and Romanticism in Mary Shelley's 'Matilda' 65

strong sense, what we depend on for our existence and what we harbor and preserve in the beings that we are.[10]

Butler's calm acknowledgement of this paradox is not an option open to Mathilda. She cannot forgive herself, but retains a vision of her own monstrosity in comparison with an unstated and repressed ideal. This ideal is not the only repressed item on Mathilda's list. When her father resists telling her what troubles him so deeply she impulsively pushes him to tell her: 'I was led by passion and drew him with frantic heedlessness into the abyss that he so fearfully avoided' (*M* 27 [ch. v]). The language of passivity, 'was led by passion' ought to make us suspicious here. Whose passion, if not that of her 'self'?

She is also responsible for intruding upon another's mental terrain as a result of an involuntary feeling. That one may be responsible for involuntary feelings, that these feelings may bear the same consequence as acts, is a paradox which Mathilda eventually comes to recognize, as we have previously seen. When this recognition first appears it is in a passage which relates not to herself, but, retrospectively, to her father, and to her misunderstanding of him. Following her guess that her father fell in love with someone 'unworthy', she asks herself:

> Could there be guilt in it? He was too upright and noble to *do* aught that his conscience could not approve; I did not yet know of the crime there may be in involuntary feeling and therefore ascribed his tumultuous starts and gloomy looks wholly to the struggles of his mind and not any as they were partly due to the worst fiend of all – Remorse.
>
> (*M* 24 [ch. iv])

In *Matilda*, then, the belief that all guilt comes from intent is ascribed to Mathilda's uneducated youthfulness; once she experiences more of the world's horrors, she becomes 'aware of the crime there may be in involuntary feeling' and applies the lesson to herself. She becomes a Romantic heroine in understanding that moral agents may become guilty, fallen without choosing to do wrong, fallen from gaining knowledge through communication with others. Especially telling is the language of her decision to follow her father after he writes to her begging forgiveness and announcing his intention never to see her again:

> He must know that if I believed that his intention was merely to absent himself from me that instead of opposing him it would be that which I should myself require – or if he thought that any lurking feeling, yet he could not think that, should lead me to him would he endeavour to overthrow the only hope he could have of ever seeing me again; a lover, there was madness in the thought, yet he was my lover, would not act thus. No, he had determined to die, and he wished to spare me the misery of knowing it.
>
> (*M* 36–7 [ch. vii])

Given the invention and ascription of intent that Mathilda makes here, and given the tentative, horrified fascination with the possibility of her own desire for her father (which yet is not openly stated, even here), we can more reasonably speculate about that desire and therefore about a way in which Mathilda is a mental actor in this text and thus capable of the 'agent's regret'[11] that drives the latter two-thirds of the novel. The fact that she is right – that her father is suicidal – only adds to her reasons for remorse. The father becomes the passive to her active by communicating to her *in writing* and then fleeing before she can respond. Having already said too much, he retreats behind written entreaty for sympathy that cannot be reciprocated, a one-way *communiqué* that avoids communication. In the end Mathilda repeats his pattern of the retreat into writing rather than speak her woes to Woodville. In copying the father's act the novel itself gets written, again confusing the moral boundaries between the incestuous pair and further preventing us from arriving at glib identifications of either as agent or victim.

The climax of the father–daughter dialogue highlights the novel's enigmas regarding power and communication. It conjures up a unique feeling of excluding the reader from a dialogue between characters to which no one else could be privy. Their mirrored desires perhaps explain why, when the father finally gives up his secret, he says almost nothing and yet she understands him completely. He is driven to say, 'Yes, yes, I hate you! You are my bane, my poison, my disgust! Oh! No, ... you are none of all these: you are my light, my only one, my life. – My daughter, I love you!' (*M* 28 [ch. v]). The reader may well pause over these lines, wonder what is the matter with them, and even read on expecting more of an explanation of them than Mathilda ever needs. What is wrong with the father saying 'I love you' to his daughter when the diction of her accusation in the preceding paragraph was 'you no longer love me'?

This aporia suggests that the father and daughter share a private language which makes them necessarily sympathetic to one another, but this necessary sympathy, the novel argues, is fraught with complications arising from the inherent inequality of their patriarchal relationship. In Mathilda's failure to intuit her father's anxiety she abandons feminine stereotypes only to be brutally punished for doing so. As Ellison notes, 'Intuition is marked as a feminine quality, just as most subjects of romantic longing are, including childhood, nature, and the demonic.'[12] (This traditional marking comes to Romanticism at least in part by way of Milton's Eve, who receives in dreams what Adam must be told in words.) In failing to act the part of the intuitive female, Mathilda assumes a particular kind of masculine selfhood, and becomes a demon possessed, like all male Romantic demons, by remorse. She thus refuses to remain within the dual female spaces of subjection: silence, and subordinated attachment to a man (her father, then Woodville). But the process of seizing subjectivity marked as masculine is a fall, not an emancipation.

The novel, then, both illustrates and criticizes the Rousseauist fear of moral knowledge which forms the headnote to this essay. Both Rousseau and Shelley acknowledge the Biblical equation of knowledge and the fall. Rousseau believes, however, that his ideal project of 'educating the whole man' through the application of reason will succeed in avoiding the dangers that he indicates. But this ideal project receives, in the failure to educate Mathilda, a melodramatic admonishment. First of all, by posing the main subject of education as female, the novel highlights the fact that Rousseau's faith in the possibility of salutary education had excluded one of the very groups Annette Baier identifies as those left on the liberal Enlightenment's margins, namely women. Secondly, the novel betrays a scepticism concerning the applicability of 'reason' to a case such as Mathilda's.

But Shelley's critique of *Emile* does not repeat Wollstonecraft's in *A Vindication of the Rights of Woman*. In one crucial respect, indeed, *Matilda* is most un-Wollstonecraftian. *A Vindication* insists that women should *not* be protected from knowledge of the world and of sex: 'Women are everywhere in [a] deplorable state for, in order to preserve their innocence, as ignorance is courteously termed, truth is hidden from them.' Instead of shielding such 'innocence', Wollstonecraft advocates the cultivation of 'modesty' or 'a reserve of reason' founded upon knowledge.[13] In *Matilda*, we find, indeed, a father who tries to protect his daughter from knowledge, and a daughter who demands that she should not be shielded from it. Yet when the daughter's demand for 'education' is met, the result is not Wollstonecraftian virtue. The truth does not empower Mathilda. In short, Shelley offers *Matilda* as an exposition of the limitations of Enlightenment faith in the saving powers of communication – not only that of Rousseau but also that of Wollstonecraft.

After the father's death, and in the course of the ensuing development of the theme of exile, *Matilda* continues and amplifies its scepticisms about language, power and gender. The plot of the ending is essentially a series of acknowledgements in which Mathilda overcomes each objection against seeking total passivity in death. In the penultimate chapter Woodville dissuades the despairing Mathilda from active suicide. His argument, vintage P.B. Shelley, starts from an assumption of scepticism. He then attempts to transcend that scepticism (which he knows she shares in) through the effort of idealism: 'We know not what all this wide world means; its strange mixture of good and evil. But we have been placed here and bid live and hope' (*M* 59 [ch. xi]). Woodville expounds P.B. Shelley's ideal of reform as the source of hope to which he clings:

> Let us suppose that Socrates, or Shakespear, or Rousseau had been seized with despair and died in youth when they were as young as I am; do you think that we and all the world should not have lost incalculable improvement in our good feelings and our happiness thro' their destruction. ... if you can bestow happiness on another; if you can give one other person only one hour of joy ought you not to live to do it?
>
> (*M* 59–60 [ch. xi])

But Mathilda is only cured of despair temporarily, feeling joy when he speaks but then reverting to the self she calls 'this monster', this 'marked creature' (*M* 61 [ch. xi]). Woodville's idealistic call to fulfil a duty to others finds its answer in Mathilda's ironic selfhood, constructed to fulfil itself only by ending itself. Mathilda cannot ascend to Woodville's masculine reformist ambition. She provides us with an alternate female script, like that of Virginia Woolf's Judith Shakespeare, in which the female voice gets silenced before its proper words can be found, as Mathilda suggests by observing herself that she is the 'source of guilt that wants a name' (ibid.). But unlike Woolf's script of active repression, *Matilda* records the internalization of a seemingly universal crushing idea – that all action is tainted – but which seems particularly damaging to the female protagonist.[14]

In the last chapter Mathilda, a solitary walker in the woods, becomes 'wrapt' in a Rousseauist 'reverie', consequently loses herself, and becomes consumptive from exposure to a rainstorm. She is pleased to be near death, as she narrates, 'I am about to die an innocent death, and it will be sweeter even than that which the opium promised' (*M* 64 [ch. xii]). Innocent because utterly passive, this death takes the form of becoming an object in a Wordsworthian natural landscape. As Mathilda writes:

> this emaciated body will rest insensate on thy [the earth's] bosom
> 'Rolled round in earth's diurnal course
>   With rocks, and stones, and trees.
> ... Your solitudes, sweet land, your trees and waters will still exist, moved by your winds, or still beneath the eye of noon, though what I have felt about ye, and all my dreams which have often strangely deformed thee, will die with me.
>
> (*M* 65 [ch. xii])

The burden of which she is now to be released is the Romantic consciousness itself, the mental activity which *Matilda*'s rigorous ethics cannot choose but consider fallen. If Mathilda's selfhood, in the end, rejects Woodville's male offering of a purpose, it supplies no female alternative except non-existence. It seems as if Mathilda dies as a creature of no gender, which is not to say a universal gender; she dies to become a rock.

As the contrast between Shelley's narrative and the narratives of the Enlightenment has shown, *Matilda* challenges both male universalism and its feminist responses within Romanticism. In particular, *Matilda* prompts us to return to the question, incisively raised by Anne K. Mellor, of whether (and how?) to distinguish between masculine and feminine modes of Romantic writing.[15] Mellor does not equate these modes strictly with the author's sex: 'the relationship between "masculine" and "feminine" Romanticism is finally not one of structural opposition, but rather of intersection along a fluid continuum'.[16] This fluidity is necessary, given, as Mellor knows, that any generalization she makes about either mode has extensive caveats. But a categorization threatens to come undone as it becomes more fluid, supple and thus more sensitive and accurate, or in other words as it comes closer to the amorphous mass of objects upon which the critic must attempt to impose order while seeming merely to discover it. We are liable to be left in a situation similar to the one Arthur Lovejoy sought to solve by proposing a multiplicity of Romanticisms;[17] if there is a multiplicity, or even a continuum, then we must employ our terminology carefully, recognizing that though opening up criticism to more works of more female authors is the most exciting phenomenon currently occurring in the study of this period, generalizing about the feminine and masculine in these authors' text invites and even assumes, all disclaimers to the contrary, an essentialism about female writing that the evidence, in our opinion, will not bear.[18]

Mellor proposes a model of Romanticism in which conflict is embedded in the masculine mode, socialisation in the feminine, and in which the masculine Romantic erotic is an act of encompassing conquest:

> the object of Romantic or erotic love is not the recognition and appreciation of the beloved woman as the independent other, but rather the assimilation of the female into the male (or the annihilation of any other that threatens masculine selfhood), the woman must finally be enslaved or destroyed, must disappear or die. ... This is not to deny the existence of powerful, independent female figures in the poetry of masculine Romanticism [here Mellor lists, among others, Beatrice Cenci] ... but only to suggest that the frequent equation of heterosexual love with erotic passion produced a desire for a total union between lover and beloved, a union that necessarily entails the elimination of otherness.[19]

As we have tried to show, *Matilda* revises Mellor's schematic by presenting a narrative in which erotic subjects do indeed elide the recognition of otherness and threaten to become mirrors to one another, but not because the masculine succeeds in absorbing and conquering the feminine. Rather, each character is destroyed by the violence of his or her own passions. Neither Mathilda nor her father can be clearly labelled the victim of the other.[20] *Matilda* squeezes agency out of a world of seeming necessity, in which everyone is a victim of all external circumstance, including the actions of other people. For Shelley in *Matilda* there are no such clear polarities between male and female as Mellor proposes, and, more importantly, no examples of true independence or freedom.

If we compare *Matilda* to a key example of male Romantic writing, Coleridge's 'The Rime of the Ancient Mariner', a narrative Shelley heard at age nine from Coleridge's own lips (Mellor, p. 11), a canonical text which exemplifies the trope of Romantic exile, a more complex and nuanced relationship between the two emerges than polarity. Coleridge's poem, like *Matilda*, undermines certainties about volition and dogmas about moral responsibility even though its narrator – the mariner himself – clings to these certainties and dogmas. The most obvious example of how the poem offers questions instead of moral decrees is the way in which the connection between shooting the albatross and the mariner's guilt is so subjectively and arbitrarily established; his guilt is at least half-created by the arbitrary causality that he and the other mariners assign to his act. But what is clear is that the Mariner *acted* and his having acted defines him as the one who will be condemned to suffer remorse. Coleridge fashions the Mariner as the modern man, swept by impulses he cannot name to commit acts he cannot understand which may or may not bear upon the mysterious events of the world. The poem suggests that action in the world is violence, and that such action inevitably betrays us. It forms the middle term in a continuum that reaches from the Biblical Cain to Shelley's novel: in Genesis Cain's action is unequivocal, his punishment absolutely stemming from his act. Coleridge destabilizes this divine equation between an action which is a cause and its effect. Shelley's text further revises Coleridge's prophecy of remorse's inevitability and universality while radically re-writing his description of action. Mathilda differs from both Cain and the Mariner in the self-consciousness by which she avoids becoming an object of sympathy. As Susan Allen Ford writes, Mathilda's 'tale is a redaction of the banishment from Eden, a fall due to sympathy, to the desire for knowledge, to speech'.[21] Because of the failure of sympathy in the scene of the father's confession, Mathilda refuses to tell her story to Woodville in person; the Mariner's compulsion to repeat, which is like a need to keep living, is nearly crushed out of her. She retains until the end her role of receiver of information. As Ellison writes: 'For the romantic subject of either gender, the feminine stereotype ... is associated with the receptive attitude in which understanding is accomplished.'[22] Mathilda rejects granting Woodville the feminine receptivity he requests but by retaining that role for herself she paradoxically carves for herself a 'masculine' independence.

The thought from *The Cenci*'s 'Preface' that 'no person can be truly dishonoured by the act of another', expresses a reaction readers might well have to Mathilda's apparent inability to distinguish herself from the consequence of her father's guilty passion. The degree to which Mathilda internalizes her father's guilt remains perplexing even to readers, who, with Bernard Williams, appreciate the moral value of a person's impulse to feel regret for bad results she didn't intentionally cause. The renewed attention moral philosophers such as Williams have given to rationally unaccountable feelings – feelings upon which we are not expected to act and which we cannot formally demand that others have – demonstrates the continued relevance of a Romantic ethics that is inherently dramatic, self-critical, and dialogic.[23]

But, as we have argued here, it is not enough simply to see Shelley as anticipating the work of Baier and Williams in complicating voluntaristic, rational models of agency. For Mathilda's reaction to her father's words must also be understood in terms of the complexity of the culture's constructions of feminine personhood. These constructions leave women stranded between the ideal of feminine pliancy that for Wollstonecraft makes women morally identical to their corrupt 'masters', and the equally problematic image of feminine virtue as a gem that keeps itself pure in an impure world. For Mathilda to meet her father's confession with detached sympathy would be to assert her independence, to achieve the ideal of an unsoiled integrity of self that returns no images of itself to others. Yet Mathilda, while not identical to her father, only finds her way to selfhood through the articulation of his desires. Shelley's revision of the interactions of male and female protagonists is thus specific to a female subject for whom the social construction of selfhood is often confused by, and at odds with, her own intermixed will to love and power.

Notes

An earlier version of this essay was jointly presented as a paper to the MLA annual conference (Toronto, December 1997).

1. Jean-Jacques Rousseau, *Emile, or On Education*, trans. Allan Bloom (New York: Basic Books, 1979) p. 96; hereafter, Rousseau, *Emile*.
2. P. B. Shelley, *Shelley's Poetry And Prose: Authoritative Texts, Criticism*, selected and edited by Donald H. Reiman and Sharon B. Powers (New York: Norton, 1977) p. 240.
3. Our starting points here are Mary Poovey's and Ruth Yeazell's analyses of the tropes of the 'Proper Lady' and the 'modest woman', which, respectively, argue that eighteenth- and nineteenth-century constructions of feminine virtue asked a woman to have no desires of her own and never to speak or act in her own name. See Mary Poovey, *The Proper Lady And The Woman Writer: Ideology as Style in the Works of Mary Wollstonecraft, Mary*

Shelley, and Jane Austen (Chicago: University of Chicago Press, 1984) and Ruth Yeazell, Fictions of Modesty: Women and Courtship in the English Novel (Chicago: University of Chicago Press, 1991).
4. See Julie Ellison, *Delicate Subjects: Romanticism, Gender, and the Ethics of Understanding* (Ithaca: Cornell University Press, 1990) p. 11; hereafter, Ellison.
5. Rousseau, *Emile*, p. 42.
6. Annette Baier, *Moral Prejudices: Essays on Ethics* (Cambridge, MA: Harvard University Press, 1994) p. 28.
7. See William D. Brewer, 'Mary Shelley and the Therapeutic Value of Language', *Papers on Language and Literature*, 30.4 (1994) 387–407.
8. See Tillotama Rajan's subtle psychoanalytic paper, 'Melancholy and the Political Economy of Romanticism', *Studies in the Novel*, 26.2 (1994) 43–68.
9. For an analysis of *Matilda* and the politics of the bourgeois family, see Mellor, pp. 191–200.
10. Judith Butler, *The Psychic Life of Power: Theories in Subjection* (Stanford: Stanford University Press, 1997) pp. 1–2; Butler's Romantic roots can be traced to her early work on Hegel.
11. The term 'agent's regret' is taken from Bernard Williams's *Shame and Necessity* (Berkeley, Los Angeles, London: University of California Press, 1993) p. 68.
12. Ellison, p. 11.
13. Mary Wollstonecraft, *A Vindication of the Rights of Woman*, ed. Carol H. Poston (New York and London: W. W. Norton, 1988) pp. 44, 83.
14. See Virginia Woolf, *A Room of One's Own* (New York, London, San Diego: Harcourt Brace Jovanovich, 1957) pp. 48ff.
15. See Anne K. Mellor, *Romanticism and Gender* (New York, London: Routledge, 1993). It ought to be noted that Mellor has explicitly labelled her ground-breaking work as 'tentative'.
16. Ibid., p. 5.
17. See Arthur Lovejoy, 'On the Discrimination of Romanticisms', *Essays on the History of Ideas* (Baltimore: Johns Hopkins University Press, 1948 [1924]) pp. 228–53. Addressing Lovejoy, Anne Janowitz writes that rather than focus on the unity or diversity of Romanticism, 'we should consider Romanticism to be the literary form of a struggle taking place on many levels of society between the claims of individualism and the claims of communitarianism'. This model allows us to 'see more clearly how self-divided British Romantic poetry has always been in its intentions' (Anne Janowitz, '"A Voice from across the Sea": Communitarianism at the Limits of Romanticism', in *At the Limits of Romanticism: Essays in Cultural, Feminist, and Materialist Criticism*, eds Mary A. Favret and Nicola J. Watson [Indianapolis, Bloomington: Indiana University Press, 1994] p. 84). See also Ellison's Introduction to *Delicate Subjects*, which theorizes the interrelations between Romanticism, gender and criticism.
18. The general problem of 'doing' feminism with or without some essentialist assumptions is one which continues to be debated among feminist writers. See, for example, Teresa de Laurentis, *Technologies of Gender: Essays on Theory, Film, and Fiction* (Bloomington: Indiana University Press, 1987).
19. Anne K. Mellor, *Romanticism and Gender*, p. 26.

20. Shelley's phrase 'victim of the state of feeling' in the 'Preface' to her editions of the *Poetical Works* of P.B. Shelley is noteworthy: 'He had been from youth a victim of the state of feeling inspired by the reaction of the French Revolution' (*M* 256). Here the ascription of agency to feeling is quite clear. The meaning appears to be that the 'temper of the times' during the period of backlash against the Revolution was one from which P.B. Shelley suffered as a youth.
21. Susan Allen Ford, '"A name more dear": Daughters, Fathers, and Desire in *A Simple Story, The False Friend,* and *Matilda*', in *Re-Visioning Romanticism: British Women Writers, 1776–1837* (Philadelphia: University of Pennsylvania Press, 1994) p. 53.
22. Ellison, p. 11.
23. Williams gives the example of the lorry driver who accidentally runs down a small child. According to Williams, while we recognize the driver's feelings of guilt as misplaced, we would be troubled if he felt no more regret over the accident than a spectator: 'We feel sorry for the driver, but that sentiment co-exists with, indeed presupposes, that there is something special about his relation to this happening, something which cannot merely be eliminated by the consideration that it was not his fault .... it would be a kind of insanity never to experience sentiments of this kind towards anyone, and it would be an insane concept of rationality which insisted that a rational person never would' (*Moral Luck: Philosophical Papers, 1973–1980* [New York and London: Cambridge University Press, 1981] pp. 28, 29). Williams's insistence that 'one's history as an agent is a web in which anything that is the product of the will is surrounded, and held up and partly formed by things that are not', resonates with earlier Romantic insights into the passivity of agency and articulations of the relationship between becoming a self and having been an accidental cause. See, for example, Frances Ferguson's essay, 'Romantic Memory' in *Studies in Romanticism*, 35.4 (Winter 1996) 509–33.

5
Mary Shelley's *Valperga*: Italy and the Revision of Romantic Aesthetics

Daniel E. White

Conceived at Marlow in 1817 but researched and written in Italy between 1818 and 1821, *Valperga: or, The Life and Adventures of Castruccio, Prince of Lucca*, tells the story of Castruccio Castracani dei Antelminelli, the early fourteenth-century Lucchese Ghibelline who by virtue of his ruthless ambition, intellect, and military leadership became captain-general of Lucca in 1316 and prince in 1320. Shelley's narrative interweaves the fictional stories of two tragic female characters, Euthanasia and Beatrice, with the nominally historical tale of Castruccio's simultaneous rise and fall from uncorrupted youth to political tyranny and spiritual destitution.[1]

Like *Frankenstein*, *Valperga* forces its reader to re-evaluate the correspondence between Romantic aesthetic categories and visions of social and political order. When turned in on itself, as in Victor Frankenstein's burning solipsistic ambition or his creature's eventual identification with the interior hell of Milton's Satan, the masculine sublime threatens both domestic tranquillity and peaceful coexistence.[2] I propose, however, that because of its roots in the Italian historical and literary landscape, Mary Shelley's second novel pushes her fiction beyond the gendered opposition of the beautiful and the sublime. Castruccio may represent a political version of Victor Frankenstein's scientific Prometheanism, but in the characters of Beatrice and Euthanasia, *Valperga* deepens Mary Shelley's depiction of the alternatives to and consequences of masculine power. In Beatrice we find a Godwinian psychological portrait of the feminine mind that accepts the self-deifying myth of masculine sublimity. In Euthanasia and her vision of Italy we discover not only the feminine alternative associated aesthetically with the beautiful, socially with domesticity, and politically with democracy, but also the possibility, at least, for another alternative, a determined revision of the sublime itself.

Critical assessments of *Valperga*, ranging from those of P. B. Shelley, William Godwin, and contemporary reviewers to those of the present, have been prompt to note that the novel is less about Castruccio than the destructive effects of this ambitious and striving masculine paradigm of egotism – P.B. Shelley called him a 'little Napoleon' (*PBSL* II, p. 353) – on the social spheres around him. The novel narrates a polemic between Castruccio's dominant political, social, and aesthetic masculine ideology and its feminine other, the values embodied by Euthanasia. This polemic significantly found its fittest expression and conclusion on Italian soil. Italy and the feminine, then, are at once the terrain and subject of the novel; *Valperga* transposes its moment and site of production onto early 14th-century Italian history, representing the contemporary post-Napoleonic moment as precluding the political and social conditions under which the author's ideology of organic reform and domestic values could be realized. The basis of this representation is the gendered opposition of the beautiful and the sublime, and although Euthanasia ultimately finds no political or personal ground on which to stand, her story opens the possibility for a different kind of power, and a different experience of sublimity.

I Italy and the feminine

Italian Romanticism, a movement fashioned largely in reaction against Napoleonic and Austrian imperialist control, constitutes the backdrop for Shelley's portrayal of the relations between masculine and feminine positions in *Valperga*. Like many Italian Romantic texts, *Valperga* is determined to deflate the representation of 'Italy' as a paradise in the Northern European imagination, a paradise of myrtles, laurels, and mountains, of love, poetry, and infinitude. Like Italian writers such as Ugo Foscolo and Giacomo Leopardi, moreover, Mary Shelley knows this land in a different sense, that of its political fragmentation and subjection first under the imperialist systems of Napoleon and then following the Congress of Vienna. Her novel, therefore, can be understood as participating in both English Romanticism's self-critique of its own aesthetic of desire and in the Italian Romantic response to the dynamics of imperialist domination. These two contexts led Shelley to represent the images and ideals of masculine romantic sublimity and individual transcendent ambition as correspondent to political and social dynamics against which much

Romantic literature and many of its writers, both male and female, explicitly struggled.

Valperga represents in striking fashion the fate of Italy and the feminine as aesthetic and political expressions of masculine desire. What Shelley saw and expressed from a female Romantic perspective was the fragmentation of the feminine into a body or nation of contradictions – at once paradise and hell, beautiful and hideous, adored and loathed, desired and feared. In *Valperga*, as well as in *Frankenstein*, this expression develops into the singular insight that such a catastrophe was in a sense the hideous progeny of a masculine and 'Romantic' imagination inscribing its desires on nature; as Victor's tutor at Ingolstadt, M. Waldman, puts it, the modern masters of science 'penetrate into the recesses of nature, and shew how she works in her hiding places' (*F* 32 [I. ii]).[3] Castruccio, too, creates his texts out of feminine nature, specifically out of women and that 'geographical expression', to borrow Metternich's 1847 phrase, Italy.

From Charlotte Smith and Mary Robinson to Laetitia Landon and Felicia Hemans, the current canon of female British Romantic writers illustrates the pitfalls of gendered identity during a period in which feminine sensibility served as one of the indices of moral virtue; similarly, the relationship between Italian Romanticism and *Valperga* suggests a parallel set of problems with respect to the political and social identities of Italy. If paradise is impossible and even dangerous when embodied in women, as articulated most forcefully by Mary Wollstonecraft, it is equally so when transcribed onto an inhabited geography, as expressed by the various counter-imperialist tones of Italian Romanticism with respect either to the largely unreformed pre-Napoleonic Italy or the war-torn, culturally colonized, and politically fragmented Italy of 1815–21. Set next to the familiar topos of Italy as a *locus amoenus*, a bower of paradise and liberation, as the destination of escape to a home 'o'er the southern moors', for instance, of Keats's lovers at the end of *The Eve of St. Agnes*, the following description of Italy as an abused and violated 'Formosissima donna' from Giacomo Leopardi's *All'Italia* (1818) offers a stark and telling contrast:

> Oimé quante ferite,
> Che lividor, che sangue! oh qual ti veggio,
> Formosissima donna! Io chiedo al cielo
> E al mondo: dite dite;
> Chi la ridusse a tale?[4]

[Alas, such wounds,
What bruises, what blood! oh, in what state do I see you,
Most beautiful woman! I cry to heaven
And to the world: Say, say;
Who reduced her to this?]

Similarly, Ugo Foscolo's epistolary novel, *Ultime Lettere di Jacopo Ortis* (1802), in the words of Shelley's own 1835 translation, resists the definition of Italy as an 'asylum': 'what can we expect except indigence and indignity.... And where shall I seek an asylum? – in Italy? Unhappy land! and can I behold those who have robbed, scorned, and sold us, and not weep with rage?'.[5] While there is neither evidence nor likelihood that Shelley read Leopardi while she was in Italy, she did read Foscolo there.[6] In many respects *Valperga* was a production of the same cultural climate in which authors such as Leopardi, Foscolo, Alessandro Manzoni, Carlo Porta, and more radical writers such as Giovanni Berchet and Silvio Pellico, both associated with the patriotic Milanese newspaper *Il Conciliatore* (suppressed by the Austrian police in 1819), voiced opposition to past and present histories of foreign domination in Italy.

Early in the novel Shelley accordingly orchestrates a rapid and dramatic deflation of any naive Romantic expectations evoked by the cultural signifier, Italy. The fifth chapter of the first volume finds her young hero, yet to become an anti-hero, crossing 'the beautiful Alps, the boundaries of his native country' (*V* 46 [I. v]), to re-enter Italy from France. The path is treacherous, and as Castruccio advances he hears the cries for help of a man who has slipped over the edge of the precipice. Given the generations of barbarians and aesthetes who had crossed these very same boundaries through the ages, it would have been all too natural for Shelley's audience to assume the unfortunate traveller to be a foreigner. Castruccio indeed assumes the same, and having rescued the stranger:

> soothed him with a gentle voice, and told him that now the worst part of the journey was over, and that they were about to descend by an easier path to the plain of Italy; 'where,' he said, 'you will find a paradise that will cure all your evils.'
> The man looked at him with a mixture of wonder, and what might have been construed into contempt.... He replied drily, 'I am an Italian.' And Castruccio smiled to perceive, that these words were considered as a sufficient refutation to his assertion of the boasted charms of Italy.
>
> (*V* 47 [I. v])

The passage deftly carries its reader across the symbolic Alps from one perspective into another, into the actual plain of Italy, to inhabit which is to be an individual in a country of the imagination ruled and defined from without – not a paradise, but heaven and hell in one. In *Valperga*, the same holds true for subjects inhabiting all such bodies of the imagination, be they geographical, political, or human. In Italian history, Shelley had found the terrain on which to represent the consequences of Romantic aesthetic and political conflicts – from Dante to Napoleon – on contemporary Europe's gendered subjects and geographies, as at least one hostile reader was quick to recognize. The *Blackwood*'s reviewer, perceiving the association between gender, politics, and aesthetics, professed first to be grieved that 'any English lady' should have been capable of writing Beatrice's heretical speech, then went on to quip: 'we are mortally sick of "orange tinted skies," "dirges," and "Dante." Another thing we are sick of, is this perpetual drumming of poor Buonaparte'.[7]

II *Valperga* and the socialization of romantic subjects

It is interesting to note that negative characterizations of *Valperga* from the 1820s onwards have consistently evoked the very aesthetic criteria against which, in part, the novel was composed. One early reviewer found in *Valperga* 'not one flash of imagination, not one spark of passion'. Richard Garnett's preface to his 1891 collection of Shelley's *Tales and Stories* declared that *Valperga* 'wants the fire of imagination which alone could have interpenetrated the mass and fused its diverse ingredients into a satisfying whole'.[8] In other words, *Valperga* fails in the same fiery terms descriptive in Shelley's first novel of those masculine desires that led to the destruction of Victor and everyone around him.[9] In *Valperga*, as in *Frankenstein*, the fire of excessive imaginative ambition is to a large extent the problem.

In this novel, Shelley conceives her characters along a range of masculine and feminine subject positions and proceeds to represent the drama of necessity, a tragedy, that she foresaw would ultimately leave the stage of the novel and, she feared, the stage of contemporary history empty. With its three protagonists Castruccio, Euthanasia, and the ardent prophetess Beatrice, along with a number of interesting minor figures such as the 'military peasant' Guinigi and his son Arrigo, Wilhelmina of Bohemia and her appointed 'papess' Magfreda, the witch Fior di Mandragola and the albino servant Bindo, *Valperga* plays out at length a drama of love and ambition within contemporary dynamics of gender and power. The story of Castruccio's education and early desires depicts the propagation of a forceful strand of male Romantic subjectivity. His masculine socialization begins at age eleven when his family is exiled from Lucca by the then-dominant Guelf party. A witness to the violence of civil discord and the misery of exile, young Castruccio:

> became inflamed with rage and desire of vengeance. It was by scenes such as these, that party spirit was generated, and became so strong in Italy. Children, while they were yet too young to feel their own disgrace, saw the misery of their parents, and took early vows of implacable hatred against their persecutors: these were remembered in after times; the wounds were never seared, but the fresh blood ever streaming kept alive the feelings of passion and anger which had given rise to the first blow.
> (V 11–12 [I. i])

'Desire of vengeance' grows into doctrines of dominance and subordination; 'implacable hatred' ensures the continuity of cyclical history alternating between tyranny and liberty, Ghibelline and Guelf – Byron's endless *'one* page' of history in the fourth Canto of *Childe Harold's Pilgrimage*, or P.B. Shelley's 'struggling World, which slaves and tyrants win' of the first Act of *Prometheus Unbound*. But while these poems position themselves against such histories, there is a facet of their aesthetic ideals, Shelley implies, by which images of sublimity reinscribe values of individual ambition which sustain repetitive cycles of political and social power. *Valperga*, like *Frankenstein*, implicates the egotism of the Promethean poet, reformer, or scientist, whether bound and cursing *or* unbound and universally loving, in the reproduction of those values that have set cyclical history in motion, or for that matter prescribed the contents of history's one page. Ever-striving desire, the *immer streben* at the heart of Castruccio, corresponds to the fiery aesthetic that for Shelley entangles the powerful figure of the Romantic artist in the relations of power he characteristically deplores.

Shelley thus locates egotism and ambition at the centre not only of the tyrannical politician but also of the figurative Romantic artist; she appropriates the character of Castruccio in order to disclose affinities between this Machiavellian paradigm[10] and the destructive powers of the Byronic ideal.[11] As Jean de Palacio notes:

Castruccio tombe en effet dans le péché le plus grave au regard de l'évangile shelleyen: celui de subordonner tout intérêt humain aux moyens égoïstes de parvenir.... Castruccio réunira en lui le lion et le renard.[12]

Anne Mellor has argued persuasively and in detail with respect to *Frankenstein* that Shelley understood this subordination of all human, or rather domestic, interests to self-advancement in the public sphere as the necessary consequence of what she calls male Romantic ideology, 'grounded as it is on a never-ending, perhaps never successful, effort to marry contraries, to unite the finite and the infinite'.[13]

These are the terms into which the young Castruccio develops, the aesthetic terms of Anglo-German Romanticism that Shelley translates into the imperialist terms of a Napoleonic vision. At age 17 Castruccio:

> would throw his arms to the north, the south, the east, and the west, crying, – 'There – there – there, and there, shall my fame reach!' – and then, in gay defiance, casting his eager glance towards heaven: – 'and even there, if man may climb the slippery sides of the arched palace of eternal fame, there also will I be recorded'.
>
> (*V* 23 [I. ii])

Years and pages later, after Castruccio has been exposed to the intrigues of the English court and the doctrines of Alberto Scoto and Benedetto Pepi, the consequences of his education have become manifest:

> It were curious to mark the changes that now operated in his character. Every success made him extend his views to something beyond; and every obstacle surmounted, made him still more impatient of those that presented themselves in succession. He became all in all to himself; his creed seemed to contain no article but the end and aim of his ambition; and that he swore before heaven to attain.
>
> (*V* 182–3 [II. vi])

Castruccio's early desire to transcend mortality and the finite by recording and deifying himself in the 'arched palace of eternal fame' leads to the politically and socially destructive expressions of that egotistical emptiness Shelley identifies as the end of masculine

Romantic desire – empty because unable to accept the humanist or domestic values of an alternative ideology on their own terms, those offered by Euthanasia.

In opposition to the inward turn of Castruccio's ambition – 'He became all in all to himself' – Euthanasia presents an externally directed ideology of domesticity and enlightened bourgeois politics. The formation of her character is modelled on the educational programme for rational womanhood of Mary Wollstonecraft's *A Vindication of the Rights of Woman* (1792) and embodies feminine ideals of sensibility found in Wollstonecraft's *Letters from Norway*. Shelley reread both books in the months before she began to work continuously on *Valperga*.[14] Euthanasia becomes the ideal 'Romantic' woman conceived from the bourgeois feminist perspective of the 1790s, a self-sufficient individual who can both think and feel, and whose thoughts and feelings lead her to an ideology of social renovation through universal love and gradual political reform through organic change.[15]

Early in the first volume Shelley strikes a dramatic balance in Euthanasia's 'sweet looks, in which deep sensibility and lively thought were pictured, and a judgement and reason beyond her years'. As a child, she learned to love *and* to read Latin. The 'polished language of Cicero' strengthens this 'judgement and reason', lending it a philosophical cast. The Roman writers awaken her 'hope of freedom for Italy, of revived learning, and the reign of peace for all the world' (*V* 18–19 [I. ii]). Upon this education is predicated an essential strand of an alternative aesthetic that unites the modern Italian Romantic with the antique and medieval past. It is not, however, the aesthetic of the self-aggrandizing Promethean but rather of the humanistic Republic of Letters: communitarian, non-élitist, democratic, at once oral, written and performative, popular and courtly, pastoral and urban, serious and prankish, orchestrated and spontaneous.

Euthanasia convenes a May court which attracts 'a multitude of *Uomini di Corte*; story-tellers, *improvisatori*, musicians, singers, actors, rope-dancers, jugglers and buffoons' (*V* 105 [I. xiii]). C*anzone*-singers mingle with fire-eaters and mimes, a rich mixture which has nurtured Dante and is later to feed the genius of Boccaccio and Chaucer. This varied entertainment testifies to the creativity of the Italian people; as the narrator comments enthusiastically: 'No nation can excel the Italians in the expression of passion by the language of gesture alone, or in the talent of extemporarily giving words to a series of actions which they intend to represent' (*V* 117 [I. xiv]). Thus Shelley asserts the continuities between medieval Italian vernacular oral culture and the Italian Romantics, between Dante and Foscolo, and connects this heritage to Euthanasia's education in Latin.[16]

But Euthanasia as a child has learned to love as well, and the other side of her humanistic education, sensibility, later culminates in expressions of the domestic affections extended to all humanity:

> to behold the heaven-pointing cypress with unbent spire sleep in the stirless air; these were sights and feelings which softened and exalted her thoughts; ... she felt bound in amity to all; doubly, immeasurably loving those dear to her, feeling an humanizing charity even to the evil.
>
> (V 180 [II. vii])

Of course, the presence of the cypress in place of the myrtle or laurel foreshadows the inevitable failure of the individual in this subject position to survive under existing conditions. Similarly, the presence of an unbidden guest, the destructive Benedetto Pepi, in the midst of Euthanasia's May festivity (itself infiltrated by malicious satirists and barely contained Guelf–Ghibelline divisions) indicates that the celebratory, familial occasion of the court is only a brief holiday or truce. It is in the representation of failed potential that Euthanasia embodies a critique of the existing order.

III 'The god undeified' and the feminine sublime

While the colonization of the masculine by the feminine may be Euthanasia's image of a utopian future – her 'hope of freedom for Italy, of revived learning and the reign of peace for all the world' – it is precisely this future that *Valperga* represents as closed-off. The historical impasse is an impersonal structure of social and political conditions that in some way makes barren, or worse, the two central human relationships in the novel. The domestic and personal bonds between Euthanasia and Castruccio and between Castruccio and Beatrice tragically fail to bear any fruit besides negation and destruction. A third kind of relationship does exist in one of the rare Romantic representations of exclusively female friendship, that between Euthanasia and Beatrice. *Valperga* represents both a heroine who refuses to conceive of herself solely in relational terms and a friendship in which two females might develop such a concept of female identity. But as with Guinigi's agrarian paradise and

Euthanasia's court, this feminine enclave provides only a temporary and profoundly inconsequential respite before the inevitable emptiness of the conclusion.

In *Valperga* all conceived generic resolutions of public and private are rejected as sterile, as politically and personally qualifying, negating, or marginalizing the individual, male or female, in the feminine position. There is, as Betty Bennett notes, 'no happy ending which one would expect of a popular romance'.[17] Rather, with the death of all female heroines, along with the male 'heroines' Guinigi and Arrigo, the stage of the novel's history is left empty but for public actions and events, themselves the hollow expressions of egotistical desire. For history to be full, *Valperga* implies, political and social conditions must be such that the private sphere can colonize the public without being fragmented and negated by a world that refuses to forego its longings and ambitions for aesthetic, social, or political thrones in the 'arched palace of eternal fame'. There are particular dangers in aspiring to an aesthetic immortality that does not spring from nor is validated by a community, but which is grounded in self-deification.

This process is exemplified by the prophetess Beatrice. The narrative depicts the consequences of uncritically accepting the self-deifying expressions of the Romantic imagination.[18] Beatrice, it has been argued, presents an unflattering portrait of the 'Romantic Poet' whose flashing eyes and floating hair persuade her, or rather him, that he alone among all humanity has drunk the milk of paradise. Thus Jane Blumberg writes that Beatrice 'is passion and creativity gone mad, the potential end result of the unrestrained and impractical Romantic imagination', while Joseph Lew states, 'she becomes a Romantic poet'.[19]

The early Beatrice, then, is a talented and creative woman who affirms for herself the novel's rendition of the dream-world inhabited by the Romantic imagination:

> she preaches, she prophesies, she sings extempore hymns, and entirely fulfilling the part of *Donna Estatica*, she passes many hours of each day in solitary meditation, or rather in dreams, to which her active imagination gives a reality and life which confirm her in her mistakes.
>
> (*V* 136–7 [II. ii])

This type of the *Donna Estatica* would have echoed for Shelley's readership the tragic career of Germaine de Staël's fictional *improvisatrice* in *Corinne ou l'Italie* (1807), which, according to her journal, Shelley was reading in November 1820, and for us prophetically anticipates the actual career of Laetitia Landon. When the *Donna Estatica* in *Valperga* crosses from the masculine position of solitary and self-referential prophet/poet to that of the feminine object of Castruccio's desire, the impossibility of this female 'Romantic' poet becomes manifest.

The source of Beatrice's poetry was an imaginative self-deification, an illusion that she was the *'Ancilla Dei'*, the chosen vessel into which God has poured a portion of his spirit' (*V* 136 [II. ii]); her renunciation of the position of prophetess for that of Castruccio's mistress involves a substitution of one false deity for another, Castruccio for herself. Before she goes to Castruccio to give herself to him for the first time, she removes from her forehead the symbolic diadem on which the words *'Ancilla Dei'* are written. He asks:

> 'Where is thy mark, prophetess? art thou no longer the *Maiden of God?'* ...
> 'I still have it,' she replied; 'but I have dismissed it from my brow; I will give it you; come, my lord, this evening at midnight to the secret entrance of the viscountess's palace'.
> (*V* 151 [II. iv])

Beatrice transfers illusions of her own divinity onto her relationship with Castruccio. Sacrificing her own position of imaginative creativity to her adoration of Castruccio, she never learns the lesson to which Shelley repeatedly returns, that attributions of divine creativity to human individuals, ourselves or others, are highly dangerous, too often serving as masks for the various faces of unrestrained ambition and power. The constancy of her illusion lies in her persistent acceptance of the masculine as all in all, as divine. This deification of the masculine, even after Castruccio has abandoned her, blinds her to the truth that at the heart of Castruccio is the mere desire for power, a desire based on lack that only requires her and the feminine world as objects of appropriation in its never-ending internalized quest for fulfilment.

In a bold and unexpected turn the narrative brings Beatrice face-to-face with a nameless essence of masculine power, linking her to the character of the same name in P.B. Shelley's tragedy, *The Cenci*. For three years, Beatrice reveals, she was imprisoned in an 'infernal house' ruled by an unnamed figure of evil who subjected her to sexual and psychological horrors unspeakable but to 'the unhallowed ears of infidels': 'What was he, who was the author and mechanist of these crimes? he bore a human name; they say that his lineage was human; yet could he be a man?' (*V* 257 [III. iv]). In that he is all too clearly a man, Beatrice's deification or demonization of him – the two are finally the same – leads to possibly the clearest account of how Shelley conceived the relation between one category of Romantic aesthetics and contemporary mechanisms of power:

> There was something about him that might be called beautiful; but it was the beauty of the tiger, of lightning, of the cataract that destroys. Obedience waited on his slightest motion; for he made none, that did not command; his followers worshipped him, but it was as a savage might worship the god of evil. His slaves dared not murmur; – his eyes beamed with irresistible fire, his smile was as death.
>
> (*V* 258 [III. iv])

This representation of power encodes the terms of Romantic sublimity – the tiger, the lightning, the cataract that destroys, eyes beaming with irresistible fire. By both imagining itself as divine and defining the sublime in its own image, masculine power aesthetically reproduces its own illusions in the minds of those it seduces and dominates. Both Castruccio and the unnamed man futilely attempt to fill their lives with the power of gods or demons over humankind. Their illusions succeed only in reflecting themselves in minds such as Beatrice's, undisciplined and mortal minds that are subject to accepting masculine power's self-deifying aesthetic representations of itself:

> Ever the dupe of her undisciplined thoughts, she cherished her reveries, believing that heavenly and intellectual, which was indebted for its force to earthly mixtures; and she resigned herself entire to her visionary joys, until she finally awoke to truth, fallen, and for ever lost.
>
> (*V* 152–3 [II. iv])

In Shelley's work, the fate of such seduced individuals is a form of negation, the emptying of oneself into the deification or demonization of a void.

The narrative of Euthanasia's love for Castruccio, however, depicts the gradual disenchantment of a female mind with the illusions imposed on it by a masculine world. Unlike Beatrice, Euthanasia finally refuses to accept the values of Castruccio's public sphere as aesthetic ideals. If the paradise projected by Beatrice for herself and Castruccio fails because of the imaginary gods and demons in which they both believe, Euthanasia's initial deification of Castruccio cannot survive in her mind alongside the political demands of her beliefs. She refuses to concede any substance or validity to the terms of public success and glory, challenging all translations of honour, fame, and dominion into aesthetic achievements. 'Romantic' notions of the beautiful and the sublime for Euthanasia are criteria that need to be evaluated in terms of the political consequences of the ideology that has produced them in its own image. In the development of Euthanasia's character, Shelley suggests first the formation of an alternative aesthetic in the image of an alternative ideology, one that comes to value peace and domestic affections, the mingling of all the arts and the talents in an ephemeral celebratory moment, over all forms of conquest, ultimately whether in the name of liberty or tyranny.

Euthanasia's initial love for Castruccio traps her in the same imaginary deification of the masculine as that which seduced Beatrice. Like the fallen prophetess, Euthanasia once 'made a god of him she loved' (*V* 79 [I. ix]). In volume two the narrative voice reflects on Beatrice's predicament, defining the constraints of a form of love that excludes the political and external world from its purely personal demands and desires. This is the description of idolatrous love that the masculine world ultimately fails to keep kindled in the heart of Euthanasia:

> even as we idolize the object of our affections, do we idolize ourselves: if we separate him from his fellow mortals, so do we separate ourselves, and, glorying in belonging to him alone, feel lifted above all other sensations, all other joys and griefs, to one hallowed circle from which all but his idea is banished; we walk as if a mist or some more potent charm divided us from all but him; a sanctified victim which none but the priest set apart for that office could touch and not pollute, enshrined in a cloud of glory, made glorious through beauties not our own.
>
> (*V* 152 [II. iv])

The description intimates that a cloud of glory may be just that, a cloud, while no matter how hallowed such a woman in love feels herself to be, she remains 'a sanctified victim'.

In other words, Euthanasia's conception of viable love does not separate individuals from political and social conditions external to their relationship. Having concluded the peace treaty between Florence and Lucca, Euthanasia makes it clear that the political terms of this treaty are also the personal conditions of the contract under which she offers Castruccio her love:

> 'Love you indeed I always must; but I know, for I have studied my own heart, that it would not unite itself to yours, if, instead of these thoughts of peace and concord, you were to scheme war and conquest.'
> 'You measure your love in nice scales,' replied Castruccio, reproachfully; 'surely, if it were as deep as mine, it would be ruled alone by its own laws, and not by outward circumstances'.
> (*V* 98 [X. xii])

In effect, Euthanasia comes to measure her love in political scales. Her initial deification of Castruccio sought a 'hallowed circle' in which 'outward circumstances' would be immaterial. This paradise crumbles when her ideals are faced with a world beyond their personal relationship, with outward circumstances that show up all too clearly the imaginary and contradictory nature of a domestic sphere co-opted into imagining itself to be the entire world. In the words of Betty Bennett: 'Their love relationship fails in political terms; a personal love would not suffice.'[20]

If in the narrative of Beatrice's destruction we are meant to understand the workings of a mechanism of power fuelled by the unfillable lack at the centre of Castruccio, the unnamed persecutor of Beatrice, and the masculine ideology they represent, it is precisely this understanding that Euthanasia gains from hearing her story. The narrator states the effect unequivocally:

> her very person was sacred, since she had dedicated herself to him; but, the god undeified, the honours of the priestess fell to the dust. The story of Beatrice dissolved the charm; she looked on him now in the common light of day; the illusion and exaltation of love was dispelled for ever.... Her old feelings of duty, benevolence, and friendship returned; all was not now, as before, referred to love alone.
> (*V* 190-1 [II. viii])

In this common light of day there are no titans or tigers, cataracts or deep Romantic chasms; there is only an actual landscape inhabited by human individuals to whom one owes the benevolence and friendship one such as Euthanasia would offer willingly to a sibling, parent, or child.

But *Valperga* does not end without pushing past this almost Manichaean opposition between the beautiful and the sublime, the feminine and the masculine. Euthanasia, after all, is identified throughout the novel with the stars, with the eternal and the infinite. There is a form of power and desire in Euthanasia, therefore, that complements her humanistic sensibility. At the opening of volume three, the narrator describes the witch Fior di Mandragola's motives in maintaining her control over Bindo: 'The love of power is inherent in human nature; and, in evil natures, to be feared is a kind of power' (*V* 229 [III. i]). Euthanasia, too, loves a form of power. Rather than to be feared, as we have seen, Euthanasia desires peace and equality for Tuscany, and these desires correspond to a negative opposition to Castruccio's destructive rule. But they also correspond to a positive identification with a kind of sublimity different from that of 'the tiger, of lightning, of the cataract that destroys', expressed most clearly in Euthanasia's discourse on music and in her heroic acts of selfless charity.

In her failed attempt to bring Beatrice back from the brink, Euthanasia counters the prophetess's impassioned madness with a celebration of music. Music, for Euthanasia:

> comes, like a voice from a far world, to tell you that there are depths of intense emotion veiled in the blue empyrean.... But more than to the happy or the sorrowful, music is an inestimable gift to those who forget all sublimer emotions in the pursuits of daily life. I listen to the talk of men; I play with my embroidery-frame; I enter into society: suddenly high song awakens me, and I leave all this tedious routine far, far, distant.
> (*V* 248 [III. iii])

Like Castruccio's dreams of glory during his childhood days on Guinigi's farm, music elevates Euthanasia above the tedium of 'daily life'. And just as in *Frankenstein* M. Waldman's natural philosophy 'penetrate[s] into the recesses of nature', music too 'seems to reveal to us some of the profoundest secrets of the universe; and the spirit, freed from prison by its charms, can then soar, and gaze with eagle eyes on the eternal sun of this all-beauteous world' (*V* 248 [III. iii]). But unlike the solipsistic desires of Castruccio's politics and Victor Frankenstein's science, Euthanasia's 'sublimer emotions', like Guinigi's 'simple yet sublime morality' (*V* 25 [I. iii]), do not preclude 'amity to all', even as they raise the individual above and beyond domestic pursuits.

Ultimately, Euthanasia's sublime desires manifest themselves in the epitome of selflessness, charity. As Castruccio's army lays siege to Florence, Euthanasia follows 'like an angel, in his track, to heal the wounds that he inflicted' (*V* 291 [III. viii]). Instead of the ministering woman of sensibility, a wife or mother, we might expect from such a description, however, Euthanasia appears in significantly more elevated terms: 'An heroic sentiment possessed her mind, and lifted her above humanity' (*V* 292 [III. viii]). Euthanasia does, then, see herself deified, in a sense, or at least recorded as a kind of hero in the 'arched palace of eternal fame', but this self-deification or transcendence depends on the most basic form of care for others. Whereas Beatrice is duped into accepting her own divinity through Bindo's genuine but deluded awe at her 'superhuman presence' (*V* 271 [III. vi]), and whereas Euthanasia's early idolatrous love for Castruccio made her 'feel lifted above all other sensations', Euthanasia now 'shed tears, as she heard the groans and complaints of the sufferers; but she felt as if she were lifted beyond their sphere, and that her soul, clothed in garments of heavenly texture, could not be tarnished with earthly dross' (*V* 293 [III. viii]). Destructive insofar as her humanity falls away while her soul rises beyond earthly woes, this experience of the infinite nonetheless gives power to benevolence. In this power, then, there is an aesthetic experience beyond the sublimity that destroys; there is the possibility, at least, for sublimity that destroys *and* preserves, like powerful music or heroic selflessness, like the infinite imaginative potentialities in *Valperga*'s feminist and Romantic representation of the Italian aesthetic.

But Castruccio's love of power remains the norm for Italy, and, *Valperga* maintains, so long as an aesthetic of desire successfully reproduces its correspondent values in undisciplined and receptive minds, political and social conditions will continue to preclude any tenable position for an uncompromised feminine subject, beautiful or sublime. Material conditions inevitably bring Euthanasia into a stalemate, the position from which any movement whatsoever will contradict the ideological terms by which she lives. Rather than see the citizens of Florence destroyed, individuals to whom she owes benevolence and friendship, she chooses to join the conspiracy against Castruccio, thereby implicating herself in the system she opposes and setting in motion the chain of events that leads to her death.

Like *The Cenci*, *Valperga* turns to an Italian historical narrative to critique the idealism we associate with *Prometheus Unbound*. Neither Beatrice Cenci nor Euthanasia can summon a Demogorgon to pull the tyrannical figure of masculine power from his throne; both must do it themselves. The point in neither case is that they should not have done so, but that they could not have done otherwise. Euthanasia knew that she was compromising her position, that her act was treacherous, but as in *The Cenci* it is significantly only the frowns of masculine figures of power that damn her for it. Castruccio's (tellingly named) deputy Mordecastelli tellingly exclaims, 'I took her for an angel, and I find her a woman; – one of those frail, foolish creatures we all despise' (*V* 311 [III. xi]). Both Euthanasia and Beatrice Cenci step out of their subject positions when those positions become untenable and unbearable, and both are inevitably destroyed:

> Earth felt no change when she died; and men forgot her.... Endless tears might well have been shed at her loss; yet for her none wept, save the piteous skies ... none moaned except the sea-birds that flapped their heavy wings above the ocean-cave wherein she lay; – and the muttering thunder alone tolled her passing bell, as she quitted a life, which for her had been replete with change and sorrow.
>
> (*V* 322 [III. xii])

Earth feels no change, and thus the novel continues, or at least there continues to be ink on the page for a brief space following the death of Euthanasia. The 'Conclusion' after the conclusion begins:

> The private chronicles, from which the foregoing relation has been collected, end with the death of Euthanasia. It is therefore in public histories alone that we find an account of the last years of the life of Castruccio.
>
> (*V* 323)

In a brief staccato march through public history *Valperga* relates the events comprised in the remainder of Castruccio's life. The deaths of Beatrice, Euthanasia, Guinigi, and Arrigo have left the stage empty of the feminine; all that remains is the public world of dominance and subordination. With the disclosure that the novel has been culled from 'private chronicles', the feminine becomes both the repository and the content of private history. With the departure of the feminine from the stage, historical plenitude evaporates, leaving behind the empty human forms of nothing to play out their cyclical struggles of individual ambition and desire, but leaving as well the alternatives that lie in the imaginative revision of aesthetic experience.

Notes

An early version of this essay was published in *Romanticism On the Net*, 6 (May 1997) <http://users.ox.ac.uk/~scat0385/valperga.html>.

1. In the preface to the first volume Shelley offers four sources for the events of Castruccio's life, including 'Machiavelli's romance', *La Vita di Castruccio Castracani da Lucca* and Sismondi's *Histoire des républiques italiennes du moyen âge*.
2. My discussion of the value placed by Shelley on organic reform and domesticity is indebted to Anne Mellor's concept of 'female Romantic ideology'. For critical representations of 'female Romantic ideologies' see Mellor's *Romanticism and Gender* (New York: Routledge, 1993) and 'Why Women Didn't Like Romanticism: The View of Jane Austen and Mary Shelley', in *The Romantics and Us: Essays on Literature and Culture*, ed. Gene W. Ruoff (New Brunswick: Rutgers University Press, 1990), hereafter Ruoff; Joseph W. Lew, 'God's Sister: History and Ideology in *Valperga*', in *Other MS*. See as well Stuart Curran, 'The I Altered', in *Romanticism and Feminism*, ed. Anne K. Mellor (Bloomington: Indiana University Press, 1988).
3. Chapter iv in texts following the 1831 edition.
4. Giacomo Leopardi, *Canti* (Firenze [Florence]: Sansoni Editore, 1988) p. 5.
5. [Mary Shelley *et al.*,] *Lives of the Most Eminent Literary and Scientific Men of Italy, Spain, and Portugal*, 3 vols (London, 1835) II, p. 358 in *The Cabinet Cyclopædia* (133 vols), ed. Dionysius Lardner.
6. According to her journal, Shelley read Foscolo's novel at some time between 12 June and 7 July 1822 (*MWSJ* I, p. 412), though it is quite possible that she had some previous acquaintance with the work. A very tenuous connection exists between Shelley and Leopardi through Lady Mount Cashell ('Mrs Mason'), Shelley's friend during her Pisan period (1820–22). Mount Cashell's salon (1827–32), the 'Accademia di Lunatici', numbered among its minor members Leopardi, who moved to Pisa in 1827. However, although he wrote some of his most celebrated poems at Pisa, there is no evidence that Mount Cashell made Shelley aware of them or of him; see *Leopardi a Pisa* (Exhibition catalogue), ed. Fiorenza Ceragioli (Milan: Electa, 1997) pp. 322–6. (I am grateful to Nora Crook for this last piece of information.)
7. [John Gibson Lockhart], 'Review of *Valperga*', *Blackwood's Edinburgh*

Magazine, XIII (March 1823) 284.
8. [Anon.], *Knight's Quarterly Magazine,* III (August–November 1824) 195; *Tales and Stories by Mary Wollstonecraft Shelley, Now First Collected, with an Introduction by Richard Garnett,* LL.D. (London: W. Paterson, 1891) p. vii. Surprisingly, even Mellor claimed that *Valperga* 'does not satisfactorily synthesize its mass of historical details, "raked," said P.B. Shelley, "out of fifty old books," into a coherent narrative' (Mellor, p. 178). This line of P.B. Shelley's is often, as here, quoted out of context both to indicate a deprecation of *Valperga* on his part and to represent the novel as an imperfect fusion of its materials. What P.B. Shelley wrote to Thomas Love Peacock on 8 November 1820, when *Valperga* was still in its formative stages, was:

> Mary is writing a novel, illustrative of the manners of the Middle Ages in Italy, which she has raked out of fifty old books. I promise myself success from it; and certainly, if what is wholly original will succeed, I shall not be disappointed.
>
> (*PBSL* II, p. 245)

He meant to emphasize the extent of Shelley's research.
9. Garnett's 'interpenetrated the mass' pointedly recalls the words of Earth's final song in *Prometheus Unbound,* IV. 370–423, and thus, by implication, contrasts Shelley's work unfavourably with that of P.B. Shelley.
10. I use 'Machiavellian' here in its 'vulgar' sense, and not as Shelley herself understood the historical Machiavelli, whom she saw as, ultimately, a democrat. For an exploration of the importance of Machiavelli for *Valperga* see Betty T. Bennett, 'Machiavelli's and Mary Shelley's Castruccio: Biography as Metaphor', *Romanticism,* 3.2 (1997) 139–51.
11. I stress the importance of seeing Castruccio as a representative *figure* of male Romantic paradigms. Even recent critical treatments of Shelley's works have fostered autobiographical readings that without fail serve to reduce her voice to the merely relative or derivative. To see Castruccio, for example, as a caricature of P. B. Shelley or Byron, or Beatrice as Claire Clairmont, is in an important way to prescribe the limits of Shelley's critique. For an extended statement of the case, see Pamela Clemit, *The Godwinian Novel: The Rational Fictions of Godwin, Brockden Brown, Mary Shelley* (Oxford: Clarendon Press, 1993) p. 141:

> Despite [an] early recognition of Mary Shelley's intellectual commitment, twentieth-century critics have interpreted her relation with the Godwin circle largely in private terms. Mary Shelley's complex position as daughter of Godwin and Wollstonecraft, then wife of Percy Shelley and friend of Byron, has lent itself to readings which posit a psychological frame of reference, excluding both the intellectual stimulus provided by the Godwin school and her independent revaluation of these concerns.

12. Jean de Palacio, *Mary Shelley dans son œuvre* (Paris: Editions Klincksieck, 1969) p. 205: 'Castruccio falls indeed into the gravest sin that pertains to the Shelleyan gospel: that of subordinating all human interest to egotisti-

cal means of achievement ... Castruccio will unite in himself the lion and the fox'.
13. Anne Mellor in Ruoff, p. 284.
14. Shelley read the first in May and the second in June 1820. She also read *Julie, ou la Nouvelle Héloïse* (1761) for the third time in February 1820, having previously read it in 1815 and 1817. A long tradition of educated female poets, novelists, and dramatists of sensibility extending back to Charlotte Smith and Hannah Cowley in the 1780s also lies behind the figure of the rational, feeling female in Shelley, who read Smith in 1816 and 1818 (*MWSJ* I, pp. 318–20, II, pp. 670, 676).
15. On the entrenchment of 'conservative nostalgia for a Burkean model of a naturally evolving organic society' in the 1820s, see Clemit, *The Godwinian Novel*, p. 177; and Elie Halévy, *The Liberal Awakening, 1815–1830*, trans. E. I. Watkin (New York: Barnes & Noble, 1961) pp. 128–32.
16. It is significant, too, that in the few instances in *Valperga* where Shelley actually introduces quotations from Romantic poets, they are unidentified and tend to be constituted as inheritors of an Italian tradition. The most striking instance occurs with 'Tis said, that some have died for love'. Not only has Shelley chosen an example of Wordsworth's experimentation with the canzone but the poet is also seen as giving voice to what the fictitious Euthanasia *had* felt six hundred years previously: 'she would exclaim as a modern poet has since done; 'Thou, thrush, that singest loud, and loud, and free ... '. Twice Shelley quotes briefly from 'Ode to the West Wind', the only poem in terza rima by P.B. Shelley to be published in his lifetime (*V* 191, 204, 233 [II. viii, II. x, III. 227]).
17. Bennett, *Evidence*, p. 363.
18. On the character of Beatrice see Barbara Jane O'Sullivan, 'Beatrice in *Valperga*: A New Cassandra', in *Other MS*.
19. Jane Blumberg, *Mary Shelley's Early Novels: 'This Child of Imagination and Misery'* (Basingstoke: Macmillan and Iowa City: University of Iowa Press, 1993) pp. 99–100; Joseph Lew, 'God's Sister: History and Ideology in *Valperga*', *Other MS*, p. 171.
20. Bennett, *Evidence*, p. 363.

6
Gender, Authorship and Male Domination: Mary Shelley's limited Freedom in *Frankenstein* and *The Last Man*

Michael Eberle-Sinatra

> [T]he man of genius lives most in the ideal world, in which the present is still constituted by the future or the past.
> (Samuel Taylor Coleridge, *Biographia Literaria*)[1]

Frankenstein, Paula R. Feldman rightly says, is:

> a novel about itself and about its author's relation to it. At its heart lies Mary Shelley's individual struggle with the act of creation, a struggle characterized by fear as much as by ambition.[2]

Ever since Ellen Moers's *Literary Women* (1976), *Frankenstein* has been recognized as a novel in which issues about authorship are intimately bound up with those of gender. The work has frequently been related to the circumstance of Shelley's combining the biological role of mother with the social role of author.[3] The creation of the Creature and Victor's attempt at transgressing the rules of nature have been widely understood as an expression of what Chris Baldick calls '[Shelley's] mixed feelings, both assertive and guilty, of the adolescent for whom fully adult identity means both motherhood and (in her circle) authorship too'.[4]

Authorship and its gendering are no less, I would argue, central thematic concerns in *The Last Man*. Indeed, both Shelley's first and her third novel evidence a struggle, in paratext and text, over whether she is to be present as a (pseudo-) male author, a female author, a usurped author or an author of indeterminate gender, a struggle in which the 'fear' and 'ambition' mentioned by Feldman in the opening quotation are key operatives.

To take ambition first: Shelley writes as the daughter of two successful and well-known authors, who is expected and encouraged to become an author herself, as she herself testifies in her Introduction to the 1831 edition of *Frankenstein*:

> My husband ... was from the very first, very anxious that I should prove myself worthy of my parentage, and enrol myself on the page of fame. He was for ever inciting me to obtain literary reputation.
> (F 176)[5]

Moreover, purely literary mothers also existed. In 1818 there was an established tradition of writers – notably Ann Radcliffe – who in the previous generation had developed gothic into a genre that an ambitious and gifted young woman might respectably attempt without thereby being 'unsexed'.

Yet Shelley frequently betrays awareness of the strains of writing in a male-oriented society where the image of woman as passive and docile, embodying beauty and delicacy, still is dominant, an awareness in which fear and insecurity are present. In one of the most interesting elements of the 1831 preface to *Frankenstein*, anxiety about being 'unsexed' is uppermost. This emerges from her attempt to answer the question which she declares most people naturally ask her: 'How I, then a young girl, came to think of, and to dilate upon, so very hideous an idea?' (F 175).[6] Nor could Radcliffe's novels have been plausibly invoked by Shelley as offering a precedent for and thus a defence of *Frankenstein*. Shelleyan gothic would certainly have incurred the censure of Radcliffe, who strongly criticized the literary use of horror (as distinct from terror or suspense) in her posthumously published 1826 article on the supernatural in poetry.[7]

Writing *The Last Man* gave Shelley the opportunity to create a space in which she could express her anxiety about her future as a writer, as well as to recount the part of her past life that she missed so terribly.[8] It also allowed her to set down in writing her sense of insecurity within London society upon her return to England in August 1823.[9] This insecurity, however, was expressed and assuaged rather than exorcized by the act of writing. Even though the publication of three novels and her husband's *Posthumous Poems* had by the mid-1820s established Shelley's fame, she seems to disclaim any role as a woman of letters. In a letter of 5 January 1828 she protested that 'my sex has precluded all idea of my fulfilling public employments' (*MWSL* II, p. 22).[10] Confined within the limits of a society that attempts to impose a passive role on women and to enclose them within the private sphere, Shelley seems to adhere, at least publicly, to the prescribed norm.

But do *Frankenstein* and *The Last Man* reflect this adherence? Or can they be perceived as working within the normative in such a way that they embody a criticism of it? Is her adoption of male protagonists and male narrators in these novels a tribute – a homage even – to the men in her life, particularly her father, P.B. Shelley and Byron, or a transgressive act encoding a protest against male domination?[11]

In engaging with these questions, I find it helpful to refer to Gérard Genette's theory of the paratext, that is, everything that does not belong directly to the literary text itself and yet can be perceived as part of the work: title page, name of the author, epigraph, dedication, preface, afterword and notes. All these materials constitute a special space 'around' the text that is both a transitional space and a transactional space.[12] Readers have access to the literary text via the preamble of the paratext. They may not pay attention to the elements constituting the paratext but these elements are nevertheless crucial to the understanding of the work.

I The title

Both titles indicate the content of the novels: *Frankenstein* is the story of Victor Frankenstein and *The Last Man* is the narrative of the last man on earth. Both end with their chief characters left 'Companionless/As the last cloud of an expiring storm',[13] Lionel Verney as last of his race, the Creature as the first and last of *his* (unnamed) race. But both titles are also the sites of strong misreading. *Frankenstein* has been famously misunderstood to refer to the Creature. I would suggest that the long-standing confusion in the mind of the public between Frankenstein as the creator, that is Victor Frankenstein, and Frankenstein the unnamed Creature, epitomizes the displacement of discourse and naming in the novel. What is not named in the text acquires an identity through the confused misinterpretation of the novel by the reader.

An analogous misinterpretation has historically dogged the title, *The Last Man*, as a result not only of contemporary reviewers' knowingness about the gender of the author but also of an ambiguity in the title itself. Although Lionel Verney, the main character of the novel, is the Last Man once the plague has eliminated the rest of humanity, contemporary readers of the novel identified Shelley, the female writer, with the narrator. The anonymous reviewer of *The Last Man* in

98 Gender

The Literary Gazette and Journal of Belles Lettres, Arts, Sciences, &c. of February 1826 exploits this paratextual information, mischievously choosing to interpret 'man' as meaning 'member of the male sex' rather than 'member of the human race' when he wonders why Shelley did not choose to name the novel *The Last Woman*. The last woman would, the reviewer claims, 'have known better how to paint her distress at having nobody left to talk to'.[14]

II The name of the author

Most critics assumed that the anonymously authored *Frankenstein* was written by a male disciple of the dedicatee, William Godwin, and several supposed this disciple to be none other than P.B. Shelley himself. The two-volume 1823 edition of *Frankenstein*, published at Godwin's instigation in order to coincide with the early theatrical adaptations of the novel, significantly changed this situation. Godwin dropped the title-page epigraph of the novel from Milton's *Paradise Lost*, as well as the dedication to himself, and identified the author as 'Mary Wollstonecraft Shelley'.[15] Thus the reading public was informed that the author of *Frankenstein* was the daughter of Godwin and Wollstonecraft and the widow of P.B. Shelley, this act rendering superfluous any repetition of the information on the title pages of Shelley's later novels. The name on the title page of *The Last Man* is 'The Author of *Frankenstein*'. This measure was undoubtedly a pragmatic one. It simultaneously associated Shelley with the Great Unknown, Walter Scott, 'The Author of Waverley', and ensured Timothy Shelley's satisfaction at not seeing his son's name in print again.

Yet I would suggest that assigning *The Last Man* to 'The Author of *Frankenstein*' also points to an unstable gendering of the novel. The 'Author of *Frankenstein*' is not assigned a gender, but referred to only as the author of a previous work which itself had an intricate history of authorship in its early version. Ultimately, it is not until the 1831 edition of *Frankenstein* that Shelley herself is able textually to assert her authorship of that work and choose to place her name on the *engraved* title page.[16] The 1823 'outing' was Godwin's choice and not hers. This new 'threshold' text allows Shelley to claim her identity as a female writer. However, she retains the freedom of unstable gendering by retaining 'The Author of Frankenstein' on the *printed* title page.[17]

III The epigraph

The subtitle of *Frankenstein*, 'The Modern Prometheus', encodes a reference to the myth of Prometheus as the creator of man/the human race. The title pages for each volume of the 1818 edition contain a quotation from Milton's *Paradise Lost* that also refers to the creation of man:

> Did I request thee, Maker, from my clay
> To mould me man? Did I solicit thee
> From darkness to promote me?
> *(Paradise Lost*, X. 743–5)

As Lucy Newlyn has pointed out, *Frankenstein* is 'a revisionary reading of *Paradise Lost*'.[18] Sandra M. Gilbert and Susan Gubar have also defined *Frankenstein* as Shelley's attempt:

> to take the male culture myth of *Paradise Lost* at its full values – on its own terms, including all the analogies and parallels it implies – and [to] *rewrite it so as to clarify its meaning*.[19]

Frankenstein is also, I would contend, a supplement to that poem and a *rifacimento*. That is to say, Shelley's work develops certain Miltonic themes further, and acts as a replacement of *Paradise Lost* and of the Prometheus myth as encountered in Hesiod and Aeschylus' *Prometheus Bound*. The result is Shelley's re-writing the myths of the creation of man as *Frankenstein* and re-writing the myths of man's subsequent extinction in *The Last Man*, an extinction which the epigraph on the volume title pages, also from *Paradise Lost*, portends:

> Let no man seek
> Henceforth to be foretold what shall befall
> Him or his children.
> *(Paradise Lost*, XI. 770–2)

In Shelley's interpretation, Man becomes his own creator insofar as Victor Frankenstein can create life and thus circumvent any divine or female participation. Man also becomes his own annihilator with his role in the proliferation of the plague, 'a spectre conjured up by xenophobia, sexism and racism', in *The Last Man*.[20] Woman (in the person of Evadne) identifies herself with destruction, and 'enacts the revenge of female power against control'.[21]

100 Gender

Shelley re-writes myths, only to produce new myths in which women are even less present than in the Miltonic epic; there is, after all, no Eve at the end of the novels, either for the Creature or for Lionel. Yet the very conspicuousness of this absence constitutes a critique of 'things as they are'. An imagined future universe of desolation in which women are *annihilated* recalls the reader to a renewed recognition of the injustice of an actual present world in which they are merely *controlled, marginalized* and *subordinated*. As Bette London remarks (specifically of *Frankenstein*, but her words apply equally to *The Last Man*): 'the presence of the novel's self-consciously male texts ... illuminate the absences they cover, to expose the self-contradictions they repress'.[22]

IV The Preface/the Introduction

Prefatory matter is both a site for contention over ownership of the novels and for the construction of an author of indeterminate gender. P.B. Shelley not only wrote the preface to the 1818 edition of *Frankenstein* but would seem to have replaced one that Shelley had previously written.[23] On 14 May 1817, Shelley wrote in her journal: 'Read Pliny and Clarke – S. reads Hist of Fr. Rev. and corrects F. write Preface – Finis' (*MWSJ* I, p. 169). As Charles Robinson notes, this entry 'suggests that MWS herself wrote a preface after she transcribed her novel' and 'it appears that it was discarded in favor of the published Preface written by PBS' (*Frankenstein Notebooks* I, lxxxv–lxxxvi). Of course there is no way of knowing the degree to which P.B. Shelley took the initiative here.[24] Nevertheless, however one reconstructs the process whereby P.B. Shelley became the one who assumed the prefatorial role of presenting the book to readers and explaining its intentions, the salient point is that Shelley did, by relinquishing this role to her husband, deprive herself of an important paratextual function of authorship.

There are various ways in which we can interpret this self-dispossession. One is to regard it as a necessary component of a literary hoax. The Shelleys had taken pains successfully to hoodwink both the publishers and the public into thinking that the gender of the author was male. The possibility of a 'young girl' writing such a story was ruled out, as the various reviews show.[25] P.B. Shelley's own review of *Frankenstein*, unpublished during his lifetime, and perhaps intended for *The Examiner*, also refers to the author as a man. He sent a complimentary copy of *Frankenstein* with an accompanying letter couched in such terms as, without telling an outright lie, might mislead Walter Scott, whose subsequent review in *Blackwood's Edinburgh Magazine* duly assumed that P.B. Shelley was the author. Shelley appears to have connived readily in this ruse. Yet once *Frankenstein* was published and was enjoying its *réclame* in the summer of 1818, she was not content to allow her position to be usurped. She was quick to write to Scott in June 1818 that she was:

> anxious to prevent your continuing in the mistake of supposing Mr Shelley guilty of a juvenile attempt of mine; to which – from its being written at an early age, I abstained from putting my name – and from respect to those persons from whom I bear it. I have therefore kept it concealed except from a few friends.
> (*MWSL* I, p. 71)

This extract reveals not only Shelley's keen desire to repossess the authorship of the novel,[26] even though it is 'a juvenile attempt', but also her consciousness of her husband and parents, 'those persons from whom I bear [my name]', who, she declares, have determined her choice not to assert her position publicly alongside them.

When, however, we turn to the 'Introduction' to *The Last Man* we encounter a fascinating instance of this reversal of gendered patterns. Instead of a preface which is actually male-authored and assumed to be so by the reading public, but which is not overtly identified as such, we have an introduction which is female-authored, known to be so by the reading public, but which is presented as written by someone of uncertain gender. The anonymous 'Introduction' corresponds perfectly to Genette's definition of a *préface crypto-auctorial*, that is to say a preface for which the author pretends not to be the author or only claims the authorship of the preface from the whole work.[27] Within the 'Introduction' Shelley presents herself as the mere editor of the novel:

> For the merits of my adaptation and translation must decide how far I have well bestowed my time and imperfect powers, in giving form and substance to the frail and attenuated Leaves of the Sibyl.
> (*LM* 9 [Introd.])

The question of gender in this introduction is particularly intriguing, as Anne Mellor comments:

neither the Author in the 'Author's Introduction' nor the 'companion' is assigned a gender. Most readers have assumed that the Author is Shelley, her companion Percy. However, the three lines quoted from the sonnet that Petrarch wrote to his dead patron Giacomo Colonna implicitly align the voice of the Author with the male gender. Is Shelley here raising the possibility of a new kind of subject in which gender is absent, or at the least, unstable, fluid, unimportant?[28]

I would assert that instability and fluidity of gender is precisely what Shelley aims at in her preface and in the novel in general, and that these qualities relate to the novel's prophetic aspect. Writing about prefaces, Derrida has remarked that 'the text exists as something written – a past – which, under the false appearance of a present, a hidden omnipotent author (in full mastery of his product) is presenting to the reader as his future.'[29] This quotation sums up Shelley's novel, which is indeed 'a past' (a narrative retelling the story of the last man), 'a present' (an author presenting her/his work to a reader), and 'a future' (a possible future for the world and civilization). By its very instability with regard to gender, the preface exemplifies Shelley's attempt at presenting to the reader a work in which the characters merge or exchange qualities (virtues or defects) conventionally assigned to one or the other sex. (In Evadne, for instance, a 'masculine' artistic genius co-exists with 'feminine' jealousy; in Raymond, 'masculine' will-to-power co-exists with 'feminine' narcissism and caprice. Idris has a 'masculine' intellect while her brother possesses a 'feminine' physical frailty.) Describing *The Last Man* as a prophecy, the preface also allows the reader to see the work as a warning against allowing history to repeat a story of the repression of women and their erasure from the record. The plague stresses this repression by the very fact that it is gendered as female in *The Last Man*, and functions both metaphorically and literally against the male domination present in the novel. The reader is stimulated to imagine an alternative future history, in which the story of woman will be fully incorporated into the story of humanity and in which repressed female energies will not return as annihilating forces.[30]

V Literary education and authorship

Turning from the paratextual to the textual, I now wish to focus on one way in which Shelley encodes within the two novels her frustration at male domination while demonstrating the importance of a literary education.[31] In *Frankenstein* literature is crucial to the Creature's education; in *The Last Man*, the same is true of the education of Lionel and his sister Perdita. Lionel, the Wordsworthian child of the Lake District at the beginning of the novel, describes this when he declares:

> I was already well acquainted with what I may term the panorama of nature, the change of seasons, and the various appearances of heaven and earth. But I was at once startled and enchanted by my sudden extension of vision, when the curtain, which had been drawn before the intellectual world, was withdrawn, and I saw the universe, not only as it presented itself to my outward senses, but as it had appeared to the wisest among men. Poetry and its creations, philosophy and its researches and classifications, alike awoke the sleeping ideas in my mind, and gave me new ones.
>
> (*LM* 27 [I. ii])

Shelley emphasizes the need for education as a key both to understanding and possible change in society through her narrator Lionel, whose intellectual awakening stimulates him to become a writer, and for whom books:

> stood in the place of an active career, of ambition, and those palpable excitements necessary to the multitude.... As my authorship increased, I acquired new sympathies and pleasures.... Suddenly I became as it were the father of all mankind. Posterity became my heirs.
>
> (*LM* 122 [I. x]).

The importance here invested in authorship shows up a major difference between Victor and Lionel. Victor illustrates the male attempt at transgressing the biological limits of his sex. Lionel's 'transgression', however, is so merely by analogy. He seems to himself to 'father' mankind in a metaphorical process of asexual reproduction. He immediately attempts to win his sister to participate in the same pursuits as he. Perdita, intellectually active but relatively uneducated, thinks at first that Lionel's craving for knowledge is only, in her words, 'a new gloss upon an old reading, and her own was sufficiently inexhaustible to content her' (LM 122 [I. x]). But when she gains access to literature she discovers that:

amidst all her newly acquired knowledge, her own character, which formerly she fancied that she thoroughly understood, became the first in rank among the terræ incognitæ, the pathless wilds of a country that had no chart.

(*LM* 123–4 [I. x])

Despite the fact that Lionel attempts gently to entice the female into the magic circle of knowledge, the relationship between them remains an unequal one: the brother is in charge of his sister's education. Perdita never, in fact, becomes an author. Her widened horizons narrow as she applies her new-found knowledge to introspection rather than outwards towards composition; she continues to behave like a Byronic heroine to whom love is 'woman's whole existence' and this is the eventual cause of her death. Under what conditions, the reader asks, could Lionel and Perdita have collaborated in a work? Each would have had to step outside a prescribed gender role – Perdita that of the love-lorn female, Lionel that of the moulder of his sister's mind. Yet Lionel, in as much as he is a fictional character, a male author created by a female author, still represents the possibility of an as-yet-unrealized un-gendered writing for a non-existent, and thus also un-gendered, readership.

In both *Frankenstein* and *The Last Man*, Shelley presents gender issues in a way that is not overtly defined. She herself seems to have taken on a position of resignation in her life as far as male dominance in society was concerned. Yet I would argue that the two novels that I have discussed belie her apparent acceptance of this state of affairs. It is precisely the expression of this accepted female passivity that Shelley writes against. And she does so by portraying her female characters as conspicuously absent or secondary. Thus, she reflects adversely upon a society where women are subordinated or relegated to separate spheres, where men think of themselves, incorrectly, as the masters of knowledge. At the same time her self-presentation as an author of indeterminate gender points towards a possible alternative future in which the conventional polite disclaimer of the female writer ('my sex has precluded all idea of my fulfilling public employments') will no longer serve any purpose. *The Last Man* could be subtitled 'Remembrance of Things to Come': the tale of Verney is to be an example of what had happened and what would happen to society, were it not to change in the direction of that alternative imagined future.

Notes

I would like to thank Charles Robinson, Joel Pace, Astrid Wind and Chris Koenig-Woodyard for their comments on earlier versions of this essay, which was also presented as a conference paper at 'Mary Shelley: Beyond Frankenstein' (University of Bristol, February 1997) and 'Mary Wollstonecraft Shelley in Her Times' (New York, May 1997).

1. Samuel Taylor Coleridge, *Biographia Literaria*, ed. James Engell and Walter Jackson Bate, 2 vols (Princeton, NJ: Princeton University Press, 1983) I, p. 43.
2. Paula R. Feldman, 'The Psychological Mystery of *Frankenstein*', in *Approaches to Teaching Shelley's Frankenstein*, ed. Stephen C. Behrendt (New York: Modern Language Association of America, 1990) p. 71.
3. Many critics have explained the absence of mothers in *Frankenstein* as due to the difficulty for Shelley of coping with her mother's death; see for instance Barbara Johnson, 'My Monster/My Self', *Diacritics*, 12 (1982) 2–10, and Stephen Behrendt, 'Mary Shelley, *Frankenstein*, and the Woman Writer's Fate', in *Romantic Women Writers: Voices and Countervoices*, eds Paula R. Feldman and Theresa M. Kelley (Hanover, N.H.: University Press of New England, 1995) pp. 69–87, hereafter Feldman and Kelley.
4. Chris Baldick, *In Frankenstein's Shadow: Myth, Monstrosity, and Nineteenth-century Writing* (Oxford: Clarendon Press, 1987) p. 32.
5. The negative side of this 'encouragement' was expressed by Claire Clairmont, who declared caustically in 1833: 'in our family if you cannot write an epic poem or a novel that by its originality knocks all other novels on the head, you are a despicable creature not worth acknowledging' (*The Clairmont Correspondence*, ed. Marion Kingston Stocking, 2 vols (Baltimore and London: Johns Hopkins University Press, 1995) I, p. 295.
6. Leigh Hunt humorously wrote of Shelley in 1837:

   And Shelley, four famed, – for her parents, her lord,
   And the poor lone impossible monster abhorred.
   (*So sleek and so smiling* she came, people stared,
   To think *such fair clay* should so darkly have dared ...);
                            ('Blue-Stocking Revels' II, lines 209–12; my emphasis)

7. Ann Radcliffe, 'On the Supernatural in Poetry', *The New Monthly Magazine*, XVI (1826) 149. Radcliffe came out in favour of terror which, according to her, makes the reader experience interest to a higher degree and of a superior kind than that excited by horror.
8. The novel is the most personal that she wrote and published during her lifetime. As Fiona Stafford notes, 'Mary Shelley's decision to embark on a novel describing the decimation of the entire human race (bar the narrator), was directly related to the traumas of losing her husband and children' (Fiona Stafford, *The Last of the Race: the Growth of a Myth from Milton to Darwin* [Oxford: Clarendon Press, 1994] p. 7).
9. She had expressed such doubts as early as 18 January 1824 when she recorded in her journal: 'I have been nearly four months in England and if

I am to judge of the future by the past and ~~future~~ the present, I have small delight in looking forward' (*MWSJ* I, p. 470). The similarity in feeling with regard to society between Shelley and Lionel Verney, the main protagonist and narrator of *The Last Man*, is expressed at the beginning of the second volume of the novel, where Verney exclaims:

> How unwise had the wanderers been, who had deserted its shelter, entangled themselves in the web of society, and entered on what men of the world call 'life,' – that labyrinth of evil, that scheme of mutual torture.
>
> (*LM* 172 [II. iv])

10. This reaction had been called out by a request from the *Ladies Museum* to feature her as one of their monthly 'portraits'. She had good reason to be suspicious of the good faith of the *Ladies' Museum*, a genteel monthly without the prestige of the Great Reviews. Two years previously it had briefly dismissed her *Last Man* with the conventional judgement that her talents were wasted on subjects 'too extravagant for common conception'. Yet her refusal is too consonant with other remarks scattered throughout her correspondence to be dismissed as an *ad hoc* response. For instance, in a letter to John Cam Hobhouse dated 10 November 1824 she commented: 'I have an invincible objection to the seeing my name in print' (*MWSL* I, p. 455).
11. She dedicated the first edition of *Frankenstein* to Godwin, and both P.B. Shelley and Byron can be seen as depicted in her novels under the various characters of Victor Frankenstein, Clerval, Adrian and Lord Raymond.
12. Gérard Genette, *Seuils*, Collection Poétique (Paris: Editions du Seuil, 1987) p. 8.
13. P.B. Shelley, *Adonais*, lines 272–3, in *Shelley's Poetry and Prose*, eds Donald H. Reiman and Sharon B. Powers (New York: Norton, 1977) p. 399.
14. *The Literary Gazette and Journal of Belles Lettres, Arts, Sciences, &c*, 473 (1826) 103. Shelley herself had anticipated such an identification in her well-known journal-entry of 14 May 1824, in which she writes: 'The last man! Yes I may well describe that solitary being's feelings, feeling myself as the last relic of a beloved race, my companions, extinct before me ...' (*MWSJ* II, p. 476–7).
15. For suggestions as to Godwin's possible motives, see note 7 of Nora Crook's contribution in this volume.
16. As Stephen Behrendt shrewdly remarks, the 1831 preface also constitutes 'a gesture of authority by which [Shelley's] own authorial voice supersedes the ventriloquistic voice of her dead husband in the [1818] preface' (Feldman and Kelley, p. 84).
17. Colburn and Bentley's Standard Novels series (in which the 1831 edition appeared) had two title pages. The engraved title page remained the same while the printed title page varied according to the dates of subsequent impressions.
18. Lucy Newlyn, *Paradise Lost and the Romantic Reader* (Oxford: Clarendon Press, 1993) p. 134. For an illuminating discussion of Shelley's use of *Paradise Lost* in *Frankenstein*, see Newlyn, pp. 133–9.

Gender, Authorship and Male Domination 107

19. Sandra M. Gilbert and Susan Gubar, *The Madwoman in the Attic: the Woman Writer and the Nineteenth-Century Literary Imagination* (New Haven and London: Yale University Press, 1984) p. 220.
20. I accept here that reading of the plague which sees its literal, biological existence as inseparable from the moral and ideological; this reading is persuasively articulated by Anne McWhir, from the introduction to whose edition of *The Last Man* my quotation is taken. McWhir argues that Raymond's will to power is unconsciously complicit with the spread of the plague: it is more than hinted that the blowing up of the plague-ridden Constantinople, which he has been besieging, releases the seeds of disease which are then disseminated by winds throughout the world (*The Last Man*, ed. A. R. McWhir [Peterborough, Ontario: Broadview, 1996] pp. xxviii–xxxii).
21. McWhir, introd. *The Last Man*, p. xxv.
22. Bette London, 'Mary Shelley, *Frankenstein*, and the Spectacle of Masculinity', *PMLA*, 108.2 (1993) 260.
23. In the 1831 Preface, Shelley writes that 'As far as I can recollect, [the preface] was entirely written by [P.B. Shelley]'. Regina B. Oost offers an enriching reading of the 1818 preface in terms of marketing technique in the 1820s, although she does not take into account the gender politics at play in P.B. Shelley's writing of the preface; see Regina B. Oost, 'Marketing *Frankenstein*: the Shelleys' Enigmatic Preface', *English Language Notes*, XXXV, 1 (1997) 26–35. Charles Robinson's edition of the *Frankenstein Notebooks* has demonstrated that P.B. Shelley's involvement is not as crucial and intrusive to Shelley's novel as some critics (such as James Rieger and the editors of the Broadview *Frankenstein*) have considered it to be; nevertheless, he is still a presence in the published text.
24. For instance, Shelley herself may have become dissatisfied with her preface and (preoccupied with her new-born daughter Clara, and fatigued with lack of sleep after the birth) delegated its rewriting to her husband.
25. *The British Critic*'s reviewer, who, alone among his peers, was aware of the true gender of the author, seems to have been given special information, but the source remains unknown.
26. Nevertheless I agree in general with Zachary Leader that, though Shelley 'may have taken authorship seriously, ... she also found it difficult to think of herself as an author, and her early journals and letters barely mention composition' (Zachary Leader, *Revision and Romantic Authorship* [Oxford: Clarendon Press, 1996] p. 185).
27. Gérard Genette, *Seuils*, p. 172. For a discussion of P. B. Shelley's use of a *préface crypto-auctorial* in his poem *Epipsychidion*, see my article 'Shelley's Editing Process in the Preface to *Epipsychidion*', *Keats–Shelley Review*, 11 (1997) 167–81.
28. Anne K. Mellor, 'Introduction', *The Last Man*, ed. Hugh J. Luke, Jr (Lincoln and London: University of Nebraska Press, 1965; new edn 1993) pp. xxiv–xxv.
29. Jacques Derrida, *Dissemination*, trans. Barbara Johnson (London: Athlone Press, 1981) p. 7.
30. In saying this, I dissent from those readings which assume that the novel demands that, within its fictive world, we accept the inevitable annihila-

tion of mankind by plague as the only possible future, without alternatives. Even if the Sybil is accepted as having absolutely true knowledge of the future, the transmission of her prophecies is carried out by a decidedly imperfect process. Some of the lost leaves may have contained material which reversed the desolate ending; the editor has pieced out the missing record with non-Sybilline material in order to make a continuous narrative and may have assembled the recovered leaves incorrectly. 'Doubtless' the editor confesses, 'the leaves of the Cumæan Sybil have suffered distortion ... in my hands' (*LM* 8 [Introd.]).

31. Shelley's mother Mary Wollstonecraft had already written about this issue in *Thoughts on the Education of Daughters* (1787) and *A Vindication of the Rights of Woman* (1792). So had several other prominent women writers, such as Catharine Macaulay in *Letters on Education* (1783) and Hannah More in *Strictures on Female Education* (1799).

7
'The Truth in Masquerade': Cross-dressing and Disguise in Mary Shelley's Short Stories
A. A. Markley

One of the most interesting aspects of the body of Mary Shelley's fiction is the remarkable frequency with which she experimented with the plot devices of identity switches, clothes changes, disguise, and cross-dressing, particularly in the case of women altering their dress in order to pass as men. The interpretative question that then arises concerns the extent to which these episodes embody a critique of the rigid gender restrictions which women have suffered under historically. By presenting women who function successfully outside their restricted gender roles, did Shelley intend to call attention to the fact that women are capable of achieving far more than societal restrictions allowed? Or, in fashioning viable plots that would hold the attention of the readership of the annuals, was she rather drawing on the reversal of societal convention achieved by the carnivalesque and the masquerade, as Shakespeare and Byron had done, in order to entertain her audience?

In coming to terms with these questions, I hope to demonstrate the extent to which Shelley as an artist was continuously involved in responding to and reworking both historical and contemporary literary traditions. The dynamic nature of her involvement in these traditions is exhibited even in her short stories, which have too often been ignored as short pieces that she tossed off – albeit by her own admission – to make ends meet in the 1820s and 1830s as she struggled to support herself and her son in England after P.B. Shelley's death.[1] Despite the fact that the tales that she wrote for annuals such as *The Keepsake* took her away from her work on the longer novels that she wished to be able to pursue full-time, they demonstrate a great amount of technical artistry. As a group, they display a profound engagement with the themes and conventions of English literature historically, and as they were changing and developing in the 1820s and 1830s.

The historical record, particularly of the 17th and 18th centuries, includes a great number of examples of women who passed as men for one reason or another, and English literature during these periods reflects a growing awareness of the phenomenon of transvestism. Women transvestites commonly were motivated by extreme romantic, patriotic, or economic factors, and were usually of a lower social class. Yet this last factor was not universal. Two unusual cases of transvestism occurred within Shelley's own circle. Lady Mount Cashell, Mary Wollstonecraft's former pupil and friend of the Shelleys during their Pisan sojourn of 1820–22, had once assumed male attire in order to study medicine at Jena.[2] In the 1820s Shelley befriended the poet Mary Diana Dods, and helped her to pass as 'Walter Sholto Douglas' in Parisian social circles in 1827 and 1828. Dods had previously used the pseudonym 'David Lyndsay' in publishing her poems in *Blackwood's*. Betty Bennett, who discovered the Dods affair and Mary Shelley's involvement, argues that her transformation into Walter Sholto Douglas allowed her to fulfil her desire to function in both literary and social circles as a man. In addition, the ruse provided a 'husband' for Shelley's friend Isabella Robinson, who had conceived a child out of wedlock. No one familiar with Shelley's history of having been almost entirely ostracized from 'proper' English society throughout her adult life would doubt her enthusiasm for shielding Isabella Robinson from the same fate, and her actions in this case undoubtedly strengthened her self-picture as a champion of her own sex.[3]

Yet while, as I shall later reaffirm, Shelley's biographical experience has importance for her experimentation with the plot device of transvestism, of more significance are literary antecedents and cultural phenomena such as the flourishing of the masquerade during the eighteenth century. With its origins stemming from the Lenten and folk festival traditions of Medieval and pre-Medieval Europe, the masquerade offered men and women of every class the opportunity to experiment with the concept of self, to hide identity behind a mask and domino, or an even more elaborate costume, and to interact with countless unknown others likewise in disguise, who might include a servant or a Duchess, a prostitute or even the king. Cross-dressing was a popular form of costume at the masquerade, as was the adoption of religious habits.

The masquerade offered the eighteenth-century fiction writer rich material for comic plot possibilities. As Terry Castle explains, it allows for a 'pattern of narrative transformation', in which characters, particularly women and members of the lower classes, can experiment with new forms of control over men and the patriarchal system. Although the repercussions of such experimentation may not be immediate or obvious as a plot unfolds, the experimentation often serves as a prelude to other and better developments.[4] The use of inversion by the eighteenth-century novelist 'may be a way of indulging in the scenery of transgression while seeming to maintain an aspect of moral probity'.[5] Novels that make use of the masquerade as an important plot device include Henry Fielding's *Amelia*, Fanny Burney's *Cecilia*, and a work which was particularly influential on members of the Godwin circle, Elizabeth Inchbald's *A Simple Story*.[6]

Still more relevant here are theatrical models. The introduction of women playing female parts on the English stage at the instigation of Charles II in 1660 continued to confuse the boundaries of gender, as well as to highlight the performativity of gender difference, as actresses often enjoyed the opportunities opened to them by wearing men's clothing off-stage as well as on.[7] Although English medieval and Renaissance sumptuary laws attempted to enforce a dress code that maintained gender distinctions, and, more importantly, the hierarchy of class distinctions, the English theatre was a continuously transgressive site in which the distinctions that these laws attempted to enforce were regularly blurred or flouted outright.

Of the many Renaissance and Restoration playwrights who experimented with the dramatic device of female-to-male cross-dressing, Shakespeare has certainly had the widest influence on later writers. There is a large body of scholarship on Shakespeare's cross-dressing heroines, and there appears to be a modern consensus that, although his representations of women in men's clothing may appear to advocate the transgression of gender boundaries, the plays actually reinforce those boundaries.[8] Portia in *The Merchant of Venice*, Rosalind in *As You Like It*, Viola in *Twelfth Night*, all assume male attire – and, with it, certain male freedoms and power – only to relinquish it in the last scene. In each case, the play ends with a traditional marriage for the heroine and a cancellation of any threat she may have posed to the status quo. The appeal of this device to Renaissance audiences has been usefully interpreted by Michael Shapiro, who credits Shakespeare and other Renaissance dramatists with using 'the illusion of multiple identities' to develop 'narrative vibrancy' in their characters' multi-layered personalities. This technique, Shapiro argues, energizes and empowers the character 'without placing her in direct conflict with patriarchal social norms' – a powerful literary technique, whatever its political implications.[9]

Jonathan Dollimore, however, would ascribe a more challenging role to cross-dressing. In his work on Jacobean drama, he uses the term 'transgressive reinscription' to describe the manner in which transvestism on the stage often can be characterized by a 'mode of transgression which seeks not an escape from existing structures', an assumption made by many modern feminist critics of these texts, 'but rather a subversive reinscription within them – and in the process a dis-location of them'.[10] In Dollimore's model, 'inversion becomes a kind of transgressive mimesis: the subculture, even as it imitates, reproducing itself in terms of its exclusion, also demystifies, producing a knowledge of the dominant which excludes it, this being a knowledge which the dominant has to suppress in order to dominate'. And 'change, contest, and struggle in part are made possible by contradiction'.[11]

Very close to Shelley's own circle were, of course, the examples of cross-dressing that Byron's works provided. In *Lara*, for example, the corsair Lara's faithful servant Kaled is revealed at the end of the poem to be Gulnare, the woman who loves him. Perhaps more influential are the multiple examples to be found in *Don Juan*, for much of which Shelley served Byron as a copyist.[12] *Don Juan* is noteworthy for its instances of both male and female cross-dressing; first in what Juan calls his 'odd travesty' (V. lxxiv. 5) where he is forced (under threat of castration) to disguise his gender and to dress as a female attendant on the lustful Sultana Gulbeyaz (V–VI). In the later cantos set in England, Don Juan encounters the Duchess of Fitz-Fulke impersonating the spectre of the 'Black Friar' in a monk's cowl, crossing the borders of both gender, religion, and the supernatural, in true masquerade fashion. Alan Richardson has argued that the incidences of cross-dressing in *Don Juan* and the reversal of sexual roles that they involve is actually 'the vehicle of a more profound questioning of the grounds of sexual difference'.[13] Susan Wolfson, however, while recognizing that cross-dressing and disguise can frequently function as 'agents of sexual disorientation that break down, invert, and radically call into question the categories designed to discriminate "masculine" from "feminine"' maintains that this does not properly occur in *Don Juan*.[14] *Don Juan*, she has argued, foregrounds the political, social, and psychological implications 'when men and women are allowed ... to adopt the external properties and prerogatives of the other' (Wolfson, p. 284). But despite the poem's questioning of male privilege, Byron ultimately tends 'to renew expressions of male power' (ibid., pp. 272, 280). In Wolfson's view, Byron's play with the borderlines of gender calls attention to those lines, but ultimately neither questions nor criticizes their existence.

In this essay, while Shelley's eighteenth-century legacy is not ignored, I shall be concentrating on that legacy chiefly as it is mediated through Shakespeare and Byron. The issues which divide Shapiro from Dollimore and Wolfson from Richardson over Shakespeare and Byron are no less applicable to her work. Her use of the plot device of cross-dressing, like theirs, calls attention to gender categories and markers of difference between the genders. At the same time, her exploitation of the device is distinctive and individual, as I hope to demonstrate.

The presence of Shakespeare may be seen as early as 1819 in the novella *Matilda*. In Chapter 2, her heroine describes her early obsession with the father whom she longed to meet: 'My favourite vision was that when I grew up I would leave my aunt, whose coldness lulled my conscience, and disguised like a boy I would seek my father through the world' (*M* 14 [ch. 2]). Mathilda's wish is not to change her gender but her clothes, thereby adopting a different 'self' that will allow her to liberate herself and to act out her fantasies. In this repeated 'vision', which includes a variety of recognition scenes, Mathilda's father always recognizes her immediately as his daughter – his first words to her always being 'My daughter, I love thee!'.

In these passages Shelley subtly alludes to familiar scenes in Shakespeare's works. Mathilda's desire to adopt men's clothing in order to go out into the world to search for her father mirrors Rosalind's cross-dressing as she embarks on her adventures in the pastoral world of Arden in *As You Like It*. Moreover, Mathilda's actual reunion with her father after a frustrating few hours lost in the woods near her home occurs in the little boat she uses to speed home to meet him; this scene alludes to Marina's reunion with her father Pericles after their long and arduous separation in *Pericles, Prince of Tyre*.

A few years after composing *Matilda*, Shelley fully developed the situation of female-to-male cross-dressing as a plot device in 'A Tale of the Passions', a story that was published in January 1823 in the second number of *The Liberal*. 'A Tale of the Passions' involves Despina, a young woman who dresses and passes as a man named 'Ricciardo' in order to take an active role in the political strife of thirteenth-century Naples; the name 'Ricciardo' is perhaps meant to recall Richiardetto of Ariosto's *Orlando Furioso*, the brother of the cross-dressing

Bradamante, who was often mistaken for him. Despina's greatest wish is to see King Charles d'Anjou of Naples unseated in favour of the young Corradino (Conradin), King Manfred's nephew, and in the eyes of her fellow Ghibellines, the rightful heir to the Neapolitan throne. Despina adopts the disguise and dress of a young man so that she can shield her identity not from her enemies, but from her friends, who would certainly prevent her from undertaking the personal sacrifice that she has planned. Shelley describes her heroine in men's dress as something of an enigma, appearing to be a slight youth of no more than 16, yet with 'a self-possession in his demeanour and a dignity in his physiognomy that belonged to a more advanced age'. Ricciardo's countenance was like 'monumental marble', with thick, curling locks of chestnut hair clustered about his brow and fair throat (*MWST*, p. 5). Similarly, Byron had described the cross-dressed Gulnare in the guise of Kaled as having a femininely white hand and smooth cheek, and, like Ricciardo, possessing an aspect of haughty pride and a 'latent fierceness' that defied his slight frame and effeminate beauty (*Lara*, I. xxvii).

Despina orchestrates her disguise as Ricciardo in order to gain an audience with Corradino's enemy Lostendardo. Knowing that Lostendardo will recognize her, she hopes to play on his known passion for her in convincing him to take a line of neutrality towards Corradino. Lostendardo declines this opportunity, however, and when Corradino is captured, he cruelly drags the dying Despina to the scene of Corradino's execution in order to force her to witness it. At this point Lostendardo himself insists that Despina be made to stay in the disguise of a young man, knowing that she will 'attract less compassion' dressed as a youth 'than if a lovely woman were thus dragged to so unnatural a scene' (*MWST*, p. 23). Thus cross-dressing is central to this story for two reasons. Despina defies contemporary Italian gender and social restrictions and disguises herself so as to become politically active, even though her means of doing so must include her reverting to a female's role in order to play on Lostendardo's attraction towards her. The character displays a remarkable facility in embodying or discarding conventional roles as needed. Secondly, Lostendardo must deny his attraction and symbolically keep Despina in her male guise in order to avoid public shame in treating a woman as he does.

In this story Shelley deftly manoeuvres her exploration of gender and identity-switching to effect a radical change in the evil Lostendardo. Despina's devotion to Corradino leaves Lostendardo permanently altered. '[A]t the summit of glory and prosperity', Shelley writes, 'he withdrew from the world, took the vows of a severe order in a convent', lived a life of 'self-inflicted torture', and 'died murmuring the names' of his former enemies and Despina (*MWST*, p. 23). From a feminist perspective, Despina's cross-dressing is conceived merely to enable her to serve her male leader, and ultimately to empower the branch of the male hegemony she chooses to support. Moreover, Lostendardo's power over her showcases the normative paradigm of male aggression despite whatever questioning of gender roles Despina may have initiated, and even charges that reassertion of dominance with a clear sexual component. From a psychological viewpoint, however, Despina's failure succeeds – albeit after her death – in crippling Lostendardo emotionally, and thus disempowering him politically. Cross-dressing may not have been the direct means of effecting this change; nevertheless Despina's strength of will and her inversion of social norms does progress her political agenda to some degree, if not in the specific way she has intended.

In her 1830 novel, *The Fortunes of Perkin Warbeck,* Shelley returns to the character of Despina and recasts her as Monina, a woman who is obsessively devoted to the cause of the putative Richard, Duke of York, otherwise known as 'Perkin Warbeck', the pretender who challenged Henry VII's right to the English throne in the late fifteenth century. From the beginning of Perkin's campaign, Monina plays Una to his Red Cross Knight, leading him through dangers and helping to plot his political course. Amazingly, she consistently defies all danger and improbability by wandering in and out of both Perkin's camp and the court of Henry VII; she disguises herself as a pilgrim in order to penetrate such unlikely places as the convent where the former queen, Elizabeth Woodville, has been imprisoned by Henry, and even Henry's own palace, where she gains the audience and the confidence of Perkin's sister, who is also Henry's queen. There is rarely a palace intrigue or a battle skirmish that Monina misses; her easy changes from women's clothing into men's prevents her from being inhibited by her gender in any way.

Like Despina, Monina's passion for a political cause takes over all other aspects of her life and personality. Despina's description of her love for the defeated Manfred prefigures much of Monina's feelings for Perkin: 'My spirit worshipped Manfred as a saint', Despina says:

> I loved the sun because it enlightened him; I loved the air that fed him; ... I devoted myself to Sibilla, for she was his wife, and never

in thought or dream degraded the purity of my affection towards him.

(*MWST*, p. 12)

Despina effectively transfers her emotions for Manfred to his heir Corradino after Manfred's death, renewing her zeal in the process. And, although dragged to the scaffold so that she will be forced to witness the execution of this latest of her beloved 'saints', Despina manages to escape this degradation and all further political disappointment by dying moments before her lord's inglorious end.

Like Despina, the furiously loyal Monina grows to love Perkin Warbeck, and Shelley again describes her feelings about him in highly idealized terms. 'His cause was her life; his royalty the main spring of all her actions and thoughts. She had sacrificed love to it – she taught her woman's soul to rejoice in his marriage with another.' '[T]he religion of her heart', Shelley continues, 'was virtuous devotion to him; ...'. Monina believes that it is better to die than to back down, asserting that were Perkin to die, she too would die in the same hour (*PW* 291 [III. iv]). Ultimately, Monina, like Despina, avoids the degradation of seeing her idol destroyed by passing into death before him.

In her portraits of Despina and Monina, Shelley exhibits women whose flexibility in terms of traditional gender roles does not represent a significant transgression or challenge to the existent hierarchy. Moreover, in these two characters she seems to explore the dangers of being single-minded and even *too* loyal and devoted to a particular cause. Monina has, in Shelley's words, 'too much self-devotion, too passionate an attachment to one dear idea, too enthusiastic an adoration of one exalted being' (*PW* 304 [III. vii]). In both Despina's and Monina's cases, the woman's passion for her political agenda is not easily distinguishable from her sexual passion for her political leader himself, the physical symbol of that agenda.

Shelley's involvement in the Mary Diana Dods case in 1827–28 seems to have given a new stimulus to the use of identity-swapping and disguise in her fiction. Two stories that she wrote and published just after the height of her experience with Dods, 'The Sisters of Albano' and 'Ferdinando Eboli', both call attention to the boundaries of race, gender and social class. Set in Italy during the Napoleonic wars, the stories were published together in *The Keepsake for 1829.* Interestingly, each tale involves siblings who experiment with exchanging identities by exchanging clothes. 'The Sisters of Albano' involves one sister's plot to switch identities in order to save the life of the other. The younger sister, Anina, falls in love with an outlaw, and is captured by French soldiers while trying to carry food to him. Thus Anina manages to transgress both her family's values concerning finding a mate within her own social station, and the law imposed on the Italians by the French military in occupation. Anina's elder sister Maria, who is a nun, visits Anina in jail and exchanges her habit for Anina's peasant clothes, in order to take her place in prison. Although the sisters hope that the French will not dare to execute a holy sister, Maria is shot before she can be rescued by Anina's lover and his bandit comrades. Anina then takes the veil permanently, filling her sister's place at the convent of Santa Chiara, and providing a double meaning for the story's title. 'God has saved me in this dress' she says, thus 'it were sacrilege to change it' (*MWST*, p. 62). Ironically, while Anina was originally willing to alter identities to escape danger, she now feels that she must permanently retain the identity that bought her freedom. In its symbolic use of the nun's habit as disguise, a common costume adopted in the masquerade, 'The Sisters of Albano' may recall the cross-dressing nun Constance de Beverley of Scott's *Marmion*, who, certainly less nobly than Maria, doffs her habit in order to pursue her man. More importantly, the story mirrors Shakespeare's *Measure for Measure*, in which the Viennese deputy, Angelo, promises to release Claudio, convicted and imprisoned on a morals charge, if Claudio's sister, the novice nun Isabella, will sleep with him. Shelley's story draws on Shakespeare's treatment of the theme of the sacrifice of one sibling for another, as well as the complexity of Isabella's dilemma as a member of a holy order.[15]

One interpretation of 'The Sisters of Albano' is to read the sisters' changing of clothing and identities as a release of the tension Anina brings about with her infraction of both family and community codes in falling in love with an outlaw and then breaking the law to protect him. Shelley demonstrates that, through Maria's self-sacrifice, Anina is reclaimed and purified, and order is restored. The story is extremely dark, however, since it results in one sister's death and the other's permanent removal from the opportunity to find happiness through human love at all. Here the anxiety about switching identities is taken to an extreme in focusing on both the danger women may face in attempting such a switch, and also on the fear that one may get stuck in the identity one may happen to borrow in attempting to escape a bad situation; that is, one may find oneself unable to change back into one's own clothes, having stepped into another's.

The companion story, 'Ferdinando Eboli', involves a complete reversal of the situation of 'The Sisters of Albano' by dramatizing a change of identity between two brothers who are poised as enemies. In this story, the good brother Ferdinand is captured, made to strip, and forced into a peasant's clothes. Soon he learns that a stranger who looks strikingly like himself has adopted his own clothing, and is impersonating him both with his military commander and with his fiancée, Adalinda. When Adalinda discovers that her supposed lover is not who he pretends to be, she is duly imprisoned in her own home by the usurper – who we learn is Ferdinand's vengeful and previously unknown half-brother, Ludovico. Unwilling to play the role of the helpless damsel in distress, Adalinda changes into a page's outfit and manages to escape her imprisonment. The story ends happily: Ferdinand is rescued when Adalinda alters *her* identity, escapes her imprisonment, finds Ferdinand, and restores order by unmasking the impersonation.

This mysterious twist on the Doppelgänger tale owes something to P.B. Shelley's early gothic novel, *Zastrozzi*, with its figure of the vengeful, illegitimate half-brother who is determined to destroy the life of his more fortunate sibling. It is easy in this case to identify the theme of changing clothes as a product of Ludovico's hatred for his legitimate brother's difference in class status, symbolized by his literal forcing of peasant's clothes onto Ferdinand. Interestingly, Shelley concludes this tale of Ludovico's transgression of class and legitimacy by tacking on an ending in which Ludovico abruptly becomes an honourable character after experiencing the compassion of Ferdinand and Adalinda. Here Shelley follows a tale of the transgression of socially prescribed boundaries not only with a reassertion of order as in the case of 'The Sisters of Albano', but also with an account of an idealized improvement on the part of the transgressing character, as in the case of Lostendardo in 'A Tale of the Passions'. She moves beyond the anxiety about identity-switching evident in 'The Sisters of Albano', and offers a happy ending to a tale of siblings who exchange clothing and social roles. As in the case of Despina, Adalinda's crossdressing can hardly be seen to have effected a major alteration in her own gender role, because it is manoeuvred merely to protect her fiancé, after which Adalinda happily embraces a traditional role as Ferdinand's wife. Nevertheless, as in 'A Tale of the Passions', the full implications of this story's experimentation with altering gender restrictions is not so easily dismissed. Adalinda's behaviour, like Despina's, contributes to a revolution in Ludovico – another paragon of aggressive and destructive male dominance. Dollimore's model of 'transgressive reinscription' applies to both 'A Tale of the Passions' and 'Ferdinando Eboli'. Despite the heroines' ultimate reinscription into the patriarchal system, their experimentation with dislocating the dominant can be read as to some extent successful.

Shelley returned to the theme of psychological metamorphosis two years later in 'Transformation', which she published in *The Keepsake for 1831*. Here she takes the situation of changing identities by changing clothes to the extreme when the narrator Guido actually exchanges his own body with that of a mysteriously powerful dwarf. Guido's many transgressions as a wayward youth are followed by an extreme crisis of identity, and his restoration to his own body at the end of the story is accompanied by a lesson learned, and an alteration of his previously profligate nature. In a convincing article that focuses on 'Transformation', as well as the work of George Sand (yet another notorious cross-dresser), Scott Simpkins has gone so far as to identify a technique used by both Sand and Shelley which he calls 'narrative cross-dressing'. Simpkins argues that Shelley uses a male narrator with the hidden agenda of craftily manipulating her readers' 'gender-oriented expectations'. While a story such as 'Transformation' may seem on the surface to support traditional male-oriented values, Simpkins suggests that it actually undermines them, as Shelley subtly uses Guido's narration of his experiences to demonstrate how one man's treatment of women is altered by a radical shift in identity that forces him to renegotiate his own identity and his orientation towards women.[16]

In many ways 'Transformation' can be read as a light rehashing of the characteristics of the Godwinian novel. Guido's confessional narrative recalls those of both Caleb Williams and Reginald de St Leon; his obsessive self-love and concern with his appearance reflect in various places the heroes of both *Fleetwood* and *Mandeville*.[17] In 'The Mortal Immortal: A Tale', published in *The Keepsake for 1834*, Shelley again reworks Godwinian conventions, this time specifically as they are developed in *St Leon*'s plot concerning the philosopher's stone and the *elixir vitae*. As the narrator, Winzy, narrates the painful story of his accidentally becoming an immortal by drinking a philtre which he took as an antidote for obsessive love, elements of disguise figure in his ageing wife Bertha's pathetic attempts to appear as youthful as her husband: '[S]he sought to decrease the apparent disparity of our ages by a thousand feminine arts – rouge, youthful dress, and assumed juvenility of manner. I could not be angry – ', Winzy says, 'Did not I myself wear a mask?' (*MWST*, p. 228). Similarly, at Bertha's behest, Winzy tries in vain to diminish the ever-increasing difference between their apparent ages by adopting a gray wig. Here Shelley effectively employs elements of disguise and inversion from the tradition of the masquerade, this time inversion of the normative categories of age, in order to foreground the agonized, if far-fetched, position of Winzy and the pathetically vain Bertha.

A year after Adalinda cross-dressed to escape her imprisonment in 'Ferdinando Eboli', Shelley returned to the device and reversed the situation in 'The False Rhyme', published in *The Keepsake for 1830*, in which a woman dons man's clothing in order to *be* imprisoned. In this story Shelley introduces the cynical King Francis I of France, who doubts the loyalty of all women, exemplified by Emilie de Lagny, a woman who had reputedly run off with her page when her husband, one of the king's boldest knights, was imprisoned on a charge of treason. The king's cynicism is altered, however, when, thanks to the agency of his sister Queen Margaret, Emilie's disappearance is ultimately explained: having exchanged clothes with her husband, she took his place in prison, allowing him to return to the war and to continue fighting in the service of the king who had wrongfully convicted him.

Emilie's true identity is revealed in a scene in which she enters Henry's court still disguised, kneels at the king's feet, and then uncovers her head, letting down 'a quantity of rich golden hair' which 'fell over the sunken cheeks and pallid brow of the suppliant'. In this passage Shelley draws heavily on similar scenes in which the true identity of a woman warrior is revealed, as in *Orlando Furioso*, when Bradamante removes her helmet, 'And all her haire her shoulders over spred,/And both her sex and name was known withall' (XXXII. lxxiv).[18] Spenser makes use of the same scene of exposure when Britomart makes her true gender known to Amoret in Book IV of *The Faerie Queene*:

> With that her glistring helmet she unlaced;
> Which doft, her golden lockes, that were up bound
> Still in a knot, unto her heeles downe traced,
> And like a silken veile in compasse round
> About her backe and all her bodie wound.
>
> (IV. I. xiii)

Again, when Britomart's helmet is knocked off by Arthegall, 'her yellow heare/Having through stirring loosd their wonted band,/Like to a golden border did appeare' (IV. VI. xx).[19]

As Emilie waits in prison dressed as a man, her husband escapes prison in her dress; both of them subverting conventional gender barriers in order to reassert the order of things after the king had made a twisted assessment of their true loyalty and worth. By the end of the story, Emilie's willingness to go to any length, or to don any costume necessary, allows her husband to achieve a military victory that would not have been possible had she not taken his place in prison. Despite the fact that the implications of a woman's willingness to step out of her gender role have been extended in 'The False Rhyme' to effect significant change not merely on the personal level, but also in the political arena, Emilie de Lagny's risk is inspired by her profound devotion to her husband and indeed to her king, and her efforts do restore her husband to a place of prominence and contribute to the military achievements of the masculine state. She is the ultimate example of the good wife. Unlike Britomart, she conquers through self-chosen inaction and suffering. There is 'more loveliness in her faded cheek' and 'grace in her emaciated form, type as they were of truest affection' than in the 'fresher complexion' of the court beauties (*MWST*, p. 120). Nevertheless, it would be wrong to dismiss Emilie's achievement as a capitulation to the patriarchal status quo without acknowledging Shelley's joke at the expense of patriarchy as embodied in Francis I, whose short-sightedness and misconceptions about women are easily exposed by the wiser Margaret.

In several instances in Shelley's writings, a woman masquerades as a pilgrim in order to travel for some particular and usually urgent purpose, as in the case of Monina, mentioned above. This sometimes represents not so much a gendered disguise, however, as a recognizable and acceptable character type. In *Valperga*, for example, the character Beatrice, in the midst of fourteenth-century Italian political strife, adopts pilgrim dress in order to ask penitential alms of the heroine, Euthanasia (*V* 184–91 [II. viii]). But the idea is developed more fully in 'The Brother and Sister: An Italian Story', which Shelley published in *The Keepsake for 1833*. Raised by her brother Lorenzo, the main character Flora grows to worship her older sibling, who is 'father, brother, tutor, [and] guardian' to the girl (*MWST*, p. 170). 'He was a part of her religion; reverence and love for him had been moulded into the substance of her soul from infancy' (*MWST*, p. 183). When Lorenzo challenges Fabian, a family enemy in Siena, he is exiled from the city for five years, and, no longer having any friends who will risk assisting him, he is forced to leave Flora under the protection of Fabian.

Flora, like many of Shelley's heroines of this period, is chiefly characterized by excessive devotion. She becomes obsessed with her brother's whereabouts and well-being after the passage of his five-year exile. Unwilling to sit and do nothing, Flora dresses in 'pilgrim's garb' and sets out to look for him. Her disguise effectively masks her identity and her purpose; it also inspires respect. Finally, as in the cases of both Despina and Adalinda, Flora's unyielding devotion to her brother and her courage in altering her identity in order to travel through Italy alone effect a change in those around her. Coming upon Fabian and Lorenzo, she dissolves the long-enduring strife between their two families. In revealing Fabian's goodness to her brother she first prepares Lorenzo for seeing the wrongfulness of his prejudice against Fabian, tellingly saying that 'to mention the name of our benefactor were to speak of a mask and a disguise, not a true thing' (*MWST*, p. 189). Charles E. Robinson has pointed out that in the fair copy manuscript Shelley's name for Flora and her title for the story was 'Angeline', which, along with longer passages describing her superhuman devotion to her brother, emphasized the 'divine' qualities of the character (*MWST*, p. 386). The significance of Flora's transgressive act, however, is weakened by the fact that it was conceived merely as a means of restoring herself to the protection of her older brother. Moreover, as in the case of Shakespeare's Viola and Rosalind, the reconciliation that Flora manages to bring about between her brother and Fabian ends with the symbolic reordering of patriarchal society and with Flora's own implied future as Fabian's bride. On the other hand, in her willingness to step out of her carefully delineated place in society, Flora single-handedly restores order to two families that had been torn apart by competing forces of masculine domination.

A similar tale is spun in 'The Pilgrims', written by Shelley for *The Keepsake for 1838*.[20] In this story a brother and sister disguise themselves as pilgrims in order to attempt to restore a long-standing breach in their family, and they manage to bring about a reunion with their estranged grandfather. In many ways 'The Pilgrims' reads as a prose rewriting of Samuel Taylor Coleridge's 'Christabel', and it provides an ending of sorts to the situation of Coleridge's unfinished poem. Desiring to patch up an old friendship that had gone wrong years before, Christabel's father Sir Leoline neglects his devotion to his daughter in favour of his desire to extend his hospitality to his long-lost friend's putative daughter Geraldine. The opening of 'The Pilgrims' alludes to 'Christabel' as Burkhardt of Unspunnen is described wandering in the forest outside his castle as night falls; the reference to an avenue of lime trees strengthens the association with Coleridge by bringing to mind his 'This Lime-Tree Bower My Prison'. The reader soon learns that, like Christabel's father Sir Leoline, Burkhardt lost his beloved wife after only a year of marriage, and was left with an infant daughter. Like Leoline, Burkhardt also allows his obsessive relationship with a rival to take precedence over his duty to his loyal daughter Ida; in this version he denounces Ida when she falls in love with and marries the son of his enemy. In a reversal of the pathetic scene in *Matilda* in which the heroine refuses to open her barred door to her anguished father and subsequently loses him, Burkhardt shuts a door on Ida's entreaties for forgiveness, and as a result, he never sees his daughter again.

As in the cases of Shelley's heroines Adalinda and Flora, the risk that Ida's children take and their use of disguise (the daughter, also called Ida, cross-dresses in her pilgrim role) allows them to effect a significant moral improvement in the other characters in the story. Nevertheless, the story does end predictably like a Shakespearean comedy or romance, with both children's marriage and a general restoration of happiness much like the fantastic manner in which *The Winter's Tale* concludes. There is, however, a silenced voice, that of Burkhardt's abused daughter Ida. We learn of the pain that her father caused her through a letter that her children bear to him, but the damage that Burkhardt has done in cursing her cannot be undone. Here masculine rage and power and the mismanagement of parental duties have obliterated the female child. That the second Ida is made chatelaine of her grandfather's castle and ultimately is raised in rank above both Burkhardt and her brother may be interpreted as a symbolic resurrection of the mother, but it cannot be a literal one. Thus while 'The Pilgrims' can be read as a simple tale in which an agonizing dissolution between parent in child is restored in the third generation, a more complex reading would suggest that the story explores, not unlike *Frankenstein*, the far-reaching effects of bad parenting and the abuses of the male hegemony, a reading that is strongly supported by the story's allusions to 'Christabel'.

These stories, like *Don Juan*, 'leave the thing a problem, like all things'.[21] Shelley's tales of cross-dressing, ending as they almost invariably do with a Shakespearean reassertion of order, indeed apparently restabilize the status quo. Nevertheless, like Byron in *Don Juan*, Shelley continually draws our attention to the often arbitrary nature of gender categories as each narrative unfolds. Perhaps we as readers should avoid privileging the endings of these tales as providing the final word on whether Shelley is or is not challenging convention, and refrain from judging that their moral consists in a reaffirmation of the fitness of things as they are. We might bear in mind that Shelley and at least part of her readership would have been aware of Godwin's distinction between *moral* and *tendency*: 'the moral tendency of a work may often be diametrically opposite to the moral end; that is, from the one pervading moral which seems to be the intended result of the fiction'.[22] The formulaic comic ending in which the dominant male paradigm is restored was a necessity demanded by contemporary editors and audiences. Yet before Shelley bows to such a demand at the last, she consistently dazzles her readers with women who boldly step out of their socially prescribed roles in order to effect change and improvement to the patriarchal world in which they live.

Notes

I am most grateful to Pamela Clemit, Anne Mellor, Donald H. Reiman, Stuart Curran, Joseph Wittreich, Jeanne Moskal, Rick Incorvati and Brian J. Meyer for their comments concerning this essay, which was first presented as a paper at 'Mary Wollstonecraft Shelley in Her Times' (New York, May 1997).

1. In a letter to Leigh Hunt dated 9 February 1824, Shelley wrote 'I write bad articles which help to make me miserable – but I am going to plunge into a novel, and hope that its clear water will wash off the <dirt> mud of the magazines' (*MWSL* I, p. 412).
2. See *The Clairmont Correspondence*, ed. Marion Kingston Stocking, 2 vols (Baltimore: Johns Hopkins University Press, 1995) II, Appendix C, p. 658. Late in her life Claire Clairmont reported to Edward Silsbee a scheme that P.B. Shelley concocted in the winter of 1821–22. According to Clairmont, the poet wished her to attempt to persuade Mount Cashell to go back into men's clothing, and pay court to and 'marry' Emilia Viviani, in order to free Emilia from her term of pre-nuptial convent imprisonment, a scheme which would then allow her to live with the Shelleys.
3. See Betty T. Bennett, *Mary Diana Dods, A Gentleman and a Scholar* (New York: William Morrow, 1991; rev. edn, Baltimore: Johns Hopkins University Press, 1994).
4. Terry Castle, *Masquerade and Civilization: the Carnivalesque in Eighteenth-Century English Culture and Fiction* (Stanford: Stanford University Press, 1986) pp. 122–5.
5. Ibid., p. 126.
6. In addition to these novels, elements of masquerade are evident in several of William Godwin's novels, a body of work to which Shelley clearly responded in her early novels *Frankenstein*, *Matilda*, and *The Last Man*, as

'The Truth in Masquerade' 125

well as in many of her short stories; I am thinking in particular of Godwin's *The Adventures of Caleb Williams*, *St Leon*, and *Fleetwood*. Additionally, cross-dressing as a literary device appears in much of the literature of Shelley's contemporaries, such as M. G. Lewis's *The Monk*, Mary Robinson's *Walsingham; or, The Pupil of Nature*, and Walter Scott's poem *Marmion*.

7. See, for example, Rudolf M. Dekker and Lotte C. van de Pol, *The Tradition of Female Transvestism in Early Modern Europe* (London: Macmillan, 1989), and Lynne Friedli, '"Passing Women" – a Study of Gender Boundaries in the Eighteenth Century', in *Sexual Underworlds of the Enlightenment*, eds G. S. Rousseau and Roy Porter (Chapel Hill: University of North Carolina Press, 1988) pp. 234–60.
8. See, for example, Juliet Dusinberre, *Shakespeare and the Nature of Women* (New York: Macmillan, 1975); Catherine Belsey, 'Disrupting Sexual Difference: Meaning and Gender in the Comedies', in *Alternative Shakespeares*, ed. John Drakakis (London: Methuen, 1985) pp. 166–90; Phyllis Rackin, 'Androgyny, Mimesis, and the Marriage of the Boy Heroine on the English Renaissance Stage', *PMLA*, 102 (1987) 29–41; Jean Howard, 'Crossdressing, the Theatre, and Gender Struggle in Early Modern England', *Shakespeare Quarterly*, 39.4 (1988) 418–40; Stephen Greenblatt, *Shakespearean Negotiations* (Berkeley: University of California Press, 1988); Marjorie Garber, *Vested Interests: Cross-Dressing and Cultural Anxiety* (New York and London: Routledge, 1992).
9. Michael Shapiro, *Gender in Play on the Shakespearean Stage: Boy Heroines and Female Pages* (Ann Arbor: University of Michigan Press, 1994) p. 217.
10. Jonathan Dollimore, 'Subjectivity, Sexuality and Transgression: The Jacobean Connection', *Renaissance Drama*, n.s. XVII (1987) 57.
11. Ibid., 61.
12. See Peter Cochran, 'Mary Shelley's Fair-Copying of *Don Juan*', *Keats–Shelley Review*, 10 (1996) 221–41.
13. Alan Richardson, 'Escape from the Seraglio: Cultural Transvestism in *Don Juan*', in *Rereading Byron: Essays Selected from Hofstra University's Byron Bicentennial Conference*, eds Alice Levine and Robert Keane (New York: Garland, 1993) p. 180.
14. Susan Wolfson, '"Their She Condition": Cross-Dressing and the Politics of Gender in *Don Juan*', in *Romantic Poetry: Recent Revisionary Criticism*, eds Karl Kroeber and Gene W. Ruoff (New Brunswick, NJ: Rutgers University Press, 1993) 268.
15. The symbolic importance of religious habits is of course complicated in *Measure for Measure* by the role of the Duke, Vincentio, who adopts the disguise of a friar throughout most of the play in order to observe life in Vienna from another point of view.
16. Scott Simpkins, 'They Do the Men in Different Voices: Narrative Cross-dressing in Sand and Shelley', *Style*, 26 (autumn 1992) 400–18.
17. For a more detailed discussion of Shelley's reworking of the conventions of the Godwinian novel in her short stories, see my article, '"Laughing That I May Not Weep": Mary Shelley's Short Fiction and Her Novels', *Keats–Shelley Journal*, 46 (1997) 97–124.
18. Ludovico Ariosto, *Orlando Furioso*, trans. John Harington (1591), ed. Robert

McNulty (Oxford: Clarendon Press, 1972), stanza lxxix in Ariosto's original. This and the succeeding Spenserian examples are found in Shapiro, pp. 212–14.
19. Edmund Spenser, *The Faerie Queene*, ed. J.C. Smith (Oxford: Clarendon Press, 1964). Shelley had originally used the figure of the woman warrior in her 1826 novel *The Last Man*, in which the Greek princess Evadne is driven by her obsessive love for Lord Raymond to enlist herself secretly among his ranks when he joins the war for Greek independence. As a result of her desperate loyalty to Raymond, Evadne ultimately dies on the battlefield.
20. The attribution of this anonymous story to Shelley is based almost entirely on the authority of Richard Garnett, who included it in his 1891 edition of Shelley's stories; see *MWST*, p. 393. It has been accepted by Robinson, with whom I concur; both style and theme are supportive.
21. *Don Juan* XVII. xiii, cited by Wolfson, p. 284.
22. These are not Godwin's actual words but an accurate (and approving) summary of his position in 'Of Choice in Reading' (pt. I, Essay xv of *The Enquirer* [1797, 1823]) by the reviewer (probably Bulwer) of 'On Moral Fictions. Miss Martineau's Illustrations of Political Economy', *The New Monthly Magazine*, XXXVII (1833) 146. Godwin instanced *Aesop's Fables* and *Paradise Lost* as examples of works where moral and tendency are opposed.

Part III
The Contemporary Scene

8
'Little England': Anxieties of Space in Mary Shelley's *The Last Man*
Julia M. Wright

> This royal throne of kings, this sceptr'd isle,
> This earth of majesty, this seat of Mars,
> This other Eden, demi-paradise,
> This fortress built by nature for herself
> Against infection and the hand of war,
> This happy breed of men, this little world,
> This precious stone set in the silver sea,
> Which serves it in the office of a wall,
> Or as a moat defensive to a house
> Against the envy of less happier lands;
> This blessèd plot, this earth, this realm, this England.
> (William Shakespeare, *Richard II*)[1]

While political geography has developed a core-periphery model of nationalism in which the core is 'politically powerful and culturally self-confident',[2] British literature of the later Romantic period often reveals a much more insecure core – a core that does not feel threatened by the peripheral 'Other' and validated by its own great traditions, as in the usual representation of national–imperial discourse,[3] but dwarfed by the sheer, almost sublime, scale of the globe it now presumes to master. Shelley's novel *The Last Man* reveals such a sense of insecurity, acting as, to some degree, an extended refutation of reassuring representations of England as a well-defended sanctuary – 'this sceptr'd isle', as John of Gaunt puts it in *Richard II*. While critics such as Alan Frost have noted the importance of 'new geographical perspectives' in the Romantic period,[4] my focus here is on the Romantic-era insecurity produced by the new sense that, in William Blake's words, 'The whole extent of the Globe is explored.'[5]

As Raymond Schwab suggests, 'Only after 1771 does the world truly become round; half the intellectual map is no longer a blank.'[6] In this newly detailed and complete global geography, Britain appears as a tiny island on a diverse and extensive sphere – and a sphere that, as the centre of a burgeoning empire, it somehow had to master. Out of this imperial necessity emerge various strategic devices for managing space. Map-making, travelogues, allegorical cartography, personifications of regions (as in John Dixon's *The Oracle, Representing Britannia, Hibernia, Scotia and America* [1774]), detailed documentation or collection (such as Joseph Banks's botanical miscellany) – all provide mechanisms for imagining, if not actually establishing, geographic control. But Shelley, as Lee Sterrenburg notes, is 'writing an obituary on the idea that the social organism has a natural imperative toward survival and improvement',[7] and such pessimism determines the representation of such imaginative control mechanisms as ultimately deceptive, if not dangerously so. By the end of the second volume of *The Last Man*, 'This fortress built by nature for herself/Against infection and the hand of war',[8] has succumbed to both.

The human need, and inability, to manage space emerges at the very beginning of Shelley's novel. In the pair of essays that close the volume, *The Other Mary Shelley*, Barbara Johnson and Audrey Fisch point to the first paragraph of the first chapter of *The Last Man*:

> I am the native of a sea-surrounded nook, a cloud-enshadowed land, which, when the surface of the globe, with its shoreless ocean and trackless continents, presents itself to my mind, appears only as an inconsiderable speck in the immense whole; and yet, when balanced in the scale of mental power, far outweighed countries of larger extent and more numerous population.... When I stood on my native hills, ... the earth's very centre was fixed for me in that spot, and the rest of her orb was as a fable.
>
> (*LM* 11 [I. i])[9]

Placing the emphasis on the 'mental power' rather than the physical, Fisch describes this as 'Verney's tribute to the superiority of England, and of the Englishman, over the world and over nature', while Johnson refers to it as an 'image of England as mental mastery, inviolable insularity, self-sufficient centrality' (*Other MS*, pp. 267, 265). But this image appears only to paste over an anxiety rooted in the physical reality which that mental mastery requires Lionel to grasp. The 'mental power' of the Englishman here reminds Lionel first of the geographical diminutiveness of England, locating him on a 'nook', a 'speck', in immensity; the primacy of that 'mental power' is reassuring, but does not erase the anxiety of being physically inconsiderable. Lionel is caught between the power to know and what is known, between the discursive construction of England as mighty and the cartographic representation of it as minute.

This tension between the infinite imagination and the scale of global geography reverberates through the novel. It is marked not only by the contrast invoked by Lionel between the 'inconsiderable speck' and the weighty 'mental power' of England, but also by the contraction, and retreat, that he executes at the end of this first paragraph: 'When I stood on my native hills ... the earth's very centre was fixed for me in that spot, and the rest of her orb was as a fable.' Imaginative contraction reshapes the globe, and Lionel's perspective, to resurrect a reassuring understanding of global geography that belonged to an earlier time – before travelogues, and before the empire extended much beyond Europe, when England could more easily be represented as its own 'little world' 'set in the silver sea'. Shelley suggests, however, that such contractions are ultimately ineffectual. At the end of *The Last Man*, Lionel turns from the imaginative contraction of space that has repeatedly failed him to an imaginative temporality independent of space. This temporality, and its denial of spatiality, can be usefully compared to the Romantic-era development of national narrative at the moment of Britain's global imperial expansion. Lionel's 'mental' management of space – imaginative contraction and then non-spatial temporality – echoes and implicitly critiques key discursive strategies for coping with imperial space as England turned outward to establish what would become the Victorian empire.

I Imaging insecurity

Lionel's anxiety about his 'little world', and his use of 'mental power' to assuage it, is echoed throughout British imperial discourse. H. Rider Haggard's adventure-driven and classically imperial novel *She* (1887), as Patrick Brantlinger suggests, is one of a cluster of late 19th-century texts which reveal 'anxieties about ... the weakening of Britain's imperial hegemony'.[10] This anxiety is in part articulated through a tension between imaginative control and spatial inadequacy. In Haggard's novel, human diminutiveness is quickly translated from the material to the spiritual, from ungraspable space to an unknowable God in whom consolation lies:

I lay and watched the stars come out by thousands, till all the immense arch of heaven was sewn[11] with glittering points, and every point a world! Here was a glorious sight by which man might well measure his own insignificance! Soon I gave up thinking about it, for the mind wearies easily when it strives to grapple with the Infinite, and to trace the footsteps of the Almighty as he strides from sphere to sphere, or deduce His purpose from His works. Such things are not for us to know.... What would it be to cast off this earthy robe, to have done for ever with these earthy thoughts and miserable desires.... Yes, to cast them off, to have done with the foul and thorny places of the world; and, like to those glittering points above me, to rest on high ... and lay down our littleness in that wide glory of our dreams, that invisible but surrounding good, from which all truth and beauty comes![12]

Here, Haggard's protagonist, Holly, lays out a Lionel-like paradigm: before the immensity of the many worlds of the night sky, 'man' is 'insignifican[t]'; but, through the transcendence of 'dream' and divinity, a form of 'mental power', he can escape his 'littleness'. More to the point, this turn away from the physical to the spiritual allows him to 'have done with the foul and thorny places of the world' – uttered in Africa, the imperial resonances of the reference are inescapable.

Attempts to mentally master space were not new in the nineteenth century. Such propagandist images as the late 16th-century painting of Elizabeth I standing on a map of Britain that is the size of a doormat use allegory to assuage such geographical anxieties and assure mastery.[13] But in the Romantic period, these anxieties were heightened. The wars with the United States, France, and Tipu in India, not to mention colonial disturbances in Ireland and imperial competition with other European nations, as well as the ever-expanding maps with fewer and fewer blank spaces, forced the British to look outward to a degree, and with an interest, for which they were ill-prepared. While Romantic-era novels, such as Jane Austen's, indicate that a journey of a few miles could seem adventurous, even dangerous, the work of empire was being done at distances of a few thousand miles.

The awareness of the problem of space is persistent in the Romantic period, as Britain hovered on the verge of consolidating and greatly extending its imperial possessions to establish the empire which Haggard's generation was so afraid to lose. Such awareness can be seen in, for instance, William Cowper's *The Task* (1785), published in the decade after Schwab's watershed year of 1771 (the year that the world is comprehended as a complete sphere). Cowper offers 'fancy' as the means by which problems of space can be mastered, but the solution remains an imaginative one without practical applications – a reassuring fantasy of control which leaves the Englishman 'still at home'. Thus, in *The Task*, we are offered 'The world contemplated at a distance' through a newspaper:

> Thus sitting, and surveying thus at ease,
> The globe and its concerns, I seem advanc'd
> To some secure and more than mortal height,
> That lib'rates and exempts me from them all.
> It turns submitted to my view, turns round
> With all its generations; I behold
> The tumult, and am still. The sound of war
> Has lost its terrors ere it reaches me. ...
> While fancy, like the finger of a clock,
> Runs the great circuit, and is still at home.[14]

Like Shelley's Lionel and Haggard's Holly, this Englishman can imaginatively manipulate scale to cope with the global; he is the centre, the globe is the circumference, and 'fancy' connects them with immediacy and without danger. Cowper's clock-hands offer an imaginative means for traversing great distances, transforming geography from real spaces of thousands of square miles to the abstract relations of a clockface in which actual measures of distance are irrelevant. Such clock-hands, like John Donne's 'twin compasses',[15] imaginatively collapse ungraspable distances through simulations of the kind defined by Jean Baudrillard. 'Ideology', Baudrillard suggests, 'only corresponds to a corruption of reality through signs; simulation corresponds to a short circuit of reality and to its duplication through signs.'[16] Geographical simulation, the imaginative collapsing of distance to envision control over it, cuts short the circuit around the globe, reducing it to the motion of 'the finger of a clock', a map in a book, or one's 'native hills'.

But journalistic reports of the progress of the American and Napoleonic wars, proliferating travel narratives, atlases, and so forth, implicitly challenged such short circuits, undermining the reassuring force of such representations of spatial management. Thus, a quarter of a century after *The Task*, Anna Laetitia Barbauld paints a picture of British cartographic insecurity against the backdrop of the earlier rhetoric of island security and imaginative containment:

> Oft o'er the daily page some soft one bends
> To learn the fate of husband, brothers, friends,
> Or the spread map with anxious eye explores,
> Its dotted boundaries and penciled shores,
> Asks where the spot that wrecked her bliss is found,
> And learns its name but to detest the sound.
> And thinks't thou, Britain, still to sit at ease,
> An island Queen amidst thy subject seas ... ?[17]

There is a key transition here, as Barbauld eschews the apparent security of the 'island Queen', for the stark reality of a map, locating Britain not allegorically but geographically. Allegory breeds confidence, eliding scale and physical difficulty in the assurance that right is might. Geography, however, especially global geography from the perspective of a tiny island, elicits only an 'anxious eye' and the fear that right needs might.

This concern about managing space emerges in concert with concern about managing populations in Romantic-era texts such as Austen's *Mansfield Park*. As Edward W. Said has noted, there is a parallel drawn – with only a difference of scale – between Sir Thomas's management of his English estate and 'his control over his colonial domain' in Antigua.[18] While Said focuses on social modes of regulation, suggesting that 'What assures the domestic tranquility and attractive harmony of one is the productivity and regulated discipline of the other',[19] the regulation of space is represented as a necessary pre-condition for social modes of regulation. In one telling episode, Fanny, Edmund and Mary Crawford go for a long walk. Since Fanny, we are repeatedly told, cannot traverse great distances well, the group must rest for a while, but Mary cannot:

> 'I must move', said she, 'resting fatigues me. – I have looked across the ha-ha till I am weary. I must go and look through that iron gate at the same view, without being able to see it so well.'
>
> Edmund left the seat likewise. 'Now, Miss Crawford, if you will look up the walk, you will convince yourself that it cannot be half a mile long, or half half a mile.'
>
> 'It is an immense distance', said she; 'I see *that* with a glance.'
>
> He still reasoned with her, but in vain. She would not calculate, she would not compare. She would only smile and assert. The greatest degree of rational consistency could not have been more engaging, and they talked with mutual satisfaction. At last it was

agreed, that they should endeavour to determine the dimensions of the wood by walking a little bit more about it.[20]

Later, Julia 'scrambled across the fence'.[21] The divisions are clear: Edmund, the hero of the piece, can judge distances and the virtuous Fanny cannot cross more than moderate distances; the dubious Mary and Julia, however, cannot (or pretend they cannot) judge distances, obey their bounds, or appropriately traverse manageable spaces. In the novel's final paragraphs, Austen again returns to space:

> ... their home was the home of affection and comfort; and to complete the picture of good, the acquisition of Mansfield living by the death of Dr Grant, occurred just after they had been married long enough to ... feel their distance from the paternal abode an inconvenience.
>
> On that event they removed to Mansfield, and the parsonage there ... soon grew as dear to her heart, and as thoroughly perfect in her eyes, as every thing else, within the view and patronage of Mansfield Park, had long been.[22]

Control is loosed at a distance – the father in Antigua, Fanny in Portsmouth, Mary in London – and re-established at the novel's end as the family retreats to the bounded circle of Mansfield Park. The issue throughout these works, from Cowper to Austen, is not the management of what lies within the space, but sustaining the ability to conceive of space and to circumscribe one's activity to an imaginable as well as manageable sphere.

II Scaling the globe

The Last Man offers an enlightening articulation of such anxiety and the imaginative mechanisms for managing it. The concern here is one not only of the infectious East or the dangerous Other, but of scale: the fear is of the relative smallness of England. The problem of spatial reference, of ratio and scale, resonates in critics' remarks on Shelley's interest in this novel with what cannot be imagined, described, or named.[23] The plague, as Snyder notes, for instance, 'defies all referential sense'.[24] Such anxiety emerges in the novel as a product of two interrelated problems.

First, commercial Britain relied on the porousness of the island's borders, indeed of all borders, in order to sustain an imperial economy, and this reliance undercuts centuries of imagining England or Britain as a moated isle, set apart from the globe and secure from invasion. This is different from the point that Nigel Leask takes from Schwab, namely that 'It was logically inevitable that a civilization believing itself unique would find itself drowned in the sum total of civilizations',[25] a point that receives its most vivid expression in Thomas De Quincey's nightmare vision of oriental civilization in *Confessions of an English Opium-Eater*. Here, the issue is the re-definition of space that imperialism required, that is, spaces defined by their connectivity rather than their borders, and by their diversity rather than their homogenizing 'sum'. In De Quincey's 'English Mail-Coach', the mail-coach routes constitute the circulatory system through which England organically coheres as a nation. In a global context, circulation – routes for trading commodities and slaves, voyages, the movement of Europeans into colonised spaces – is the means by which England, or Britain, defined its ideological, commercial, and imperial place within an international geography rendered coherent and manageable through such circulatory routes. Moreover, as Homi K. Bhabha argues, 'the racist discourse of colonial power [is] constructed around a "boundary dispute".... [T]he construction of the colonial subject in discourse, and the exercise of colonial power in discourse, demands an articulation of forms of difference',[26] a point that extends to the cartographical construction (or 'simulation') of the global space as a collection of disparate regions linked only by those cohering routes.[27]

Secondly, the imperial geography was global, and England, a bare dot on the world map, seemed physically inadequate to the task of controlling continents, sub-continents and nations many times greater in size. As Lionel puts it, bringing together the geographical reality of England's relative size and the imperial necessity of situating England within the global circulatory context, British ships 'stem the giant ocean-waves betwixt Indus and the Pole for slight articles of luxury' (*LM* 248 [II. i]).

In *The Last Man*, imperial possessions are identified with ungraspable dimensions: 'The vast cities of America, the fertile plains of Hindostan, the crowded abodes of the Chinese' (*LM* 184 [II. v]). Shelley's image of China here echoes De Quincey's nightmarish vision of the populous East, sublime in the Burkean sense as De Quincey describes the Orient with such phrases as 'the vast age of the race and name', 'immemorial tracts of time', 'swarming with human life', 'vast empires', and 'the enormous population'.[28] But the images are insistently spatial – whether vast, fertile, or crowded, whether cities, plains, or homes, space and its characterization are key. It is in *Suspiria de Profundis* rather than *Confessions of an English Opium-Eater* that one of De Quincey's childhood reminiscences best illustrates the geographic anxiety revealed in Shelley's novel. The young scholar orders a 'general history of navigation, supported by a vast body of voyages' of an undetermined number of volumes and quickly becomes terrified of the scope of his bibliographical obligation, imagining himself responsible for the purchase of thousands of volumes:

> when I considered with myself what a huge thing the sea was, and that so many thousands of captains, commodores, admirals, were eternally running up and down it, and scoring lines upon its face so rankly that in some of the main 'streets' and 'squares' (as one might call them) their tracts would blend into one undistinguishable blot, I began to fear that such a work tended to infinity. What was little England to the universal sea?[29]

The problem here is managerial, as in *Mansfield Park*, and it explicitly pivots on the management of space rather than populations.

Throughout Lionel's bleak narration, there is a persistent concern with the unmanageability of large spaces and the insignificance of the human within them. Lionel's 'inconsiderable speck', England, becomes even smaller as it is placed on an insignificant world, 'this little globe' (*LM* 154 [II. ii]). Anticipating Holly's vision of the night sky in *She*, Lionel declares;

> What are we, the inhabitants of this globe, least among the many that people infinite space? Our minds embrace infinity; the visible mechanism of our being is subject to merest accident. Day by day we are forced to believe this.... In the face of all this we call ourselves lords of the creation, wielders of the elements, masters of life and death, and we allege in excuse of this arrogance, that though the individual is destroyed, man continues for ever.
> (*LM* 182 [II. v])

Here the nationalist claim of the first chapter to insuperable 'mental power' becomes mere *hubris* in the face of material reality. Raymond typifies this *hubris* in his declaration:

> The prayer of my youth was to be one among those who render the

pages of earth's history splendid; who exalt the race of man, and make this little globe a dwelling of the mighty.

(*LM* 154 [II. ii])

Maps and globes insistently mark the vulnerability that such 'arrogance' denies, especially as the progress of the plague, and the question of England's false sense of security, is traced:

> We wept over the ruin of the boundless continents of the east, and the desolation of the western world; while we fancied that the little channel between our island and the rest of the earth was to preserve us alive among the dead. It were no mighty leap methinks from Calais to Dover. The eye easily discerns the sister land; they were united once; and the little path that runs between looks in a map but as a trodden footway through high grass. Yet this small interval was to save us.
>
> (*LM* 195 [II. vi])

Geographical anxiety is intimately connected with the rising sense of powerlessness in the novel. As the plague progresses, space becomes less manageable. Maps are inadequate, characters self-consciously turn from wide-ranging maps to focus on small regions in those maps, retreats and searches are alike fruitless, the empire's contact with its colonies is lost, and even the sanctity of the English country estate proves fictional as the plague invades and all falls into ruin: in one such scene, 'the deer had climbed the broken palings, and ... grass grew on the threshold' (*LM* 201 [II. vii]). Traditionally managerial geographic representations, from maps to the topographic literary tradition, as well as devices such as fences, prove falsely, if not dangerously, reassuring. In England, the house of an astronomer who 'liv[ed] only in the motion of the spheres' is 'assigned to the invading strangers' – that is, the Irish who colonize England – who abuse or destroy his astronomical instruments and calculations, and leave his 'globes defaced' (*LM* 237 [II. ix]). The plague carves its own tracks, defacing the globe and crossing national boundaries enforced by political will and military might for centuries but revealed, through the plague, to be mere lines on a map.

III Contracting empire

In *The Last Man*, Shelley, in the only overt allusion to Jonathan Swift's

'Little England' 139

dystopian vision of an Englishman confronting an expanding world, does not mention Lilliput, but Brobdignag (*LM* 183 [II. v]): Shelley's Englishman is belittled by a world of Titanic proportions, and the most belittled Englishman typifies ineffectuality. In one of the more provocative resonances in the novel, Shelley describes Ryland, as the plague pushes him to panic and flight from his duty as Lord Protector, as 'contracted':

> He scarcely appeared half his usual height; his joints were unknit, his limbs would not support him; his face was contracted .... Perpetual fear had jaundiced his complexion, and shrivelled his whole person. I told him of the business of the evening, and a smile relaxed the contracted muscles.
> (*LM* 191, 198 [II. vi])

Ryland shrivels as his inability to deal with a crisis of such scale is made manifest, but Lionel tries to take control of his relative size: he contracts his vision, locating himself within a smaller space.[30]

During the battle scenes, Lionel is unable to see effectively because of the distances he is required to see across, so he concedes defeat. He writes:

> When I came to the reality, and saw regiments file off to the left far out of sight, fields intervening between the battalions, but a few troops sufficiently near me to observe their motions, I gave up all idea of understanding, even of seeing a battle.
> (*LM* 142 [II. i])

Shelley emphasizes the anxiety produced by large-scale, and especially global, geography by representing the reassuring power of the smaller space, the space that contains only England or, as in the first chapter, Lionel's 'native hills' within England. It is Lionel who repeatedly executes such contractions of vision: 'I spread the whole earth out as a map before me. On no one spot of its surface could I put my finger and say, here is safety. ... I contracted my view to England' (*LM* 204 [II. vii]). Much later in the novel, as Lionel, now one of the last three human beings left alive, faces a storm, he once again contracts his vision: 'The vast universe, its myriad worlds, and the plains of boundless earth which we had left – the extent of the shoreless sea around – contracted to my view – they and all that they contained, shrunk up to one point' (*LM* 342 [III. ix]).

Lionel's imaginative contractions recall that contraction executed in Austen's *Mansfield Park*, as the characters of the novel retreat from the vast distances that separate them from paternal control – distances motivated and defined by the colonial reach – to remain within the confines of the Park. But in Shelley's more pessimistic novel this contraction to the imaginable space fails, and it fails because that space is not isolatable. The imperial centre cannot be the sea-girt isle. While the plague proves the penetrability of the English borders most viscerally, this penetrability is a consequence of the permeability demanded by the 'reciprocity of commerce' so important to the formulation of Englishness as well as to the sustenance of the English economy: as the plague which is to depopulate the globe approaches Europe, Shelley pauses to note that the English are 'a commercial people' (*LM* 185, 182 [II. v]). When trade is halted to enforce the quarantine, England collapses under the weight of its own dependence on empire:

> Our own distresses, though they were occasioned by the fictitious reciprocity of commerce, encreased in due proportion. Bankers, merchants, and manufacturers, whose trade depended on exports and interchange of wealth, became bankrupt.... The very state of peace in which we gloried was injurious; there were no means of employing the idle, or of sending any overplus of population out of the country. Even the source of colonies was dried up, for in New Holland, Van Diemen's Land, and the Cape of Good Hope, plague raged.
>
> (*LM* 185 [II. v])

Shelley's novel here not only anticipates England's economic problems because of the loss of its imperial holdings in the early 20th century, but reveals the growing 'anxieties of empire', to use Leask's phrase, in her era. But these anxieties are predicated on British dependence rather than oriental threat. Again, this is symptomatic of a recurring sense of anxiety in the period. Barbauld's *Eighteen Hundred and Eleven*, for instance, warns, 'thy Midas dream is o'er;/The golden tide of Commerce leaves thy shore'.[31]

In *The Last Man*, the frame of geographical reference cannot be contracted. England is an 'inconsiderable speck' on an unimaginably large sphere lost in infinite space, but because it is the centre of a global empire even the act of narration cannot separate it from that unimaginable expanse – the national narrative depends upon its expansionism and commercial endeavours, depends on the production of such volumes as those ordered by the young De Quincey. The only reassurance lies in a 'mental power' that transcends the physical; and the progress of the plague, and the social chaos that accompanies it, insists upon the inability of the mental to transcend the physical, especially the physical that is out-of-scale. Mental power is finally just another unknown land, another unimaginable space: Lionel valorizes 'the universe within' and figures human minds as the 'terræ incognitæ, the pathless wilds of a country that had no chart' (*LM* 123–4 [I. x]). Raymond's lack of self-reflection is represented as another *terra incognita*:

> while Raymond had been wrapt in visions of power and fame, while he looked forward to entire dominion over the elements and the mind of man, the territory of his own heart escaped his notice....
> (*LM* 93 [I. vii])

Instead of the easy ascendancy of the mental over the geographic, we are left with incommensurable spaces – geographical, mental, emotional, the social and the self – that remain distinct, independent, and ungraspable.

IV Turning to 'the space of time'

Spatially and materially, the English are nothing; however, Shelley suggests, temporally and textually ('we call ourselves lords of the creation'), they convince themselves of the converse. As the essays in Bhabha's influential volume, *Nation and Narration*, demonstrate, the nationalism that emerged in the Romantic period is dependent on narratives of coherence and continuity; and, as postcolonial studies of space have indicated, empire is dependent on effective modes of geographical representation. Graham Huggan, for instance, has noted the 'exemplary role of cartography in the demonstration of colonial discursive practices', where 'the reinscription, enclosure and hierarchization of space' in maps 'provide an analogue for the acquisition, management and reinforcement of colonial power'.[32] But in the Romantic period, the sense that 'The whole extent of the Globe is explored' was a relatively new one. The growing priority of narrative as the temporal articulation of national greatness and coherence arguably compensates for the geographical anxiety raised by this new sense of global (and imperial) scale, locating the nation within the intangible linearity of historical narration rather than the expansive, unmanageable, multiply connected spaces of the globe. These conflicting senses of time and space, and the place of the human within them, are crucial to the reconfiguration of national-imperial representation during the consolidation of empire that followed the domestic and imperial turmoil of the early Romantic period. In *The Last Man*, this concern with national temporality emerges in concert with the novel's non-linear and apocalyptic historiography,[33] as temporality is revealed to be, like spatiality, a paradigm through which to establish, or lose, control.

At the end of Shelley's novel, Lionel, like characters in other Last Man narratives from the period, anticipates late Victorian 'anxieties about the ease with which civilization can revert to barbarism or savagery'.[34] He 'fed like a wild beast', took no shelter, and did not change his clothes for days (*LM* 350 [III. x]) – symptoms of a regression to the bestial in which 'a ceaseless, but confused flow of thought, sleepless nights, and days instinct with a frenzy of agitation, possessed [him]' (ibid. 350). He becomes, in short, a 'wild-looking, unkempt, half-naked savage' (*LM* 352 [III. x]), recalling his declaration, when he confronts his last-ness and loneliness, that he would willingly socialize with the 'wild and cruel Caribbee, the merciless Cannibal' (*LM* 352, 347 [III. x, ix]). Moreover, throughout these final pages, Lionel refers to the world as an island and, specifically, as an island associated with 'primitive' inhabitants: he compares himself to Robinson Crusoe, 'both thrown companionless – he on the shore of a desolate island; I on that of a desolate world', and refers to himself as 'islanded in the world, a solitary point, surrounded by a vacuum' (*LM* 347 [III. ix]). In other words, Lionel figures his isolation through the imperial discourse of primitive islands which threaten the civility of the European castaway, through the rhetoric of 'going native'. But Lionel, unable to hope for rescue from the blank space in which he finds himself, reclaims his civility through temporality.

After confronting the fact that 'the world was empty; mankind was dead', Lionel laments:

> neither change of place nor time could bring alleviation to my misery ... I must continue, day after day, month after month, year after year, while I lived. I hardly dared conjecture what space of time that expression implied.
>
> (*LM* 351 [III. x])

'Little England' 143

Given the geographic anxieties which pepper the novel until this point, this translation of space from the geographical to the temporal ('the space of time') is provocative. And it precipitates Lionel's conversion from despair to hope, and from barbarity to renewed civility:

> Why talk of days – or weeks – or months – I must grasp years *in my imagination*, if I would truly picture the future to myself – three, five, ten, twenty, fifty anniversaries of that fatal epoch might elapse – every year containing twelve months, each of more numerous calculation in a diary, than the twenty-five days gone by – Can it be? Will it be? – We had been used to look forward to death tremulously – wherefore, but because *its place* was obscure? But more terrible, and more obscure, was the unveiled course of my lonely futurity. I broke my wand; I threw it from me. I needed no recorder of the inch and barley-corn growth of my life, while my unquiet thoughts created other divisions, than those ruled over by the planets – and, in looking back on the age that had elapsed since I had been alone, I disdained to give the name of days and hours to the throes of agony which had in truth portioned it out.... My thoughts had been of death – these sounds spoke to me of life.
> (*LM* 354–5 [III. x]; my emphases)

Lionel here rejects the temporal divisions dictated by spatial entities – the same entities named in expressions of human insignificance, that is, the stars and planets – to 'grasp years in [his] imagination'. In other words, rather than contracting his vision, as he does throughout the novel, he alters his temporality, defining it imaginatively rather than astronomically, once again exerting his 'mental power'.

The imagination reappears throughout the final pages as a consoling mechanism, as a means by which to evade physical inadequacy, and Lionel continues to inflect it temporally rather than spatially. In Rome, for instance, Lionel muses on the city's 'power ... over the imaginations of men' (*LM* 356 [III. x]):

> If those illustrious artists had in truth chiselled these forms, how many passing generations had their giant proportions outlived! and now they were viewed by the last of the species they were sculptured to represent and deify. I had shrunk into insignificance in my own eyes, as I considered the multitudinous beings these stone demigods had outlived, but this after-thought restored me to dignity in my own conception. The sight of the poetry eternized in

these statues, took the sting from the thought, arraying it only in poetic ideality.

(*LM* 357 [III. x])

While the imaginative can 'eternize', and so dignify the insignificant human, this consolation remains tenuous. In one telling passage, Verney explicitly contrasts the power of the imaginative with the power of the spatial:

> [I] reflected how the Enchantress Spirit of Rome held sovereign sway over the minds of the imaginative, until it rested on me – sole remaining spectator of its wonders.[35]
>
> I was long wrapt by such ideas; but the soul wearies of a pauseless flight; and, stooping from its wheeling circuits round and round this spot, suddenly it fell ten thousand fathom deep, into the abyss of the present – into self-knowledge – into tenfold sadness.... The generations I had conjured up to my fancy, contrasted more strongly with the end of all – the single point in which, as a pyramid, the mighty fabric of society had ended, while I, on the giddy height, saw vacant space around me.
>
> (*LM* 359 [III. x])

In the novel's final paragraph, Verney places himself within the imaginative. Finding the 'monotonous present ... intolerable', the very present he associates with an 'abyss' and 'vacant space', he prepares to set sail, but into the 'wild dreams' that 'ruled [his] imagination' (*LM* 365, 359, 365 [III. x]). Poetry is on board – Homer and Shakespeare are 'the principal' of his books – as he prepares to read rather than map the globe:

> I shall witness all the variety of appearance, that the elements can assume – I shall read fair augury in the rainbow – menace in the cloud – some lesson or record dear to my heart in everything'.
>
> (*LM* 365 [III. x])

In this legible rather than mappable globe, temporality is irrelevant ('the moon waxes or wanes' [*LM* 365]) and Lionel is situated within the visibility of the supernatural rather than the cartographic: 'angels, the spirits of the dead, and the ever-open eye of the Supreme, will behold the tiny bark, freighted with Verney – the LAST MAN'. At the moment of Lionel's greatest spatial insignificance, he becomes most imaginative and, in ways reminiscent of Haggard's Holly, spiritual.

While Haggard refers to the feeble human 'vessel' being 'shattered into fragments' by the magnitude of the truths that it cannot grasp,[36] Shelley offers a narrative that is itself shattered into fragments, dramatizing this failure to contain through the prefatory fiction in which an editor collates the Sibyl's leaves. The textual fragments, 'piles of leaves, fragments of bark, and a white filmy substance', are 'Scattered and unconnected', so the editor 'links' them, like a mosaic, to 'giv[e] form and substance to the frail and attenuated Leaves of the Sibyl' (*LM* 7-9 [Introd.]), piecing together the tiny, individual fragments to give them, collectively, greater material weight. But the lesson that those collected fragments convey renders this piecing together ironic: while Raymond, Lionel, and others in the novel imagine the human collectivity having the power to supersede the insignificance of the individual, the pressure of the narrative against this claim is relentless. Shelley offers us an Englishman coping with an almost sublime terror of geographic scale – one man lost in immensity – by situating himself imaginatively and temporally rather than cartographically, recalling the articulation of national narrative at the moment in which the English were beginning to grasp the scale of the globe over which they aspired to claim imperial range.[37] In Shelley's novel, compensatory strategies – from the pastoral ideal embodied at Windsor to the imaginative power of narrative, from spatial contraction to temporal inflection – are revealed only in their failures, as Lionel moves from one imaginative simulation to another, redefining his location to evade the threatening spatiality, and size, of the globe. These strategies mark not confidence, but false reassurances as the fear of global space in the novel emerges in concert with a suspicion of the temporal as history comes to an end.

In *The Last Man*, the centre has a structural authority that its spatial insignificance (as a dimensionless point) belies. Shelley offers astronomical instruments, globes, and calculations that are destroyed by reverse colonization and the astronomer's inability to focus on the local (*LM* 237 [II. ix]) – by the incompatibility of centre and circumference. Time and history stop with the man who is 'last' because of the spatial relationships that they cannot contain or circumscribe – or even effectively simulate. And the last man who repeatedly contracts his gaze from an immense sphere to his native space finds himself a wanderer in that nightmarish immensity, his sanity – and his English civility – threatened by the scale of the trackless continents he must now traverse.

146   *The Contemporary Scene*

Notes

An earlier version of this essay was presented as a paper to the NASSR Conference 'Romanticism and its Others' (McMaster University, October 1997).

1. William Shakespeare, *The Tragedy of Richard the Second*, II.i.40 (*The Complete Works*, gen. eds Stanley Wells and Gary Taylor [Oxford: Clarendon Press, 1988]).
2. E. Spencer Wellhofer, '"Things Fall Apart; the Center Cannot Hold": Cores, Peripheries and Peripheral Nationalism at the Core and Periphery of the World Economy', *Political Geography*, 14.6–7 (1995) 503.
3. The emphasis on the traditions of the imperial centre has its roots in Whig history and the so-called 'romantic nationalism' – a term often used by historians and political scientists – which it produced; this connection is especially clear in the writings of Edmund Burke, and his *Reflections on the Revolution in France* in particular. Anna Laetitia Barbauld offers a typical articulation of this view of the nation's past:

    > The Englishman conversant in history has been long acquainted with his country. He knew her in the infancy of her greatness; has seen her, perhaps, in the wattled huts and slender canoes in which Cæsar discovered her; he has watched her rising fortunes, has trembled at her dangers, rejoiced at her deliverances, and shared with honest pride triumphs that were celebrated ages before he was born; he has traced her gradual improvement through many a dark and turbulent period, many a storm of civil warfare, to the fair reign of her liberty and law, to the fulness of her prosperity and the amplitude of her fame.

    ('On the Uses of History', in vol. II of *Memoirs, Letters, and a Selection from the Poems and Prose Writings of Anna Lætitia Barbauld*, ed. Grace A. Ellis [Boston: James R. Osgood and Company, 1874] p. 401; hereafter Ellis.)

    For discussions of this model, see, for instance, Benedict Anderson, *Imagined Communities: Reflections on the Origin and Spread of Nationalism*, rev. edn (New York: Verso, 1991); Anthony D. Smith, 'Neo-Classicist and Romantic Elements in the Emergence of Nationalist Conceptions', in *Nationalist Movements*, ed. Anthony D. Smith (London: Macmillan, 1976), and the essays in *Nation and Narration*, ed. Homi K. Bhabha (New York: Routledge, 1990). This form of nationalism is by no means the only one circulating in the Romantic period – I address this subject in my essay, '"The Nation Begins to Form": Competing Nationalisms in Morgan's *The O'Briens and the O'Flahertys*', *English Literary History* (Winter, 1999). But it is predominant, and is especially critical to reactionary and imperialist discourses.
4. Alan Frost, 'New Geographical Perspectives and the Emergence of the Romantic Imagination', in *Captain James Cook and His Times*, eds Robin Fisher and Hugh Johnston (Seattle: University of Washington Press, 1979) pp. 5–19.
5. William Blake, *Milton; A Poem*, in *The Complete Poetry and Prose of William*

Blake, ed. David V. Erdman, newly rev. edn (Toronto: Doubleday, 1988) 25.18.
6. Raymond Schwab, *The Oriental Renaissance: Europe's Rediscovery of India and the East, 1660–1880*, trans. Gene Patterson-Black and Victor Reinking, foreword by Edward W. Said (New York: Columbia University Press, 1984) p. 16 (hereafter Schwab). Paul A. Cantor associates Shelley's view of an imperially connected global geography with modernity itself in his essay 'The Apocalypse of Empire: Mary Shelley's *The Last Man*', in *Iconoclastic Departures: Mary Shelley after Frankenstein*, eds Syndy M. Conger, Frederick S. Frank and Gregory O'Dea (Madison: Fairleigh Dickinson University Press, 1997) p. 195, hereafter *Iconoclastic Departures*.
7. Lee Sterrenburg, '*The Last Man*: Anatomy of Failed Revolutions', *Nineteenth-Century Fiction*, 33 (1978) 332.
8. William Shakespeare, *The Tragedy of Richard the Second* II.i.43–4.
9. This passage is quoted at greater length in Barbara Johnson, 'The Last Man' and Audrey A. Fisch, 'Plaguing Politics: AIDS, Deconstruction, and *The Last Man*', in *Other MS*, pp. 264–5 and p. 267 respectively.
10. Patrick Brantlinger, *Rule of Darkness: British Literature and Imperialism, 1830–1914* (Ithaca: Cornell University Press, 1988) p. 229.
11. Thus in the first book edition (1887) of *She* (Karlin's copytext, see below) and others; altered to 'strewn' in the 1890s.
12. H. Rider Haggard, *She; A History of Adventure*, ed. Daniel Karlin (Oxford: Oxford University Press, 1992) pp. 117–19, hereafter Haggard, *She*.
13. I refer to the Ditchley portrait of Elizabeth I (1592). For a discussion of this portrait in the context of the construction of cartographic authority, see Richard Helgerson, 'The Land Speaks: Cartography, Chorography, and Subversion in Renaissance England', in *Representing the Renaissance*, ed. Stephen Greenblatt (London: University of California Press, 1988) pp. 330–1.
14. William Cowper, *The Task*, IV.94–101, 118–19 in *Poetical Works*, ed. H.S. Milford, 4th edn, with corrections and additions by Norma Russell (London: Oxford University Press, 1971).
15. John Donne, 'A Valediction: forbidding mourning', line 26.
16. Jean Baudrillard, *Simulacra and Simulation*, trans. Sheila Faria Glaser (Ann Arbor: University of Michigan Press, 1997) p. 27.
17. Anna Laetitia Barbauld, *Eighteen Hundred and Eleven*, in Ellis II, pp. 114–15.
18. Edward W. Said, *Culture and Imperialism* (New York: Vintage Books, 1994) p. 87.
19. Ibid., p. 87.
20. Jane Austen, *Mansfield Park*, ed. Tony Tanner (Harmondsworth: Penguin Books, 1966) p. 123.
21. Ibid., p. 128.
22. Ibid., p. 457.
23. See, e.g. Morton D. Paley, 'Mary Shelley's *The Last Man*: Apocalypse Without Millennium', *Keats–Shelley Review*, 4 (1989) 1–25 and Robert Lance Snyder, 'Apocalypse and Indeterminacy in Mary Shelley's *The Last Man*', *Studies in Romanticism*, 17 (1978) 435–52. Snyder suggests that the plague is a 'grotesque enigma mocking all assumptions of order, meaning, purpose, and causality. It is, in short, an irreducible phenomenon that

both challenges and defines the limits of rational understanding' (pp. 436–7).
24. Snyder, p. 440.
25. Schwab, p. 18; quoted in Nigel Leask, *British Romantic Writers and the East: Anxieties of Empire* (Cambridge: Cambridge University Press, 1992) p. 11.
26. Homi K. Bhabha, 'Difference, Discrimination, and the Discourse of Colonialism', in *The Politics of Theory*, eds Francis Barker, Peter Hulme, Margaret Iversen, and Diana Loxley (Colchester: University of Essex, 1983) p. 194; a significantly revised version of this essay appears as 'The Other Question: Stereotype, Discrimination and the Discourse of Colonialism' in Bhabha's book, *The Location of Culture* (London: Routledge, 1994) pp. 66–84. Bhabha's view offers a useful counterpoint to Schwab's heralding of 'the beginning of world history' in the late eighteenth century, when 'The times were swarming with navigators, scholiasts, collectors, and moralists who equipped themselves with a patchwork image of men from all times and countries, and who unwittingly heralded the census of all humanity from which modern man seeks self-understanding' (Schwab, p. 17). Bhabha's work suggests that perhaps the image was required to be a 'patchwork' one, as well as to appear 'unwitting'.
27. Edward W. Said has noted that the very division into East and West is an artificial one; see *Orientalism* (New York: Random House, 1978) p. 5. But it is specifically a discrimination of the kind to which Bhabha points. As Jason Haslam suggested to me in a conversation after I presented a version of this essay in a department colloquium series, the transformation of 'east' and 'west' from directions into regions dividing geographical space is itself a mechanism of spatial management – a critical step in the creation of a grid through which to impose order and institute difference.
28. Thomas De Quincey, *Confessions of an English Opium-Eater*, in *Confessions of an English Opium-Eater and Other Writings*, ed. Aileen Ward (New York: Caroll and Graf, 1985) p. 95.
29. Thomas De Quincey, *Suspiria de Profundis*, in *Confessions of an English Opium-Eater and Other Writings*, p. 157.
30. Cantor suggests that 'the course of the narrative involves a massive process of contraction.... Shelley progressively narrows her narrative horizons from the worldwide network of imperialism and trade to England ... to isolated villages ... to groups of human beings ... to the pseudo-family grouping of Lionel, Adrian, and Clara, and finally to the Last Man' (*Iconoclastic Departures*, p. 199). This contraction is more specifically one of depopulation – tracing the transition from the state-communities of empire to nation and then village, and then from the more informal communities of survivors to a family and, finally, a lone individual – but it is played out on a constant sphere. Beginning with a 'worldwide network' in which far-flung populations are multiply connected by the varied and intersecting routes of trade and empire, recalling the infinite lines of De Quincey's feared voyages, the novel ends with one man cutting a single circuit through the global space. It is, in short, a question of ratio: in this, as in so much in the novel, the human has a declining ability to oversee and manage space.
31. Anna Laetitia Barbauld, *Eighteen Hundred and Eleven*, in Ellis II, p. 115. Here

Shelley echoes contemporary suggestions that those complicit in colonial exploitation are corrupted by the colonial system itself rather than contact with the colonized. See, for instance, such varied texts as Barbauld's 'Epistle to William Wilberforce', Eliza Fenwick's *Secresy*, and Samuel Taylor Coleridge's 'Fears in Solitude'. Cantor briefly discusses the 'metaphorical link between the plague and the spirit of modern commerce' in Shelley's novel (*Iconoclastic Departures*, p. 198).
32. Graham Huggan, 'Decolonizing the Map: Post-Colonialism, Post-Structuralism and the Cartographic Connection', *Ariel*, 20 (1989) 115.
33. Gregory O'Dea addresses the anti-linearity of the text, noting:

> The text forms a tapestry of past, present, and future in that it relates the future of various pasts, various pasts of the present, and so on: the prophetic history becomes a Gordian knot of time as 'a moving image of eternity', in which human distinctions between past, present and future have little purpose
> ('Prophetic History and Textuality in Mary Shelley's *The Last Man*', *Papers on Language and Literature*, 28 [1992] 293)

34. Brantlinger, *Rule of Darkness*, p. 229.
35. 'Spirit of Rome' corrected from 'Spirit or Rome', a misprint in *MWS Pickering*.
36. See Haggard, *She*, p. 118.
37. This also oddly recalls Cowper's use of the clock hand to link the English centre with the global circumference.

9
Mary Shelley and Walter Scott: *The Fortunes of Perkin Warbeck* and the Historical Novel

Lidia Garbin

The change of direction from the 'Gothicism' of *Frankenstein* (1818) to the 'historical romance' of the later novels *Valperga* (1823) and *Perkin Warbeck* (1830) represents a shift in Mary Shelley's narrative from invented fantasy to genuine, though represented, history. This step obviously removed her from the literary domain which gave her fame with *Frankenstein* and consequently from the popular response which her masterpiece had attracted. Why did Shelley deviate from Gothic writing? And, with regard to her fourth novel, what prompted her to dramatize the adventures of the Yorkist pretender? The answer to this second question will help to explain Shelley's turn to historical writing.

From a purely political perspective, it is often maintained that the subject matter chosen by the historical novelist appeals to the reading public because of its relevance to contemporary politics. The novelist's choice of a historical topic for a fiction is then seen as a kind of 'escapism': writers write about the past because they cannot write about the present. In the case of the greatest historical novelist of the Romantic period, Walter Scott, the recourse to past and often remote events represented a sort of retreat from the major social and political issues of his time. Scott's withdrawal from the present, however, was not absolute because he managed to raise, if indirectly, the great questions of his age by relating events of the past which advanced parallel issues.[1]

All her life, Shelley was attracted by, and involved in, contemporary matters but her 'dormouse' nature, which made her reluctance to expose herself to the public increase after the death of P.B. Shelley, prevented her from taking an active part in open political and social debate.[2] Distrust for the personalities of those with whom she might have to ally herself could also have played a part. The revulsion against the Philosophical Radicals that she expressed later in her life offers another possible reason for her reserve and detachment from the public arena:

> But since I lost Shelley I have no wish to ally myself to the Radicals – they are full of repulsion to me. Violent without any sense of justice – selfish in the extreme – talking without knowledge – rude, envious & insolent – I wish to have nothing to do with them.
> (*MWSJ* II, p. 555)

Being far from the 'here and now', historical fiction became the means through which Shelley could express her political anxiety, and in this she found a mentor in Scott, despite Scott's quite different politics.

The view that Shelley and Scott wanted to deliver through their historical narratives was similar insofar as it derived from the general belief that the main purpose of historical fiction was to leave a moral legacy to successive generations. Both writers started from the assumption that, as Shelley affirmed in her Preface to *Perkin Warbeck*, 'Human nature in its leading features is the same in all ages' (*PW* 6 [Preface]). This statement strongly recalls Scott's famous avowal in the 'Introductory' chapter to *Waverley* (1814) that he had endeavoured to throw:

> the force of [his] narrative upon the characters and passions of the actors; – those passions common to men in all stages of society, and which have alike agitated the human heart, whether it throbbed under the steel corslet of the fifteenth century, the brocaded coat of the eighteenth, or the blue frock and white dimity waistcoat of the present day.[3]

The notion that one can always get universal lessons out of the past derives from the belief that human life is conditioned and guided by a set of essentially common circumstances. At the same time, Shelley was well aware of the human failure to learn from the past. In one of her frequent interventions in the narrative through the voice of the narrator, she emphasizes this point by laconically commenting that 'the wise have taught, the good suffered for us; we are still the same' (*PW* 275 [III. i]). If we apply this classical notion of a universal human nature to Scott's Romantic Waverley Novels and to *Perkin Warbeck*, a process of deduction allows us to transfer to the present the observations applied to a forgotten past, and the message of the historical novel becomes paradigmatic both of a universal condition and of the contemporary situation. What, then, was Shelley's aim in recalling the adventures of the Yorkist pretender?

Perkin Warbeck opens on the day which marked the end of the War of the Roses with the victory of the Lancastrians over the Yorkists at Bosworth Field on 22 August 1485, and ends after the execution of Perkin Warbeck in 1499. Shelley adopted the theory according to which Perkin Warbeck was the true Richard, Duke of York, the youngest son of Edward IV, who had escaped his uncle's attempt to murder him, survived his brother and become the rightful heir to the throne of England. The author was aware that this thesis was questionable, and that many believed it to be actually false, but, as she stated in her Preface to the novel, her immediate aim was to impress 'on [her] reader's mind ... that whether [her] hero was or was not an impostor, he was believed to be the true man by his contemporaries' (*PW* 5). Shelley's conception of narrative 'art' was therefore fairly independent of the historical 'truth' and gave her a certain freedom of interpretation. As regards *Perkin Warbeck*, however, her historical adaptation did not contribute to the success of the novel. Had the reader been left in some doubt as to Perkin's identity, as in *Frankenstein* where the duality of creator/Creature keeps the reader in suspense to the last, or as the Renaissance dramatist John Ford had done in his own play on Perkin Warbeck, the novel would have probably met greater praise and a larger popular response.

The fictionalization of Perkin Warbeck as the true Richard of York, however, allowed Shelley to attack both usurped and legitimate monarchy and absolutist power.[4] If her recourse to history is similar to Scott's, her political reading is here the opposite of his. Although Shelley's Richard is the rightful heir to the throne of England, his actions to obtain recognition as such by chivalric standards are viewed as illegitimate and fallacious. Shelley's condemnation of usurped and legitimate monarchy derived from her view that both Henry VII and Richard failed in what they should have been able to achieve as leaders – namely, the realization of the common weal. The positive image we are at first offered of Richard is subverted when his wife, Lady Katherine Gordon, who, in many critics' opinion, is a self-portrayal of the author,[5] 'aim[ed] at restricting the ambitious York to mere privacy' and realizes 'that power failed most, when its end was good' (*PW* 291 [III. iv]). Katherine perceives that her husband's obsession with the crown will not grant him a victory and wishes to convince him to abandon his dreams of glory and power, since these cannot be achieved without recourse to bad means.

At the core of *Perkin Warbeck* is a yearning for social and political reforms which originates in Shelley's upbringing in a radical environment. The rejection of the status quo and the hope for a better future based on justice are expressive of the author's commitment to a cause which had seen in P.B. Shelley and his circle its major exponents, and which viewed the suffering of the masses and the lower classes in the early nineteenth century as the result of a misgovernment caused by individual and oligarchic power.[6]

There were also other reasons behind Shelley's shift in narrative path. P.B. Shelley's unexpected death in 1822 had left Shelley emotionally exhausted and alone to cope with financial difficulties. A continuing need for money (the feature which was to cause so much harsh criticism against Scott after Thomas Carlyle's complaint that Scott had made a trade of literature), led Shelley to consider the demands and the expectations of the 19th-century reading public.[7] A predilection in contemporary taste for the kind of narrative offered by the Waverley Novels showed her the path to follow, one which she had already attempted with a degree of commercial success. Her previous historical novel, *Valperga; or, The Life and Adventures of Castruccio, Prince of Lucca* (1823)[8] had been far better received than *The Last Man* (1826), which had succeeded in pleasing neither the admirers of *Frankenstein* nor that novel's detractors. As Bonnie R. Neumann reports, the *Ladies' Monthly Museum*, reviewing *The Last Man*, had urged Shelley to write 'on subjects less removed from nature and probability'.[9]

When she treated historical subjects, Shelley did not resort so directly to her own imagination as she had done in *Frankenstein* and in *The Last Man*. *Perkin Warbeck* is built out of material taken from previous works, mainly historical sources – some of which she acknowledged in her Preface – including Bacon, Hall, and Holinshed. It is more instructive, however, to consider which sources she did not acknowledge. She did not mention John Ford's *The Chronicle History of Perkin Warbeck* (1634) though we know she had acquired a copy of this play in February 1828 and her narrative obviously depends on it, as the six chapter-tags she took from it testify.[10] She did not refer to Shakespeare either, but 30 mottoes to the chapters are taken from his work and several characters derive from, or are modelled on, correspondent Shakespearean prototypes. Another unacknowledged source, and the most striking omission, is Scott himself, her literary precursor in the field of historical writing. Although there are no overt allusions to Scott in *Perkin Warbeck*, the novel is clearly indebted to him both for its conception and its style. This is supported by a letter Shelley sent to the Scottish novelist on 25 May 1829, asking for any information on any works or manuscripts he may know on the historical Perkin Warbeck. There is no evidence that Scott answered her enquiry, and whether he did or not is not relevant to the present discussion. What is of special interest here is the tone of Shelley's letter. She apologizes to Scott for 'troubling' him with her request:

> it is almost impertinent to say how <incongruous> foolish it appears to me that I should intrude on your ground, or to compliment one all the world so highly appretiates –
>
> (*MWSL* II, p. 78)

Shelley's reference to her attempt to write historical fiction as 'foolish' may be a way of parrying any comparison with Scott, for whose work she expressed admiration, but it also discloses her uneasiness and lack of assurance in handling historical material.

Shelley's appreciation of Scott emerges from her regular reading of his novels, a practice in which she was often joined by her husband. Given their distance from the politics of Scott, it is surprising that the radical Mary and P.B. Shelley read the Waverley Novels, often as soon as they were published and some even two or three times, as Shelley's entries in her journal record.[11] The Shelleys showed respect and esteem for Scott, whom Mary styled as a 'liberal man' (*MWSL* I, p. 120). When P. B. Shelley sent him a copy of *Frankenstein* in 1818 for reviewing, thus furthering the general misconception about the authorship of the novel, he implied a high regard for Scott's liberal views as a literary critic (*PBSL* I, p. 590).

One of Mary Shelley's favourite novels by Scott was *Ivanhoe*, which she read twice, first, in June 1820 in two days and again in two days in December 1821 (*MWSJ* II, p. 672). *Ivanhoe* enters the narrative of *Perkin Warbeck* both as a medieval romance relating the adventures of a chivalric hero and as an example of Scott's use of the past for political purposes. The most obvious analogy between *Ivanhoe* and *Perkin Warbeck* resides in their subtitle, 'a romance', which indicates at once what genre they belong to. Like many romances, in fact, the two novels are set in a remote past and relate the adventures of a young man who is dispossessed of what is his own by right. Both *Ivanhoe* and *Perkin Warbeck*, however, trespass the limits set by their literary genre by focusing on the clash generated by the meeting of love with political ambition and by giving an appraisal of the ideals and paraphernalia of chivalry. The connection between the two novels is reinforced by the presence of a hero who epitomizes the contrast between these opposing drives.

Muriel Spark has characterized the protagonist of Shelley's novel as 'a mixture of Ivanhoe, Shelley, and Ford's Perkin Warbeck'. However, when she goes on to describe him as 'a rebel'[12] she is only partly correct. Unlike the historical Perkin Warbeck who *was* a rebel (and, historians now agree, a fake as well) Shelley's hero is far from being one. Inasmuch as he is not a rebel, he is like Ivanhoe. Like Ivanhoe he has a chivalrous and naive nature. Richard and Ivanhoe likewise fight against an established order which they do not recognize as being legitimate. Ivanhoe helps to restore Richard the Lion-Heart, England's rightful king and therefore places himself against the establishment; Richard of York's claim to the throne inevitably leads him to play the insurrectionary. Like many of Scott's heroes, Richard is caught between two worlds, but whereas Scott's characters from Edward Waverley onwards, after hesitating between two opposite factions, finally choose the most secure side, Richard's ambition prevents him from accepting a compromise and he dies. His quixotic quest for the crown renders him unsuccessful both in the political world and in his private life. He is the representative of an obsolete chivalry who fails to realize that times have changed, and his naivety contrasts strikingly with the craftiness of the wily politician Henry VII.[13]

But when Spark describes Richard as 'fighting a reactionary cause' and William A. Walling writes that '[Richard] is really an advocate of what we can only call "reactionary" policies'[14] I demur. The obsolete is not necessarily the reactionary; there is a sense in which chivalry can be seen as progressive. According to William D. Brewer, who has analysed the impact of William Godwin's views on chivalry on *Perkin Warbeck*, Shelley associated what was to her the positive ideal of chivalry with the elevation of women and with a, perhaps utopian, precapitalistic world.[15]

Again, while I agree with Walling when he states that 'caught between two worlds [Richard] functions effectively in neither' I find his argument too absolute when he calls him an 'impossibly absurd' hero and accuses the character of 'incoherence'.[16] The crux of Walling's argument is that Richard is made to play the part of both a reactionary and a proto-revolutionary:

In wishing to turn the clock back on the world view which has triumphed on Bosworth Field, Richard fails to realize that the age of martial heroism is dead: the grandeur of chivalry has been succeeded by the cunning policy-making of Henry VII. And yet, at the same time, Richard represents the insurrectionary tactics of a still later world view which eventually culminated (if it has culminated) in the French Revolution.[17]

I would dispute Walling's view of Richard as 'incoherent' by suggesting that in him his creator wanted to portray her own twofold vision of the past. In the 'chivalric' Richard, Shelley described the ideal human being whose positive nature would help to make the world a better place. In the numerous narratorial comments which run through the text, however, she also presented him as a negative example whose actions prejudiced the welfare of his countrymen. In her portrayal of Perkin/Richard, who combines ideal capabilities with bad actions, Shelley presents a human being no more incoherent than her own Frankenstein – and indeed, a personality more representative of 'mankind' in his inconsistency than Scott's Ivanhoe.

Ultimately, the parallel between *Perkin Warbeck* and *Ivanhoe* does not depend on the resemblance between their heroes, which on the whole remains vague; it finds, instead, major support in the two female characters who enter Richard's life and in whom Shelley expressed her vision of women's double role in the public and private spheres of life.

Monina de Faro and Lady Katherine Gordon are visibly modelled on Scott's Rebecca and Rowena and are therefore often contrasted with one another:

> Nothing beautiful could be so unlike as these two fair ones. Katherine was the incarnate image of loveliness, such as it might have been conceived by an angelic nature; ... Monina, – no, there was no evil in Monina; if too much self-devotion, too passionate an attachment to one dear idea, too enthusiastic an adoration of one exalted being, could be called aught but virtue.
>
> (*PW* 304 [III. vii])

Monina, 'the humble daughter of a Moorish mariner' (*PW* 291 [III. iv]), shows many traits in common with Rebecca, the daughter of a Jew.[18] Like Rebecca, she is endowed with 'some little skill in surgery' (*PW* 98 [I. xii]) which allows her to rescue Richard from death a few times, just as Rebecca often saves Ivanhoe's life. Both Monina and Rebecca are in love with the hero and would risk their lives for his sake, but the hero loves someone else. Katherine's debt to her predecessor, Rowena, besides emerging from her physical appearance, appears from her being 'a girl of royal birth, bred in a palace, accustomed to a queen-like sovereignty over her father's numerous vassals in the Highlands' (*PW* 290–1 [III. iv]).[19]

The contrast between a dark woman and a fair woman has become a recurrent motif in literature and cinema. Scott's pairing of dark and bright heroes and heroines has been extensively analysed.[20] In the Waverley Novels, the dark woman is usually portrayed as sensual and passionate, the fair woman is, on the contrary, secure and safe and the one the hero eventually chooses. In *Ivanhoe*, the hero cannot have the dark heroine because she is a Jewess, therefore an outcast, and a union with her would be disruptive of the social order. In *Perkin Warbeck*, by contrast, there are no apparent motives for Richard's rejection of Monina's love.[21] Like Rebecca, Monina is the passionate spirit who prompts the hero to action and to the fulfilment of his ambition, she is the prototype of the 'modern' woman.[22] Monina distinguishes herself from Rebecca, however, in that her commitment to the cause of the White Rose shows a lack of the rationality which is conspicuous in Scott's Jewess.[23]

The roles played by Monina and Katherine are also similar to the roles played by Scott's heroines. Monina, like Rebecca, is active in helping the man she loves to fight for his 'rights' whereas Katherine, like Rowena, prefers not to act publicly and keeps a reserved conduct. Surprisingly, Shelley shares Scott's views on the role of the two women and while praising and expressing admiration for the dark beauty's passion and commitment to the man she loves, in the end she identifies happiness with the fair beauty's choice of domestic quiet and resignation.[24]

The character of Sir Robert Clifford and a few episodes recalling correspondent scenes in Scott's novel further confirm the parallel between the two works. Like Brian de Bois Guilbert, Clifford nourishes an inexplicable hatred for the hero which is increased by the awareness that the woman he loves, or rather, desires, is in love with his rival. Although Clifford's passion for Monina is not fully developed, he would marry Monina and fly with her just as Bois Guilbert proposes to Rebecca to fly to Palestine with him.[25] The medical knowledge which Monina has obtained from some Spanish monks allows her to heal Richard's wounds as the 'balsam' that Rebecca received from Miriam allows her to heal the wounded Ivanhoe.[26] The passage where Richard is met by Clym of the Lyn and his outlaws in the forest recalls the similar episode in Scott's novel where Richard the Lion-Heart and Wamba are rescued by Robin Hood and his companions.[27]

This is but a short list of parallels. A careful reading of Shelley's novel brings out more evidence to support her recourse to *Ivanhoe* and to Scott's technique. A brief allusion to Shakespeare becomes then necessary, almost compelling, for Scott's own novels and their immediate acclaim depended upon his use of Shakespearean allusion and scale. One form of intertextuality uncovers another.

Shakespeare is a strong presence in *Perkin Warbeck*. Not only did Shelley rely on his plays for the construction of the plot and for the portrayal of characters but she also made clear her allegiance to historical drama by a consistent use of chapter-mottoes taken from his works. She had not used this device before in a novel and would use it only in *Lodore* (1835) thereafter.[28] Did she derive it from Scott's famous chapter-tags? It is difficult to give a definite answer; the use of tags as mottoes for the chapters was also frequent among Gothic writers with whom Shelley was of course well acquainted. Ann Radcliffe, in particular, made an extensive use of Shakespearean epigraphs.[29] Scott's use of the device in the Waverley Novels is, however, more constant than Radcliffe's; it is suggestive that in *Perkin Warbeck* 30 chapters out of 58 are prefixed by a Shakespearean quotation.[30]

Significantly, when Shelley gave her critical judgement of Scott, in line with most of her contemporaries, she linked his name with that of the Elizabethan dramatist.[31] In her review of her father's *Cloudesley: A Tale* (1830), she expressed the belief that 'a certain degree of obedience to rule and law is necessary for the completion and elevation of our nature and its productions' (*M* 203).[32] In her view:

> of all writers, Shakspeare, whom the ignorant have deemed irregular, is the closest follower of these laws, for he has always a scope and an aim, which, beyond every other writer, he fulfils.
>
> (*M* 203)

Shelley's judgement of Shakespeare was openly in accordance with the Romantics' idea of 'organic form' which she thought Scott had not managed to achieve:

> Sir Walter Scott has not attained this master art; his wonderful

genius developes itself in individual characters and scenes, unsurpassed, except by Shakspeare, for energy and truth; but his wholes want keeping – often even due connexion.

(M 203)

Shelley's criticism of Scott may be applied to Shelley herself as a historical novelist: in *Perkin Warbeck* she did not reach Shakespeare's 'art' either, for, as a whole, her novel also 'wants keeping'. But the positive side of her judgement also applies: like Scott's, her individual characters and scenes are developed with 'energy and truth'.[33]

The political layer of the novel, with its displaced attack on contemporary nineteenth-century power-structures, and the proposition of a doctrine of love as a possible answer to the problems of all ages, are certainly indicative of Shelley's political and social beliefs. And it is thus that the character of Katherine Gordon can be viewed as the author's surrogate self, in particular in the last chapter, which Muriel Spark has viewed as Shelley's 'apologia'.[34] But we cannot understand *Perkin Warbeck* unless we also see that it stands in Scott's shadow and that Shelley is deeply sympathetic to the method of Scott's works.[35] It is especially in her experimentalism, and the consequent intertextual practice that we see her relation to Scott and, through Scott, to Shakespeare. The 'escapist' view of history in *Perkin Warbeck* which allowed its author to reflect over the present by relating events of the past is just one of Scott's legacies in Shelley's historical writings. Scott's 'Waverley' novels dealt with historical events which, sometimes explicitly, sometimes obscurely, exerted a certain bearing on the present. Scott hoped he would instil a moral lesson into his readers through the portrayal of the past. In a similar manner, although her political aim was different, and more obviously radical than Scott's, Shelley hoped that her representation of the past in which 'the wise have taught; the good suffered for us' would leave a trace on her readers' minds and hopefully make them different and better human beings.

Notes

Earlier versions of this essay were presented at 'Beyond Frankenstein' (University of Bristol, February 1997) and published in *Romanticism On the Net*, 6 (May 1997) <http://users.ox.ac.uk/~scat0385/warbeck.html>.

160 The Contemporary Scene

1. Shakespeare's history plays, which are often regarded as the literary ancestors of historical novels, always presented historical events which attracted big audiences; similarly, the themes favoured by Scott in his narratives are always emblematic of the way great historical events affect the life and destiny of human beings.
2. See her letter to Lord Byron of 16 November 1822:

> It is a painful thing to me to put forward my own opinion. I have been so long accustomed to have another act for me; but my years of apprenticeship must begin. ... I would, like a dormouse, roll myself in cotton at the bottom of my cage, & never peep out'
>
> (*MWSL* I, p. 288)

In her journal entry for 21 October 1838 Shelley gave her reasons for not joining the political debate:

> I have not argumentative powers. ... I do not feel that I could say aught to support the cause efficiently – besides that on some topics (especially with regard to my own sex) I have am far from making up my mind. ... When I feel that I can say what will benefit my fellow creatures, I will speak, – not before.
>
> (*MWSJ* II, p. 554)

3. Walter Scott, *Waverley; or, 'Tis Sixty Years Since*, ed. C. Lamont (Oxford: Clarendon Press, 1981) p. 5.
4. In her introduction to *MWS Pickering*, Betty T. Bennett notes that *Perkin Warbeck* was published in 1830, in the year of the revolution in France for which Shelley expressed great admiration (*MWS Pickering*, 1, pp. xiii–lxx, lvi).
5. See in particular Muriel Spark, *Mary Shelley* (London: Constable, 1987) p. 210.
6. According to Betty T. Bennett, *Valperga* and *Perkin Warbeck* '[were] written in the tradition of social reform, particularly influenced ... by Godwin and Wollstonecraft' (Bennett, *Evidence*, p. 356).
7. See T. Carlyle, 'Sir Walter Scott', in *Critical and Miscellaneous Essays* (London: Chapman and Hall, 1839; 1869) VI, p. 50:

> Station in society, solid power over the good things of this world, was Scott's avowed object; towards which the precept of precepts is that of Iago, *Put money in thy purse* ... in this nineteenth century, our highest literary man, who immeasurably beyond all others commanded the world's ear, had, as it were, no message whatever to deliver to the world; wished not the world to elevate itself, to amend itself, to do this or to do that, except simply pay him for the books he kept writing.

In the early 19th century, Scott's efforts to pay off his debts through writing was seen as utterly moral, and only later was it condemned from an aesthetic point of view.

8. *Valperga*, although influenced by Scott and set in 14th-century Italy at the time of the fights between Guelfs and Ghibellines, is in some respects not the kind of historical novel that Scott had popularized. Its main plot, in fact, is concerned more with the personal stories of Euthanasia and Beatrice than with the struggle for power of the two opposed Italian factions; the impact of this struggle on the general character of the people is not developed fully. See Safaa El-Shater, *The Novels of Mary Shelley* (Salzburg: Institut für Englische Sprache und Literatur, 1977) p. 126. For a discussion of *Valperga* as a political allegory, see William A. Walling, *Mary Shelley* (Boston: Twayne Publishers, 1972) pp. 51–71, hereafter Walling. Stuart Curran argues that Shelley's divergence from Scott's model testifies to a deliberate and confrontational strategy on her part. 'In *Valperga*, she appropriates ... the characteristics of *Ivanhoe* and turns them to radically divergent ends from Scott's' (*Valperga*, ed. and introd. Stuart Curran [New York and Oxford: Oxford University Press, 1997] p. xvii).
9. Bonnie Rayford Neumann, *The Lonely Muse: a Critical Biography of Mary Wollstonecraft Shelley* (Salzburg: Institut für Anglistik und Amerikanistic, 1979) p. 215. Neumann quotes from the review of *The Last Man* published in *The Ladies' Monthly Museum*, XXIII (March 1826) 169.
10. In a letter to John Murray of 19 February 1828, she acknowledged receipt of 'Mr. Gifford's edition of Ford', which had appeared in 1827 (*MWSL* II, p. 27).
11. According to her journal, she read *The Antiquary, Guy Mannering, Ivanhoe*, and *Rob Roy* twice, and *Waverley* three times; see 'The Shelleys' Reading List' (*MWSJ* I, p. 672). Shelley's love for Scott's work appears from her reading *Ivanhoe, Waverley, The Antiquary,* and *Rob Roy* in the space of a week, from 12 to 20 December 1821; see *MWSJ* I, pp. 387–8.
12. Spark, p. 205.
13. Shelley describes Henry VII as a 'bitter enemy' of chivalry (*PW* 210 [II. x]).
14. Walling, p. 104.
15. William D. Brewer, 'William Godwin, Chivalry, and Mary Shelley's *The Fortunes of Perkin Warbeck*', *Papers on Language & Literature*, 35.2. By contrast, Bennett affirms that 'the standards of the chivalric social-political code, [were] repugnant to Mary Shelley and to those who influenced her' (Bennett, *Evidence*, p. 365).
16. Walling, p. 104.
17. Walling, pp. 103–4. Bennett agrees with Walling that Richard's goal is reactionary but argues that 'there is little reason to see him as a precursor of anti-monarchical revolutionary tactics' because his 'avowed goal is ... to rule as a benevolent but absolute monarch' (Bennett, *Evidence*, p. 366).
18. Cf. Scott, *Ivanhoe: a Romance*, ed. Graham Tulloch (Edinburgh: Edinburgh University Press, 1998), pp. 71–2 for the description of Rebecca. All further references are to this edition.
19. Cf. *Ivanhoe*, pp. 43–4 for the description of Rowena.
20. See, for instance, A. Welsh, 'Blonde and Brunette', *The Hero of the Waverley Novels* (New Haven and London: Yale University Press, 1963) pp. 70–82.
21. The main obstacle to a marriage between Ivanhoe and Rebecca is her religion, which prevents any feeling of affection on the part of Ivanhoe; see *Ivanhoe*, p. 235. In *Perkin Warbeck*, Richard's love for Monina encounters

no religious obstacles since Monina, although of Moorish origins, has been brought up a Christian. Richard's feelings for her turn into brotherly affection when he meets Katherine; see *PW* 231 (II.xiii). Walling states that Richard 'rejects the love of Monina, ... because she is a commoner' but this argument does not find any evidence in the text (Walling, p. 103).

22. Brewer (see above, n.15) sees Monina as a 'political agitator' who '[u]nlike Katherine, ... refuses to limit herself to traditionally feminine roles.'
23. Rebecca's view on 'the laws of chivalry' clearly contrasts with Monina's exalted feelings:

> and what is it, valiant knight, save an offering of sacrifice to a demon of vain-glory, and a passing through the fire to Moloch? ... Glory? ... alas, is the rusted mail which hangs as a hatchment over the champion's dim and mouldering tomb – is the defaced sculpture of the inscription which the ignorant monk can hardly read to the inquiring pilgrim – are these sufficient rewards for the sacrifice of every kindly affection, for a life spent miserably that ye may make others miserable?
>
> (*Ivanhoe*, p. 249)

24. In the characters of Katherine and Monina, Shelley may be portraying, perhaps unconsciously, herself and Claire Clairmont.
25. Cf. *PW* 198 (II.ix) and *Ivanhoe*, p. 342.
26. Cf. *Ivanhoe* where Isaac informs us that Rebecca's skill comes from a Jewess: 'the lessons of Miriam, daughter of the Rabbi Manasses of Byzantium, whose soul is in Paradise, have made thee skilful in the art of healing, and that thou knewest the craft of herbs, and the force of elixirs'. Later in the narrative Monina temporarily reanimates Queen Elizabeth with 'a precious balsam given her by the monks of Alcala-la-Real in Spain' (p. 231); see *PW* 132 (I. xvi [error for xvii]).
27. This episode is preceded by an allusion to Richard the Lion-Heart; cf. *PW* 321 [III. x] and chapter 40 of *Ivanhoe*.
28. We may add to the tally the mottoes she supplied for some chapter-headings of Trelawny's *Adventures of a Younger Son* (1831), which she edited. She had also made occasional use of mottoes to head her tales from as early as 1824.
29. About one third of the mottoes of Radcliffe's *The Italian* are taken from Shakespeare.
30. The Shakespearean epigraphs are taken from the following works: *Richard II*, *Richard III*, *3 Henry VI*, *2 Henry VI*, *King John*, *The Rape of Lucrece*, *Henry V*, *1 Henry IV*, *Two Gentlemen of Verona*, *Antony and Cleopatra*, the *Sonnets*, and *Two Noble Kinsmen*. Most Scott scholars have noticed his constant use of chapter-tags but so far only Dieter A. Berger has attempted an assessment of this technique in '"Damn the Mottoe": Scott and the Epigraph', *Anglia*, C (1982) 373–96.
31. There is a 'history' of parallels between Scott and Shakespeare which begins in Scott's own time and has continued through the nineteenth and twentieth centuries.
32. *Blackwood's Edinburgh Magazine*, XXVII (May 1830) 711–16. This review is also excerpted in *The Mary Shelley Reader*, eds Betty T. Bennett and Charles

E. Robinson (New York and Oxford: Oxford University Press, 1990) pp. 372–6.
33. For an astute yet sympathetic assessment of Shelley's style in *Perkin Warbeck*, see Spark, pp. 199–212.
34. Spark, p. 210. Diverging from Spark, in the General Introduction to *MWS Pickering*, Bennett reports that Katherine's concluding monologue has been viewed:

> as an abandonment by Mary Shelley of her reformist ideals.... Mary Shelley's sorrow at P.B. Shelley's death resonates in Katherine's apologia, but Katherine's sphere remains personal within the established system, whereas Mary Shelley continued, in her own writing and in her editing of P.B. Shelley's works, to actively promote reform.
> (Bennett, *MWS Pickering* 1, p. lvi)

35. Shelley's recourse to Scott therefore was not limited to the 'romance' side as Jean de Palacio and Sylva Norman have suggested; see Bennett, *Evidence*, p. 355.

10
Mary Shelley and the Lake Poets: Negation and Transcendence in *Lodore*
David Vallins

> What though the radiance which was once so bright
> Be now for ever taken from my sight,
> Though nothing can bring back the hour
> Of splendour in the grass, of glory in the flower;
>   We will grieve not, rather find
>   Strength in what remains behind;
>   In the primal sympathy
>   Which having been must ever be;
> In the soothing thoughts that spring
>   Out of human suffering;
>   In the faith that looks through death,
> In years that bring the philosophic mind.
>   (*William Wordsworth*)[1]

The view of Mary Shelley's fiction as expressing her rejection of the political, philosophical, and aesthetic values of male Romantics has gained widespread currency in recent years. In an influential essay of 1980, Mary Poovey argues that *Frankenstein*, in particular, depicts Romantic optimism and individualism, and the Romantic idealization of imagination, as governed by a fundamental egotism which endangers the 'self-denying energies of love' on which domestic relationships depend. Whether they celebrate the advancement of knowledge and freedom or the unique value and insight of the individual imaginative act, she suggests, male Romantics are primarily engaged in an 'egotistical drive to assert and extend the self' whose destructive consequences Shelley illustrates in *Frankenstein*.[2]

The reason for the destructiveness of this quest, moreover, is not only that it ignores the real interests of others, and especially the maintenance of the domestic unit, but also that in the absence of social regulation, individual desire is characterized by a 'fateful fraternity with death' analogous to that which Schopenhauer associates with the reality underlying civilized illusion.[3] Though largely endorsing this view of Romantic egotism, however, Poovey also notes that a comprehensive rejection of the self-assertiveness which, she argues, is essential to artistic creation would undermine even Shelley's exposure of the dangerous pretences underlying Romantic optimism. Hence, she suggests, Shelley adopts various strategies – including a hyperbolic emphasis on the inevitability of the disasters flowing from her Romantic characters' self-indulgence and dishonesty – to conceal the creative individualism involved in her depiction of them. Only through a self-effacement and indirectness which disguises her complicity in what she criticizes can Shelley effectively counter the more destructive egotism of her male contemporaries.[4]

The ambivalence which characterizes Poovey's description of Shelley's strategies, however, is relatively absent from Anne Mellor's more recent treatment of these themes. Male Romantics generally, Mellor suggests, express a desire 'to guide mankind toward salvation, to participate in the Infinite I AM, and to destroy the mind-forged manacles of society'; yet each of these aims reveals the 'rampant egoism' which was also manifested in their financial, domestic, and sexual irresponsibilities (Mellor, p. 79). In seeking revolutionary political change, imaginative transcendence, and philosophical or scientific progress, she argues, male Romantics elevate the pursuit of individual power and pleasure above the interests of the family unit (Mellor, pp. 79–82). In identifying with the spirit underlying the natural world, moreover, they seek to 'erase' the female identity traditionally associated with nature, while the pursuit of scientific progress exemplified by Frankenstein and Walton involves an attempt to 'conquer and subdue' a natural world envisaged by analogy with 'a passive female who can be penetrated in order to satisfy male desire' (Mellor, pp. 111–12).[5]

By interpreting Shelley's writing primarily in terms of gender, however, critics have often obscured the ways in which not only her political and philosophical values but also the distinctive sensibility which they reveal, coincide with those of leading male Romantics. Among recent interpreters of Shelley, Martin Willis is unusual in noting the extent to which her response to contemporary science and philosophy in *Frankenstein* coincides with the Romantic rejection of materialism which Coleridge particularly exemplifies, and that, far from opposing the attitudes of male Romantics generally, she in fact recommends precisely the 'humility and respect' before the mysteries of nature which not only Coleridge and Wordsworth, but also Humphrey Davy had encouraged.[6] That Shelley's view of Coleridge in particular was latterly (at least) a positive and sympathetic one, moreover, is suggested by her descriptions of several characters in *Lodore* and *Falkner* whose passion for 'abstruse metaphysics' and 'ancient learning' is combined with the qualities of sympathy and self-control so conspicuously lacking in her Byronic anti-heroes.[7] Since her criticism of Byron's and P.B. Shelley's values and behaviour plays so prominent a part in many analyses of Shelley's writing, indeed, it is perhaps surprising that her coincidences with the mature Lake Poets – who like Shelley herself had rejected the radical optimism and materialism associated with revolutionary France – have not been more widely noted.

In addition to these resemblances, however, Shelley's fiction repeatedly evokes experiences of loss, disappointment, and creative compensation which, though originating at least partly in her tragic experiences as a bereaved wife and mother, nevertheless closely parallel those described by the later Coleridge and Wordsworth. In Shelley as in these male writers, I will argue, the loss of youthful optimism is accompanied not only by the moral and political conservatism which, Poovey and Mellor have argued, becomes increasingly prominent in her later writing, but also by the view of creative and intellectual effort as compensating for the disappearance of a youthful 'joy' resembling that evoked in Wordsworth's 'Intimations of Immortality'.[8] The analogies with Wordsworth are more extensive than this, however, since Shelley's fiction also emphasizes the importance of a sympathetic devotion to the interests of others, and of those 'little, nameless, unremembered, acts/Of kindness and of love' which 'Tintern Abbey' describes as forming the 'best portion of a good man's life', and which Wordsworth repeatedly celebrates in preference to the pursuit of large-scale political or social change.[9]

Hence not only Shelley's political and philosophical values but also the patterns of sentiment which they reveal, have much in common with those of first-generation Romantics who had rejected the Enlightenment ideals later espoused by Byron and P.B. Shelley.[10] Though several of her male characters are unambiguously self-indulgent and destructive, moreover, the intensity with which she often describes their transition from optimism to pessimism suggests a far greater identification with their experience than most critics seem to recognize. In her last two novels particularly, Shelley's descriptions of her characters' sufferings are marked by degrees both of empathy and of relevance to her own experience that distinguish them from the merely negative view of Romantic optimism which Mellor describes her as expressing. Though Lodore and Falkner are clearly responsible for their own and others' suffering, and though their function in her writing is partly to teach the importance of self-restraint and sympathy for others, they are also invested with key elements of Shelley's own emotional life, and thus disrupt the dualism of male and female qualities presented by several recent critics. Her passionate identification with their sense of loss and of inevitable fate, indeed, suggests that Shelley not only displaces onto these characters the guilt which, in a truly moral universe, ought to have preceded her own misfortunes, but also uses them partly to justify her suffering in terms of a misguided optimism she shared with male Romantics, and of an inevitable transition from joyful innocence to sorrowful experience – albeit soothed by diverse consolations – which parallels that described by Coleridge and Wordsworth.

Hence her later novels act as compensations for suffering in three principal ways: firstly through the process of imaginatively re-creating her experience, in which she seems to have found a palliative quality resembling that which Coleridge attributed to philosophical effort, and which Wordsworth attached to what James Averill calls the 'imaginative projection of human suffering'; secondly through criticism of the Romantic egotism and irresponsibility from which she felt her afflictions had resulted (and Poovey's theory of a countervailing 'assertiveness' in Shelley is particularly relevant here); and thirdly through seeking justifications for her misfortune in a shared experience of inevitable loss and disappointment.[11] At the same time, however, her later fiction recommends precisely the transcendence of loss through sympathy and faith which Wordsworth celebrates in my epigraph; and the gradually increasing prominence in her writing of a process of compensation and recuperation resembling the 'drama of suffering, death and resurrection' which Morton Paley finds in Coleridge's later poetry is among the most important features of her creative development.[12]

These resemblances to certain aspects of Coleridge and Wordsworth are especially prominent in *Lodore*. Precisely what significance should be attached to the title of the novel is not made explicit, yet it was by this time so well known as the name of the 'celebrated cataract' above Derwentwater as clearly to invoke the Lake Poets, all of whom refer to it at some point in their works.[13] More specifically, Shelley's description of Lord Lodore's response to that other 'celebrated cataract', Niagara Falls, has important features in common with Coleridge's descriptions of the Lodore waterfall, which was the focus of an anecdote he used on several occasions to illustrate the widespread misuse of aesthetic terms. 'In a Boat on the Lake of Keswick,' he wrote in the notes for his 1808 lectures on poetry, 'I was looking at the celebrated Cataract of Lodore, then in all its force and greatness – a Lady of no mean Rank observed, that it was sublimely beautiful, & indeed absolutely pretty' – a comment which, he argues, seeks to identify quite different forms of pleasure and aesthetic experience.[14] In his essays 'On The Principles of Genial Criticism,' published in *Felix Farley's Bristol Journal* in 1814, the anecdote reappears. In this version, the lady's observation is said to be prompted by Coleridge's initial remark that the cataract 'was in the strictest sense of the word, a sublime object', and the setting is described more amply:

> Many years ago the writer ... was gazing on a Cataract of great height, breadth, and impetuosity, the summit of which appeared to blend with the sky and clouds, while the lower part was hidden by rocks and trees ... [15]

Though Coleridge gives no detailed explanation of why Lodore is 'in the strictest sense ... sublime', his emphasis on its 'great height, breadth, and impetuosity', and on its appearing 'to blend with the sky and clouds' recalls both Burke's and Kant's descriptions of the sense of incomprehensible power or vastness produced by objects incompletely viewed or understood.[16] Whether or not Shelley was familiar with this passage in Coleridge, it parallels several aspects of her description of Lodore's response to Niagara, where he pauses with his daughter Ethel shortly before his fatal duel with Hatfield. 'One day,' she writes, '[Lodore] stood watching that vast and celebrated cataract, whose everlasting and impetuous flow mirrored the dauntless but rash energy of his own soul' (*L* 81 [I. xiv]). The image not only transfers Coleridge's emphasis on the vastness and 'impetuosity' of the waterfall to Lord Lodore himself, but also resembles the image of the 'life-ebullient stream' which, in his periodical *The Friend*, Coleridge uses to symbolize the infinite and irrepressible powers of nature and the human mind.[17] In addition to resembling Coleridge's or Wordsworth's identification with the spirit of nature, however, Lodore's response to the waterfall recalls the hyperbolic – and implicitly suicidal – desire to *merge* oneself with nature which Manfred expresses in Byron's drama. 'A vague desire of plunging into the whirl of waters agitated him', Shelley writes, much as Manfred vaguely regrets not having 'stood ... beneath' Mount Rossberg during the disastrous landslide of 1806.[18] That it should be Lodore – himself named after the best-known cataract in England – who dreams of merging with the waters of Niagara Falls, moreover, is a notably ironic symbol of the Romantic desire for transcendence which he exemplifies elsewhere in the novel. Hence his Romantic quest has more ambiguous implications than those which Coleridge or Wordsworth usually attach to it.

Perhaps the most important feature of Lodore's character, indeed, is the hedonism or self-indulgence which Shelley had earlier made a distinctive quality of Lord Raymond, the Byron-figure in *The Last Man*. In particular, Lodore's ill-fated marriage to the young Cornelia arises from a need to stifle his cloyed appetite for sensual pleasure, and Shelley's description of his motivations makes explicit the morality underlying her less direct, if no less forceful, criticisms of Romantic optimism in *The Last Man*. In the midst of the self-indulgence of the rich, she writes:

> the eternal law which links ill to ill, is at hand to rebuke and tame the rebel spirit; and such a tissue of pain and evil is woven from their holiday pastime, as checks them midcourse, and makes them feel that they are slaves. The young are scarcely aware of this; they delight to contend with Fate, and laugh as she clanks their chains. But there is a period – sooner or later comes to all – when the links envelop them, the bolts are shot, the rivets fixed, the iron enters the flesh, the soul is subdued, and they fly to religion or proud philosophy, to seek for an alleviation, which the crushed spirit can no longer draw from its own resources.
>
> (*L* 58 [I. xi])

As one who is not among 'those whose situation in life obliges them to earn their daily bread' (ibid., 58), as Shelley puts it, Lodore's self-indulgence reflects in an exaggerated form that which she attributes to Lord Raymond in *The Last Man*. More importantly, the pattern whereby suffering necessarily follows the self-indulgence arising from Lodore's prosperity, reveals a morality which is both fatalistic and puritanical. Shelley's comparison of this thwarting of youthful optimism with a form of imprisonment interestingly echoes that in

Wordsworth's 'Intimations of Immortality', albeit without the countervailing sense of a transcendent unity with the divine.[19] This fatalism, however, is connected here not only with a puritanical view of pleasure and of wealth but also with an insistent claim that human beings do not possess the freedom which male Romantics had repeatedly argued that they do. Whereas Coleridge and his German sources claimed that man transcends all definition, and is the source as much as the product of the physical world, Shelley describes mankind as bound by iron laws analogous to the physical necessities which, with obvious disapproval, she describes Lodore as having temporarily escaped.[20]

The flight to 'religion or proud philosophy' which she describes as the destiny of those who have recognized their imprisonment reflects not only Shelley's implicit judgement of the Romantic poets, but also certain aspects of their experience and practice. Coleridge, who frequently described such a flight from loss, disappointment, and cloying self-indulgence as the source of his own philosophizing, clearly provides the most obvious Romantic instance of this principle, and Shelley's reference to 'proud philosophy' seems to echo Coleridge's description of his metaphysical reflections in lines 56–7 of 'The Eolian Harp' as 'Bubbles that glitter as they rise and break/On vain Philosophy's aye-babbling spring' (*CPW* I, p. 102). These lines themselves, indeed, interestingly resemble those from Coleridge's 'Ode to Tranquillity' which Shelley proposed to her publisher as a motto for the second chapter of the novel, where Lodore is himself described as fleeing from sorrow into the consolations of Platonic philosophy.[21] The lines in question are 'The bubble floats before/The spectre stalks behind' – in which the 'bubble' signifies the 'idle hope' through which we flee from the 'spectre' (or in Shelley's version, 'shadow') of 'dire Remembrance.' In a well-known passage of *The Friend*, moreover, Coleridge not only describes how self-indulgence necessarily gives way to a disgust which he interprets as its natural punishment,[22] but also argues that the only 'preventive ... remedy, [or] counteraction' to this cycle is a philosophical 'habituation of the intellect to clear, distinct, and adequate conceptions concerning all things that are the possible objects of clear conception', after which we should reserve our 'deep feelings' for sublime ideas such as those of 'Freedom, Immortality, [and] God' (*Friend* I, pp. 105–6). Not only Coleridge's distinctive combination of philosophy and religion, therefore, but also the purifying and liberating function he attributes to it have almost exact parallels in Shelley's description of Lodore. That she is referring to this Coleridgean model, indeed, is further suggested by the striking resemblance between her proposed motto and the passage immediately following Coleridge's description of the naturally waning motives of 'habitual vice.' 'No object,' he writes, 'not even the light of a solitary taper in the far distance, tempts the benighted mind from before; but its own restlessness dogs it from behind, as with the iron goad of Destiny' (*Friend* I, p. 106). Not only is this sentence almost identical in its ideas and images with her proposed motto but the passage it derives from also describes precisely the flight from cloying self-indulgence into religion and philosophy which she depicts as the ultimate destiny of the hedonist. The only important difference is that whereas Coleridge describes this movement as morally necessary, Shelley describes it as little more than automatic, and almost as an extension of the self-indulgence which precedes it, thus implicitly problematizing the religious or philosophical faith which it engenders.

Coleridge, therefore, seems almost certain to have been Shelley's chief model for this pattern, to which in her description of Lodore she attaches the ironic implication that the sublime ideas invoked by Coleridge, and others like him, are little more than a flight from discomfort. That the passage from his 'Ode to Tranquillity' also held a more personal significance for her, however, seems to be confirmed by her use of the same quotation in a journal-entry of 1824, where it evokes her own experience of inescapable loss following the death of her husband (*MWSJ* II, pp. 472–3). A passage in the fictional editor's introduction to *The Last Man* further suggests that Shelley's view of such a flight from suffering into philosophical or creative effort was not wholly unsympathetic. Her own work, of course, is distinctly more literary than philosophical; yet, she writes:

> such is human nature, that the excitement of mind was dear to me, and that the imagination, painter of tempest and earthquake, or, worse, the stormy and ruin-fraught passions of man, softened my real sorrows and endless regrets, by clothing these fictitious ones in that ideality, which takes the mortal sting from pain.
> (*LM* 8–9 [Introd.])

Shelley's very Coleridgean statement here reminds us that although Coleridge described philosophy as compensating for the intolerableness of imaginative creation, his best-known description of this process reveals precisely the imaginative powers he claims it would be intolerable to use, and thus suggests that poetry shares the therapeutic function he attributes to philosophy.[23] In describing literary creativity as a source of consolation analogous to religion and philosophy, therefore, Shelley expresses substantial identification not only with Coleridge, but also with those who, like Lodore before his marriage to Cornelia, have discovered the limitations of their youthful optimism.

That the transition from optimism to pessimism was the most important experience underlying her later fiction, indeed, is emphasized by the passage immediately following her description of Lodore's flight from his cloying pursuit of sensual pleasure. 'This hour! this fatal hour!' she writes:

> How many can point to the shadow on the dial, and say, 'Then it was that I felt the whole weight of my humanity, and knew myself to be the subject of an unvanquishable power!' This dark moment had arrived for Lodore. He had spent his youth in passion, and exhausted his better nature in a struggle for, and in the enjoyment of, pleasure. He found disappointment, and desired change.
>
> (*L* 58 [I. xi])[24]

That it is Lodore's pursuit of 'pleasure' – or, as she even more emphatically puts it, 'the enjoyment' of pleasure – that leads to his disappointment cannot conceal the connection of this passage with the experience of loss which dominates much of Shelley's fiction. Though Lodore's hedonism is obviously depicted as a negative quality, Shelley nevertheless seems passionately to identify with his experience of disappointment, and to represent it as in certain ways a universal one.

As we have seen, Shelley suggests that her own response to such experiences was to recreate them in an imaginary or idealized form. The response she describes Lodore as adopting is apparently quite different, yet reveals fascinating analogies with that which she attributes to herself. Lodore's alternative to sensual pleasure, she writes, was to seek to impose his will upon Cornelia, whom he found like 'white paper to be written upon at will, ... a favourite metaphor' she adds, 'among those men who have described the ideal of a wife' (*L* 41 [I. vii]). Though ostensibly highlighting the anti-social qualities of a character in whom, as in Lord Raymond, self-indulgence is combined with self-deception and the pursuit of power, Shelley's description of Lodore's attitude towards Cornelia is interestingly paralleled by her characterization of Elizabeth Raby in *Falkner*. 'Elizabeth's mind', she writes:

> was of that high order which soon found something congenial in study. The acquirement of new ideas – the sense of order, and afterwards of power – awoke a desire for improvement.
>
> (*F* 39 [I. vi])[25]

The sense of power which Elizabeth acquires from studying is clearly analogous to the consolation which Shelley describes herself as deriving from the imaginative recreation of her experiences. More importantly, however, the process of writing which produces this consoling sense 'of order, and afterwards of power' is reflected, metaphorized, or 'idealized' in Shelley's description of Lodore's view of Cornelia. That he should regard her as resembling 'white paper to be written upon at will' appears to be no accident: Shelley's process of literary creation involves a pursuit of order and power which at once parallels that which she attributes to the Byronic characters in her fiction, and compensates for the suffering she feels that their real-life models inflict. Once their deaths have both removed this imposition and stolen the ideal they represented to her, however, Shelley seeks to 'soften ... real sorrows and endless regrets', as she puts it, by 'clothing them in that ideality which takes the mortal sting from pain' – that is, by engaging in a displaced imitation of the pursuit of power which she attributes to male Romantics. This imitation, however, itself reshapes them into figures who, like Lodore, are not only exploitative and hedonistic, but also destined to die as a result of their irresponsibility and lack of judgement. Shelley, that is, decisively takes control of the male Romantics in her fiction, and re-presents them in allegories informed and moralized by her own experience of loss and disappointment. Her comparison of Lodore's exploitativeness to the process of writing, indeed, highlights the idealized nature of such characters in her fiction: though Byron's and P.B. Shelley's careers provide much on which to base such images, the original (or originary) writing is at least as clearly Shelley's as it is theirs.

The effect of the experience of loss which is so prominent in Shelley's later fiction, therefore, is not to transform her view of male Romantics, but rather to give her writing a more overtly didactic form by highlighting the complicity of self-indulgence with self-deception, and by contrasting the harmfulness of these tendencies with the beneficial effects of sympathetic self-sacrifice. Her identification of the former as masculine and the latter as feminine qualities, however, is sometimes exaggerated by her critics. According to Kate Ellis, for example, Lodore's flight to America in order to escape a duel with Count Casimir emphasizes his 'poor judgement of women' and the destructive nature of the 'code of masculinity that emphasizes abstract honor over concrete relationships.' Lodore's reason for fleeing to America, however, is not merely the code of honour which, in fact, would require him to fight Casimir, but also the fact that Casimir is his illegitimate son – a fact which certainly highlights his previous irresponsibility, yet which also forces him to abandon British society precisely because of the impossibility of seeming to behave honourably. Had he privileged the honour code over 'concrete relationships', there would have been no dilemma for him and no need to fly – he would have fought his son.[26]

The difficulty of identifying moral weakness and transgressiveness with 'masculine' qualities, moreover, is highlighted by Lady Lodore's second marriage to Horatio Saville – a man, as Mellor notes, 'of empathy and benevolence, who acknowledges that the claims of a child can take precedence over ... [those] of a husband'.[27] Saville, indeed, is one of several models in *Lodore* of the selflessly empathic and benevolent character which Shelley contrasts with that of the young Lodore, and implicitly with the Byronic anti-heroes of *Frankenstein* and *The Last Man*. He is distinctive, however, in combining virtues which several critics have described as characteristically feminine – or represented by Shelley as being so – with a passion for 'abstruse metaphysics' which, in addition to being an obviously Coleridgean trait, is also among the transgressive and masculine qualities which Mellor associates with Frankenstein's careless pursuit of knowledge and power (Mellor, p. 79). Shelley herself seems conscious of a certain paradox in connecting such enthusiasms with the selflessness and self-control which Saville also demonstrates in outstanding degrees – a fact which lends support to William Veeder's theory that her fiction recommends a unification of the qualities she often represents as distinctively masculine and feminine.[28] Saville, she writes:

> was a being fashioned for every virtue and distinguished by every excellence; to know that a thing was right to be done, was enough to impel Horatio to go through fire and water to do it.... At school he held the topmost place, at college he was distinguished by the energy with which he pursued his studies; and these, so opposite

from what might have been expected to be the pursuits of his ardent mind, were abstruse metaphysics – the highest and most theoretical mathematics, and cross-grained argument, based upon hair-fine logic; to these he addicted himself. His desire was knowledge; his passion truth; his eager and never-sleeping endeavour was to inform and satisfy his understanding.

(*L* 113–14 [II. ii])

A philosopher who is at once so passionate in his studies and so tolerant, selfless, and sympathetic as Shelley elsewhere affirms clearly disrupts the dualistic vision not only of gender-identities, but of character-traits in general, which much of her fiction seems to propagate.[29] Clearly, Saville's studies are not of the kind that tend 'to weaken [one's] affections', as those of Frankenstein are shown to do; yet they are also of precisely the metaphysical and (implicitly) dialectical character which Mellor in particular describes as characterizing a 'masculine Romantic ideology' (Mellor, p. 79), and as seeking to 'erase' female identity.[30]

Not only Saville's qualities, however, but also those of Fanny Derham, and of Elizabeth Raby in *Falkner*, demonstrate that the pursuit of knowledge need in no sense be associated with selfishness, violence or transgression. Far from breaking any moral law, the Romantic metaphysician represented by Saville, and the lovers of academic study represented by Fanny and Elizabeth, are both ideally free from the negative qualities which *Frankenstein* and several of its interpreters associate with the pursuit of knowledge. The explanation of this difference, however, appears to lie not in any transformation of Shelley's values, but rather in the predominantly scientific rather than metaphysical nature of Frankenstein's interests. In seeking practical control over the forces of life, that is, Frankenstein more obviously identifies with Enlightenment values rather than with the interests of Wordsworth and especially Coleridge, whose emphasis on the ultimate incomprehensibility of the universe parallels that implied in the allegorical *débâcle* of *Frankenstein*.

The fact that Saville's metaphysical interests so strikingly parallel those with which Coleridge was associated, moreover, suggests that Shelley must have had the latter in mind when devising this character. As early as 1797, Coleridge's fascination with the 'maze of metaphysic lore' had been described in a poem by Anna Barbauld; and Saville's fascination with 'abstruse metaphysics' closely parallels Coleridge's descriptions of his 'abstruse research', though the emphasis on its power to suppress uncomfortable emotions is more prominent in Shelley's descriptions of Lodore.[31] Not only Saville's habit of referring to 'some unexplained passage in Plato the divine, or some undiscovered problem in the higher sciences', indeed, but also his physical attributes and the attitudes of his admirers parallel those described by several of Coleridge's acquaintances, especially Thomas Carlyle. Though 'his noble purposes and studious soul, demanded a frame of iron' Shelley writes, 'he had one of the frailest mechanism'. 'The sparkling eye, the languid step, and flushed cheek of Horatio Saville, were all tokens that there burnt within him a spirit too strong for his frame' (L 114–15 [II. ii]).[32] Her description of him as 'addicted' to abstruse metaphysics seems to hint at Coleridge's physical addiction. His cousin Villiers's habit of waiting on him 'as an inferior spirit may attend on an archangel' recalls not only Lamb's description of Coleridge as resembling 'an Arch angel a little damaged' (an image repeated in Hazlitt's 'anticipatory review' of Coleridge's *The Statesman's Manual*), but also the image of the 'sage' of Highgate later evoked by Carlyle.[33] Like Carlyle's memoir of Coleridge, Shelley's description of this feverish, incomprehensible, and idolized genius may be at least partly ironic, and Veeder highlights her later comment that 'the quick alternations of [Saville's] gaiety and seriousness were often ludicrous from their excess' (L 170 [II. xi]).[34] Rather than characterizing his behaviour in general, however, this quality is in fact the first symptom of the breakdown of his marriage to Clorinda, and most of Shelley's references to Saville are unambiguously positive, implying substantial admiration for, and sympathy with, the advocates of Romantic idealism, and especially with Coleridge.[35]

Her suggestion in an earlier passage of *Lodore* that every individual is the 'slave' of a natural law which 'crushes' all who seek to resist it, however, seems hyperbolically to invert the Romantics' celebrations of transcendence and individual freedom, and implicitly associates them with the destructive forms of self-indulgence demonstrated by Lodore. Her enthusiastic description of Saville's philosophy and the consolations of Romantic thought which Coleridge also illustrates, therefore, do not seem to imply an identification with Romantic idealism in general, but rather with those aspects of it whose dependence on experiences of loss or disappointment parallels Shelley's creative compensation for her own misfortunes.[36] The aspect of Romanticism she most vividly illustrates in *Lodore* is precisely that evoked by the passage from Wordsworth quoted in my epigraph – namely a sense of the power of sympathy, thought, and creative endeavour to alleviate those sufferings which, in Wordsworth's vision as in hers, the progress of life seemed inevitably to generate.

Notes

Earlier versions of this essay were presented at 'Beyond Frankenstein' (University of Bristol, February 1997) and 'Mary Shelley: 'Parents, Peers, Progeny' (APU and OU, Cambridge, September 1997).

1. 'Ode: Intimations of Immortality from Recollections of Early Childhood', lines 176-87, *The Poetical Works of William Wordsworth*, eds E. de Selincourt and Helen Darbishire, 5 vols (Oxford: Oxford University Press, 1940-49) IV, p. 284; hereafter *WPW*.
2. Mary Poovey, 'My Hideous Progeny: Mary Shelley and the Feminization of Romanticism', *PMLA*, 95 (1980) 332-4.
3. Ibid., p. 336. The comparison with Schopenhauer is my own, yet is clearly suggested by Poovey's phrase. See, for example, Christopher Janaway, *Schopenhauer* (Oxford: Oxford University Press, 1994) pp. 83-6.
4. Mary Poovey, 'My Hideous Progeny', pp. 332-3, 344-6.
5. See also Anne K. Mellor, *Romanticism and Gender* (London: Routledge, 1993) pp. 65-6, 85-90, 96.
6. Martin Willis, 'Frankenstein and the Soul', *Essays in Criticism*, 45.1 (1995) 28-9 and 33-4.
7. See especially the descriptions of Fanny Derham and Horatio Saville in *Lodore* 79 and 113-14 [I.xiv, II.ii]) and of Elizabeth Raby in *Falkner* 39 [I.vi], discussed below. Shelley's descriptions of Fanny and Elizabeth are also discussed in William Veeder, *Mary Shelley and Frankenstein: the Fate of Androgyny* (Chicago: Chicago University Press, 1986) pp. 159-61, hereafter Veeder.
8. And also, of course, in 'Tintern Abbey', which, as James Averill notes, dramatizes a process of 'compensation for the passing of youthful vision' which 'has specifically to do with the imagination's projections of human suffering', and hence, I would argue, is particularly analogous to Shelley's vision in her later novels. See especially *WPW* II, p. 261, lines 83-92, and James H. Averill, *Wordsworth and the Poetry of Human Suffering* (Ithaca, NY: Cornell University Press, 1980) p. 236.
9. *WPW* II, p. 260, lines 33-5. See also, for example, Wordsworth's celebration of the benevolent patrician Beaupuy, to whose democratic ideals he attaches only a secondary importance compared with his commitment to 'human welfare' and the service of the poor. (William Wordsworth, *The Prelude 1799, 1805, 1850: Authoritative Texts, Context and Reception*, eds Jonathan Wordsworth, M.H. Abrams, Stephen Gill [New York: Norton, 1979] pp. 328-9 and 338-9)
10. See, however, P.B. Shelley's ambivalent view of contemporary science in *A Defence of Poetry* (*Shelley's Prose: or, The Trumpet of a Prophecy*, ed. David Lee Clark [London: Fourth Estate, 1988] p. 293), hereafter *Shelley's Prose*.

178 *The Contemporary Scene*

11. For Coleridge's descriptions of the palliative effects of philosophical effort see especially 'Dejection', lines 87–93, *Poetical Works*, ed. E. H. Coleridge, 2 vols (Oxford: Oxford University Press, 1912) I, p. 367 (hereafter *CPW*), and S.T. Coleridge, *Biographia Literaria*, eds James Engell and W. Jackson Bate, 2 vols (Princeton: Princeton University Press, 1983) I, p. 17. See also Robert Lance Snyder, 'Apocalypse and Indeterminacy in Mary Shelley's *The Last Man*', *Studies in Romanticism*, 17 (1978) 449 on how 'the long process of seeing [*The Last Man*] through to its completion enabled [Shelley] ... to objectify her experience and surmount the dejection accompanying her loss'.
12. See Morton D. Paley, *Coleridge's Later Poetry* (Oxford: Clarendon, 1996) p. 131.
13. For references to Lodore in Wordsworth and Southey, see *WPW* IV, 207 ('Inscriptions' XV: 'For the Spot Where the Hermitage Stood on St Herbert's Island, Derwent Water', where the sound of Lodore is described as accompanying St Herbert's meditations 'on everlasting things'), William Wordsworth, *A Guide Through the District of the Lakes in the North of England* (Malvern: Tantivy Press, [1948]) p. 88n, which mentions Lodore as among the elements of the 'sublimity' surrounding Derwentwater, and Southey's 'The Cataract of Lodore: Described in Rhymes for the Nursery', in *Poems of Robert Southey*, ed. Maurice H. Fitzgerald (London: Henry Frowde, 1909) pp. 348–9. For other instances of allusions by Wordsworth and Coleridge to the Falls of Lodore, see Lisa Vargo's introduction to *Lodore* (Peterborough, Ontario: Broadview, 1997), p. 22.
14. S.T. Coleridge, *Lectures (1808–19) on Literature*, ed. R.A. Foakes, 2 vols (Princeton: Princeton University Press, 1987) I, pp. 34–6.
15. S.T. Coleridge, *Shorter Works and Fragments*, eds H.J. Jackson and J.R. de J. Jackson, 2 vols (Princeton: Princeton University Press, 1995) I, p. 362.
16. See Edmund Burke, *A Philosophical Enquiry into the Origins of our Ideas of the Sublime and Beautiful*, ed. James T. Boulton (Oxford: Blackwell, 1958, 1987) pp. 58–64, and Immanuel Kant, *The Critique of Judgement*, trans. J.C. Meredith (Oxford: Clarendon Press, 1952) pp. 99–105.
17. S. T. Coleridge, *The Friend*, ed. Barbara E. Rooke, 2 vols (Princeton: Princeton University Press, 1969) I, p. 519; hereafter *Friend*. For further images connecting springs and fountains with the 'general Spirit of Life' expressed in human intellect and creativity, see *Collected Letters of Samuel Taylor Coleridge*, ed. E.L. Griggs, 6 vols (Oxford: Clarendon Press, 1956–71) I, p. 349 and III, p. 171. For further evidence of Shelley's acquaintance with *The Friend* (with which she was familiar as early as 1814), see my discussion of Coleridge's 'Ode to Tranquillity' below.
18. See Byron, *Complete Poetical Works*, ed. Jerome J. McGann, 7 vols (Oxford: Clarendon Press, 1980–93) IV, p. 65 (lines 99–100) and IV, p. 472.
19. See *WPW* IV, p. 281, lines 58–76.
20. A point made no less emphatically in Falkner's description of his kidnapping of Alithea as involving an attempt to usurp the power of God; see *FN* 176–7 (II. xi).
21. An extract from Marvell's translation from Seneca emphasizing peaceful retirement rather than flight from sorrow was eventually chosen. Shelley appears to have had difficulty in obtaining an early edition of *The Friend*

Mary Shelley and the Lake Poets 179

which contained the version of 'Ode to Tranquillity' that she wanted; see *MWSL* II, pp. 196–7 and notes, and *CPW* I, p. 361.
22. 'This is indeed the dread punishment attached by nature to habitual vice, that its impulses wax as its motives wane' (*Friend* I, p. 106).
23. See especially Paley, *Coleridge's Later Poetry*, pp. 2–6 on this point; also *CPW* I, pp. 366–7 and Coleridge, *Biographia Literaria*, I, p. 17. The fact that the fragments supposedly reassembled in *The Last Man* were written on 'Sibylline leaves' (*LM* 7 [Introd.]), moreover, clearly encodes a reference to Coleridge, whose volume of that title (published in 1817) was the first in which 'Dejection' appeared.
24. For a strikingly similar passage, see part of Falkner's account of the events preceding his crime:

> Thus was I led to the fatal hour; a life of love, and a sudden bereavement, with *such a thing* the instrument of my ruin! A contempt for the order of the universe, a stern demoniacal braving of fate, because I would rule, and put that right which God had let go wrong.
> (*FN* 177 [II. xi])

25. This passage recalls P.B. Shelley's statement in *A Defence of Poetry* that 'The functions of the poetical faculty are twofold: by one it creates new materials of knowledge, and power, and pleasure; by the other it engenders in the mind a desire to reproduce and arrange them according to a certain rhythm and order' (*Shelley's Prose*, p. 293).
26. See *L* 56 (I.x): 'It is a tragedy ... brought now to its last dark catastrophe. Casimir is my son. We may neither of us murder the other.' See also Kate Ferguson Ellis, 'Subversive Surface: the Limits of Affection in Mary Shelley's Later Fiction' in *Other MS*.
27. Mellor, *Romanticism and Gender*, p. 69.
28. See especially Veeder, pp. 16–17 and pp. 159–61 on this point.
29. See also her reference to 'the earnestness of [Saville's] affections, and the sensibility that nestled itself in his warm heart' (*L* 114 [II. ii]).
30. See *F* 38 (I.iii); Mellor, *Romanticism and Gender*, pp. 29, 89–90, 96.
31. Anna Laetitia Barbauld, 'To Mr [S. T.] Coleridge' (1799), in *Women Romantic Poets*, ed. Jennifer Breen (London: Dent, 1994) pp. 84–5, *CPW* I, p. 367 and Coleridge, *Biographia Literaria* I, p. 17. Shelley's fuller characterization of Saville's metaphysics – 'He had no desire but for knowledge, no thought but for the nobler creations of the soul, and the discernment of the sublime laws of God and nature' (*L* 114 [II. ii]) – makes the connection with Coleridge still clearer.
32. See also Carlyle's description of how, in Coleridge, 'a ray of heavenly inspiration struggled ... with the weakness of flesh and blood', of the 'radiant and moist' face with which he spoke, and of how 'in walking, he rather shuffled than decisively stept' (*The Works of Thomas Carlyle*, ed. H.D. Traill, 30 vols [London: Chapman & Hall, 1896–99] XI, pp. 54–60). Veeder notes that Saville's 'tall ... thin and shadowy' figure, together with his imaginative detachment and the sound of his voice, all recall aspects of P.B. Shelley (Veeder, pp. 74–5). Yet, I would argue, other factors make the analogy with Coleridge more prominent.

180 *The Contemporary Scene*

33. Shelley, who had been acquainted with both Lamb and Hazlitt, is likely to have been aware of their characterizations of Coleridge. As Edwin Marrs points out, Lamb's description (in a letter to Wordsworth) quotes ironically from Milton's description of Satan in *Paradise Lost*, I.589–99; see *The Letters of Charles and Mary Lamb*, ed. Edwin W. Marrs, Jr, 3 vols (Ithaca: Cornell University Press, 1975–78) III, pp. 215, 217n. For Hazlitt's version of the same image see *The Complete Works of William Hazlitt*, ed. P.P. Howe, 21 vols (London: Dent, 1930–34) VII, p. 118. The phrase 'anticipatory review' occurs in *The Letters of Charles and Mary Lamb* III, p. 198. For Coleridge as the sage of Highgate, see *The Works of Thomas Carlyle* XI, pp. 52–3.
34. Quoted in Veeder, p. 68. The paragraph from which Veeder takes this comment also describes Saville as having 'a tact, a delicacy, a kind of electric sympathy in his disposition, that endeared him to everyone that approached him' (*L* 169 [II. xi]).
35. I would also argue that her political views were not far apart from those of Coleridge in the 1830s; Shelley, though still classing herself as a friend to liberalism, had made an ideological journey from youthful radicalism towards conservatism analogous to that made by Coleridge. See, for example, her well-known critique of Political Radicalism in a journal-entry of October 1838 (*MWSJ* II, p. 554–5).
36. See especially Thomas McFarland, *Paradoxes of Freedom: the Romantic Mystique of a Transcendence* (Oxford: Oxford University Press, 1996) pp. 37–8 and pp. 61–2 on these aspects of Coleridge and Wordsworth.

11
Lodore: a Tale of the Present Time?

Fiona Stafford

Only in very recent years has Shelley's fifth novel, *Lodore*, begun to receive anything resembling sustained critical attention. Although greeted enthusiastically by its first reviewers in 1835, and subsequently scrutinized by scholars in search of biographical insights into Percy Bysshe Shelley, it remained out of print for much of the twentieth century. However, with two scholarly editions now in print, one in paperback,[1] it is becoming one of the chief beneficiaries of the increased interest in and availability of Shelley's work. This interest had been growing steadily since the late 1970s, with the emergence of feminist criticism and, more specifically, the new editions of Shelley's better known novels, her *Letters* and her *Journals*. As she has ceased to be seen as a 'one-book' woman, or merely as an appendage to her husband, recent studies such as those by Anne K. Mellor and Katherine Hill-Miller have been willing to move beyond *Frankenstein* to explore the treatment of family dynamics or the 'sexual education' of women in the later fiction.[2] *Lodore* has proved to be particularly amenable to such readings.

But, as with *Frankenstein*, it is fruitful to extend the consideration of politics in *Lodore* beyond issues of gender and to address others raised by the novel's engagement with current affairs. This is especially pertinent, given the period in which *Lodore* was written. While it would not be altogether true to say that critics have been unaware of this dimension, it has not yet received full recognition. Since Shelley began her novel in the early months of 1831, and was describing it as 'nearly finished' in January 1833 (*MWSL* II, p. 183), its composition coincided with one of the most significant periods of British political history. In a letter of December 1830, immediately preceding that in which she makes the first reference to *Lodore*, Shelley described the current state of turmoil: 'The people *will* be redressed – will the Aristocrats sacrifice enough to tranquillize them – if they will not – we must be revolutionized'(ibid., p. 124). During the summer, France had 'redeemed her name'; and the news of the July Revolution meant that pressure for Parliamentary Reform in Britain was becoming intense. With the accession of William IV, and the collapse of the old Tory government, it seemed that at last the iniquities of the electoral system might be redressed. Although Lord John Russell's Bill was to meet with determined opposition, violent revolution was avoided and the Reform Act finally passed in June 1832.

When Shelley completed her novel, she planned to call it 'Lodore – a tale of the present time',[3] and although the subtitle was subsequently dropped, it affords valuable insight into her attitude to the work in 1833. Unlike *Valperga* and *Perkin Warbeck*, which had adopted carefully researched historical settings, or *The Last Man*'s futuristic vision of the 21st century, *Lodore* is set in the early 1830s and fixed firmly by internal details. The first chapter reveals that the birth of the eponymous Henry Fitzhenry, Lord Lodore, had occurred at about the time of his father's promotion to the aristocracy, 'towards the close of the American War' and that when the action of the novel opens, he has 'reached the mature age of fifty' (*L* 6, 8). Lisa Vargo has noted that Lodore goes to 'the Illinois' in about 1818, the year in which Morris Birkbeck published his popular *Letters from Illinois*.[4] Further details are scattered throughout the text to confirm that the fictional account is meant to coincide roughly with the period of composition between 1831 and 1833, even though descriptions of the major public events are generally avoided.

It is possible to regard the contemporary setting as nothing more than an attempt by Shelley to capitalize on the prevailing popularity of novels describing fashionable London life. Since the mid-1820s her publisher, Henry Colburn, had been flooding the market with 'silver-fork' fiction, which revelled in representations of the family relationships, financial fluctuations, marital successes and failures of English high society. Edward Bulwer's *Pelham* of 1828 was perhaps the single best-selling work of this kind, but dominating the genre was undoubtedly Catherine Gore who, between 1830 and 1833, produced *Women as They Are, or the Manners of the Day*, *Pin Money*, *The Tuileries*, *Mothers and Daughters: a Tale of the Year 1830*, *The Opera*, *The Fair of May Fair*, *The Sketch Book of Fashion*, and *Polish Tales*, each in three volumes. Although *Lodore* can be linked to earlier fiction, and explicitly evokes a host of well-known English poems and plays through its epigraphs and allusions, Shelley's depictions of the English aristocracy in contemporary London, complete with references to Almack's, the King's Theatre and a network of West End streets, has obvious affinities with the work of her popular contemporaries.

The desire to conform to the popular taste of the day, however, was not merely a question of following fashion or courting respectability. The extreme difficulties that beset the contemporary book trade resulted in great pressure being put on writers to produce something saleable in order to be published at all. In August 1831, Shelley offered various ideas to John Murray to be considered for a possible volume in his 'Family Library', but none was accepted. Over Christmas, she worked on the manuscript of her friend Edward John Trelawny's *Adventures of a Younger Son*, advising him to remove 'Certain words & phrases', and even entire scenes, for fear of putting off a potential publisher, commenting:

> The burnings – the alarms – the absorbing politics of the day render booksellers almost averse to publishing at all – God knows how it will all end, but it looks as if the Autocrats would have the good sense to make the necessary sacrifices to a starving people.
>
> (*MWSL* II, p. 120)

Despite her sympathy for the 'starving people', the very unrest that helped create the pressure for Parliamentary Reform was also contributing to the virtual paralysis of the booktrade. As Alan Horsman has commented: 'In 1832, writers, from Wordsworth down, found that anxiety about the state of the realm limited public interest in imaginative literature.'[5] The massive political uncertainties made booksellers excessively cautious about investing in new fiction, while the terrible decline of Sir Walter Scott, worn out by overwork after the collapse of Constable and Co. in 1826, seemed a frightening symbol of the current plight of the contemporary writer.

For if the book trade was suffering from what Thomas Dibdin described as 'Bibliophobia' ('Fear is the order of the day ... the fear of Reform, of Cholera, and of BOOKS'),[6] the prospects for those dependent on writing for their own survival was even bleaker. In 1831, Shelley had to support not only herself as a widow, but also Percy Florence, who had now reached the age of 11 and was just starting at Harrow. Her applications to her father-in-law, Sir Timothy Shelley, were unsuccessful, and within a year she was forced to contemplate moving out of London, in order to reduce her own expenses and thus meet those of her son.[7] Nor could she expect any help from her father, William Godwin, who was in fact a further source of financial anxiety, as she confessed to Charles Ollier in the very letter announcing her intention to embark on *Lodore*:

> I have been considering what you say – and I feel sure that you will think I do wisely in giving up any idea of making a proposal now. According to the account you give, things can never be worse than now – unless London were on fire – Meanwhile I will write the novel as I proposed – You will kindly be on the *look out for me* & if a *lucky moment* occur you may bring my book forward as being in hand – Or when it is done as you approve the plan, I shall as usual depend on your good offices for bringing it forwards, & making the requisite arrangments. Do you agree with me that this is the best way?
>
> I am very anxious about Trelawny's – You will let me know something about it as soon as you can –
>
> Do you think that in any arrangement for the Ct Journal I could take a part? – It has struck me several times that I might do something in that way. Frankly what you tell me of the state of things, of the truth of which there are too many signs fills me with disquietude for my Father, who depends on his pen – And I should be so glad to be doing anything that was a certain gain – If I knew *what was wanted*, if any thing is wanted, I think I could be of service – I would engage for an <essay> Article every week – either a light one or on any given subject that was wanted – Will you propose this to Bentley I should be very much obliged to you –
>
> (*MWSL* II, p. 125)

Lodore was thus conceived in response to circumstances that seemed to threaten not only Shelley and her immediate family but also the entire literary world of 1831. To see it as a cynical attempt at popular fiction, as a book written purely for the marketplace, is however, to miss many of the more subtle and interesting ways in which it reflects 'the present time'.

Lodore is, not surprisingly, a book preoccupied with money – and especially with the difficulties arising for those who find themselves suddenly bereft of financial support – but in addition to the obvious biographical resonances, the concern is typical of the period in which it was written. As Edward Bulwer observed in his contemporary analysis *England and the English*, the fashionable novels of the third decade were in themselves symptoms of the 'moral spirit of the age' since they represented a blurring of traditional class boundaries:

> In proportion as the aristocracy had become social, and fashion allowed the members of the more mediocre classes a hope to outstep the boundaries of fortune, and be quasi-aristocrats themselves, people eagerly sought for representations of the manners which they aspired to imitate, and the circles to which it was not impossible to belong.
>
> (*England and the English*, p. 287)[8]

Rather than expressing sympathy with the upper echelons of society, however, Bulwer perceived in such novels signs of serious discontent:

> Few writers ever produced so great an effect on the political spirit of their generation as some of these novelists, who, without any other merit, unconsciously exposed the falsehood, the hypocrisy, the arrogant and vulgar insolence of patrician life.
>
> (Ibid., p. 288)

Silver-fork fiction, in Bulwer's eyes, was by no means frivolous escapism, but rather an inherently political genre, its power arising from the very popularity enjoyed among readers beyond the social sector it depicted:

> Read by all classes, in every town, in every village, these works ... could not but engender a mingled indignation and disgust at the parade of frivolity, the ridiculous disdain of truth, nature, and mankind, the self-consequence and absurdity, which, falsely or truly, these novels exhibited as a picture of aristocratic society.
>
> (Ibid., p. 288)

Bulwer found the fiction of the 1820s and 1830s packed with evidence of a corrupt aristocracy, whose influence could be seen infecting the whole of British society. The 'lively novels' of Mrs Gore, for example, gave a 'just and unexaggerated picture of the intrigues, the manoeuvres, the plotting and counterplotting' that characterized the peculiarly English practice of 'marketing' unmarried women, itself an effect of the national obsession with wealth and titles (*England and the English*, pp. 85–6).

Shelley's unsympathetic portrayal of Lady Santerre, the 'oily flatterer' whose desperation to marry off her daughter and thus escape a penniless widowhood, appears to accord well with Bulwer's denunciation of the contemporary custom of 'open match-making' which 'encourages the spirit of insincerity among all women, – "Mothers and Daughters," – a spirit that consists in perpetual scheming, and perpetual hypocrisy' (pp. 85–6). It is, after all, Lady Santerre who initially orchestrates the marriage between Cornelia and Lord Lodore and subsequently ruins it by constant interference and fixed resistance to her daughter's desire to accompany her husband and their child into exile in America.

Despite the apparent conformity to popular literary trends, however, it is clear that Shelley's conception of the 'mothers and daughters' in *Lodore* was not confined to her portrayal of Lady Santerre and Cornelia, but concentrated much more strongly on the relationship between Lady Lodore and her lost daughter, Ethel. In a letter of January 1833 to Ollier, she described her new novel in the following way:

> A Mother & Daughter are the heroines – The Mother who after safrifising [sacrificing] all to the world at first – afterwards makes sacrifises not less entire, for her child – finding all to be Vanity, except the genuine affections of the heart. In the daughter I have tried to pourtray in its simplicity, & all the beauty I could muster, the devotion of a young woman for the husband of her choice – The disasters she goes through being described – & their result in awakening her Mother's affection, bringing about the conclusion of the tale.
>
> (*MWSL* II, p. 185)

If *Lodore* drew on the current of modern society novels, its criticism of the English aristocracy was by no means as incidental as Bulwer's account of the genre implies; Shelley appears to have set up the caricatured figure of the scheming Lady Santerre largely to form a contrast with the self-sacrifice that eventually results from her daughter's love for her own child. Through the mask of silver-fork fiction, it is thus possible to discern not only a serious attempt to explore the deepest human emotions, but also an underlying conviction that despite the fear of poverty, 'a tyrant, whose laws are more terrible than those of Draco', love is ultimately more powerful than money (*L* 40–1 [I. vii]). While *Lodore* is very much a 'tale of the present time', in both its adoption of the most popular contemporary genre of fiction, and in its

'*Lodore*': *a Tale of the Present Time?* 187

preoccupation with the pernicious effects of the British class system, it nevertheless retains a belief in the power of the suffering individual, and in transcendent human values, that harks back to the literature of the Romantic period.

The depiction of Lodore himself is fraught with ambiguity; for although the first volume suggests strong criticism of the aristocracy, there are also indications of a less severe attitude that seems to complicate any overt political message. The opening pages of the novel are hardly complimentary to the family of Fitzhenry, whose influence on the village of Longfield is quite disproportionate to their 'moderate income of fifteen hundred a-year', and has developed only because of its remote location 'in the flattest and least agreeable part of the county of Essex'. Nor is the family's influence on the village merely a question of social status; and the comment that 'half of it belonged to them, the whole voted according to their wishes' is particularly barbed, given the abolition of Pocket Boroughs in the Reform Act (*L* 6, 5 [I. i]).[9] The political dimension is further emphasized by the recent creation of the peerage. Rather than being an ancient aristocratic line, the title has been bestowed on Fitzhenry's father for services in the American war, but it is also made clear that his successful naval career had depended on his own father's services to the government: 'In a contested election, his father was the means of insuring the success of the government candidate, and the promotion of his son followed' (*L* 6 [I. i]). Indeed, Shelley's creation of Lord Lodore has elements in common with Bulwer's description of 'The Aristocracy' published in 1832, which included an account of the 'usurer' whose wealth enabled him to purchase the rotten borough of Old Sarum, and thus to attract first the interest of the Prime Minister and then a baronetcy.[10] Bulwer's attack on the new class of 'gentlemen', whose titles have been acquired through wealth rather than honour, and whose children are 'taught to detest being called the son of a rich merchant, and to aspire to become the devoted and inseparable friend of the profligate and spendthrift peer', finds abundant support in the story of Henry Fitzhenry, whose father's newly acquired title renders him 'a demigod among the villagers' (*L* 29 [I. v]). He is educated at Eton and Oxford where he befriends Derham, 'the younger son of a rich and aristocratic family', but leaves the university without a degree, gripped by 'the mania of travelling' (*L* 33 [I. vi]). Even after the death of his father, the new Lord Lodore fails to remain on his estate, and after years on the Continent, returns to Britain filled with 'gnawing discontent; energy rebuked and tamed into mere disquietude, for want of a proper object'

(*L* 38 [I. vii]). It is largely boredom and inactivity that allow him to be inveigled into the disastrous marriage to Cornelia Santerre, and the unfulfilling life of theatres and party-going in London.

As a comment on the English aristocracy, the portrayal of Lord Lodore's career could hardly be less positive. Nor is Shelley content with making moral comments through the voice of the narrator, for the consequences of Fitzhenry's misspent youth are rapidly embodied in the figure of his illegitimate son, Count Casimir, who appears in London and forms a close friendship with the beautiful young Lady Lodore. An intense confrontation follows, but although Lodore strikes Casimir in public, he refuses to meet his son in a duel and is forced to flee the country in disgrace. In America, he becomes part of a community founded on a basis entirely different from the class-ridden society of Britain, and although he retains a degree of isolation from the rest of the settlers in the Illinois, he gradually learns to appreciate their qualities:

> Personal courage, honesty, and frankness, were to be found among the men; simplicity and kindness among the women. He saw instances of love and devotion in members of families, that made him sigh to be one of them; and the strong sense and shrewd observations of many of the elder settlers exercised his understanding.
>
> (*L* 13 [I. ii])

Despite the peace of the Illinois, however, when his teenage daughter, Ethel, begins to attract admirers, Lodore reacts impulsively and decides to return to Britain. In New York, his past rears up once again, as he overhears an American giving a mocking account of his own quarrel with Casimir, and in the ensuing duel, Lodore is killed.

In the context of 1832, Lodore's story can be read as a moral tale, emphasizing the evils consequent upon an irresponsible life of idle self-indulgence. The position of privilege, acquired through inheritance rather than merit, spoils a man of considerable natural ability and leads ultimately to his premature death. The situations of his daughter, wife, and sister, too, left with little financial and no moral support, also seem to demonstrate that the consequences of Lodore's shortcomings reach far beyond his own self-destructive career. The very circumstances of Lodore's death are also loaded with significance, since the duel was a symbol of aristocratic society. By the early nineteenth century, the combined forces of evangelism and utilitarianism had begun to render duelling a relic of the feudal past in which the ruling élite had regarded themselves as above the law, guided instead by misplaced notions of honour.[11] To depict an English Lord being killed in a duel by an American thus had particular meaning in the context of the Reform movement, especially since Lodore's life exactly spans the period between the end of the War of Independence and the great Act of 1832. It is as if his personal history links the two public events, the fatal duel representing the eventual victory of democracy over a degenerate aristocracy. Indeed, the very title awarded to his father in the fight against American freedom proves the ultimate downfall of Lodore, not only as a result of the pride it engenders, but because it is the thought of the title that triggers the provocative words of his opponent, Hatfield:

> 'Lodore!' cried one of the by-standers; 'Fitzhenry was the name of the man who took the Oronooko.'
> 'Aye, Fitzhenry it was,' said Hatfield, 'Lodore is his nickname. King George's bit of gilt gingerbread, which mightily pleased the sapient mariner. An Englishman thinks himself honoured when he changes one name for another. Admiral Fitzhenry was the scum of the earth – Lord Lodore a pillar of state. Pity that infamy should so soon have blackened the glorious title!'
>
> (*L* 90 [I. xvi])

In Britain, the title had transformed the family of Fitzhenry, because of the elevation in social status; but in the eyes of the republican, the change was nothing but a false veneer, hiding the real nature of the man beneath the name. Ironically, it is Hatfield's mocking speech, describing the 'infamy' of the confrontation with Casimir Lyzinski, that makes Fitzhenry resume his title for the first time in 12 years, with an assertiveness reminiscent of Hamlet in the fifth act: 'I am Lord Lodore!' (*L* 90 [I. xvi]). Any beneficial effects gained from the settlement in the Illinois are instantly erased, as Lodore announces his title and dies.

Lodore, 'a tale of the present time' can thus be read not merely as a novel suited to the taste of the day, and packed with contemporary detail, but as a much more profound reflection on recent political history. Just as the narratives of *Frankenstein* and *The Last Man* have been interpreted as imaginative responses to the French Revolution and its aftermath,[12] so *Lodore* can be seen, in part at least, as an allegory of the Reform Movement. The problem with such a reading, however, is that the novel is much more complicated than the paraphrase and selective quotation above might imply. For although Lodore is heavily criticized, with his wealth, title, character and prejudices all shown up as destructive to himself and his family, he is also the most interesting and powerful character in the novel. His childhood may be excessively privileged, but he is also:

> a fine, bold, handsome boy – generous, proud, and daring; he was remembered, when as a youth he departed for the continent, as riding fearlessly the best hunter in the field, and attracting the admiration of the village maidens at church by his tall elegant figure and dark eyes; or, when he chanced to accost them, by a nameless fascination of manner, joined to a voice whose thrilling silver tones stirred the listener's heart unaware.
>
> (*L* 7 [I. i])

At Eton, too, the criticism of the 'self-idolizing boy' is balanced by his heroic protection of the sensitive Derham, whom he rescues from corporal punishment, thus incurring his own expulsion. Lodore's faults are serious enough, but Shelley's strategy is not to invite ridicule, so much as sympathy and regret. He is a Byronic figure, and his very title – so disastrous in terms of the narrative – nevertheless associates him with the great forces of the natural world. Although the idea is not made explicit, waterfalls resound in the background of the first volume of the novel, because the cataract of Lodore was one of the great attractions of the English Lake district in the early 19th century. It is only in America, shortly before his death, however, that the connection emerges, as Lodore confronts Niagara, 'that vast and celebrated cataract, whose everlasting and impetuous flow mirrored the dauntless but rash energy of his own soul' (*L* 81 [I. xiv]).

The idea of Lodore as an embodiment of natural energy seems far from Hatfield's perception of the corrupt aristocrat, and so by the time that their encounter takes place, the reader's sympathies are fully engaged by the Romantic figure of the English nobleman. The narrator's comment on duelling, too, gives little sense that the conflict results from Lodore's aristocratic code of honour, but seems rather a sign of American backwardness:

> Duels, that sad relic of feudal barbarism, were more frequent then than now in America; at all times they are more fatal and more openly carried on there than in this country.
>
> (*L* 90 [I. xvi])

The association of America with feudal barbarism seems oddly contradictory to the natural equality depicted in the Illinois, and yet towards even this apparently idyllic community, there are hints of a less positive attitude. For although Lodore's image of himself as a 'china vase' threatened by 'collision with the brazen ones around' (*L* 13 [I. ii]), seems indicative of his self-alienating pride,[13] the explicit allusions to *The Tempest* seem to equate Lodore and Ethel with Prospero and Miranda, while the American settlers are cast as Calibans.

Shelley's knowledge of America was very different from her firsthand experience of Italy, and must have been influenced by conversation with people who had visited the country, and by accounts published by British writers. Although she may have developed a favourable impression from the reports of friends such as the social reformer, Frances Wright, or Edward Trelawny, who was 'America-mad',[14] as well as from liberal journalists who looked to the United States as a symbol of democracy, the early 1830s also saw a wave of writing on America that was rather less enthusiastic. Indeed, Thomas Hamilton's *Men and Manners in America* (1833) was written in alarm at the admiration of America displayed by British reformers:

> I found the institutions and experience of the United States deliberately quoted in the reformed Parliament, as affording a safe precedent for British legislature, and learned that the drivellers who uttered such nonsense, instead of encountering merited derision, were listened to with patience and approbation, by men as ignorant as themselves.[15]

In response to such attitudes, Hamilton set out to expose the misconception of America as 'the land of liberty and equality', by giving a detailed account of his own perceptions of American society: 'there is as much practical equality in Liverpool as New York. The magnates of the Exchange do not strut less proudly in the latter city than in the former; nor are there wives and daughters more backward in supporting their pretensions. In such matters legislative enactments can do nothing' (p. 65). Frances Trollope was similarly struck by the inequalities she witnessed in the United States, and beneath her apparent snobbery about 'Domestic manners', is a real sense of injustice at the fate of the native Americans and, even worse, of slaves:

> The effect produced upon English people by the sight of slavery in every direction is very new, and not very agreeable, and it is not the

less powerfully felt from hearing upon every breeze the mocking words 'All men are born free and equal'.[16]

Any idea of America leading the world to a better system of government, and with it to universal liberty and equality, seemed seriously flawed in the light of the growing consciousness of social inequality in the United States.

The problems articulated in *Lodore* are thus typical of British experience in the early 1830s, when the existing social structure was clearly unjust and out of date, but alternative models seemed inadequate and unattractive. The story of Lord Lodore contains not only a political allegory of Reform, but also a lingering attachment to the past, and an attraction to the Romantic heroism that seemed threatened by the brave new world of legal equality. For although he disappears from the novel after the first volume, 'his memory is the presiding genius of his daughter's life, and the name of Lodore contains for her a spell that dignifies existence in her own eyes' (*L* 312 [III, Conclusion]).

Shelley's reasons for abandoning her subtitle are not recorded, and may reflect nothing more than the delay between completion and publication, which lessened its immediacy. Whatever the reason, however, her comment on the change is strangely appropriate to the complicated feelings engendered by the Reform Act of 1832. In a letter to Ollier she suggested that he ask Godwin about the title, commenting 'He has a very good judgement about Titles, & might make some lucky suggestion. – "A Tale of the Present Times" does not quite please me yet what exchange it for?' (*MWSL* II, p. 206). By 1834, titles of all kinds no longer semed to please the British public. But it was not clear how the British aristocracy with their inherited wealth and names were to be replaced, or indeed, whether the new world ushered in by the Reform Act promised any real improvement on the old.

Notes

A version of this essay was read at 'Mary Shelley: Parents, Peers, Progeny' (APU and OU, Cambridge, September 1997) and another was published in *Romanticism*, 3.2. (1997) 209–19.

1. The paperback here referred to is Lisa Vargo's admirable edition of *Lodore* (Peterborough, Ontario: Broadview Press, 1997), which appeared after my original essay was written (hereafter, Vargo).

'Lodore': a Tale of the Present Time? 193

2. See Mellor (1988); Katherine C. Hill-Miller, 'My Hideous Progeny': Mary Shelley, William Godwin, and the Father–Daughter Relationship (Newark and London: Associated University Presses, 1995); see also Kate Ferguson Ellis, 'Subversive Surfaces: The Limits of Domestic Affection in Mary Shelley's Later Fiction', in Other MS (1993) and Vargo's introduction to Lodore, especially pp. 29–39.
3. To Charles Ollier, 21 November 1833, MWSL II, p. 196.
4. Vargo, pp. 27–8.
5. Alan Horsman, The Victorian Novel (Oxford: Clarendon Press, 1990) p. 2.
6. Thomas Dibdin, Remarks on the Present Languid and Depressed State of Literature and the Book Trade (London, 1832) p. 9.
7. See her letter to William Whitton, 24 January 1832 (MWSL II, p. 153).
8. Edward Bulwer, England and the English (1833), rpt ed Standish Meacham (Chicago and London: University of Chicago Press, 1970).
9. See P. Brantlinger, The Spirit of Reform: British Literature and Politics, 1832–1867 (Cambridge, Mass. and London: Harvard University Press, 1977); A. Briggs, The Age of Improvement, 1783–1867, rev. edn (London and New York: Longman, 1979).
10. 'The Aristocracy', New Monthly Magazine, xxxv (August 1832) 164–5.
11. V.G. Kiernan, The Duel in European History (Oxford: Oxford University Press, 1989) pp. 204–42; J. Kelly, 'That Damn'd Thing Called Honour': Duelling in Ireland 1570–1860 (Cork: Cork University Press, 1995) pp. 223–77.
12. See for example, Lee Sterrenburg, 'The Last Man: An Anatomy of Failed Revolutions', Nineteenth Century Fiction, 33 (1978) 324–47; 'Mary Shelley's Monster: Politics and Psyche in Frankenstein', The Endurance of Frankenstein, eds G. Levine and U.C. Knoepflmacher (Berkeley: University of California Press, 1979) pp. 143–71; Pamela Clemit, The Godwinian Novel: the Rational Fictions of Godwin, Brockden Brown, Mary Shelley (Oxford: Clarendon Press, 1993); Paul A. Cantor, Creature and Creator: Myth-making and English Romanticism (Cambridge: Cambridge University Press, 1984).
13. The allusion is to Aesop's fable of the vases, one of china, one of brass, washed away in a storm; see 'The Two Jars' in William Godwin, Fables, Ancient and Modern, 2 vols (London, 1805) II, pp. 112–16.
14. So described in a letter to Maria Gisborne, 24 August 1832 (MWSL II, p. 171). Mary Shelley met Frances Wright in 1827 and corresponded with her regularly during the period when Lodore was being written.
15. Thomas Hamilton, Men and Manners in America (Philadelphia, 1833), preface.
16. Frances Trollope, Domestic Manners of the Americans, 2 vols (London, 1832) II, p. 15. Although, as Betty Bennett has pointed out (MWSL II, pp. xxi–xxii), Shelley disapproved of Trollope's attack on Frances Wright, she may have been influenced by other aspects of the account. A later reference to 'Mrs Trollope's description of the Americans' in Rambles in Germany and Italy (London, 1844) is in its context suggestive of some degree of endorsement of Trollope (TW 149 [Rambles I, Letter xii, p. 143]).

Part IV
The Parental Legacy

12
The Corpse in the Corpus: *Frankenstein*, Rewriting Wollstonecraft and the Abject

Marie Mulvey-Roberts

> Abjection ... is an alchemy that transforms death drive into a start of life, of new significance.
> (Julia Kristeva, *Powers of Horror*)[1]

> For we think back through our mothers if we are women.
> (Virginia Woolf, *A Room of One's Own*)[2]

Frankenstein has been frequently read as the hideous progeny of a number of parenting texts written by Mary Shelley's actual parents, Mary Wollstonecraft and William Godwin. Such readings take the monstrosity of the book beyond Victor Frankenstein's scientific ingenuity with the decomposing parts of corpses to Shelley's literary ingenuity in recomposing parts of the corpus of her parents' texts into the body of her own (monstrous) text. I have chosen to dwell in this essay on the process of recomposition of the mother's texts,[3] invoking Julia Kristeva's theory of abjection to show how *Frankenstein* – and other items in the corpus of Shelley's works – reinscribe the horror of the equation between birth and decay, the maternal body and the mother's cadaver. But this corpus is not only a monstrous patchwork quilt of the mother's writings. It functions as a palimpsest on which Shelley wrote a narrative of exhumation, purification, rebirth, and reunion.

For Kristeva, the maternal body and the infant to which it has given birth may both be symptoms of 'the abject'. The abject simultaneously attracts and repels the subject who, in order to take up a symbolic position as a speaking subject, must disavow modes of corporeality, especially in what is deemed 'unacceptable, unclean or anti-social'.[4] The subject must, therefore, disown part of itself. This may be applicable whether the mother's body is 'unclean' in the aftermath of birth or decaying in death, whether the infant is alive or still-born. The abject, according to Kristeva, can never be completely exiled or fully obliterated but persists in occupying the boundaries of a subject's identity. It threatens the apparent unity of the subject with disruption or possible dissolution, becoming a space, an abyss at the borders of the subject's identity, a hole into which the subject may fall. Punning on the Latin verb *cadere* 'to fall' and 'cadaver', Kristeva expatiates on how bodily wastes must fall or be cast out in order for life to continue.

The corpse, the supreme examplar of the abject, is described by Kristeva, as:

> the most sickening of wastes ... a border that has encroached upon everything.... It is death infecting life. Abject. It is something rejected from which one does not part, from which one does not protect oneself as from an object. Imaginary uncanniness and real threat, it beckons to us and ends up engulfing us.
>
> (Kristeva, pp. 3–4)

The suppression of the maternal body sets up the conditions for writing. As Helga Geyer-Ryan, a critic influenced by Kristeva's thought, has written: 'The resurrection of the maternal body from the pre-Oedipal space would ... always be the presentation of a corpse lying concealed beneath the appearance.'[5]

Not only is the cadaver or maternal body the abject; so too is the placenta, the life-blood link between mother and infant, malfunctioning of which is also one of the causes of puerperal fever. 'Frozen placenta, live limb of a skeleton, monstrous graft of life on myself, a living dead. Life ... death ... undecideable', writes Kristeva.[6] In a section in *Powers of Horror* entitled 'Life? A Death', she refers to Ignaz Semmelweis's observation that 'puerperal fever is the result of the female genitalia being contaminated by a corpse; here then is a fever where what bears life passes over to the side of the dead body' (Kristeva, pp. 3–4).

Shelley's sense of her own birth as writing her mother's death warrant, it has often been observed, underwrites the production of *Frankenstein*. For Mary Wollstonecraft, the maternal body, at the moment when it gave birth to the future Mary Shelley, was also soon to be the dying body. In post-parturition, the inability of

Wollstonecraft's body to expel the placenta spelled death from puerperal fever. Mrs Blenkensop, the midwife Wollstonecraft had chosen, was willing to use nature's method and wait for the spontaneous expulsion of the placenta. After two hours, as this had not taken place, she urged Godwin to call in a male practitioner. He summoned Dr Lewis Poignand who carried out an emergency procedure involving the manual removal of the placenta. Whether infection, which led to septicaemia and the onset of death, was introduced by this intervention, or was due to another cause, is disputed,[7] but the important point is that the retained placenta was seen as the initiating factor by the practitioners concerned. What nourishes the foetus, in this case, is seen here as eventually killing the mother 11 days after childbirth.

In Shelley's work we find a similar paradox: that which gives life also kills. The abject hovers on the borders of the *Frankenstein* text in which the monster can be read as a spectre of the maternal body as well as Frankenstein's monstrous child. *Frankenstein* is a parasitic text, being both necrophobic and necrophiliac, that feeds off the nurturing parenting texts that have given it life. Shelley's fears of being subsumed by the identity of her mother – since the subject must keep the abject at a distance in order to define itself as a subject – is also a resistance to being swallowed up by her mother's texts. At the same time, the daughter wishes, while still retaining her identity, to retain a life-blood link to her mother's body, and maternity provides a partial resolution to this conflict of desire. Kristeva claims that maternity positions woman in a kind of corporeal contiguity with her own mother which satisfies infantile desire to bear her own mother a child. In addition to this, Kristeva points out: 'By giving birth, the woman enters into contact with her mother; she becomes, she is her own mother; they are the same continuity differentiating itself.'[8] For a daughter to gestate and bring forth a book, especially when the mother is or was a writer, is to sublimate this process. The monster that Victor composes out of corpses can be seen as exemplifying a sublimation through art of Wollstonecraft and Shelley's return to the symbolic prior to the moment of separation. The text of *Frankenstein* is a rebirthing sublimated through Victor's animation of dead bodies.[9] Through the Frankenstein monster, Shelley expiates her matricidal guilt in having caused the death of her mother through her own birth.

In the words of the Kristevan epigraph to this essay, 'Abjection ... is an alchemy that transforms death drive into a start of life, of new significance.' In Shelley's work, but most clearly in *Frankenstein*, one finds four distinct modes of transformation of the abject of the maternal body: *incorporation, defecation, resuscitation* and *the quest leading to reunion*. These do not form a sequential series, but are different attempts at dealing with the 'matter'.

Shelley inclusion of her mother's corpus within the body of her own texts is a topic that has already received limited critical attention with respect to *Frankenstein*. Elisabeth Bronfen and Anne Mellor, for instance, have treated the monster's disquisition as a continuation of Jemima's narrative in Wollstonecraft's unfinished novel, *The Wrongs of Woman or, Maria* (1798).[10] But there are many more such mothering texts informing Shelley's novel. Among them are Wollstonecraft's novella *Mary* (1788) and her *Thoughts on the Education of Daughters* (1787). In *Mary*, Wollstonecraft's description of a heroine being haunted by the corpse of a suicide mother prefigures her daughter's nightmare at Villa Diodati, as recalled in the Introduction to the 1831 edition of *Frankenstein*. Here Shelley describes how the hideous corpse is for 'the pale student of unhallowed arts' the cradle of life (*F* 179). (It is tempting to read into this Shelley's sense of being her own mother's cradle of life and concomitant bringer of death.) In *Mary*, Wollstonecraft writes:

> Mary saw her dead body, and heard the dismal account; and so strongly did it impress her imagination, that every night of her life the bleeding corpse presented itself to her when she first began to slumber.... The impression that this accident made was indelible.[11]

This nightmare appears later in the famous passage in *Frankenstein* when Victor gives his fiancée Elizabeth Lavenza the proverbial kiss of death, whereupon 'I thought that I held the corpse of my dead mother in my arms; a shroud enveloped her form, and I saw the grave-worms crawling in the folds of the flannel' (*F* 40 [I. iv]). It is also present in the sickening scene where Frankenstein refuses to 'give birth' to the half-made-up adult female who (he anticipates) would have been mother to 'a race of devils', but tears it apart. He lays up the remains in a basket and sinks it in the sea, returning the abject to the abyss where it 'belongs' (*F* 129–32 [III. iii]).

Thoughts on the Education of Daughters is *Frankenstein*'s most obvious parenting text. It had been written for Wollstonecraft's first daughter Fanny.[12] In her pedagogical treatise, Wollstonecraft's insistence that the mother is the best person to educate a child when it comes into the world, has a dire, unstated message for the motherless child, a message liable to have made Shelley, the daughter Wollstonecraft never knew, feel triply deprived. She would have been deserted not only by her first teacher, but also by her mother, and been betrayed by the author herself. In the opening chapter, Wollstonecraft notes: 'As I conceive it to be the duty of every rational creature to attend to its offspring, I am sorry to observe, that reason and duty together have not so powerful an influence over human conduct, as instinct has in the brute creation.'[13] On reading this, Shelley is likely to have reflected upon her own maternal deprivations, which she dramatizes through her account of the upbringing of the creature in her *bildungsroman*. Wollstonecraft's endorsement is not of a maternal instinct, but rather that of a mother's 'rational affection for her offspring'.[14] Parents are advised to subdue their own passions in the upbringing of a child. In *Frankenstein*, Victor displays no 'rational affection' for his creature nor an ability to subdue his own passions. The points of departure from Wollstonecraft's precepts about child rearing can be seen in *Frankenstein* as resulting in monster rearing. The Creature's upbringing is a strange completion of 'Letters on the Management of Infants' (1798) a book planned by Wollstonecraft but of which she completed only a fragment.[15]

Not only does Shelley incorporate and expiate: she purifies. Both in *Frankenstein* and outside *Frankenstein*, her work may be seen to function as the textual equivalent for the rite of lustration, of purification of the abject, a rite which, according to Kristeva, had been traditionally accommodated by religion (in, for example, the 'churching' of women after childbirth). I have called this process 'defecation' as it is the word that Shelley herself chose to use on occasion.[16] By 'defecation', here, we are to understand a symbolic cleansing not merely from 'child-bed taint', but from the decay of her mother's posthumous reputation into that which is deemed anti-social. Wollstonecraft's vilification in Richard Polwhele's poem of 1798 as an 'unsex'd female',[17] is a positioning which Shelley embraced through her authorship of *Frankenstein* (a book sent into the world in male attire, a tale written in a 'masculine' style by male narrators). But she also reacted against it, and her reaction involves her in attempting to dispel and to disown it. Thus in her last novel *Falkner* (1837), we are told that the heroine, Elizabeth Raby, by learning needlework, neatness and order as well as more masculine studies 'escaped for ever the danger she had hitherto run of wanting those feminine qualities without which every woman must be unhappy – and, to a certain degree, unsexed' (*FN* 40 [I. vi]). The process of disowning the unacceptable is most marked in Shelley's reconstruction of Wollstonecraft's life in her father's biography.[18] By de-monsterizing her now demonized mother, she portrays, or should I say *betrays,* her as a kind of depoliticized social reformer whose female radicalism is not even mentioned. Yet, betrayal though it might be, the process of defecating or sanitizing Wollstonecraft's reputation is an attempted form of reconciliation between mother and daughter, a rite of lustration.

The raising of Wollstonecraft from the dead is a metaphor that, deriving from her actual rescue and revival from drowning, manifests itself as her textual resuscitation in her daughter's novels. Wollstonecraft's posthumous reputation was scandalous not only for her 'unsexing' but also for her attempted suicides. Not only does Shelley's attempt to resurrect the dead mother; but she also symbolically resuscitates the suicidal mother, a resuscitation of the rescuscitated. The impression made on Shelley when she read her father's account in his *Memoirs of the Author of 'The Rights of Woman'* (1798) of her mother's attempts to take her own life must have been no less indelible than the account of her death.[19] Moreover, we find the following fragments of a suicide narrative in *Frankenstein*: attempted rescue and revival from a watery grave; expressed regret at having been made to live; activity as an antidote to sweet oblivion.

The remains of the half-made female monster resurface, as it were, from the abyss of Victor's mind, transformed into his dead friend, whose dark eyes and long lashes resemble so potently those of his own dead mother (*F* 140 [III. iv]). When Clerval's body is discovered, it is thought to be 'the corpse of some person who had been drowned, and was thrown on shore by the waves; but, upon examination, they found that the clothes were not wet, and even that the body was not then cold' (*F* 135 [III. iv]). He is then taken into a woman's cottage where he is placed in bed and rubbed in a vain effort at revival. Similarly rubbing is applied to Victor to revive him after he has been pulled exhausted from the sea. This last incident has often been related to Shelley's journal entry for 19 March 1815, where she records a dream about her dead baby; 'Dream that my little baby came to life again – that it had only been cold & that we *rubbed it before the fire* & it lived' (*MWSJ* I, p. 70; my italics), and of course, the body of the dead baby is itself an 'abject' in the text. But warming and rubbing was also a standard procedure for reviving the drowned as advocated by The Royal Humane Society.[20]

In the *Memoirs of the Society Instituted at Amsterdam in favour of Drowned Persons,* which had been translated into English by Thomas Cogin in 1773, it is claimed that 'upwards of a hundred and fifty persons, may, with the strictest propriety, be said *to have been raised from the dead'*.[21] Various methods of resuscitation are described, some extremely odd, such as the use of tobacco clysters.[22] One of the directors of the Amsterdam Society was called Johann Goll Van Frankenstein. Could this be yet another source of the name of Shelley's Victor?[23] Victor also practises raising from the dead, albeit by first reconstituting his subject from parts of dead bodies taken from charnel houses; furthermore, the methods of reviving the drowned as practiced by 18th-century humanitarians converge with Victor's scientific methods of reanimating a corpse.

The Amsterdam society was a predecessor of the British Royal Humane Society, which adopted many of its procedures. In the 1796 report of the Royal Humane Society, these appear, gathered into verses headed 'Restoration of the Apparently Dead'. One method which has a strong link with *Frankenstein* was the use of electricity. In the Introduction to the 1831 edition of *Frankenstein*, Shelley speculates that for her ghost story 'Perhaps a corpse would be re-animated; galvanism had given token of such things: perhaps the component parts of a creature might be manufactured, brought together, and endued with vital warmth' (*F* 179). The same method of resuscitation was used as for victims of drowning, sometimes referred to as 'aquatic suffocation'.[24] By what method Wollstonecraft was revived it is impossible to tell. We do know that, owing to the pain of it, she resolved never to try and drown herself again.[25]

After throwing herself off Putney Bridge into the Thames in 1795, Wollstonecraft blamed her failure to drown herself on her rescuers for bringing her back to life saying: 'I have only to lament, that, when the bitterness of death was past, I was inhumanly brought back to life and misery.'[26] After being nursed through a life-threatening fever, Victor also complains: 'Why did I not die? More miserable than man ever was before, why did I not sink into forgetfulness and rest? ... But I was doomed to live' (*F* 137 [III. iv]).

For both Wollstonecraft and Victor Frankenstein, travel northwards is an alternative to the euthanasia of suicide by laudanum. Wollstonecraft's first suicide attempt in 1795 had been a half-hearted over-dose of laudanum. Subsequently, she set out for the Northern Utopia of Scandinavia at the instigation of Imlay. According to Claire Tomalin, he had suggested the business trip as 'a curious half-solution'[27] to her own self-destructive urge. Victor takes a 'double dose' on board ship returning from Ireland – in order ostensibly to sleep, but in his unhinged state of mind an accidental overdose would be a welcome quietus. The thirst for action later dispels his need to seek the oblivion offered by the drug, and he pursues the monster across the Arctic regions. In *Frankenstein*, Shelley not only continued Wollstonecraft's journey northward to the North Pole but also completed the journey to Switzerland that her mother never made. Shelley's visit to the Swiss Alps and her invocation of their sublimity in *Frankenstein* evokes Wollstonecraft's description in her *Short Residence* of her encounter with the sublime in Norway. (Similarly her 1817 *History of a Six Weeks' Tour Through a Part of France, Switzerland, Germany and Holland* – co-written with P.B. Shelley – and *Rambles in Germany and Italy in 1840, 1842, and 1843* of 1844 take as their models Wollstonecraft's own travel writing.)

The quest for the expelled abject and reunion with it are another form of catharsis for matricidal guilt; in Shelley, this quest converges with the Female Gothic quest for the missing mother and the Romantic quest for lost origins. Both Shelley and her creature are motherless offspring, who set out to re-discover their origins and parentage. The creature, for example, browses through Victor's laboratory notes in a bizarre parody of the way in which, as Chris Baldick has argued, Shelley would have read about her own birth in her father's *Memoirs* of Wollstonecraft.[28] She had been conceived in December 1796 which is the month in which the action in *Frankenstein* begins. Furthermore the outer narrative framework of the novel spans a gestation period of nine months from the first letter to the last. The fictional Victor's death on 11 September 1797 is made to take place on the day after the date that Wollstonecraft died.[29]

Like her first novel, *Frankenstein*, Shelley's last novel *Falkner* encrypts a quest-narrative for the dead mother. Significantly, *Falkner* opens with a child protecting her mother's grave from a mysterious stranger. There is another exhumation of a dead mother whose 'pale, wise spirit checked, guided, and whispered sage lessons' to the narrator (*FN* 178 [II. xi]). The eponymous hero attempts suicide after causing the death of his beloved Alithea Rivers. The infant Elizabeth Raby rescues him. At one point he laments:

> I lost my mother before I can well remember. I have a confused recollection of her crying – and of her caressing me – and I can call to mind seeing her ill in bed, and her blessing me; but these ideas are rather like revelations of an ante-natal life, than belonging to reality.
>
> (*FN* 157 [II. ix])

At times is tempting to read into *Falkner* a reflection of Shelley's own abandonment in childhood and subsequent identification with the motherless monster:

> Since my birth – or at least since I had lost my mother in early infancy, my path had been cast upon thorns and brambles – ... cold neglect, reprehension, and debasing slavery; to such was I doomed. I had longed for something to love –
>
> (*FN* 162 [II. x])

Falkner's mother, however, is not the subject of the quest. This is displaced onto Alithea Rivers, and the quester is the young man who falls in love with Elizabeth, a P.B. Shelley-like character called Gerard Neville. He turns out to be the son of Alithea Rivers. To uncover the cause of her death becomes his obsession, and the upshot of his search is a return of the dead mother slightly less grisly though no less grim than that in *Frankenstein*. All that remains of her body are 'discoloured bones, and long tresses of dark hair, which were wound around the skull' (*FN* 215 [III. iii]).

The nearest that Shelley comes to addressing directly the longing for merging with the lost mother is in her mythological drama *Proserpine*, written in 1820, a year in which Shelley reread her mother's *Posthumous Works*.[30] It is more often discussed as a story of a mother's search for a lost daughter (two years earlier Shelley had experienced separation from her own daughter, Clara, through death), and of course it is that too. But the significant opening line is the plea made by the eponymous heroine to Ceres, 'Dear Mother, leave me not!' (*M* 73). Marjean D. Purinton points out that:

> Proserpine's identity requires a loss, a separation from the mother, and yet as a 'natural' and 'normalized' female body, Proserpine is expected to become a maternal body – the obligation to reproduce being the function that verifies women's social value.[31]

It is in this respect that the daughter takes on her mother's role. Rather than be parted from her daughter, Ceres threatens to descend with her into the darkness of the underworld. The separation of mother and daughter is a form of death, represented by Proserpine's descent into Hades. As Purinton notes, 'Hades is the universal receiver of bodies – a receptacle, and Proserpine's drama transforms the abject of the female body to mystery.'[32]

In death, Shelley was reunited with her mother in 1851 in accordance with her last wishes to be buried with her parents. Her daughter-in-law, Lady Jane Shelley, decided to have her buried at St Peter's Church in Bournemouth. Here too were destined the bodies of Godwin and Wollstonecraft. Though these were exhumed from their grave at St Pancras, Shelley's supposedly detested stepmother, the second Mrs Godwin, was left unceremoniously behind.[33] That the episode can be read as a legitimized version of Victor's grave-robbing may be why the rector of St Peter's refused to bury the disinterred bodies. Ensconcing herself in her carriage in front of the hearse, Lady Shelley refused to move until the rector relented. Eventually he agreed and allowed the gravedigger to lower the coffins into their grave. Taking place in the dead of night, the burials were marked by no ceremony. Moreover, even though Wollstonecraft had been acknowledged as the author of the *Vindication* on her tombstone, no reference was made at the grave of Mary Wollstonecraft Shelley that she had ever been the author of *Frankenstein*. On the outside of the churchyard wall one can find the place to which the plaque proclaiming her authorship has been exiled. For that information, one must step outside the boundaries of the consecrated ground, to the symbolic space occupied by the abject.

Notes

I would like to thank Carolyn Williams, Marion Glastonbury, Pamela Clemit and Major General Christopher Tyler, C.B., Secretary of The Royal Humane Society, for their generous help. Earlier versions of this essay were presented as papers at 'Romantic Generations' (University of Leeds, July 1997) and 'Mary Shelley: Parents, Peers, Progeny' (APU and OU, Cambridge, September 1997).

1. Julia Kristeva, *Powers of Horror: An Essay on Abjection*, trans. Leon S. Roudiez (New York: Columbia University Press, 1982) p. 15; hereafter Kristeva.
2. Virginia Woolf, *A Room of One's Own* (London: Harcourt Brace, 1957) p. 79. Of Wollstonecraft, Shelley noted: 'The memory of my Mother has always been the pride & delight of my life; & the admiration of others for her, has been the cause of most of the happiness I have enjoyed' (*MWSL* II, pp. 3–4).
3. There is still much to be said on this theme with respect to her father's texts. *St Leon* (1799), the story of a Rosicrucian who, like Victor Frankenstein, has acquired a secret sway over life and death is one of the most striking examples of Godwinian influence; see Marie [Mulvey] Roberts, *Gothic Immortals: the Fiction of the Brotherhood of the Rosy Cross*

(London: Routledge, 1990) pp. 37–45; Marilyn Butler is among the critics who have recognized the importance of this work for *Frankenstein* (see her introduction to *Frankenstein* (Oxford World's Classics: Oxford University Press, 1993). There are also parallels between Victor who fathered and constructed his creature and Shelley's father who helped construct her as a woman and writer (I owe this point to Marion Glastonbury).

4. Elizabeth Gross, 'The Body of Signification', in *Abjection, Melancholia and Love: the Works of Julia Kristeva*, eds John Fletcher and Andrew Benjamin (London: Routledge, 1990) p. 86.
5. Helga Geyer-Ryan, *Fables of Desire: Studies in the Ethics of Art and Gender* (Oxford: Blackwell, 1994) p. 198.
6. Quoted by Elizabeth Gross, 'The Body of Signification', p. 95.
7. See Vivien Jones, 'The Death of Mary Wollstonecraft', *British Journal of Eighteenth-Century Studies*, 20.2 (Autumn, 1997) 191–2.
8. Julia Kristeva, *Desire in Language: a Semiotic Approach to Literature and Art* (Oxford: Blackwell, 1982) p. 239. For Shelley the inscription of herself as author was not only an attempt to resuscitate her mother; it was also an erasure of her own experience of monstrous birthing encoded within her body, her first baby (a girl) who died after only thirteen days of life. Emily Sunstein (Sunstein, p. 97) speculates tentatively that Shelley might have intended to call this baby girl 'Mary Wollstonecraft'. The significance of this trauma for Shelley was first articulated by Ellen Moers, in her much discussed reading of *Frankenstein* as a 'birth myth' (Ellen Moers, *Literary Women* [Garden City: Doubleday, 1976]).
9. Godwin's interests in raising the dead are evident from his collection of esoteric biographies entitled *Lives of the Necromancers* (1834). Included in these are the alchemists whom Victor adopted as mentors. It is not surprising to find Shelley resurrecting her parents for the revised version of *Frankenstein* while working on a short memoir of her father which appeared as an introduction to the Bentley's Standard Novels edition of *Caleb Williams* in the same year (1831).
10. Elisabeth Bronfen, 'Rewriting the Family: Mary Shelley's *Frankenstein*', in *Frankenstein, Creation and Monstrosity*, ed. Stephen Bann (London: Reaktion Books, 1994) p. 34 and Anne K. Mellor, 'Righting the Wrongs of Woman: Mary Wollstonecraft's *Maria*', *Nineteenth-Century Contexts: an Interdisciplinary Journal*, 19.4 (1996) 420–2.
11. Mary Wollstonecraft, *Mary, a Fiction* [with *The Wrongs of Woman; or, Maria, a Fragment*] eds James Kinsley and Gary Kelly, World's Classics (Oxford: Oxford University Press, 1980) p. 6.
12. Fanny Godwin, in October 1816, was to write herself out of the family plot into the text of Shelley's masterpiece as the lonely and misunderstood monster. This was an argument put forward by Maurice Hindle in a paper called 'Victim of Romance: The Life and Death of Fanny Godwin' presented at the conference 'Romantic Generations', University of Leeds, July 1997.
13. Mary Wollstonecraft, *Thoughts on the Education of Daughters*, ed. Janet Todd (Bristol: Thoemmes Press, 1995) pp. 1–2.
14. Ibid., p. 5.
15. It would have covered such areas as pregnancy, bathing, lying in, the first

208 *The Parental Legacy*

    month, diet and clothes, the following three months, and the first two
    years of the baby's life; see *A Wollstonecraft Anthology*, ed. Janet Todd
    (Oxford: Polity Press, 1993) pp. 59–60.
16. 'To defecate life of its misery and its evil, was the ruling passion of his soul'
    (Shelley on P.B. Shelley, in the 'Preface' to her editions of his *Poetical Works*
    (*M* 255).
17. Reprinted in part by Vivien Jones, *Women in the Eighteenth Century:
    Constructions of Femininity* (London: Routledge, 1990) pp. 186–9.
18. Shelley was working on her 'Life of Godwin' from 1836 to 1839 or 1840.
19. Godwin points out that from the end of May to the beginning of October
    1795, Wollstonecraft was prompted to attempt suicide twice as a response
    to Gilbert Imlay's rejection of her; see Godwin, *Memoirs of the Author of
    'The Rights of Woman'*, p. 255.
20. See Marie Mulvey-Roberts and Carolyn Williams, 'The Inanimate Mass
    Hath Breathed the Breath of Life: Abjection, Resuscitation and
    Frankenstein', *Women's Writing* (forthcoming). Nora Crook has pointed out
    to me that Robert Thornton's compilation *Medical Extracts*, which P.B.
    Shelley ordered in 1812, contains a long section entitled 'Of the Institution
    of the Humane Society for the Recovery of Persons Apparently Dead' in
    which the processes of resuscitation advocated by the society and by John
    Hunter, Thomas Beddoes and Thornton himself are detailed (*The
    Philosophy of Medicine, Being Medical Extracts* [etc.], 2 vols, 5th edn [London:
    Sherwood, Neely and Jones, 1813] II, pp. 49–79). Electricity, heat and friction
    are all mentioned, as is alcohol. (Frankenstein is rubbed with brandy
    and given some to drink.) *Medical Extracts* stresses that techniques for the
    resuscitation of the drowned are based on those used to revive persons in
    the torpor caused by extreme cold. This book probably lies behind P.B.
    Shelley's note to *Queen Mab* (1813) 'I will beget a Son': 'the Humane
    Society restores drowned persons, and because it makes no mystery of the
    method it employs, its members are not mistaken for the sons of God.'
    There are connections to be made between *Frankenstein*, Wollstonecraft
    and the suicide by drowning in December 1816 of Harriet Shelley (whose
    body was carried to a Receiving Station of the Royal Humane Society,
    where the inquest later took place); see vol. 4 of *Shelley and His Circle*, ed.
    K.N. Cameron, [Cambridge, Mass., Harvard University Press, 1970]
    pp. 777–9). These, however, lie outside the scope of this essay.
21. *Memoirs of the Society Instituted at Amsterdam in favour of Drowned Persons for
    the Years 1767, 1768, 1769, 1779 and 1771*, trans. Thomas Cogin (London:
    G. Robinson, 1773) p. iii.
22. The recommended method of resuscitation was to approach the rear end
    and 'blow into the intestines through a tobacco-pipe, a pair of bellows, or
    the sheath of a knife, cutting off the lower point' (*Memoirs of the Society
    Instituted at Amsterdam in favour of Drowned Persons for the Years 1767,
    1768, 1769, 1779 and 1771*, p. 3). Only in a footnote on page 4 is it
    noted that it also very effective to blow forcefully into the lungs. In
    'Restoration of the Apparently Dead' (The Royal Humane Society, *Annual
    Report* [1796] p. 9), the technique is strongly urged where other methods
    have failed:

> *Tobacco-smoke* has often prov'd, indeed,
> Of wond'rous use, in cases of such need.
> Try ev'ry means, not even this neglect,
> With this herb's fumes the bowels to inject.
> Thrice administer the same within the hour;
> And, if it proves inadequate in power,
> To clysters of this pungent herb apply,
> Or other juice of equal potence high.

A version of 'Restoration of the Apparently Dead' was included, for learning by heart, in William Mavor's *The English Spelling Book* (1801), an educational work which went into many editions and which was still being reprinted in the 1840s. By a curious coincidence, Mavor's son was a co-publisher of *Frankenstein*. *Medical Extracts* stated that the 'steam of some warm stimulating substances' conveyed to the stomach would, through sympathy, gently assist recovery. This was evidently the rationale for the treatment.

23. Ibid., p. 12. I am entirely indebted to Carolyn Williams for this point and these leads. Radu Florescu has argued strongly in favour of the alchemist Dippel of Castle Frankenstein in Darmstadt as the source of the name (see Radu Florescu, *In Search of Frankenstein*, rev. edn [London: Robson Books, 1996]). But the two are not mutually exclusive.

24. The Royal Humane Society, *Annual Report* (1796) p. 10. In 'Restoration of the Apparently Dead', the verse on 'Electricity' reads:

> Likewise, th' *electric fluid*, when death doth reign,
> And stagnant life is cold in very vein,
> (Drawn from the choice – the best of Nature's fires)
> A kindly warmth, a gentle heat inspires;
> Breathes thro' the whole a vivifying strife,
> And wakes the torpid powers to sudden life,
> Yet more: the *shock* of life is oft the test,
> When all who're present are of doubt possest:
> Let fly the sudden shock: if life remain,
> Contractions, spasms, instantly are plain.

25. See Godwin, *Memoirs of the Author of 'The Rights of Woman'* p. 250. I have been unable to track down her rescue in the records of The Royal Humane Society Report for 1795 possibly because several of the female suicide attempts by drowning that are listed bear no name. Neither does the name, Mrs Imlay, which she called herself, nor that of Wollstonecraft, appear among those who joined in a parade for those rescued from the watery grave.

26. *Collected Letters of Mary Wollstonecraft*, ed. Ralph M. Wardle (Ithaca: Cornell University Press, 1979) p. 317. For a discussion of Wollstonecraft's suicide attempts see Janet Todd, *Gender, Art and Death* (Oxford: Polity, 1993) pp. 102–19. Carolyn Williams has suggested that when Wollstonecraft said that she had been 'inhumanly' rescued, she was making a reference to unwanted intervention by The Royal Humane Society.

210 *The Parental Legacy*

27. Claire Tomalin, *The Life and Death of Mary Wollstonecraft* (London: Harcourt Brace Jovanovich, 1974) p. 179.
28. See William Godwin, *Memoirs of the Author of 'The Rights of Woman'*, ed. Richard Holmes (Harmondsworth: Penguin, 1987) p. 265, and Chris Baldick, *In Frankenstein's Shadow: Myth, Monstrosity, and Nineteenth-Century Writing* (Oxford: Clarendon press, 1987) p. 31.
29. See Mellor, pp. 54–5 and *Frankenstein Notebooks*, I, p. lxv and n. I accept the arguments of Robinson and Mellor that the chronology of *Frankenstein* is at least partly realistic and that the narrative ends in September 1797.
30. See *MWSJ* II, p. 684. There are textual clues which support a biographical identification of Wollstonecraft with Ceres and Shelley with Proserpine. P.B. Shelley in the *Revolt of Islam* (1818) which he dedicated to his wife, made a tribute to her parentage in the line; 'With thy beloved name, thou Child of love and light' (line 9). Ceres refers to her daughter as 'child of light' (*M* 87 [II.166]). Proserpine responds by declaring her mother to be 'dearer to your child than light' (*M* 88 [II.192]).
31. Marjean D. Purinton, 'Polysexualities and Romantic Generations in Mary Shelley's Mythological Dramas *Midas & Proserpine*', Mary Shelley Special Issue, *Women's Writing* 6.3 (1999).
32. Ibid.
33. For a challenge to this stereotypical view, see Harriet Devine Jump, 'Monstrous Stepmother: Mary Shelley and Mary Jane Godwin', Mary Shelley Special Issue, *Women's Writing* 6.3 (1999).

13
Rehabilitating the Family in Mary Shelley's *Falkner*
Julia Saunders

When Mary Shelley began writing her last novel, *Falkner*, she did not know that the book was to be overshadowed by an ending of another sort. During the course of its composition, her father, William Godwin, passed away. As her life was ushered in under the shadow of the death of one radical parent, so her literary life as a novelist came to an end with the passing of the other. Her relationship with her father had often been turbulent, but also central to her creativity as he had supported her career as a writer with his advice and ideas and it is significant that she never produced another full length work of fiction after his death. Many of her father's radical ideas – and those of her equally famous mother – provided material for Shelley's imagination and intellect; indeed, her novels reveal new depths when read as an engagement with Shelley's inheritance as the literary heir of her parents, William Godwin and Mary Wollstonecraft, the two leading radicals of the 1790s. It was the ideas of the radicals of the past, rather than those of her own era, that formed her intellectual milieu. By the time she wrote *Falkner*, the radical agenda of her parents' generation had become muted and mutated in the work of the daughter, but its presence is still felt in both form and content.

For many literary critics, the later works of Shelley represent an ideological retreat from her bold, speculative writing of the 1820s in which she confidently tackled themes as ambitious as world government, science and history. For Pamela Clemit, the widowed Shelley lost her way, lacking 'any stable system of values from which to conduct an authoritative cultural analysis'.[1] For Anne Mellor, '[Shelley's] later novels suffer from her obsessive need to idealize her husband and the bourgeois family' (Mellor, p. 39) – implying that Shelley rejected her inheritance of radical social experimentation and joined the chorus of praise for traditional family values. Biographical evidence is often brought in to support this view as Shelley recorded her dislike of the radicals of her own era (some of whom had once been friends and acquaintances of her deceased husband), calling them 'Violent without any sense of justice – selfish in the extreme – talking without knowledge – rude, envious and insolent' (*MWSJ* II, p. 555). Personal dislike of particular radicals, however, did not equal a rejection of all radical ideas. On the contrary, Shelley also wrote that she had 'never written a word in disfavour of liberalism' (ibid., p. 554). Shelley's kind of radicalism was in a sense 'out of date' – it was not that of her peers in the 1820s and 1830s, but that of her parents' generation. In the era of the Great Reform Bill, her radicalism was not directed at the reform of institutions but at the education of the individual. It was no wonder that her contemporaries did not understand her politics: she was still reflecting on the unfinished agenda of a quarter of a century ago; their agenda had moved on.

The last disciple of an old movement, Shelley was an isolated figure in intellectual circles of Victorian England, even more so when her last ally – her father – passed away. She struggled hard to retain the optimism needed to support a belief in the efficacy of radical reform. Optimism had not been in such short supply in the heady aftermath of the French Revolution, the heyday of her parents' generation, but it had since ebbed away as the new dawn had been followed by a reactionary day. Aside from the chastening political realities of post-1815 Europe, Shelley had little cause for personal optimism; life had dealt her many hard blows. Her own recipe for reform was a bleaker one than that of her more sanguine contemporaries. She approved the end of radical reform but was not convinced that the means (i.e. political agitation) suggested by her peers was the right course of action:

> I beleive [*sic*] that we are sent here to educate ourselves & that self denial & disappointment & self controul are a part of our education – that it is not by taking away all restraining law that our improvement is to be achieved – & though many things need *great* amendment – I can by no means go so far as my *friends* would have me.
>
> (*MWSJ* II, p. 554)

Her father in his great work of the 1790s, *Political Justice*, had also started from the premise that reform should begin with the education of the individual. However, Shelley's statement contains a specifically gendered outlook on radicalism missing from her father's work. Hers was a muted view of life's possibilities – particularly of those open to women. This attitude is present even in her early works, but made more explicit in her last two novels. Her pessimistic view of life draws on her maternal rather than paternal inheritance, sounding a note distinctly familiar to the readers of the 1790s female Jacobin novelists. Mary Hays's Emma Courtney and Wollstonecraft's Mary and Maria, for example, all learn in the harsh school of experience that the best that can be hoped from life is to learn self-control, self-denial and to bear disappointment. In one representative moment in *The Memoirs of Emma Courtney*, the heroine tries to persuade her suicidal husband of the virtues of self-control rather than rash actions, attempting to effect change in the individual, rather than society at large. She writes to him on learning of his murder of his illegitimate child:

> Let us reap wisdom from these tragical consequences of *indulged passion*! It is not to atone for the past error, by cutting off the prospect of future usefulness – Repentance for what can never be recalled, is absurd and vain, but as it affords a lesson for the time to come – do not let us wilfully forfeit the fruits of our dear-bought experience![2]

Her advice has no effect on her husband but Emma takes her own lesson to heart, telling her story retrospectively as a lesson in the folly of indulging one's passion on an unworthy object. A similar moral could be drawn from the story of Wollstonecraft's heroine Maria. Though the novel is unfinished, the plot indicates that Maria has wasted her affection during her imprisonment on a flawed man. He is not able to rise to the heights that Maria does for him: she stands up in court to defend her adulterous love; he – as many of the sketched endings suggest – is destined to abandon her. A generation later, Shelley reiterates the same message in her novels: indulging their respective passions, Frankenstein destroys his family, Falkner his beloved Alithea and Raymond his wife and mistress. The female radicals shared an acute sense of the cost of ideals on the family: they saw themselves not as Promethean free agents, but embedded in a web of responsibilities. The fall of one individual brings the rest crashing down with him.

Thus, with this tempered view of life, Shelley could not go as far as her 'friends' would have her. However, she remained loyal to a 1790s brand of radicalism, if not the formulas of the new generation.

Evidence for this can be found in *Falkner* – a novel that reviewers were quick to identify as essentially 'Godwinian' in spirit.[3] Contained in the seemingly benign form of a sentimental romance is a far from innocuous critique of society's morals and mores. In *Falkner*, Shelley castigates the aristocracy as well as questioning the values of the middle-class structure that was emerging to replace the traditional pre-eminence of the gentility: the bourgeois family – both familiar targets of her parents' generation. Constructing a social alternative, however, is a costly business, involving a rehabilitation of these old family structures on new principles. *Falkner*, and its immediate predecessor *Lodore*, differ from Shelley's earlier novels in that they suggest that such a social alternative is possible. The holocaust of families that ends the majority of her 1820s fiction is replaced by the prospect of life carrying on in a reformed family circle.

At the centre of *Falkner* lies the domestic circle of Rupert Falkner and his adopted daughter, Elizabeth. This is not a bourgeois ideal family as some critics suggest. In a 'normal' family each member is part of a web of relationships, acting as daughter, wife, mother or son, husband, father. In *Falkner* this pattern is disrupted and Shelley concentrates instead upon one single strong tie – father to daughter. Usually family ties depend on blood relationships; this concept underpins both aristocratic and bourgeois inheritance traditions. Shelley replaces blood with gratitude. This quality rules the moral world of the novel from the frontispiece quotation to the conclusion of the tale. Repeatedly society in its various forms tells Elizabeth that in the absence of a blood tie she owes no duty to Falkner. When Falkner is plunged into disgrace, she would be forgiven for claiming her 'own' name of Raby and escaping the scandal attached to the destroyer of Alithea Neville. Lady Cecil and Mrs Raby come to Elizabeth on the news of Falkner's arrest for murder with the expectation that Elizabeth will renounce her relationship to her adopted father, be 'restored to her place in society, and punishment would fall on the guilty alone' (*FN* 230 [III. vi]). Both these women have many admirable qualities, but, unlike Elizabeth, they are unable at this point in the story to rise above the conditioning of their upbringing. Even Falkner, despite years of loyal filial service from Elizabeth, believes society's dictate that Elizabeth should abandon him to be the best and the most likely resolution. Elizabeth, however, has more radical notions of what is right and she refuses to sink into the behaviour demanded and expected of her. Her upbringing has been unorthodox and has freed her to act from conviction rather than convention. Filial duty in her understanding is something which is earned by the parent, and is not the result of biology. Refusing Mrs Raby's belated attempt to entice her into the respectable circle of her natural family, Elizabeth remarks:

> I have no wish to speak of the past; nor to remind you that if I was not brought up in obedience to you all, it was because my father was disowned, my mother abandoned; and I, a little child, an orphan, was left to live and die in dependence.... Then, young as I was, I felt gratitude, obedience, duty, all due to the generous benefactor who raised me from this depth of want, and made me the child of his heart.... I am his; bought by his kindness; earned by his unceasing care for me, I belong to him – his child – if you will, his servant – I do not quarrel with names – a child's duty I pay him, and will ever.
>
> (*FN* 233 [III. vii])

Shelley provocatively gives Elizabeth words that are unsettlingly religious in flavour, employing the notion of salvation to a human object of devotion. Elizabeth not only breaks the bounds of conventional behaviour, but also risks shocking Mrs Raby and Lady Cecil by her near blasphemous use of the sacred. The strong language, however, serves to convey to her listeners in a style familiar to them, imbued with religious authority, the imperative sense of duty – a sacred bond she cannot break. This language crops up at other key moments of the plot when Elizabeth, in order to stay with Falkner, reiterates her sense that she has been 'bought' or 'saved' by him. He cannot shake off his devotee so easily. Another such moment comes on the eve of Falkner's departure for the Wars of Independence in Greece, the moment when Falkner first tries to separate his fate from that of his charge. She responds to his attempt to go alone, 'You have earned me – you have bought me by all this kindness' (*FN* 52 [I. viii]). In this relationship, stronger in the novel even than the tie of love that links Elizabeth to Gerard Neville, Shelley constructs the family on a new footing. She adopts the premise that relationships should be based on more substantial values than a blind adherence to the creed that blood is thicker than water. By doing so, Shelley picks up a central theme of the social reform agenda of her parents' generation.

One of the most contentious sections in her father's *Political Justice* (1793) was that advocating a utilitarian estimate of relationships, illustrated by the example of saving Fénelon from a house-fire, rather than his maid, even though she may be your mother or sister, on the basis that 'that life ought to be preferred which will be most conducive to the general good'.[4] This was a startling claim and one that Godwin conceded in later life did not pay sufficient attention to natural affections. However, the central point remained: that the reformed individual should not be bound by empty conventions, but should look at each person in terms of their true worth. In his novel *Hermsprong*, a fellow 1790s radical, Robert Bage, reflects this attitude in his handling of filial duty. His heroine, Caroline Campinet, flees her father's house to escape a forced marriage. Hermsprong, the new man of radicalism nurtured in the wilds of America, tries to reason with the convention-bound Caroline as she undergoes terrible pangs of remorse for abandoning what the world would term her filial duties. He asks, 'In what part of Lord Grondale's conduct to you, can you recognise the care and tenderness of a father?'[5] In *Falkner*, Shelley takes this question a further logical step. If Grondale has failed to earn his daughter's duty by his cruelty and neglect, Falkner has 'bought' the freely given devotion of his adopted daughter through his care and support – doubly so because he extended his protection to an orphan with no claim on him. Gratitude forms ties thicker than blood.

Gratitude is not a word commonly associated with the 1790s radical agenda, possibly because it was co-opted by the anti-Jacobins as an anti-revolutionary quality. For Edmund Burke, for example, kindness and gratitude were the cement of society: the upper classes were expected to show charity to their less fortunate neighbours; the lower classes were to respond with gratitude – and thus society was to be knitted together. Shelley's gratitude has none of these Burkean overtones: neither gratitude, nor its outward expression of loyalty, are accorded to the upper classes. On the contrary, *Falkner* dissects the moribund aristocracy and finds it wanting. Aristocracy is attacked on two fronts. The most sustained criticism is reserved for the Rabys, an old Catholic family and Elizabeth's natural protectors. Such is the narrow prejudice of the family that they cast off Elizabeth's father for his apostasy and renounce all responsibility for his child while she remains with her mother. Shelley gives the internal moral bankruptcy of the aristocracy an external expression. Oswi Raby, the head of the clan, focuses all the prejudice and selfishness in his own person. He is described as looking 'shrivelled, not so much by age as the narrowness of his mind', 'self-important in heart', with 'an incapacity to understand that any thing was of consequence except himself, or rather, except the house he represented' (*FN* 141 [II. vi]). He is the cankered heart hid in the beautiful surroundings of aristocratic Belleforest. Oswi is blind to the true value of others. He interprets Falkner's attempt to reconcile Elizabeth to the Rabys as the act of a man casting off an embarrassment. Nobility for him is a dry sum of family blood and religious faith; he had no conception of true nobility of character – a quality Elizabeth possesses in abundance. Oswi's aristocracy is a monster, devouring its younger sons and daughters to favour the heir; a dying institution headed for senility, as is Oswi himself.

Shelley finds a second more subtle aristocratic target in the hero himself. Falkner, despite his many compensating qualities, suffers from an ungovernable temper. This is the fatal flaw that leads him into the impulsive abduction of Alithea – an act which results in her death, the embittering of her son, and the perpetual remorse of Falkner. The blame for this fault is placed squarely in the sad circumstances of Falkner's upbringing. The root of evil in the environment of Falkner's youth is inherited wealth. The son of a younger son, Falkner suffers at the hands of his wastrel father who lives extravagantly in the false expectation of an inheritance. When this expectation is disappointed, his father sinks into abject misery and violence, presenting a pitiful role model for his son. On his father's death, Falkner is sent to the hostile environment of his uncle's aristocratic household. Falkner remarks:

> My habits were bad enough; my father's vices had fostered my evil qualities – I had never learnt to lie or cheat ... but I was rough, self-willed, lazy, and insolent. ... From the very first, I was treated with a coldness to which a child is peculiarly sensitive ... I grew imperious and violent ... I was disobedient and reckless.
> (*FN* 159 [II. ix])

His uncle does no more for him than provide for his material needs; his moral and emotional education is completely neglected. The aristocracy fail to nurture their children, producing dangerous rebels rather than well-adjusted family members. Despite the positive influence of the humble officer's wife, Mrs Rivers, and her daughter, Alithea, the first people to look on the young man with any care or compassion, Falkner remains essentially the child of his aristocratic upbringing – reckless and violent. Only the calamity of Alithea's death exposes his conduct to his own conscience in its true light. Even then, the violence continues as he seeks by various stratagems to end his own life. This story of the perversion of an essentially good character by an aristocratic education finds many echoes in Godwin's work, particularly in *Caleb Williams* and *St Leon*. The 1790s radicals, and their late disciple, Shelley, shared the belief that it was the system that made the man and – as aristocracy was a pernicious system – it should be reformed, or else the production of such damaged characters would be perpetuated.

The 1790s radicals reached a variety of conclusions as to what was necessary to reform society. Bage and Thomas Holcroft tended to concentrate on large abstract reforms in familial structures and national institutions. Godwin in his novels moved to a position in which reform was to start very much at home. St Leon's error, for example, can be interpreted as a betrayal of his domestic loyalties in search of impossible public ends, though selfishness, the lust for power and greed play no small part in his disastrous career. All his attempts to use his infinite wealth and immortality to improve the lot of his fellow men result in disaster. The novel teaches that the natural scale of reform is to start with oneself. Shelley shared the belief that any change must first happen on the personal level. Reform or rehabilitation begins on this premise in *Falkner* – and the agency is female.

By some definitions, Shelley's view of female power is more limited than that of her mother's generation. When she does portray independent women of the kind her mother described in *Maria* and *A Vindication of the Rights of Woman*, they are 'dead-ends' in society's terms. Euthanasia, the castle-state ruler of *Valperga*, and Fanny Derham, the scholarly daughter in *Lodore*, are both childless and single, forming no family lines of liberated daughters. Their futures are effaced from the narrative – Euthanasia by death, Derham by a tantalizing obscurity or lack of prophetic vision on the part of the narrator. Her story is not for this era of reform. However, Shelley does not reject this kind of liberated femininity: both characters, though 'failures' in worldly terms, are spiritual successes. Euthanasia may lose the battle as a political leader, but her untarnished reputation illuminates in an unflattering light the series of betrayals that make up the sum of Castruccio's path to power. Fanny Derham, with her loyalty, intelligence and competent independence, hovers at the edge of the plot of *Lodore*, suggesting another way for young women than the kind of femininity chosen by Ethel. Her potential as a role model, however, is not developed. The world as Shelley depicts it is not yet ready for her.

In *Falkner* Shelley constructs a form of feminine power that can exist successfully within society *and* change it to answer the emotional needs of the female. The first task of the female is to rehabilitate the aristocracy. Despite her swingeing criticism of aristocratic upbringings, Shelley appears paradoxically to hanker after some of the more noble concepts that it engenders. For example, in contrast to the disapproving description of the 'bourgeois' criminal justice route chosen by Sir Boyvill to prosecute his wife's destroyer, Gerard's desire to meet Falkner 'honourably' in a duel is treated sympathetically, almost with approval. This contrasts interestingly with the treatment given to the duel fought by Lord Lodore in Shelley's previous novel: the narrator calls duels 'that sad relic of feudal barbarism' (*L* 90 [I. xvi]). Aristocratic values are given a second favourable airing at the conclusion of *Falkner* when Gerard opts for a different kind of noble combat to describe his decision to reconcile himself to Falkner: 'Knights of old,' he tells Elizabeth;

> after they fought in right good earnest, became friends, each finding, in the bravery of the other, a cause for esteem. Such is the situation of Rupert Falkner and myself; and we will both join, dear Elizabeth, in making him forget the past, and rendering his future years calm and happy.
>
> (*FN* 298–9 [III. xx])

Gerard turns the courtroom into the jousting field, creating for himself a satisfying language in which to excuse and explain his decision. He adapts the conventions of the past to the needs of an unconventional present. In doing so, he demonstrates how traditions can be made to serve the needs of the present generation.

It is the female characters of the story, however, that are responsible for forcing the reconciliation of the aristocratic past with their family needs. Oswi Raby is replaced in the second half of the narrative by his daughter-in-law, Mrs Raby. Though brought up to share the sense of Raby pride, Mrs Raby understands the true meaning of nobility in a way the now senile Oswi never did. Risking public condemnation for giving her countenance to a man of dubious reputation, she reasons as follows as she invites Falkner and Elizabeth to her home in the aftermath of the scandalous trial:

> when Providence brings before us two selected from the world as endowed with every admirable quality, we allow a thousand unworthy considerations, which assume the voice of prudence, to exile us from them.... Such companions will teach my children

better than volumes of moral treatises, the existence and loveliness of human goodness.

(*FN* 289 [iii. xviii])

Mrs Raby realizes that nobility is a living quality – not a dry sum – and thus she begins to rehabilitate her own family on a new basis. Belleforest under her guidance finds a nobility at its heart to match the beauty of its architecture and woody glades.

Without belittling Mrs Raby's contribution to the moral sea-change governing kinship structures, the novel awards the prize of most effective female reformer of the family, both in its bourgeois and aristocratic form, to Elizabeth. Her power is a strange one because it poses as submission. Elizabeth, like Ethel in *Lodore*, has much of the disciple in her, following the strong male. However, in Elizabeth's case, it soon becomes apparent that as Falkner's supposed servant, she wields great mastery over him. This starts on their first acquaintance when, as a little child, she holds back his arm as he attempts suicide: her presence forces him to live against his will. She does so, not to save his life – the infant does not understand the full implication of the adult's action – but to stop him desecrating the grave of her mother. Her power over him thus begins with her assertion of her right to defend the female territory. In later tussles, the physical territory of the mother's grave is replaced by the emotional territory of the daughter. Society grants more duties than privileges to women, but Elizabeth gladly assumes the role of daughter. She demands in return that she must be granted the right to fulfil the role, to preserve her female territory on all occasions and not only when it is convenient for others to let her do so. On every occasion when Falkner tries to separate from her for her own good, as he defines it, she uses her claim of filial devotion to obtain permission to stay with him, even if this means going to war or joining him in his prison cell. The female uses her 'duty' of sacrifice, turning it into a powerful tool to shape her environment. The chief test of this power comes at the conclusion of *Falkner* when Elizabeth refuses to choose between her adopted father and her lover, placing the responsibility not on her will but on the involuntary demands of filial duty. This abnegation forces those around her to conform to her emotional needs: Gerard formulates the knightly language so that he can accept her tie to the man who destroyed his mother, and thus joins the *ménage à trois* which places Elizabeth at the emotional centre.

Described in this way, Elizabeth is in danger of sounding calculating and manipulative. To leave the reader with this impression would be to misrepresent her. Rather, what the process shows is that female duties, such as sacrifice and obedience, can be configured into strengths. A comparable situation can be traced in *Lodore*: Ethel commands a new moral authority through her sacrifice to follow her husband's fortunes in debt. Lady Lodore, having lost the status of mother and wife, regains both when she sacrifices her income to help her estranged daughter and son-in-law out of their difficulties. By expecting nothing in return, Lady Lodore regains everything.

The strong female characters of *Lodore* and *Falkner* in some respects symbolize the genre which contains them. The deceptively innocuous form of the sentimental romance, dealing with the 'female' sphere of courtship, family and domesticity, appears less threatening than the ambitious scope of *Frankenstein*, *The Last Man*, and of her earlier histories. In the early novels, Shelley threw down the gauntlet to the reviewers to consider her with the same intellectual rigor accorded to a man writing in these traditional masculine genres. However, her sentimental romances of the 1830s explore more challenging territory than that normally associated with a feminine courtship novel, smuggling into the drawing room unorthodox ideas in an inoffensive guise. Similarly, the meek, dutiful daughters of Shelley's last two novels appear to conform to the emerging Victorian icon of womanhood: the Angel of the home. They could safely be received as visitors in the best households. They seem conventionally feminine, reigning supreme in a small domestic circle but reliant on a male for support and guidance. Not for them are the uncontainable energies of a Beatrice, the prophetess of *Valperga*, or the statesmanship of an Euthanasia. Yet to judge Ethel and, more particularly, Elizabeth on their superficial appearance is to miss the process whereby Shelley reinvents the feminine. She takes conventions of female behaviour and turns them into tools to shape the family environment.

Though not representing the extreme liberated femininity of Fanny Derham or Euthanasia, Elizabeth, Ethel and Lady Lodore all realize a significant part of the Wollstonecraftian agenda for women within the bounds of the male-dominated society of their day. Wollstonecraft, after all, did not see her reformed womankind acting in isolation: her aim was for woman to become 'a rational creature useful to others, and content in its own station'.[6] Women were to be useful primarily – and with immediate effect – as wives, daughters and mothers, as well as, more hypothetically, professionals, doctors, midwives and so on. This is a radical philosophy which runs counter to the male Romantic ethos of self-definition – the ethos of the sons of Jacobinism after *The Rights of Man* – whose most famous Promethean figures were P.B. Shelley and Byron. The Promethean version of Romanticism has long enjoyed the reputation of representing the radical thought of the second generation of Romantic writers. This is only half the story. While the writing of Byron and P.B. Shelley breathes the spirit of liberty and daring, Shelley's novels reflect on the power that can be gained for the female through sacrifice and self-control, a truth her mother realized in *Rights of Woman*. This is at best a partial kind of freedom, because it is circumscribed by the patriarchal society in which the female lives; but it is – more importantly – a liberty which women may reach without being ostracized from the community.

Shelley's last two novels differ from her earlier works in that they conclude with a happy ending centred in the rehabilitated family, whereas *Frankenstein* and *The Last Man* both cruelly strip away all possibility of domestic peace. The early apocalyptic Shelley has modulated into an author content with less extreme positions. It is not sufficient to explain this change by claiming that she was merely responding to her audience demand for a positive resolution; the optimism is not imposed on the end but worked out through the course of the narrative, suggesting Shelley was engaged in more than an authorial afterthought. Her earlier novels chart the frustration of many of the big ideals of the radical agenda, for example the defeat of republicanism in *Valperga* and *The Last Man*. In contrast, her last two novels represent a reconciliation of progressive ideas with the possible. The Promethean figures of radicalism had perished early on in their dazzling careers; it was left to their less ambitious female friend to continue the debate on a more humble scale, grasping from the jaws of defeat small victories for radical ideas.

Notes

1. Pamela Clemit, *The Godwinian Novel: the Rational Fictions of Godwin, Brockden Brown, Mary Shelley* (Oxford: Clarendon Press, 1993) p. 187.
2. Mary Hays, *Memoirs of Emma Courtney* (1796), new edn (London: Pandora, 1987) p. 192.
3. See the useful discussion of contemporary reviews of *Falkner* in Pamela Clemit's introduction to the Pickering edition of the novel (*MWS Pickering*, 7, pp. x–xi).
4. William Godwin, *An Enquiry Concerning Political Justice* (1793); facsmile rpt,

introd. Jonathan Wordsworth, 2 vols (Oxford: Woodstock Books, 1992) I, p. 82.
5. Robert Bage, *Hermsprong* (1796), ed. P. Faulkner (Oxford: Oxford University Press, 1985) p. 218.
6. Mary Wollstonecraft, *A Vindication of the Rights of Woman* (2nd edn 1798) ed. C.H. Poston (New York: W. W. Norton & Co., 1975) p. 61.

14
Public and Private Fidelity: Mary Shelley's 'Life of William Godwin' and *Falkner*

Graham Allen

I Mary Shelley's 'Life of William Godwin'

William Godwin, as we know, left Mary Shelley in charge of looking over his manuscripts after his death in 1836, and of deciding 'which of them are fit to be printed, consigning the rest to the flames'. Betty Bennett writes:

> Mary Shelley began this project, which she never completed, by organizing the three chapters of memoirs written by Godwin and collecting, organizing, and commenting on copies of his letters.
> (*MWSL* II, p. 270n.2)

Somewhere along the line, however, this project stretched beyond that of editing Godwin's papers and grew into what we might call a hybrid project: an edition of unpublished work including his own memoirs, but also a memoir by Shelley herself. As Shelley describes it to Tom Cooper in early 1837:

> My father's Memoirs – Consisting of a portion of autobiography regarding his early years – a great many letters from & to him – with notes by myself to connect & explain – will be in two Octavo Volumes.
> (*MWSL* II, p. 284)

Note that Shelley calls the project 'My father's Memoirs'. In a rather famous letter to Trelawny around the same period, she called the work 'my Father's life' (*MWSL* II, p. 280). Shelley's 'Life of William Godwin', is a hybrid work, somewhere between an edition and a biography or memoir. It consists of manuscripts strewn throughout the Abinger Collection in the Bodleian Library; a series of manuscripts which do not eventually amount up to anything we can call a text.[1] As Syndy Conger has also pointed out, the 'Life of William Godwin' is also something of an enigma. Despite the publisher Colburn having made a contract with Shelley to publish the work, mention of the project seems to peter out after the letter to Trelawny in January 1837. It had apparently been superseded by the editing of P.B. Shelley's poetry and then his prose for Edward Moxon. Yet, in 606/4 there is a note (perhaps to herself) dated 'Richmond 6 May 1840' which, if it does refer to the 'Life of William Godwin', is puzzling. This note states that 'there are many letters to be considered' but that there is not 'anything to add'. Since Shelley's commentary in 606 does not stray much beyond the 1790s, how can she say that there is nothing to add?

Enigmatic and baffling as it is, the series of manuscripts relating to this project is of great importance on a number of levels. They represent a crucial source of material of and about Godwin, as biographers of that author have demonstrated.[2] But they are also fascinating as a largely unread text (using that word *sous rature*) by Shelley herself. As my reading seeks to demonstrate, an acquaintance with Shelley's 'Life of William Godwin' can offer us new perspectives on her approach to such issues as biography and fiction as well as providing us with new ways of interpreting her later novels, especially her last novel *Falkner*.

In her memoir, save for a few comments and references, Shelley stays mainly with the early life and work of Godwin. One way of responding to the 'Life of William Godwin' might be to argue that it is mainly a presentation of Godwin's own autobiographical pieces (which do not stretch beyond the 1790s),[3] and that once Shelley is left without Godwin's own notes on his life, apart from the sparse Journal, she cannot find her way to proceed further. This approach might then develop the argument that this fact demonstrates Shelley's confusion between editing her father's work and writing a memoir of his life. Whatever we think about this, it is certainly clear that Shelley did, at one stage, intend to pass beyond Godwin's own autobiographical sketches and write a 'life', and there is fascinating material, for example, in the penultimate division of 606 and also in 532 on Godwin and Wollstonecraft's relationship and their friends' and acquaintances' reaction to their marriage.

This point, however, might suggest another thesis as to why Shelley left the project uncompleted; that is, that as she passed from Godwin's actual autobiographical work out into the late 1790s and beyond, the subject matter began to draw far too close to home for her to continue. To write a full 'commentary' on Godwin's life would obviously mean dragging herself and her own difficult and at times publicly infamous life into the story. Indeed, one begins to wonder how it is possible for Shelley even to imagine writing a memoir or life of her father, at a time, of course, when she is still struggling with the Shelley family, is under instructions not to publish P.B. Shelley's work or his life, and is channelling most of her energy (under these constraining circumstances) into giving her son the best education and future prospects she possibly can. The small memoir she contributed to the 1831 Colburn and Bentley edition of *Caleb Williams* seems to suggest the extent of the possible in this respect.

I would argue that there is a fundamental aporia within the twin functions of editing and memorialization for Shelley when confronting this project; an aporia which gives us a clue as to why it was left unfinished. In a letter to Mary Ellen Peacock, dated 3 February 1835, in which she discusses Moxon's proposal for an edition of P. B. Shelley's poetry, Shelley refers to the idea of writing a 'life' of the poet and states:

> the *life* is out of the question – but in talking over it the question of letters comes up – You know how I shrink from all *private* detail for the public – but Shelley's letters are beautifully written, and every thing *private* could be omitted.
> (*MWSL* II, p. 221)

Again, in a letter to Mary Hays dated 20 April 1836 discussing the project, she writes: 'There is nothing more detestable or cruel than the publication of letters meant for one eye only' (*MWSL* II, p. 270). In fact, this aversion to publishing 'private' letters or the 'private' portions of letters is reiterated so many times that it is clearly a major principle for Shelley with regard to editorial work and memorialization. The memorialist and editor clearly have a duty of fidelity towards the 'private' expressions of the subject-author; a duty, that is, to keep them private. Yet, another principle of Shelley's with regard to the art of editing and of memorialization is that, as she puts it in 606 (speaking of Godwin's own Memoirs): 'The briefest outline written by the man himself contains more real information in matters of biography, than pages of uncertain guesses.' Putting that point even more concisely, Shelley writes (again in 606) that she is: 'of opinion that one word written by the man himself is more characteristic than pages of enquiry as to his character'. This second principle seems at least potentially to contradict the first. The contradiction in fidelity – fidelity to the author–subject's 'privateness', fidelity to the author-subject's actual words and life – is largely caused by a clash between Shelley's own understandable abhorrence of the making public of private utterances and a contrary, Godwinian notion of history and biography.

Referring to the 'best and most exalted' men, Godwin writes in his 'Essay of History and Romance':

> I am not contented to observe such a man upon the public stage, I would follow him into his closet. I would see the friend and the father of a family, as well as the patriot. I would read his works and his letters, if any remain to us. I would observe the turn of his thoughts and the character of his phraseology. I would collate his behaviour in prosperity with his behaviour in adversity. I should be glad to know the course of his studies, and the arrangement of his time. I should rejoice to have, or to be enabled to make, if that were possible, a journal of his ordinary and minutest actions.[4]

Godwin, of course, lived up to such notions by providing propitious conditions for those, his daughter at their head, who would insure his own posthumous immortality. In 606 Shelley refers to Godwin's own desire for posthumous fame, and there is a good deal of evidence in her 'Life of William Godwin' that she wishes to be true to her father's notions about and desires for memorialization; as we see, for example, in the passage she writes about introducing private letters into her memoir. Shelley writes of her decision to 'suppress' 'a reasonable number' of Godwin's correspondence, since in modern society, with inventions such as 'the two penny post', a 'private man's life' and relations with his 'friends' is often carried out not by oral communication but by 'pen ink and paper'. Having noted this, Shelley writes that:

> to give the notes and letters a man receives, ^as well as writes^ is to [tell?] the subjects on which his heart is set – which occupy his thoughts – and influence him to sadness or enjoyment. Most of the letters I print however are from celebrated people – nor do I insert any that do not derive an interest from the writer, from the subject, or from the ~~style in whi~~[ch] light it throws on my father's feelings and opinions.

(dep.c.606)

I do not think I need to spell out the uneasiness which this passage displays. It would seem that to write her father's 'life' it is necessary to follow him into his closet; and yet such an adventure is fraught for Shelley (as it surely is for any daughter) with anxieties and ambiguities. One of Shelley's major problems, in fact, is that when we follow her father into his closet the people we meet there are very much public figures. How do you arbitrate between the private and the public when the people in the author-subject's private life are 'celebrated people'? More problematically still, many of those members of the inner circle do not seem to make any distinction between private attachment and general principles. So thoroughly do Godwin and his circle live up in their correspondence to the philosopher's notions of the sincere and frank expression of the truth, the cutting through of social decorum and enfeebling etiquette, that Shelley is forced to criticize them. She writes of the 'very ^disputative^ air' of his own and his friends' correspondence, and notes how they practised a system in which 'silence usually announced approval' whilst 'when they thought it right to express disapprobation' they did so in writing. The problem with this system, as Shelley states, is that the '^impetus^ of composition added to the fervour of a love of truth, and the eye and voice of the friend not being there to check and soften, the rounded sentences ^often^ gathered asperity as they rolled along'. Shelley suggests that '[a]n opposite system were certainly best' (dep.c.606).

What is particularly interesting here is Shelley's understanding of what happens to private utterance when presented through the medium of writing. Writing, even the supposedly private writing of correspondence, is dangerously anonymous, dangerously cut off from the softening presence of the addressee. Writing, unlike oral communication (communication *in the presence of the Other*), has an impetus and even a logic of its own. It controls, transforms, and even disfigures sentiment, the tie/relationship to the Other. It involves us in an economy of relations and significations in which what we might call the *bodily referent* is lost.

It would seem that the dangerous anonymity and autonomous impetus of writing requires strict control. And yet, of course, Shelley writes this in the context of presenting, or preparing to present, the very kind of written communication she wants to censure. In writing her father's 'life' Shelley is forced, or would be forced, to bring private correspondence into the public domain. And more, this very correspondence is of a type which disrupts the wished-for division between private and public expression, private and public relations.

The problem Shelley faces is not simply one of writing; it is essentially one of reading, of interpretation. This issue is, of course, at the very centre of Godwin's political and philosophical radicalism. In 532 Shelley writes of Godwin's 'axiom that truth adequately illustrated must prevail'. And again: 'It was an axiom of the new philosophy that no mind could refuse truth if adequately demonstrated'. In 606 she transcribes a letter by Godwin which includes the statement that '& you will find, that – Give to a state but liberty enough, & it is impossible that vice should exist in it'. She comments:

> That any one should in the sincerity of his heart entertain this beleif seems strange – but my father did – it was the basis of his system, the very key stone of the arch of Justice, by which he desired to knit together the whole human family.
> (dep.c.606)

Shelley finds Godwin's idealism 'somewhat astounding' because she, to a greater degree than her father ever did, understands what I would call the logic of naming, or of the public name.

For Godwin, history is understandable in analogy with, indeed is structurally coincident with, the legal process. In *Political Justice*,[5] in letters in 227, and again in his 'Essay of History and Romance', Godwin draws together history-writing and legal trials by way of emphasizing the doubtfulness of 'evidence'. He writes:

> Nothing is more uncertain, more contradictory, more unsatisfying, than the evidence of facts. If this be the case in courts of justice, where truth is sometimes sifted with tenacious perseverance, how much more will it hold true to the historian?[6]

Godwin, of course, knew all about public trials, and it is significant to note that Shelley spends a considerable amount of time in 606 dealing with the treason trials of 1793 and 1794 in which the defendants were placed on capital charges for what were, at the very worst, no more than acts of seditious libel. She describes the build-up to these trials in great detail, and transcribes liberally from Godwin's correspondence and particularly from his *Cursory Strictures on the Charge Delivered by Lord Chief Justice Eyre*.[7] That text greatly influenced the outcome of the 1794 trial (which involved Holcroft, Horne Tooke, et al), as Shelley painstakingly demonstrates, and she rounds off her account of this glorious episode in her father's life with the eulogistic: 'It was for the cause that he contributed – for the cause that he contended – for the cause that he felt glad of writing. His own personal glory mingled little with these higher emotions' (dep.c.606).

Thus, at the centre of Shelley's fragment 'Life' of her father we find a celebration of an act of writing which manages to control public naming, which manages to so shape and direct language that it brings about the public recognition and vindication of truth rather than error, of correct rather than defamatory naming. An act of writing, no less, that manages to publicly attach the correct name to its bodily referents.

If the 1794 sedition trials are Godwin's greatest authorial achievement (in the sense of negotiating the process of public naming) then his worst performance in this regard is surely his composition and publication of *Memoirs of the Author of 'The Rights of Woman'*, not forgetting of course his publishing of Wollstonecraft's *Posthumous Works* including her private correspondence (particularly with Imlay). Richard Holmes makes the connection between the *Cursory Strictures* and the *Memoir* of Wollstonecraft in his edition of the latter text.[8] Holmes also discusses how Godwin's *Memoirs* of Wollstonecraft brought that author to public trial and unwittingly found her guilty, unwittingly allowed for the attachment to its subject of a defamatory public name. It is worth remembering here the first paragraph of Godwin's 'Preface' to his *Memoirs* of Wollstonecraft, and particularly its rather tortuous penultimate sentence:

> I cannot easily prevail on myself to doubt, that the more fully we are presented with the picture and story of such persons as the subject of the following narrative, the more generally shall we feel in ourselves an attachment to their fate, and a sympathy in their excellencies.[9]

Such a refusal to doubt, or to acknowledge the misrepresentations and ideological transformations consequent on the act of writing, is not, we might wish to follow Shelley in saying, likely to help 'knit together' either a micro – or the macro – 'human family'.

In 606, there is a discussion of her parents' relationship in which, significantly, Shelley lays at least part of the blame for the adverse reactions to their marriage among certain of Godwin's friends on the tone of Godwin's previous writings, specifically *Political Justice*. She concludes her discussion of this issue with the following:

~~Strangely enough~~ ^Yet in fact^ all Mr. Godwin's inner & more private feelings were opposed to ^the supposed gist of^ his doctrines. ~~No one respected the virtue of women more or demanded that~~ ^The former were all strongly enlisted in the side of female virtue^ ...

(dep.c.606)

It is hardly fanciful to see here a veiled reference to the troubled conclusions of Godwin's *Memoir* of Wollstonecraft. Elsewhere in 606 Shelley paraphrases statements in Godwin's fragment 'Analysis of Own Character' which bespeak Godwin's own lack of 'sensibility' and inability to 'readily participate in the pains & pleasures of others'.

If Godwin's 'inner and more private feelings' connected him to a 'female virtue' associated with Wollstonecraft, we can justifiably assume (taking 606 and related deposits as evidence) that Shelley saw his *Memoir* of Wollstonecraft as stemming from that side which lacked sensibility. Part of that limitation, as the publication of the *Memoir* and the *Posthumous Works* of Wollstonecraft dramatically demonstrated, was an inability to imagine the manner in which readers would respond to the publication of private facts and biographical details.

I am suggesting something more than this, however. Shelley, in composing the 'life' of her father, finds herself entering into exactly the same process her father had so unsuccessfully entered in 1798. In memorial writing the private 'name' – as I will call the bodily referent – is made public and so is put on trial and in that trial is frequently (as in the case of Wollstonecraft) found guilty, transformed beyond all recognition. Godwin's editing and memorialization of Wollstonecraft was intended to be an act of fidelity, yet it sent her name into a public sphere only for that name to become separated from any relation to its bodily referent. If the name of Wollstonecraft became a commodity, a token of political and economic exchange-value, then Godwin's memorialization and editing of Wollstonecraft greatly helped that process.

There is a very telling moment quite early on in *Falkner* in which Shelley articulates directly one of the principal themes of the novel as a whole. Just before Neville enters into Falkner's and Elizabeth's world, and so begins the process whereby the past returns, the narrator writes the following:

> It is a singular law of human life, that the past, which apparently no longer forms a portion of our existence, never dies; new shoots,

as it were, spring up at different intervals and places, all bearing the indelible characteristics of the parent stalk; the circular emblem of eternity is suggested by this meeting and recurrence of the broken ends of our life.

(*FN* 43 [I. vii])

Throughout *Falkner* the Biblical notion of the sins of the fathers being visited on their children and their childrens' children is never very far from our minds. And in a manner in which we come almost to expect in studying Shelley's life and reading her work, such a theme uncannily anticipates the experience of composing a life of her father. Which is to say, how can Shelley write such a life without replicating the very trauma (the publication and reception of Godwin's *Memoirs* of Wollstonecraft and of her private letters) which she wishes to avoid? Thinking about the project in this sense takes us back to the letter of January 1837 to Trelawny, after which mention of the project drops out of the letters.

The prospect arises in the letter to Trelawny of a kind of transgenerational recurrence of the same: the publication of a memoir ruining the public name of the mother (in this case Shelley herself) and thus ruining the 'prospects' of the child.[10] The return to an original trauma opens up before Shelley as she contemplates writing her father's 'life'. Writing the beloved's memoir should be an act of private fidelity made public. However, Shelley comes to see that no memoir can be secure in its fidelity, since it can lead to defamation of the subject's name, the potential severance between that name and its private (bodily) referent. More than this, defamation of the name can set off a series of repetitions in which each generation suffers the same trauma, the same subjection to public trial and its verdict of guilt.

II The Return of/to the Mother: Mary Shelley's *Falkner*

Falkner is a novel about private motive and public scandal, public naming. It is a novel about how the past returns, but also, as Shelley explained to Maria Gisborne, it is a novel about 'fidelity' (*MWSL* II, p. 260). Above all, it is a novel about 'vindication', that word of all words which bespeaks the connection between memorialization and legal trials. Shelley wrote on a number of occasions of how quickly the novel came to her in composition, of how it almost wrote itself. And when we read it this becomes understandable; it is so structurally neat. A son quests to vindicate his mother; a daughter seeks to protect and then clings to the belief that her father should be vindicated; the son and the daughter love; the secret but finally exposed connection between the mother and the father requires, in terms of social decorum, that the daughter and the son remain forever divided. How to resolve such an apparently irresolvable problem? How to bridge the gap between private feeling and public naming?

Much of what has so far been said about *Falkner* rests on an examination of Shelley's treatment of what she calls in *Lodore* the daughter's 'sexual education' by the father (*L* 218 [III. ii]). Thus, the novel is seen as stemming from the author's own biography, specifically her 'excessive and romantic' and yet highly ambivalent relationship to her father. But such a biographical approach to the novel needs to be reconsidered. Biography does not explain such a text; biography, rather, is part of what this novel is about, part of its subject.

The most uncanny portion of the novel involves the public unearthing of the body of Neville's dead mother. In fact, it is possible to argue that in a novel which slowly unravels (through first-person and third-person accounts, oral communication, public and private documents) the origins of a crime against a mother and so vindicates that mother's public name, this unearthing of the literal maternal body is part of the story I have been articulating so far.

Focusing on this central crises in the novel foregrounds the importance of the character of Gerard Neville, a figure frequently down-played in critical discussions of *Falkner*. Neville and Elizabeth Raby, can, in fact, be viewed as mirror images of each other, both having lost what the other yet has (Elizabeth having lost a blood parent, Neville a loving, nurturing parent) and thus both still possessing what the other lacks. The novel is designed so that the vindication of Neville's mother's public name must involve the defamation of Elizabeth's father's name. One cannot, it would seem, protect and preserve the name of the father without perpetuating and consolidating the unjust defamation of the mother. If there are biographical dimensions to this novel then, surely, we must recognize the relation between the novel's author and the character of Neville as much as we recognize the relations between that author and Elizabeth Raby.

Neville is a character who, like the infant Elizabeth, is destined to continually return to the physical site of the dead mother's body. The 'tale' of how the mother was lost is told a number of times and in a number of contexts; in Chapter xvii of Volume I, Lady Cecil, in her account of Neville's life, first tells of how Neville had recounted the event to his nurse. This traumatic event, which has already been described by Falkner in his narrative (not submitted to any reading until Chapter ix of Volume II), has to be retraced by Neville for the benefit of the barristers working on behalf of his father, Sir Boyvill, in Chapter ii of Volume II. After the harrowing experience of giving testimony in the House of Lords in the divorce case brought by Sir Boyvill, Neville, still merely 'a boy of eleven' (*FN* 121 [II. ii]), flees his father's house and heroically returns to the site of trauma. Neville returns to Dromore, Cumberland, the scene of his mother's traumatic loss, with the same belief as the infant Elizabeth Raby at the novel's beginning, that in making such a return (unknowingly, for Neville as yet, to the mother's grave) 'he should again be restored to her' (ibid.).

We should, of course, remember that Neville's mother's name, Alithea, literally means 'truth'. Alithea is a mother-figure whose name, despite its literal meaning, is, after her death, publicly defamed, branded as *false*, *untrue*. Neville's story, in the stages of the novel before Falkner's narrative is offered up for interpretation, reads like a classic case in traumatic memory. As Cynthia Chase writes, meditating on the story of Tancred and Clorinda which Freud employs as touchstone for his theory of trauma: 'trauma is not locatable in the simple violent or original event in the individual's past, but rather in the way that its very unassimilated nature – the way it was precisely *not known* in the first instance – returns to haunt the survivor later on.'[11]

Neville, the infant child left behind on his mother's inexplicable disappearance (abduction by 'the stranger', Falkner), returns constantly to the site of this loss searching for a mother whose very name embodies the object of his search. Yet, until Falkner's narrative is read and the origins of that disappearance are explained, the return is merely a return to a place of empty signifiers. Falkner's narrative returns Neville once more to the lone hut and 'skeleton tree' he had seen, as a boy of eleven, near to the scene of his inexplicable loss. Falkner's narrative, that is to say, literally places the mother's body in its previously unknown grave; and yet, at the moment it uncovers the truth it covers that body over, concealing it from public view:

> I wrapped her in her cloak, and laid her in the open grave. I tore down some of the decaying boughs of the withered tree, and arching them above her body, threw my own cloak above, so with vain care to protect her lifeless form from immediate contact with the soil.
>
> (*FN* 191–2 [II. xiii])

Falkner's narrative is not, for Neville, a revelation of a new truth, but an uncanny returning to a place he has already viewed: 'Gerard felt sure he had seen and marked that very spot' (*FN* 212 [III. ii]), and as the major participants in the drama collect round the literal 'spot', at the beginning of Volume III, Neville enacts a return worthy in its uncanniness of inclusion within the literature of traumatic repetition. In what is perhaps the novel's central scene, Alithea's body is unearthed as father, son, and others watch on:

> At length some harder substance opposed their progress, and they worked more cautiously. Mingled with sand they threw out pieces of dark substance like cloth or silk, and at length got out of the wide long trench they had been opening. With one consent, though in silence, everyone gathered nearer, and looked in – they saw a human skeleton. The action of the elements, which the sands had not been able to impede, had destroyed every vestige of a human frame, except those discoloured bones, and long tresses of dark hair, which were wound around the skull. A universal yet suppressed groan burst from all. Gerard felt inclined to leap into the grave, but the thought of the many eyes all gazing, acted as a check; and a second instinctive feeling of pious reverence induced him to unfasten his large black horseman's cloak, and to cast it over the opening. Sir Boyvill then broke the silence: 'You have done well, my son; let no man lift that covering, or in any way disturb the remains beneath. Do you know, my friends, who lies there? Do you remember the night when Mrs. Neville was carried off? The country was raised, but we sought for her in vain. On that night she was murdered, and was buried here.'
>
> (*FN* 215 [III. iii])

Sir Boyvill's endorsement of his son's act of concealment is far more ambiguous than he realizes. Since what appears like a move from literary repetition (Neville has frequently been associated with a kind of inverted version of Hamlet) to an act of private fidelity (the concealment of the mother's dead body from the public gaze) is itself a literary repetition of Falkner's own narrative. Concealment and exposure, private and public fidelity, have become so confused in this scene that to cover over (keep private) the body of the mother becomes the repetition of an act of concealment which must, if the mother is to be vindicated, be exposed. To protect the previously exposed (defamed) mother, Neville must resist his father's desire for a new public trial, a trial which will expose (defame) the name not only of Falkner, but also of Elizabeth. Yet, to resist such a public exposure of the father's and thus Elizabeth's name, would be for Neville to risk repeating the very trauma (defamation of Alithea's name) his whole life has been spent in attempting to heal and undo.

Neville is forced to return twice more to his mother's grave: first, in an official investigation instigated by his father, for the purpose of bringing Falkner to trial; second, under a desperate compulsion to find some truth within the war of fidelity to which events have brought him:

> His mother's decaying form lay beneath the sands on which he was stretched, death was there in its most hideous form.... He had demanded from Heaven the revelation of his mother's fate, *here* he found it, here in the narrow grave lay the evidence of her virtues and her death; – did he thank Heaven? even while he did, he felt with bitterness that the granting of his prayer was inextricably linked with the ruin of a being, as good and fair as she, whose honour he had so earnestly desired to vindicate.
>
> (*FN* 221 [III. iv])

If Shelley's *Falkner*, as I am suggesting, fictionalizes and thus returns us to the history and reception (and thus the trauma) of her own father's narrative (memoir) of her mother, then we might begin to see another fictional splitting of biographical referents in this novel: that part of Godwin which sought to vindicate the 'Author of *The Vindication of the Rights of Woman*' corresponding to the character of Neville, that part of Godwin which effected the defamation of Wollstonecraft's name corresponding to Falkner. And yet, just as Neville cannot simply be read as an uncomplicatedly positive contributor to the vindication of female names (the mother's or Elizabeth's), just as Neville is ambiguously caught in a process of public naming and traumatic *returning* which appears beyond his own control, so Falkner's actions are ambivalent, beyond his own intentions and desires.

Falkner himself, like Neville, is haunted throughout with his own traumatic process of returning to Alithea's dead body. From the moment, at the beginning of the novel, in which, reading Mrs Raby's letter to Alithea, Falkner hears Alithea's 'voice from the grave' (*FN* 22 [I. iii]) to the scenes after the public reception of his narrative, Falkner is confronted with the fact that his name, and his part in the defamation of Alithea's name, must have a devastating influence on the fortunes of his adopted daughter, Elizabeth. Falkner, in fact, is a figure to whom the past clings tenaciously; a figure who is destined to suffer, and to make those he loves suffer, *the return*, as the novel's narrator makes plain.[12]

In the scene in which Falkner awakes to face public trial for his crime against Alithea, Wollstonecraft's mother's death-bed words – words which Godwin tells us in his *Memoir* Wollstonecraft returned to again and again (and words which her daughter, as we know, also returned to on more than one occasion) – are, as it were, unearthed once more: 'The court clock, meanwhile, kept measure of the time that passed; the hands travelled silently on – *another turn, and all would be over*; – and what would then be?' (FN 283 [III. xvi]; my emphasis).[13]

In *Falkner*, then, the mother's name is a contested signifier which produces, in the major male protagonists, an experience of repetition which seems beyond resolution. One should remember that two things bring this narrative to its denouement: the unearthing of the mother's dead body; the publication [*sic*] of the father's narrative, a narrative which centres on the history of that maternal body, its death and its public defamation. Reading the novel in this way opens up the possibility of a critical metalepsis with regard to *Falkner*; the possibility, that is, of *returning* Shelley's novel *Falkner* to her 'Life of William Godwin'. The composition of the third volume of *Falkner* was, of course, punctuated by the death of Godwin. I am suggesting, however, that *Falkner*, in ways more significant than the literal, is *about* the 'Life of William Godwin'; or rather, it is *about* the problems (discursive, social, private) confronted by the author of that later fragment.

Falkner's narrative itself centres on the events which have led up to the defamation of the mother's name; it tells of the father's part in that traumatic event. Written as a kind of suicide note while Falkner seeks death in the Greek Wars of Independence, it is a text which, like all texts, takes on new significance in new contexts. Indeed, Falkner's intentions for his narrative, as explained to Elizabeth, might well strike the reader as overdetermined and, as the plot of Shelley's novel so painstakingly suggests, impossible to effect.[14] By the time the narrative is finally presented to those whom Falkner has injured it faces a seemingly impossible task: to vindicate Alithea, while also vindicating Falkner, satisfying both Neville and Sir Boyvill, while not injuring, by association, Elizabeth.

In *Falkner*, as in Shelley's own life, the character and the history of the mother can only be learnt by reading the father's textual account.

It is difficult, in fact, as one reads Falkner's description of Alithea herself, not to recall (return to) the descriptions of Wollstonecraft scattered through Godwin's *Memoir*, and particularly in its problematic conclusion. Rather like Godwin in that famous ending, Falkner attempts, rather less nervously than Godwin, to capture the essence of the mother's character; an 'essence' which in both cases is centred in intuition, spontaneity, and sensitivity:

> She had two qualities which I have never seen equalled separately, but which, united in her, formed a spell no one could resist – the most acute sensitiveness to joy or grief in her own person, and the most lively sympathy with these feelings in others. I have seen her so enter heart and soul into the sentiments of one in whom she was interested, that her whole being took the colour of their mood; and her very features and complexion appeared to alter in unison with theirs.
>
> (*FN* 162 [II. x])

Like Godwin, Falkner misjudges the effect his narrative will produce: he thinks, on a practical level, it will lead to a duel with Neville and thus a noble death for himself (a final, unequivocal, repayment for his crime against Alithea and her son). However, while Falkner's narrative *speaks* of his contribution to the mother's fall, the response by its readers, its public reception, serves to redeem her. Elizabeth's reaction is the model of daughterly fidelity: 'He is innocent!' (*FN* 194 [II. xiv]). Sir Boyvill's, until his death-bed confession of 'the truth', is the model of worldly and litigious defensiveness: 'from the beginning to the end it is a lie' (*FN* 211 [III. ii]). Neville, the novel's Hamlet-figure, caught between fidelity to his mother's public name and private love for Elizabeth, wanders in his interpretation between credulity and scepticism. The novel's resolution of its principal oppositions only emerges as Neville, spurred on by his love for Elizabeth and his growing recognition of the nobility of Falkner himself, learns to find the truth (and thus his mother, Alithea) in Falkner's 'tale' rather than in a public trial which will, in judging the innocence or guilt of the father, return public attention once again to the trial of the mother's name. As he says: 'For many years I devoted myself to discovering my mother's fate. I have discovered it. Falkner's narrative tells all.... This trial is but a mockery' (*FN* 259 [III. xii]).

Falkner's narrative reverses the reception of Godwin's *Memoir of Wollstonecraft*. It performs that most difficult of all authorial tasks: the public narrating of a life which does not betray the subject into a reversal of its true identity, which manages to retain the coincidence between the name and its bodily referent. More than this, however, Falkner's narrative vindicates the mother's name without defaming the father's. In this sense it defeats the economic logic of naming which the plot of *Falkner* exhibits but ultimately transcends: the logic, that is, of 'evidence' and 'justice' in which two parties in a trial cannot both be judged innocent, in which a perceived 'crime' demands retribution, in which all investments require a *return*.

Falkner encrypts the traumatic defamation of the mother's public name by the father into its narrative structure, its rhetoric, its thematics, and its intertextual dimension. It does this partly, as I have suggested, by separating Shelley's own position into that of a son and a daughter, a separation which allows Shelley to develop a narrative presentation of that trauma in which a son's quest to vindicate the mother's defamed name can be placed *alongside* a daughter's quest first to protect and then to vindicate, or seek for the vindication, of the father's name. In that process, *Falkner* as a novel brings into its field of representation the discursive and psychological problems confronted by Shelley when attempting to write a 'life' of her father. But it does this by separating functions which cannot be so separated in that later project.

Elizabeth's desire to forge a 'link' (*FN* 77 [I. xiii]) between Falkner and Neville (between the father's party and the mother's, if you will) is for most of the novel structurally unimaginable; it is so because, in *Falkner*, the economy of family relations are all posited (structured around) the original, public event of the defamation of the mother's name. The economy of these families – which should be based upon the free exchange of private feeling (what in *Lodore* is styled 'the unlimited and unregretted exchange') – is ruptured by that public naming of the mother. This naming, which is the product of a public economy (involving scandal, legal trial, the legal separation of public names, i.e. divorce), is not – despite the brave words of political radicals – analogous to but in fact opposed to that private economy of filial relations Shelley's work imagines. In *Falkner*, as in *Lodore*, society is not 'the whole human family' but is rather 'knit[ted] together' by a system of relations and exchanges which threaten to 'unknit' the private relations of particular families. The Raby family, re-entrance into which must be for Elizabeth at the expense of her social ties to Falkner, are only the most obvious examples in this novel of a system constructed on the logic of the public name. A 'little word', we should remember, let loose by her husband, turns 'the tide of public feeling' and transforms the name of Alithea into its exact opposite:

> she, who had been pitied and wept as dead, was now regarded as a voluntary deserter from her home. Her virtues were remembered against her; and surmises, which before would have been reprobated almost as blasphemy, became current as undoubted truths.
>
> (*FN* 102 [I. xvii])

Mary Poovey writes that in *Falkner*:

> the father figure ... is actually being humbled by a daughter for crimes committed against the mother. In fact, as we explore the sources of energy of this novel, it seems that Mary Shelley is concerned at least as much with punishing the father as with defusing the threat he now poses to the daughter's future.[15]

The greatest threat posed by the father to the daughter, as we have seen, is that in encouraging an act of public fidelity he threatens the daughter with a return to the trauma of public naming into which he has already been instrumental in placing the mother. Yet *Falkner* is not simply a product of this father–daughter process of threat and resistance. It minutely anatomizes the very logic of public naming which generates that process.

Like Ethel in *Lodore*, Elizabeth Raby employs a language of fidelity which reverses the logic of public naming by troping upon, and thus inverting, its very terms. The narrator early in the novel employs such economic terms to figure Elizabeth's love for Falkner: 'Elizabeth believed that she could never adequately repay the vast obligation which she was under to him' (*FN* 55 [I. ix]). Confronted with the choice between fidelity to her father or relinquishing his name in favour of adoption within the Raby family, Elizabeth states defiantly:

> It is a lesson I have been learning many years; I cannot unlearn it now. I am his; bought by his kindness; earned by his unceasing care for me, I belong to him – his child – if you will, his servant – I do not quarrel with names – a child's duty I pay him, and will ever.
>
> (*FN* 233 [III. vii])

As in *Lodore*, *Falkner* presents us with a resolution dependent on an act of love and fidelity which seeks no return. In both novels a vision of love rooted in an unconventional, 'wild' education outside of the confines of dominant society is pitted against that society's logic of economic returns. In *Lodore*, Lady Lodore's anonymous gift of her estate and moneys to Ethel and Villiers insures their union, and finally wins her family and love. In *Falkner*, inspired by Elizabeth's unwavering fidelity, Neville's inclusion of her into the 'consultations' between himself and Falkner, an act which defies the logic of exchange (here the gift of Falkner's 'daughter' *in return* for the loss of a mother), allows for the final resolution.

To view such a narrative resolution as a wish-fulfilment – a wish-fulfilment which at once humbles the father while idealizing the values of bourgeois family relations – is perhaps true enough.[16] Yet it remains a half-truth. Since *Falkner* also stands as a critique of the very social systems which generate such desires and idealized visions of familial relations.

Falkner, I have been arguing, is a meta-memoir, in that it can contain within its representational field the public domain into which non-fictional memorialization passes unprotected. *Falkner* avoids what I am calling 'the return' by thematizing it and re-presenting it. The return, of the trauma of the defamation of the mother's name, is restaged in this novel, and is thus resisted. In other words, in *Falkner*, Shelley practices a form of fidelity which she knew, and would know again, was impossible outside of the realm of fiction. The movement from public trial to private negotiation dramatized in the concluding part of the novel fictionalizes a movement from public to private fidelity which Shelley had herself to return to in the editorial and memorial work which, after the novel's completion, immediately enveloped her. *Falkner*, we might say, lives up to Godwin's ideas about biography, since it represents a more successful (more fideistic) history than, as Shelley knew, any memoir can.

Notes

My research has been helped by a grant from The President's Fund, U.C.C. I would like to thank Lord Abinger for his permission to cite from The Abinger Collection, The Bodleian Library, and Dr B.C. Barker-Benfield for his help as Senior Assistant Librarian, Department of Western Manuscripts, Bodleian Library. An earlier version of this essay was given as a paper at 'Mary Shelley, Parents, Peers, Progeny' (APU and OU, Cambridge, September 1997).

242 *The Parental Legacy*

1. The main deposit is housed in the Abinger Shelley Collection in the Bodleian Library as dep.c.606. Other deposits which contain related material include dep.c.227, dep.c.607, dep.c.532/8, dep.b.226/1, dep.b.228, dep.c.602, dep.c.674, and dep.c.810. For other discussions of Shelley's manuscript, see Clara Tuite and Judith Barbour, 'William and Mary: Muse, Editor, Executrix in the Shelley Circle', in *The Textual Condition: Rhetoric and Editing*, eds Maurice Blackman, Francis Muecke and Margaret Sankey (Sydney: LCP, 1995) pp. 92–109. I have also been greatly helped by Syndy McMillen Conger's 'Multivocality in Mary Shelley's Unfinished Memoirs of her Father', delivered to the Fifth British Association of Romantic Studies Conference, 'Romantic Generations', at The University of Leeds on 24–27 July 1997.
2. See, for example, C. Kegan Paul, *William Godwin: His Friends and Contemporaries*, 2 vols (London: Henry S. King and Co, 1876) and William St Clair, *The Godwins and the Shelleys: the Biography of a Family* (London: Faber and Faber, 1989).
3. For Godwin's autobiographical writings, see *Autobiography, Autobiographical Fragments and Reflections, Godwin/Shelley Correspondence, Memoirs*, ed. Mark Philp (vol. 1 of *Collected Novels and Memoirs of William Godwin*, 8 vols [London: William Pickering, 1992]).
4. Godwin, 'Essay of History and Romance' in *Educational and Literary Writings*, ed. Pamela Clemit pp. 294–5 (vol. 5 of *Political and Philosophical Writings of William Godwin*, 7 vols [London: William Pickering, 1993], hereafter Godwin, *Politics and Philosophy*).
5. Godwin, *Enquiry Concerning Political Justice and Its Influence on Modern Morals and Happiness*, ed. Issac Kramnick (Harmondsworth: Penguin, 1985) pp. 653–4.
6. Godwin, *Politics and Philosophy*, 5, p. 297.
7. For *Cursory Structures*, see *Political Writings*, ed. Mark Philp, researcher Austin Gee, vol. 2 of Godwin, *Politics and Philosophy*.
8. Godwin, *Memoirs* in Mary Wollstonecraft and William Godwin, *A Short Residence in Sweden and Memoirs of the Author of 'The Rights of Woman'*, ed. Richard Holmes (Harmondsworth: Penguin, 1987) p. 44. See also Mitzi Myers, 'Godwin's *Memoirs* of Wollstonecraft: The Shaping of Self and Subject', *Studies in Romanticism*, 20.3 (1981) 299–316.
9. Godwin, *Memoirs of the Author of 'The Rights of Woman'*, p. 204.
10. See *MWSL* II, pp. 280–1.
11. See Cathy Caruth, *Unclaimed Experience: Trauma, Narrative, and History* (Baltimore and London: Johns Hopkins University Press, 1996) pp. 3–4.
12. See *FN* 140 [II. vi].
13. See Godwin, *Memoirs of the Author of 'The Rights of Woman'*, p. 213; see also Janet Todd, ed., Mary Wollstonecraft, *Mary, Maria*; Mary Shelley, *Matilda* (Harmondsworth: Penguin, 1992) p. xix.
14. See *FN* 64–5 (I. xi).
15. Mary Poovey, *The Proper Lady and the Woman Writer: Ideology as Style in the Works of Mary Wollstonecraft, Mary Shelley and Jane Austen* (Chicago and London: University of Chicago Press, 1984) p. 163.
16. For a discussion of the values of bourgeois family relations in *Falkner*, see Poovey, *The Proper Lady*, and Julia Saunders's essay (Chapter 13) in this volume.

Index

Aeschylus
 Prometheus Bound, 99
Africa, 132
Alfieri, Victor, 19
Allen, Graham, xxiv, xxv, 224–42
America, 47, 48, 49, 132, 136, 174, 186, 188, 190, 191, 192, 216
Amsterdam Society, 203
Anderson, Benedict, 146
Antigua, 134, 135
Ariosto, Ludovico
 Orlando Furioso, 113, 120, 126
Austen, Jane, 92, 132, 135
 Mansfield Park, 5, 134, 135, 137, 140, 147
 Persuasion, 47
Averill, James, H., 167, 177

Bage, Robert, 218
 Hermsprong, 216, 223
Baier, Annette, xxii, 58, 59, 67, 72, 73
Baldick, Chris, 19, 95, 105, 204, 210
Barbauld, Anna Laetitia, 133, 134, 175
 Eighteen Hundred and Eleven, 134, 140, 147, 148
 'Epistle to William Wilberforce', 149
 'On the Uses of History', 146
 'To Mr [S. T.] Coleridge', 179
Barbour, Judith, 242
Baudrillard, Jean, 133, 147
Beddoes, Thomas, 208
Behrendt, Stephen, 105, 106
Belsey, Catherine, 125
Bennett, Betty T., xx, xxii, xxv, 84, 93, 94, 110, 124, 160, 161, 163, 193, 224
Bentley, Richard, 3, 226
Berchet, Giovanni, 78
Berger, Dieter A., 162
Bhabha, Homi K., 136, 141, 146, 148

Birbeck, Morris
 Letters from Illinois, 182
Blackwood's Edinburgh Magazine, 20, 79, 92, 101, 110, 162
Blake, William
 Milton, 129, 146
Blenkesop, Mrs, 199
Blumberg, Jane, xxv, 84, 94
Boccaccio, Giovanni, 82
Bohls, Elizabeth A., 18, 19
Brantlinger, Patrick, 131, 147, 149, 193
Brewer, William D., 73, 155, 161, 162
Briggs, A., 193
British Critic, 107
Bronfen, Elisabeth, 200, 207
Brooks, Peter, 30, 37
Bulwer, Edward, xxiii, 39–54, 126
 Devereux, 41
 Disowned, The, 41, 42, 52
 England and the English, 40, 41, 184, 185, 186, 187, 193
 Eugene Aram, 41, 44, 45
 'Life of Schiller', 53
 Paul Clifford, 40, 41, 42, 53
 Pelham, 41, 43, 52, 182
Bunnell, Charlene, xxii, xxvi
Burke, Edmund, 168, 216
 Reflections on the Revolution in France, 146
 A Philosophical Enquiry into the Origins of our Ideas of the Sublime and the Beautiful, 178
Burney, Frances, *Cecilia*, 111
Butler, Judith, 64, 65, 73
Butler, Marilyn, xxii, 7, 18, 207
Byron, George Gordon, Lord, xxiii, 41, 45, 53, 93, 97, 106, 109, 113, 114, 123, 160, 166, 173, 178, 222
 Childe Harold's Pilgrimage, 18, 44, 80

Don Juan, 44, 112, 123, 125, 126
Lara, 112, 114
Manfred, 169

Campbell Orr, Clarissa, xxvi
Cantor, Paul A., 147, 148, 149, 193
Carlyle, Thomas, 43, 153, 160, 176, 179, 180
Caruth, Cathy, 242
Cashell, Lady Mount, 92, 110, 124
Castle, Terry, 110, 124
Chamounix, 28
Chase, Cynthia, 234
Chaucer, Geoffrey, 82
China, 136
Cicero, 82
Clairmont, Claire, 44, 45, 93, 105, 124, 162
Clemit, Pamela, 42, 53, 93, 94, 193, 211, 222
Cochran, Peter, 125
Cogin, Thomas
  Memoirs of the Society Instituted at Amsterdam in favour of Drowned Persons, 202, 208
Colburn, Henry, 3, 182, 225, 226
Coleridge, Samuel Taylor, xxiii, 71, 164–80
  Biographia Literaria, 95, 105, 178, 179
  Christabel, 122, 123
  'Dejection', 178, 179
  'Eolian Harp, The', 170
  'Fears in Solitude', 149
  Friend, The, 168, 170, 171, 178, 179
  Lectures (1808–19), 178
  'Lime-Tree Bower My Prison, The', 123
  'Ode to Tranquility', 170, 171, 178, 179
  'On the Principles of Genial Criticism', 168
  Rime of the Ancient Mariner, The, 59, 70, 71
  Shorter Works and Fragments, 178
  Statesman's Manual, The, 176
Colonna, Giacomo, 102
Conger, Syndy M., 225, 242
Constantinople, 25

Cooper, Tom, 224
Courier, 52
Cowley, Hannah, 94
Cowper, William, 149
  Task, The, 132, 133, 135, 147
Crabb Robinson, Henry, 19
Cronin, Richard, xxi, xxiii, 39–54
Crook, Nora, xix–xxvi, 3–21, 53, 92, 106, 208
Curran, Stuart, 92, 161

Dante, Alighieri, 79, 82, 83
Davy, Humphrey, 166
De Laurentis, Teresa, 73
De Quincey, Thomas, 136, 141
  Confessions of an English Opium-Eater, 136, 137, 148
  'English Mail-Coach', 136
  Suspiria de Profundis, 137, 148
Defoe, Daniel
  Robinson Crusoe, 142
Dekker, Rudolf M., 125
Derrida, Jacques, 35, 37, 38, 102, 107
Dibdin, Thomas
  Remarks on the Present Languid and Depressed State of Literature and the Book Trade, 183, 193
Disraeli, Benjamin, 44, 46
  Vivian Grey, 43
Dixon, John
  Oracle, Representing Britannia, Hibernia, Scotia and America, The, 130
Dods, Mary Diana ('Walter Sholto Douglas' – 'David Lindsay'), 110, 116
Dollimore, Jonathan, 112, 113, 125
Donne, John, 'A Valediction', 133, 147
Dunn, Jane, 53
Dusinberre, Juliet, 125

Eberle-Sinatra, Michael, ix–xi, xx, xxii, 95–108
Edinburgh Review, 44, 45, 49, 53
Eliot, George, 51, 52
  Amos Barton, 51
  Middlemarch, 51
  'Morality of *Wilhem Meister*, The', 51, 54

Ellis, Kate Ferguson, 174, 179, 193
Ellison, Julie, 58, 67, 71, 73, 74
El-Shater, Safaa, 161
England, xxiii, 25, 29, 40, 44, 45, 48, 59, 96, 105, 109, 112, 129, 130, 131, 134, 135, 136, 137, 138, 139, 140, 148, 152, 169, 182, 187, 188, 189
Europe, 16, 20, 44, 79, 110, 140, 212
Examiner, 100

Feldman, Paula R., 53, 95, 105
Felix Farley's Bristol Journal, 168
Fenwick, Eliza
  Secresy, 149
Ferguson, Frances, 74
Fielding, Henry
  Amelia, 111
Fisch, Audrey A., xix, 37, 130, 147
Florence, 88, 90
Florescu, Radu, 209
Ford, John
  Chronicle History of Perkin Warbeck, The, 152, 153, 155, 161
Ford, Susan Allen, 71, 74
Foscolo, Ugo, 76, 78, 83, 92
France, 20, 78, 132, 160, 166, 182
Franci, Giovanna, 36, 38
François, Anne-Lise, xxii, 57–74
Frank, Frederick S., xx, xxv
Frankenstein, Johann Goll Van, 203
Fraser's Magazine, 43, 44, 53
Freud, Sigmund, 30, 234
Friedli, Lynne, 125
Frost, Alan, 129, 146

Garber, Marjorie, 125
Garbin, Lidia, xxiii, 150–63
Garnett, Richard, 79, 126
  Tales and Stories by Mary Wollstonecraft Shelley, 93
Gaskell, Mary, 19
Genette, Gérard, xxii, 97, 101, 106, 107
Geneva, 8, 13
Geyer-Ryan, Helga, 198, 207
Gifford, William, 161
Gilbert, Sandra M., 99, 107
Gisborne, Maria, 193, 232

Gittings, Robert, 53
Godwin, Fanny, 200, 207
Godwin, William, 4, 15, 18, 21, 42, 45, 51, 76, 93, 97, 98, 106, 124, 155, 160, 184, 192, 197, 199, 206, 211, 216, 218, 224–42
  Caleb Williams, 18, 21, 41, 42, 125, 207, 218, 226
  Cloudesley, 158
  Cursory Strictures on the Charge Delivered by Lord Chief Justice Eyre, 229, 230, 242
  Enquiry Concerning Political Justice, An, 14, 212, 215, 222, 229, 230, 242
  'Essay of History and Romance', 227, 229, 242
  Falkland, 41
  Fleetwood, 19, 119, 125
  Lives of the Necromancer, 207
  Mandeville, 14, 15, 20, 119
  Memoirs of the Author of 'The Rights of Woman', 202, 204, 208, 209, 210, 230, 231, 232, 236, 237, 238, 242
  'Of Choice in Reading', 126
  St Leon, 19, 125, 206, 218
  Thoughts on Man, 14, 15, 20
  'Two Jars, The', 193
Goldsmith, Steven, 38
Gore, Catherine, 185
  Fair of May Fair, The, 182
  Mothers and Daughters: a Tale of the Year 1830, 182
  Opera, The, 182
  Pin Money, 182
  Polish Tales, 182
  Sketch Book of Fashion, The, 182
  Tuileries, The, 182
  Women as They Are, or the Manners of the Day, 182
Greece, 30, 215
Greenblatt, Stephen, 125
Grenada, 40
Gross, Elizabeth, 207
Gubar, Susan, 99, 107

Haggard, H. Rider, *She*, 131, 132, 133, 137, 145, 147, 149

246 *Index*

Halévy, Elie, 94
Hamilton, Thomas
  Men and Manners in America, 191, 193
Haslam, Jason, 148
Hays, Mary, 226
  Memoirs of Emma Courtney, 213, 222
Hazlitt, William, 176, 180
Helgerson, Richard, 147
Hemans, Felicia, 77
Hill-Miller, Katherine, 181, 193
Hindle, Maurice, 19, 207
Hobhouse, John Cam, 106
Hogg, Thomas Jefferson, 53
Holcroft, Thomas, 218, 229
Holmes, Richard, 230
Homer, 144
Hook, Theodore
  Maxwell, 18
Horsman, Alan, 183, 193
Howard, Jean, 125
Huggan, Graham, 141, 149
Hunt, Leigh, 124
  'Blue-Stocking Revels', 105
Hunter, John, 208

Il Conciliatore, 78
Illinois, 48, 182, 188, 191
Imlay, Gilbert, 203, 208
Inchbald, Elizabeth
  A Simple Story, 111
India, 132
Ireland, 132, 203
Irving, Washington, 52
Italy, xxii, xxv, 6, 75–94, 116, 191

Janaway, Christopher, 177
Janowitz, Anne, 73
Jeffrey, Francis (Lord Kames)
  Essay on the Principles of Morality, 20
Johnson, Barbara, 105, 130, 147
Johnson, Samuel, 17
Jones, Vivien, 207, 208
Jump, Harriet Devine, 210

Kant, Immanuel, 59, 168
  Critique of Judgment, The, 178

Karloff, Boris, 17
Keats, John, 52
  Endymion, 53
  Eve of St. Agnes, The, 77
Keepsake, The, xxii, 52, 109, 116, 119, 120, 121, 122
Kelly, J., 193
Keswick, 168
Kiernan, V. G., 193
Knight's Quarterly Magazine, 21, 93
Knoepflmacher, U. C., xix, xx
Kristeva, Julia, 197, 198, 199, 201, 206, 207

Ladies' Monthly Museum, 106, 153, 161
Lamb, Caroline, 53
Lamb, Charles, 176, 180
Landon, Laetitia Elizabeth, 77, 85
Lardner, Dionysius
  Cabinet Cyclopedia, xxiv, xxvi, 20
Leader, 54
Leader, Zachary, 107
Leask, Nigel, 136, 140, 148
Leopardi, Giacomo, 76, 77, 78
  Canto, 92
Levine, George, xix, xx
Lew, Joseph, 84, 92, 94
Lewis, Matthew
  Monk, The, 125
Liberal, 113
Literary Gazette and Journal of Belles Lettres, Arts, Sciences, &c., 98, 106
Liverpool, 191
Locke, Don, 21
Lockhart, John Gibson, 20, 92
London, 27, 47, 48, 59, 135, 183, 188
London Magazine, 53
London, Bette, 100, 107
Lovejoy, Arthur, 69, 73
Lucca, 80, 88

Macaulay, Catherine
  Letters on Education, 108
Macdonald, D. L., 18
Maginn, William, 43
Manton, Jo, 53
Manzoni, Allsandro, 78
Markley, A. A., xxii, xxvi, 109–26

Marlow, 75
Marrs, Edwin, 180
Mavor, William
 English Spelling Book, The, 209
Mazzeo, Tilar, xxvi
McFarland, Thomas, 180
McWhir, Anne, 38, 107
Mellor, Anne K., xix, xx, xxii, 10, 11, 19, 63, 69, 70, 73, 81, 92, 93, 94, 101, 107, 165, 166, 167, 174, 175, 177, 179, 181, 193, 200, 207, 210, 211
Meyers, Mitzi, 242
Milner, H. M., 21
Milton, John, 4, 36
 Paradise Lost, 35, 67, 75, 98, 99, 106, 126, 180
Moers, Ellen, 95, 207
Monthly Magazine, 22, 37
Moore, Thomas, 52
More, Hannah
 Strictures on Female Education, 108
Moxon, Edward, 225, 226
Mozes, Daniel, xxii, 57–74
Mulvey-Roberts, Marie, xxiv, 197–210
Murray, John, 40, 161, 183

Naples, 33, 113, 114
Napoléon I, 76, 79
Neumann, Bonnie R., 153, 161
New Monthly Magazine, 41, 52, 105, 126, 193
New York, 188, 191
Newlyn, Lucy, 99, 106
Niagara, 168, 169, 190
Norman, Sylva, 163
Norway, 204

O'Dea, Gregory, xx, xxv, 149
Ollier, Charles, 40, 52, 184, 186, 192, 193
Oost, Regina, 107
O'Rourke, Jane, 21
O'Sullivan, Barbara Jane, 94
Owen, Robert Dale, 6, 19
Owenson, Sydney, Lady Morgan,
 O'Briens and the O'Flahertys, The, 146

Palacio, Jean de, xxi, xxv, 18, 80, 93, 163
Paley, Morton D., 37, 147, 167, 178, 179
Paul, C. Kegan, 242
Peacock, Mary Ellen, 226
Peacock, Thomas Love, 93
Peake, Richard Brinsley
 Presumption or the Fate of Frankenstein, 7, 8
Pellico, Sylvio, 6, 78
Peru, 40
Petrarch, Francesco, 102
Pisa, 92
Plato, 176
Poignand, Lewis, 199
Polwhele, Richard, 201
Poovey, Mary, xx, xxii, 18, 72, 164, 165, 166, 167, 177, 240, 242
Porta, Carlo, 78
Purinton, Marjean D., 205, 210

Quarterly Review, 18, 40

Rackin, Phyllis, 125
Radcliffe, Ann, 96, 158
 Italian, The, 162
 'On the Supernatural in Poetry', 105
Rajan, Tilottama, 73
Reynolds, Joshua, 52
Richardson, Alan, 112, 113, 125
Richardson, Samuel
 Clarissa, 60
Rieger, James, 18, 107
Robinson, Charles E., xx, xxii, xxv, 100, 107, 122, 126, 210
Robinson, Isabella, 110
Robinson, Mary, 77
 Walsingham, 125
Rome, 31, 32, 144
Rousseau, Jean-Jacques, 50, 67, 68
 Emile, 57, 58, 67, 72, 73
 Julie, ou la Nouvelle Héloïse, 94
Royal Humane Society, xxiv, 202, 203, 208, 209

Sadleir, Michael, 53
Said, Edward S., 134, 147, 148

248 *Index*

Sand, George, 119
Saunders, Julia, xxiv, 211–23, 242
Scandinavia, 203
Scherf, Kathleen, 18
Schlegel, Friedrich, 38
Schopenhauer, Arthur, 165, 177
Schor, Esther H., xix
Schwab, Raymond, 130, 132, 136, 147, 148
Scotland, 59
Scots Magazine and Edinburgh Literary Miscellany, 21
Scott, Walter, xxiii, 53, 98, 150–63, 183
  Antiquary, The, 161
  Guy Mannering, 161
  Ivanhoe, xxiii, 154, 156, 157, 158, 161, 162
  Marmion, 117, 125
  'Review of *Childe Harold's Pilgrimage*', 18
  'Review of *Frankenstein*', 101
  Rob Roy, 161
  Waverley Novels, 154, 157, 158, 159
  Waverley, 151, 160, 161
Scott-Kilver, Diana, 53
Semmelweis, Ignaz, 198
Shakespeare, William, 68, 109, 111, 113, 144, 153, 158, 159, 160, 162
  Antony and Cleopatra, 162
  As You Like It, 111, 113
  Hamlet, 18, 235
  1 Henry IV, 162
  Henry V, 162
  2 Henry VI, 162
  3 Henry VI, 162
  King John, 162
  Measure for Measure, 117, 125
  Merchant of Venice, The, 111
  Rape of Lucrece, The, 162
  Richard II, 129, 146, 147, 162
  Richard III, 162
  Sonnets, 162
  Tempest, The, 191
  Twelfth Night, 111, 122
  Two Gentlemen of Verona, 162
  Two Noble Kinsmen, 162

Winter's Tale, A, 123
Shapiro, Michael, 111, 113, 125
Shelley, Harriet, 208
Shelley, Lady Jane, 206
Shelley, Mary
  'Brother and Sister: An Italian Story, The', 121
  'English in Italy, The', 6
  'False Rhyme, The', 120, 121
  'Ferdinando Eboli', 116, 117, 119, 120
  Falkner, xx, xxiv, 41, 42, 166, 173, 175, 177, 179, 201, 204, 211–23, 224–42
  Fortunes of Perkin Warbeck, The, xx, xxiii, 40, 115, 150–63, 182
  Frankenstein, xix, xxi, xxiv, xxv, 3–21, 23, 39, 63, 75, 77, 79, 80, 81, 89, 95–108, 123, 125, 150, 152, 153, 154, 164, 165, 174, 175, 181, 189, 197–210, 221, 222
  History of a Six Weeks' Tour, 6, 19, 204
  'Invisible Girl, The', 52
  Journals, 6, 19, 37, 41, 92, 94, 100, 106, 151, 154, 160, 161, 171, 202, 212
  Last Man, The, xx, xxi, xxii, 22–38, 42, 95–108, 125, 126, 129–49, 153, 169, 171, 174, 179, 182, 189, 221, 222
  Letters, xxvi, 6, 10, 11, 19, 40, 41, 52, 96, 101, 106, 124, 154, 160, 161, 181, 182, 183, 184, 186, 192, 193, 224, 226, 232, 242
  'Life of William Godwin', xxiv, 21, 208, 224–42
  Lodore, xx, xxi, xxiii, 39–54, 158, 164–80, 181–93, 214, 218, 220, 221, 233, 239, 240, 241
  'Madame Rolland', 20
  Matilda, xx, xxii, xxv, 57–74, 113, 123, 242
  Maurice, xix
  Midas, 210
  'Mortal Immortal: A Tale, The', 119

'Pilgrims, The', 122, 123
Proserpine, 205, 210
Rambles in Germany and Italy, xxiv, 19, 20, 193, 204
Short stories, 109–26
'Sisters of Albano, The', 116, 117, 118
'Tale of the Passions, A', 113, 118, 119
'Transformation', 119
Valperga, xx, xxii, 43, 51, 53, 54, 75–94, 121, 125, 150, 153, 160, 161, 182, 218, 221, 222
'Vittoria Colonna', xxiv
Shelley, P. B., xxiii, 14, 20, 41, 51, 53, 68, 72, 76, 93, 97, 98, 100, 102, 106, 107, 109, 124, 150, 151, 152, 154, 163, 166, 173, 181, 222, 225, 226
  Adonais, 97, 106
  Cenci, The, 4, 53, 57, 58, 71, 85, 91
  Defence of Poetry, A, 177, 179
  Epipsychidion, 107
  Laon and Cythna (The Revolt of Islam), 4, 210
  Letters, 76, 93, 154
  Mask of Anarchy, The, 30, 37
  'Ode to the West Wind', 94
  Posthumous Poems, 41, 96
  Prometheus Unbound, 80, 91, 93
  Queen Mab, 208
  'Review of Frankenstein', 13, 17
  Zastrozzi, 118
Shelley, Sir Timothy, 40, 98, 183
Sibyl, 16, 22, 23, 26, 32, 33, 34, 38, 101, 107, 145
Simpkins, Scott, 119, 125
Sismondi, J. C. de
  Histoire des républiques italiennes, 92
Smith, Anthony D., 146
Smith, Charlotte, 77, 94
Snyder, Robert Lance, 135, 147, 148, 178
South America, 16
Southey, Robert, 'The Cataract of Lodore', 178
Spain, 162
Spark, Muriel, xx, xxv, 155, 159, 160, 161, 163

Spenser, Edmund
  Faerie Queene, The, 120, 126
St Clair, William, 18, 242
Staël, Germaine de, 19
  Corinne ou l'Italie, 6, 11, 19, 40, 85
Stafford, Fiona, xxi, xxiii, 105, 181–93
Sterne, Laurence, 4
  Sentimental Journey, A, 19
Sterrenburg, Lee, 130, 147, 193
Strawson, Galen, 21
Sunstein, Emily W., xx, xxv, 207
Swift, Jonathan, 138
Switzerland, 7, 204

Thackeray, William Makepeace, 43, 44, 45
Thomas, Sophie, xxi, xxii, 22–38
Thornton, Robert
  The Philosophy of Medicine, Being Medical Extracts, 208, 209
Tieck, Ludwig, 18
Todd, Janet, 209
Tomalin, Claire, 203, 210
Tooke, Horne, 229
Trelawny, Edward John, 191, 224, 225, 232
  Adventures of a Younger Son, 162, 183, 184
Trollope, Frances
  Domestic Manners of the Americans, 191–2, 193
Tuite, Clara, 242

Vallins, David, xxiii, 164–80
Van de Pol, Lotte C., 125
Vargo, Lisa, xxvi, 178, 182, 192, 193
Veeder, William, 174, 176, 177, 179, 180
Virgil, 34
Viviani, Emilia, 124
Volney, Constantin François de, 8

Wales, 48
Walling, William A., 155, 153, 161, 162
Wellhofer, E. Spencer, 146
Welsh, A., 161
White, Daniel E., xxii, xxiii, 75–94

Index

Whitton, William, 193
Williams, Bernard, 71, 72, 73, 74
Williams, Carolyn, 208, 209
Williams, Edward, xxiii
Williams, Jane, 53
Willis, Martin, 165, 177
Wolfson, Susan, 112, 113, 125, 126
Wollstonecraft, Mary, xix, xxiv, 51, 62, 68, 72, 77, 93, 98, 110, 160, 197–210, 211, 221, 231, 236, 238
   'Letters on the Management of Infants', 201
   Letters Written during a Short Residence in Sweden, Norway, and Denmark, 82, 204
   Mary, 200, 207, 213, 242
   Posthumous Works, 205, 230, 231
   Thoughts on the Education of Daughters, 108, 200, 207
   Vindication of the Rights of Woman, A, 61, 67, 73, 82, 108, 206, 218, 222, 223
   Wrongs of Woman, or Maria, The, 200, 213, 218, 242
Woolf, Virginia, 68, 73, 197, 206
Wordsworth, William, xxiii, 41, 53, 94, 164–80, 183
   Guide through the District of the Lakes in the North of England, A, 178
   'Inscription XV', 178
   'Ode: Intimations of Immortality from Recollection of Early Childhood', 166, 170, 177
   Prelude, The, 177
   'Tintern Abbey', 166, 177
Wright, Frances, 6, 19, 191, 193
Wright, Julia, xxi, xxiii, 129–49

Yeazell, Ruth, 72, 73

Made in United States
North Haven, CT
03 September 2022